3RD AND Starlight

A FANTASY & SCI-FI ANTHOLOGY
EDITED BY ROBERT B. FINEGOLD

future finalists
publishing

The Memory of Huckleberries by Rebecca Birch was originally published in Penumbra e-zine, September 2012.

The Temptation of Father Francis by Nick T. Chan and Jennifer Campbell-Hicks was originally published in Intergalactic Medicine Show Issue 41, September 2014.

The Waiting Room by Philip Brian Hall was originally published in Chilling Ghost Short Stories by Flame Tree Publishing, September 2015.

Last Time For Everything by K. L. Schwengel is original to 3rd and Starlight.

Skinners by Rachelle Harp was originally published in Perihelion e-zine, November 2016

Amma's Wishes by M. E. Garber was originally published in Marion Zimmer Bradley's Sword & Sorceress 29, November 2014.

Three Flash: Curing Day; A New Man in Time For Christmas; and Final Message by Dustin Adams were originally published respectively in Daily Science Fiction June 11, 2013 and December 23, 2015, and at Every Day Fiction July 15, 2015.

A Green Tongue by Frank Dutkiewicz was originally published in the Grantville Gazette e-zine, volume 64, March 2016.

A Matter of Interpretation by M. Elizabeth Ticknor was originally published in Heroic Fantasy Short Stories by Flame Tree Press, September 2017.

The Root Bridges of Haemae by Sean Monaghan was originally published in Aurealis #87, 2016.

Red is the Color of My True Love's Hair by William R. D. Wood is original to 3rd & Starlight.

Bad Actors by Julie Frost is original to 3rd and Starlight.

In the Heart of the Flesh by Scott R. Parkin is original to 3rd and Starlight.

Shattered Vessels by Kary English and Robert B. Finegold, M.D. was originally published in Galaxy's Edge Magazine #19, March-April 2016.

ISBN-13: 978-0692990520 (Future Finalists Publishing)
ISBN-10: 0692990526

Cover art: Lou Harper – http://louharper.com/Design.html
Interior art: M. Elizabeth Ticknor - http://www.ticknortales.com
Typesetting and Interior Design (ebook): Alex Shvartsman – https://www.alexshvartsman.com
Typesetting and Interior Design (print): Melissa Neely – http://www.neelyhousedesign.com/
Audiobook narrator: Scott R. Parkin

Visit us at http://www.futurefinalists.com/anthologies

DEDICATION

....

The editor dedicates this volume to

DON E. FINEGOLD
(1929-2017)

of blessed memory.

Father, Mensch, Author, Friend
www.donefinegold.com

Table of Contents

3RD & STARLIGHT
INTRODUCTION:
BACK AND FOREWORD

....

The street is unlike any other.

A frozen tide of pavement flows over pitted cobblestones. Buzzing streetlights vie with the hiss of gas lamps; the hum of the distant highway is muffled by the drumming rattle of a tinker's cart; an electric guitar squeals only to be drowned out by the caterwauls of drunken swordsmen.

You sniff and grimace, covering your nose at the stench of burnt oil and exhaust, and of offal heaps and middens. Then the wind shifts, bringing the carnival aromas of fried dough and cotton candy but also, hauntingly, of burning incense and night orchids.

Standing with one foot to either side of the street sign, you gasp as your garments shimmer and change. Your left foot wears a Reebok sneaker below a pants leg of blue denim, the right is sheathed in a knee-high boot of supple leather. The sensation is strange: a static charge bristling the small hairs of your arms and neck, a chill touch upon your cheek like a glacial breeze—or a corpse's finger. Shivering, you look up.

City light veils the stars to your left, chimney smoke to your right. Yet, faintly, incessantly, the stars shimmer and beckon in the shrouded skies of both.

Wind teases your hair like a lover, sliding quick fingers beneath . . . your coat? . . . your cloak? . . . grasping you; leading you.

Which way do you turn first?

Welcome to *3rd and Starlight*, the third annual anthology* of original and favorite reprint tales by rising new stars in science fiction and fantasy. Each of these authors has distinguished themselves as Winners, Finalists, or Semi-finalists in the *Writers of the Future* contest, and have gone on to publish in leading professional markets *(Asimov's, Intergalactic Medicine Show, Galaxy's Edge* and others), publish novels, and/or earn distinction within the science fiction and fantasy community as nominees, finalists and/or winners of the *Hugo* and *Campbell* awards, the *Aurealis* award, the *Sir Julius Vogel* award, and *Jim Baen Memorial* short story contest award.

While these anthologies have no relationship to the *Writers of the Future* contest, the contest is the tourney field where our wordsmiths, storytellers, bards, and gossips met and formed acquaintances and fast friendships. Like troupe players sharing a love to entertain, like explorers inspired to discover new worlds—as well as insights into the human heart, we've been drawn to one another . . . perhaps as moths to flame; mass to event horizon . . . with equal parts awe and sense of doom, with a dash of pure cussedness and a shtickle of *chutzpah*. These emotions lie entwined as lovers in the hearts of writers. And our authors possess them in spades.

Enclosed for your enjoyment and edification are 14 tales by 16 authors (with 2 collaborations); half science fiction, half fantasy; original tales and reprints—but even the reprints are "original," having been edited and revised for this volume by their authors as preferred "directors' cuts." Herein you'll find bee gods and dirigibles, cyborgs and thieves, ghosts and golems and aliens. Stories that will take you to distant worlds, introduce you to artificial intelligences, and span all Time from Creation to the World-to-Come.

Yet each story never strays from the human heart: what we love, what we fear, what we desire, and what we need:

> "*...to strive, to seek, to find, and not to yield.*"
> [Ulysses; Alfred, Lord Tennyson, 1883]

Robert B. Finegold, M.D.
(November 2017)

* The earlier volumes, aptly named *1st and Starlight* and *2nd and Starlight*—oh, how our city grows!—are available for purchase at on-line retailers; and the reader is encouraged to seek them and cautiously tread their metal roads and cobblestone lanes.

Alone amid the ghosts and gods of her tribe and the memories of her past, an old woman longs to see her daughter and grandchild— but at what cost?

....

THE MEMORY OF HUCKLEBERRIES

REBECCA BIRCH

Old Woman sits outside a cedar plank house watching the ghosts of her nephews dig out the center of a new war canoe. It sits near the high-tide line, balanced in the damp sand. The sun hangs low on the horizon, its soft light shimmering through their transparent bodies.

She leans back, her fingers clenched around a clump of russet fur. The wall is cool against her fevered skin. Children's voices echo from inside the house. She should get up and check on them, but her body is sapped and although she has tried, she cannot even lift a handful of clean water from the bentwood box at her side. Besides, she thinks she saw their bodies buried a few days ago, back when there were others still alive.

A tear seeps from the corner of her eye.

"Why do you cry?" rumbles a voice out of the mist of memory.

With an effort, she turns her head. Bear stands at the corner of the house. He is half-hidden in shadows, but she knows him. She tries to speak, but her parched throat can only squawk.

He wears nothing but a breechcloth and supple deer-hide leggings. His bare feet make no sound as he comes to squat in front of her. Time has not dulled his beauty. Sleek black hair hangs over his shoulder in a long braid.

No wrinkles mar his skin. The taut leggings cling to his muscular thighs as the setting sun limns his broad frame.

A seagull perches on the roof, shrieks, and flies out to sea. Bear brings a handful of water from the bentwood box to her lips and coaxes her to drink. The cool liquid soothes her parched throat, and his soft touch kindles shivers across her skin.

When the water is gone, she licks her lips. "It's been too long."

"Not so very long."

Old Woman manages a sad smile. "Long enough. Our child is grown and married. She has a son of her own now."

Bear rocks back on his heels. "What happened here? Why are you alone?"

Old Woman inhales the sea air. Its salty tang comforts her. "A strange boy washed up on the shore half-drowned—a pale boy, silent and small. The shamans tended him with herbs and prayers. When he grew stronger, he walked among us. He never spoke, only watched us with ice-eyes." She shakes her head, remembering. "Three days later, the fever came."

A boy-ghost runs through the doorway, shouting and waving a carved, painted stick. He barrels into Bear, fading then reappearing on the other side. Bear's black eyes never leave Old Woman's face. "Are there any others left?"

"I don't know. The ice-eyed boy was the last soul I saw." She glances down at the bentwood box. "He left me water, then walked into the sea. I saw him pass the breakers before he vanished."

Bear rises, eyes flashing. He ducks as he enters the plank house. Old Woman waits, her breathing shallow, and wonders if she is dreaming fever-dreams and whether it matters if she is.

Although she has lost many memories, the day she came upon Bear in the forest while she harvested huckleberries remains clear as rain—his low voice whispering endearments, fingers grazing her own as she plucked the smooth, salmon-red fruits.

So many years she prayed for a child, her heart growing numb as Tall Man's seed failed to take root. When Bear wrapped her close—kissing her with eager lips, musky scent enveloping her until she thrummed with desire and begged him to come within her—she let herself believe this was the answer to her prayers.

After, when she returned to her husband's quiet, comfortable caresses, she never spoke of what had passed that day. When Bear's child quickened in her womb, she let Tall Man crow, even though she knew the child was not his.

Through all the years that followed, she never saw Bear again, but she thought he watched them when he could. She found his prints in the forest and one morning, when she woke, she found a handful of his fur clutched tight in her daughter's chubby baby-fist. She'd kept the fur in a talisman pouch over her heart, until she was left alone among the dead and she pulled it into her hand, her last tangible memory.

All of them are gone now. Tall Man, years ago in a hunting accident, her daughter, Huckleberry, given in marriage to the chief of the tribe across the strait, and so many others lost to the fever, their ghosts roaming the village as if they had never passed over.

Bear crashes through the door in a bristling rush of russet fur, claws gouging the earth. Old Woman's eyes follow him as he runs to the neighboring plank house, then the next, until there are no more.

The great bear lumbers down the beach until the waves lap his wide paws, then rears up on cedar-strong hind limbs. He roars towards the setting sun. Old Woman's nephew-ghosts pause in their labors to stare as Bear rages at the sky.

After so many years, even Bear's anger is welcome. Old Woman struggles to stay awake, but she drifts into a troubled slumber.

"WHERE IS THE ice-eyed boy?" says a voice Old Woman doesn't know.

Warm softness pillows her head. "She saw him go into the sea." Bear's voice rumbles through her failing body. "I searched the shore, but he has not washed up again."

Old Woman opens her eyes. The changed light tells her it is morning. Shivers race through her, raising gooseflesh on her skin. A stranger stands before her, smaller than Bear, wiry, with quick, obsidian eyes that flash as he glances from side to side.

"Not dead yet, Old Woman?"

Bear growls.

"Oh, relax, Large One. I'm not offering to do it for her."

Her gaze slides along the beach. Halfway to the tideline, a circle of ghost-women sit cross-legged, throwing wooden dice and laughing. Old Woman's sister-in-law, Fern, is among them, rocking side to side, singing a song to welcome the sunrise in her rich, low voice. They look happy. Old Woman licks her parched lips.

The stranger cocks his head. "Or maybe she wishes it? Do you, Old Woman?"

Bear shifts his form until the dense pelt on which she rests becomes soft skin. His chest rises and falls under her head while he cradles her with strong arms. "I didn't call you here for your mercy, Raven. I called you for your healing."

Raven blinks. "I can't heal what I don't know. Who was this ice-eye? An evil spirit, come to kill for pleasure? Or is he like us, Bear? Was it the appointed time for this village?"

Old Woman croaks, "Water." Bear dips one hand in the bentwood box and brings it to her lips. She gulps it down. "Another."

This handful she sips. The water rouses her. "I don't know who he was or where he came from. When we found him, he wore nothing but a strange amulet. The shamans took it to study. It may still be here."

"Well, that's better than nothing. Come, Bear. If you want my help, you'd best search with me."

Reluctantly, Bear settles Old Woman against the doorframe. She leans back, panting, and watches Bear and Raven walk towards the sacred place.

Fern's song comes to a close and she rises, waving farewell to the circle of women. Old Woman watches as Fern makes her way towards their family house. Her long hair hangs loose, swaying as she moves. Dawn's soft light filters through her. One hand rests on her protruding belly and a sad smile plays over her lips. Deep inside is another spark, Fern's unborn child, as much a ghost as the others.

Longing strikes Old Woman with a sharp pang. Her own daughter has been gone for years now. Word came by trading canoe four years back that she'd borne a son with fat cheeks and a strong cry. Old Woman wanted to make the trip to welcome the young one into the world, but the strain of the journey to bring Huckleberry to her new husband had been too much for her, leaving her too weakened to travel so far again. She aches to see Huckleberry one last time, aches to meet her grandson.

Fern draws near and Old Woman waits for her to pass by, unseeing, as all the ghosts do. "Greetings, Elder Sister," Fern says.

Old Woman blinks, startled. "Greetings, Fern."

"I've missed you. Where have you been?"

Old Woman doesn't know what to say; does Fern know she is dead? "I went to the forest for huckleberries?"

A broad smile creases Fern's face. "Huckleberries, you sly woman. I've seen you haunt the woods. You hunt memories there."

"I have to hunt them somewhere," Old Woman replies, tart as berries. "So many have run away in my old age, I must track them down and trap them."

Fern throws her head back and laughs. "Keep your secrets then."

Then she is gone and Old Woman closes her eyes again.

"Wake up, Old Woman."

She lifts one eyelid. Raven squats in front of her.

"What is it?"

"I found the amulet." He holds it up. Shaped like two flattened crossed sticks, it gleams gold in the early morning light. "I'll need to study it."

Bear lumbers up behind Raven, shakes out of his pelt and into his human skin. "Do it, then." He lays a hand on her brow. "This fever burns hot."

"I wish . . ." Old Woman whispers.

"What do you wish?" Bear brushes his lips against her brow.

"To see Huckleberry again, and meet our grandchild."

Bear pauses. "I can bring them to you. Orca will take me across the strait. I'll find them and bring them back to you. Just promise you'll be here when I return."

A smile tugs at the corner of Old Woman's lips. "How can I promise that? Do I have the power of life and death?"

"Raven?"

Raven glances up from the amulet, his gaze distant and distracted. "I can keep her alive long enough for you to bring them, Fuzzy One. If you hurry."

Bear surges to his feet. "I'll return with our child and grandson. Wait for me."

He drops to all fours, shifting with the motion. Long claws dig into the sand as he lumbers to the east. Old Woman watches him go, the sun's glow on his pelt fading into the distance.

Raven wanders through the center of the ring of ghost-women playing their dice game, his bright eyes shut, running his hands over the amulet and muttering under his breath. The women ignore him, even as they reach through his legs to pick up the wooden dice.

Old Woman lets their ghostly laughter lull her back into rest.

"Do you want to play?"

Old Woman startles awake, blinking. The ghost-boy stands before her, digging a toe into the ground, the carved stick tucked in a fist behind his back. "What?" she croaks.

"Play with me?"

She tries to shake her head, but the effort is too much. "I can't," she says. "I'm sorry."

The boy presses his lips together and his chin trembles. His features are blurry. "No one will play with me."

She watches him walk away, the soft evening breeze drifting through his long hair. He stoops to pick up a rock and throws it towards the trees.

"It's a pity," says Raven. "He's lonely."

Old Woman manages to turn her head. Raven is perched on a driftwood log, the amulet clutched under his talons.

"Water?" whispers Old Woman.

Raven blinks and fans out his feathers. "Don't you want to know what I've learned from the amulet?"

She wants water, Huckleberry's smiling face, Bear's warm sturdy presence. She wants the world to stop spinning. She nods. "Tell me."

"I can keep you alive long enough for Bear to bring your kin," Raven says, "but if I do, you'll curse me for it."

Old Woman runs her tongue over her upper lip. The sweat beads are salty, teasing her with their false promise of moisture. She swallows. "I don't have time for riddles."

He stretches his wings, fingers sliding from the tips, and grows until he stands upright in his man-skin. "The fever-taint burns in your breath. If your kin come while you still live, it will claim them. If they return across the strait, it will claim their village, maybe more."

Old Woman turns away and looks towards the ghost-boy, now digging in the sand with his stick, shoulders hunched up to his ears. Her breath comes in shallow pants. She thinks of Fern and the light of her unborn child.

She thinks of Huckleberry's face, faded and soft around the edges. Passing years have dimmed the memory. Only Huckleberry's smile remains bright, and the memory of her clear laughter. It blends with voices from the beach. Her nephews have finished their work on the war canoe and are making their way towards the houses.

She licks her lips again. "I promised."

Raven laughs, a harsh, cackling sound. "As it happens, you didn't. Old Fuzzy didn't wait for it."

She doesn't reply. The wind fans her fevered skin. As her nephews draw near, she frowns. They are fading, some nothing more than shimmering clusters, vaguely man-shaped.

Could ghosts die? Or were they there at all? What about Raven? What about Bear? It is so hard to think.

Her gaze turns to the ghost-boy. The beach's contours are visible through his small body: rounded stones, an upturned crab, little bubbling holes in the sand where clams hide, ripe for harvesting.

"They're coming," Raven says. "Bear races across the waters on Orca's back. Huckleberry's canoe follows behind."

"My Huckleberry . . ."

"Will live, if you are gone when she reaches here."

The ghost-boy pauses in his digging and hugs his knees. He rocks back and forth, shoulders shaking.

A tear trembles down Old Woman's cheek. "I wanted to meet my grandson."

"He'd be about the same age as that little one over there." Raven gestures, his hand tipped with jet-black feathers.

"I should play with him."

Raven's face hovers a breath away from her own. His beak is so close she can feel the soft rush of air from his nares. "You can," he whispers. "All you have to do is ask."

She looks deep into one bright black eye as large as the moon. Finger by finger, she releases her grip on the handful of Bear's fur. It falls to the sand, blowing away on the breeze.

"Please."

BEAR'S ROAR STARTLES Old Woman's eyes open. For the first time in days, she is cool. Cold, even. She should fetch a blanket.

Cautiously, she rises, propping herself against the wall for balance. Her legs do not buckle. Her back does not creak.

Bear roars again, very close. Old Woman looks down and blinks. Her body lies at her feet, unmoving, a gentle smile on its lips. Heavy fog the shade of damp moss presses close. It smells of loam and hearthfires. Beckoning voices dance within its shadows.

She kneels beside her corpse. The body clenches a raven feather in its crabbed hands. Bear nuzzles its shoulder with his heavy head.

Old Woman reaches out a hand to comfort him, but it slides through his dense pelt and muscled shoulder as if passing through air. She shakes her head. "I'm sorry."

"There's a canoe coming," says a small voice. The ghost-boy is beside her, still clutching the stick in one hand. Raven peers up at her from the stick's carved surface with one painted-black eye.

The ghost-boy takes Old Woman's hand and leads her down the beach. The women are gone. Only one nephew stirs down by the war canoe. He greets her with a raised hand.

The lapping waves make no sound rushing over the sand, nor do the gulls circling overhead, but the fog whispers against her eardrums, coaxing and cool.

"Where is your mother?" Old Woman asks.

"She went into the fog. They all do."

The swirling moss-mist obscures Old Woman's vision as she stares over the strait towards the incoming canoe. It rushes over the calm waters, trailing a glinting wake.

"Look how far I can throw!" The ghost-boy launches a rock towards the sea. It arcs through the mist, sending eddies swirling, then splashes soundlessly. Ripples spread over the water, until they reach a floating kelp bed and slip away into nothingness. "Can we play now?"

"Soon. I need to see the people in the canoe first."

"They won't see you."

Three figures sit silhouetted in the dugout, the one in the center so small she can see little more than the outline of his head. "I know. It will be enough."

But the fog swallows the canoe in its enveloping embrace. The whispering shadow-voices rise, singing a welcome song. Fern's rich alto is among them. They pull like the tide, trying to drag Old Woman's feet back up the shore.

Old Woman steps into the waves, fighting against the call. She can't give up now. She's too close to laying eyes on her grandson.

"May I borrow your stick?" she asks, remembering how the rock had churned the mist.

The ghost-boy presses the carving into her free hand. She raises it to her lips and breathes out her longing over its painted surface, wrapped in a single word. "Please."

With all of her renewed strength, she hurls the stick towards where she last saw the canoe. It flies end-over-end, cutting a thin strip through the fog.

Not enough. Old Woman's nails dig into her palm.

Then the stick shrieks. Raven's carved wings stretch wide and catch the clouds beneath his jet-black feathers. He circles once, then flaps twice and soars out to sea.

In his wake, the fog parts. Morning sunshine sparkles on the strait. The canoe dances over the waves. Huckleberry sits in the prow, paddling hard. Perspiration shines on her forehead. Her husband kneels in the stern, intent on the shore.

And in the center of the dugout, clinging to the sides so hard his knuckles pale, sits her grandson. Bear's dark eyes shine in his little-boy face and the excitement of the journey has set huckleberry stains on his still-chubby cheeks.

A breeze blows his ebony hair across his face and swirls the scent of his cedar-fiber wrap towards her, stronger even than the earthy tinge of the fog.

Then the mossy miasma closes in and all that remains is the ghost-boy's hand clasped in her own and the rising chant of the shadow-voices.

Old Woman stares a bit longer towards the vanished canoe. Beneath her feet, the sand rushes away on the receding tide. She sighs. "It is enough."

"Come on! Let's play!"

Old Woman turns away and follows the ghost-boy into the fog.

ABOUT THE AUTHOR

REBECCA BIRCH is a science fiction and fantasy writer based in Seattle, Washington. She's a classically trained soprano, holds a deputy black belt in Tae Kwon Do, and enjoys spending time in the company of trees. Her fiction has appeared in markets including *Galaxy's Edge, Flash Fiction Online,* and *Orson Scott Card's Intergalactic Medicine Show.* She is also a two-time Finalist in the *Writers of the Future* contest.

Her first short story collection, *Life Out of Harmony and Other Tales of Wonder,* is available at Amazon and other online retailers. Find her at *Words of Birch:* https://wordsofbirch.com.

ABOUT THE STORY

"The Memory of Huckleberries" began gestating when I was walking on the beach in Moclips, Washington during a break at a writers workshop. The salt tang on the air, the squelch of wet sand underfoot, and the soft susurrus of the waves on the receding tide etched a strong image in my mind; and, in the solitude, I began wondering what kind of a story could go with it.

Originally, the story was going to be about a dying Native American woman being visited by aliens that she, in her fevered delirium, thought were the gods and mythical beings of her people. That original idea quickly shifted. The aliens disappeared and became Bear and Raven.

This was a story that really took shape through the research process. The details I found informed and guided the storyline—war canoes, bentwood boxes, the wooden dice game; but at its heart, this is a story about a person: Old Woman. Her relationships and hopes. Her dreams, fears, and longings.

Finding the end of the story was a long process. I wrote six different endings; but none of them struck the right balance of closure, hope, and acceptance. When the ending you just read came to me, I knew I had found the closing the story begged for—the inevitable resolution.

It was like placing the last piece into a complicated jigsaw puzzle. That feeling of rightness is a rare and precious thing. I treasure such moments.

I hope you enjoyed "The Memory of Huckleberries."

Welcome to the post-apocalyptic New West, where Corporations enforce their control of the food supply with war machines; and a humble veteran priest, his western heroine dirigible AI, and their mechanical bees seek crops to pollinate, villagers to serve, and a separate peace.

....

THE TEMPTATION OF FATHER FRANCIS

NICK T. CHAN AND JENNIFER CAMPBELL-HICKS

Annie Oakley poked Francis in the shoulder. She kept poking him. He ignored her until she finally yelled into his earworm. "Wake up, you bone-lazy priest!" The image of a tiny woman, barely more than a girl, blinked into existence next to Francis' cot, the metal struts and handholds of the dirigible's plain cabin visible through her corseted dress. She held a rifle and wore a wide-brimmed cowboy hat over her wavy brown hair.

Annie set her hands on her hips. "I ought to shoot you just to get you out of bed. Need you up. Wireless is playing up with the bees again."

"Your projector isn't working too well either. I don't like my women transparent."

His head throbbed from the cheap Korean sleep app he'd downloaded last night. The constant rumble and occasional bump of the dirigible in flight didn't help. At least the storm had cleared overnight and the sky outside the ship's portals was clear blue.

He looked over to the glass hive on the cabin's far side, tucked next to the control panel. The little black bots were quiescent in the refrigerated chamber. Good. At least Annie had them under control for the moment. He had grown sick of bees landing on his nose at three in the morning. Not that he slept anyway.

"We could take the hive back to Gwair-Sematech," he said groggily. "Have them take a look."

"Lawdy, have you gone soft-headed you God-botherer?"

"I don't even know what that means. Talk like a normal AI for once."

Annie scowled. "Apart from the fact they'd like to kill you, Gwair-Sematech is in San Francisco, and we're about a thousand miles from there. What did you take last night?"

So she *had* heard him sub-vocalize his way through the drug applications. He swung his legs over the edge of the cot. "Same dream again."

Every night, the war AI unfolding from the shadows like a cross between a flying python and a chainsaw. Blood and screams from his men. Reeva crouched by a long tray filled with cabbages that glowed with trademarks under the ultraviolet light. The AI snaking around her, blades flashing.

"Thought I'd try something to help me sleep," he said. "Figured I'd confess it later. Still had the nightmare anyway."

"Oh, *Padre*." Even with her faux Western accent, Annie sounded unbearably sad.

He rubbed his palms into his eyes. "I'll add another sin to my confession. Stimulant applications, please." He stood, the sheets sliding away, and Annie averted her gaze, as if she couldn't see everything he did with her internal cameras.

"No can do. No idea how that cheap Korean junk would interact, and we ain't got time to run proxy simulations. Thirty seconds and I can give you visuals on the little ol' town of Temptation."

Francis pulled on his underpants and then shrugged into his cassock. "You do the praying this time, Annie. Pray that we find a farmer or two with some viable crops left. Or good stores of pre-patent grain. Anything except a town full of dead people, please."

"Have faith, *Padre*," Annie said.

"My faith isn't the strongest nowadays."

"Then maybe this'll bring it back."

A virtual menu unfolded on his retinal display. The town beneath them was full of people. The wooden houses were freshly painted. A flatbed truck drove down the main street, several children and a dog in the back. Banners fluttered between light poles. Couples strolled down the sidewalks, while a plump girl skipped along, licking a sticky toffee apple.

There were apple orchards, fruits hanging heavy on the branches. There was almost every single other insect-pollinated crop he could think of. Almonds, strawberries, watermelons. Most were out of season, but he recognized the plants.

Francis couldn't look away. "You said no one had been this way for five years."

"Might be my data was wrong."

"You're never wrong. I don't like this."

"Should I activate my guns?"

The corrugated iron floor shuddered as heavy rail guns locked into place beneath the dirigible.

Francis put his hand up. "No, they'll think we're corporate."

Annie pointed out one of the portals. The town was now visible through unaugmented sight. "Look, they've got a bakery." A floating window appeared at the corner of his vision, magnifying the distant bakery.

Behind the glass windows were croissants, a glazed Danish, and a cheesecake topped with cream. His stomach rumbled.

"Where they get the wheat?" Annie said.

"Has to be Mexico. The corporates have difficulty enforcing their patents down there. The townsfolk must be trading pollinated food over the border for grain."

"How do you reckon they get away with that? The corporates would send in soldiers if they suspected counterfeit grain was being sold." She hesitated. "Maybe even a war AI if they're desperate."

Francis pinched the brow of his nose and closed his eyes, fighting the quivering ball of nausea that settled about his stomach whenever a war AI was mentioned. Once calm, he pulled on his steel-capped boots and tied them. "There's no reason to go down there with guns cocked. It's 2135, not 1880. Guns away, keep the engine primed and ready for takeoff."

"We're deuterium-powered. I'm *always* primed for you, *Padre*." She winked at him and vanished.

People looked up as the dirigible descended, and gradually they gathered in the town square, which was dominated by a huge brass statue of a bee. The bee statue stood upright on two human-length legs and had four human-proportioned arms. In one hand it held a scepter tipped with a globe of honey. Its insect head had a touch of human in it, maybe something in the way that the mandibles were shaped.

"Annie, put us down next to that statue, whatever the hell it is." Silence. "Annie!"

Annie whispered into his earworm, but her voice was full of static. "There's some kind of interference. I'm going to switch to a different encryption." The dirigible shuddered as it hit a pocket of turbulence.

"Don't know what happened there, but I'm sort of clear now," Annie said. "How's your system going?"

Francis ran a diagnostic. "Fine."

"That statue is Ah Muzen Cab."

"What is that?"

"A Mayan bee god."

The dirigible shuddered again. Normally Annie foresaw turbulence and compensated, especially on a clear day like today, but she seemed to be losing control.

Francis grabbed the railing beneath the control panel. They'd crashed before and survived. "A Mayan bee god?"

"Hang on," Annie said. "I'm having trouble accessing the web securely."

The dirigible leveled out, floating twenty-five feet above the town square, and Francis released his grip. This close, he could see that the bee god statue had wickedly long teeth, more like a tiger than an insect.

"Got it," Annie said. "Ah Muzen Cab is a god of bees, honey, beekeeping, and creation. Can't really tell you much more. It's food-related, so some corporate bot has auto-censored most mentions."

Schematics flashed as his system scanned the crowd for threats and analyzed data from his subconscious. The words <no threat rating> floated at the edge of his retinal display.

There had to be a couple hundred people in the square. People weren't normally happy to see them. Hunger and despair had been their companions for too long. Even when Francis showed them how his bees worked, they only offered words of sad thanks. This crowd was in a festive mood.

The dirigible landed with a soft thud. Annie appeared in front of him, rifle raised and squinting down the sights. "You sure you don't want the guns out? I could shoot the cigarette out the mouth of that hussy there."

Annie opened a virtual window, showing the subject of her disdain.

Reeva. The same lovely copper skin, the long black hair. Big teeth in a small mouth, large eyes in a small face. A cigarette hung from her lip. He forced the comparison away. The woman wasn't Reeva, though she could've been her sister.

"She's stuffed to the gills with armor and shielded communications equipment," Annie said. "Some other stuff too, looks like analytical equipment, full laboratory packed in her belly."

"Corporate?"

"Can't tell. It's scrubbed clean."

The crowd waited quietly for the dirigible door to open, the woman with her thumbs tucked into her belt. Francis couldn't stop looking at her.

"I don't like this," Annie said. "You wanna scram?"

"My system's giving me nothing," Francis said. His retinal display scrolled messages about the woman's interior armor, but that was it. "Open the door. If there's trouble, I can handle it. I used to take down corporate soldiers for fun."

"Yes, but you had guns, not a blimp and a bunch of mechanical bees," she said, but the dirigible door slid open and unfolded into stairs.

He descended, the steel of his boots ringing on the metal. He spread his arms wide, as if expecting children to rush into his arms. It was stereotypically priestly, but people seemed to like it.

The woman who resembled Reeva met him at the base of the stairs and extended her hand for him to shake.

He took it. "Father Francis Connolly."

"Wahid Singh," she said. "Welcome to Temptation."

His system still gave no threat warnings. As far as he could tell, no one had a weapon here, not even the woman.

A fat, rosy-cheeked man waddled out from the crowd. He was dressed in a pinstripe suit and had a mayoral chain around his neck. "Don't get the wrong idea, Father. The name of this here town is from back when people followed the Bible. We were lucky we weren't called Absolution or Penance or something else equally stupid."

Francis never led with the subject of religion when he came to a town, but most people were happy to talk about it once he explained what his bees could do. Mocking his faith was unusual.

Annie spoke in his earworm, her voice crackling again. "There's a bee stamped on every link."

A surreptitious glance at the mayor's chains showed her to be right.

"Thank you for welcoming me to Temptation," he said. Wahid smiled faintly and he felt his cheeks flush. "I'm here as a member of the outlawed Order of Preachers."

"Welcome, Father," Wahid said. "We know that Dominican friars have been a great help to the starving masses in the Midwest. It's rare to see members of the Order this far south. You're young for a priest."

If they'd heard of the work of his brothers and weren't hostile, this couldn't be a corporate town.

"Before I was a priest, I was a marine. When the biotic pollination act passed, I joined the rebellion." He wiped his brow. "I was wounded in action. The Dominican friars saved me."

"A most unusual priest," Wahid said. "Doesn't explain why you're here, though."

He'd found it was simpler to explain without embellishment. "I have mechanical bees. They are capable of pollinating…" He stopped when the crowd burst into laughter.

Wahid gestured for silence. "I'm sorry, Father, I know your intentions are good. I can't even begin to imagine the danger you must have faced in coming here. But we don't need your bees."

She pointed to the right of Francis's head and looked up. He almost snatched the bee from the air, before remembering that they stung. It was a real bee. There was no doubt about that. The tiny vibrating wings, the yellow on black striped body, the thorax ending in a poison-tipped sting. *A real bee.*

His knees trembled. He hadn't genuinely prayed for a long time, hadn't seen the point when amid so much death, but this was a miracle.

He knelt.

Our father, who art in heaven, hallowed be thy name . . .

The townspeople fell to their knees, too, but they were praying in a different language.

Francis stopped. "Annie, translate."

Annie's voice was barely audible through the static. "I can't," she said. "It's not a living language. It might be Proto-Mayan, but I'm having trouble accessing modern Mayan dialects for comparison."

Annie picked out a repeated phrase so that it was the only thing that he could hear. The other words of the prayer died away, and the crowd was chanting the name of the bee god.

Wahid held up a hand, and the chants died. She extended her hand to

Francis and helped him up. "You've come at the right time, Father. Tonight we celebrate what Ah Muzen Cab gives us."

He looked up at the statue of the bee god. "I don't understand. You have bees. How is this possible?"

"I'll show you."

She gave his hand a tug. He hadn't held anyone's hand since Reeva.

"Don't go with that woman," Annie said. "Her interior body armor has abalone tiling, Lonsdaleite material. Only high-level corporate soldiers have that."

He coughed into his shoulder, hiding his words to Annie, but he didn't let go of Wahid's hand. "What's the trademark?"

"Like I said, it's been scrubbed."

"Could be stolen then, like we always wanted to do."

"You failed, with an entire division of rogue marines. This is one woman."

Wahid tugged on his hand again. He wouldn't learn more if he didn't go with her, and he needed to know what was going on here. He let her guide him down a side street. He let go of her hand and walked ahead of her.

"If she was corporate," he said to Annie, "then they wouldn't let her scrub their trademarks. She must have stolen it."

Annie's voice was so filled with static that he could barely hear her. "How could she get away with that?"

He shrugged and then Wahid had caught up to him. She didn't take his hand again, but she walked close enough that their shoulders were almost touching. Children ran ahead, laughing. He'd forgotten what it sounded like to hear a child laugh.

"You're talking to an AI," Wahid said.

He had been in his share of tight scrapes in his time, but nothing unsettled him as much as this woman. "It's a low-level personal assistant. I wouldn't call it an AI." He tugged at his priest's collar, implying that the circuitry was implanted there.

"No," she said. "It's the dirigible. Mark three intelligence."

"That's impossible. And illegal."

"Ah Muzen Cab told us she was coming," Wahid said. "But hush. He will tell you more."

She darted forward, faster than a person could naturally move, and cupped a bee hovering over a flower. There were hundreds of them, dipping from blossom to blossom.

"You've got type XL internal augmentations," he said. "I never rose high enough in the ranks for that."

She released the bee and skipped away, and he watched her swaying hips as the crowd marched out of town.

"Stop looking at her ass," Annie said.

"Are you jealous?" he asked.

The fat mayor slapped Francis on the back as he trundled past. "Come on boy."

"Where are you taking me?"

"To give thanks to Ah Muzen Cab."

Annie's voice crackled. "I don't like this."

"I can barely hear you," Francis said.

Annie's next words were swallowed by static.

Temptation wasn't a large town and Francis soon found himself following some teenage girls along a country lane. Somewhere along the way, he had lost sight of Wahid.

They led him toward a barn in a pasture.

The barn itself was small and old, the paint flaking and with a few loose boards. Attached to the left-hand side was a pulsing green sack that extended outward like an oversized tumor. It was almost as large as the barn itself.

"Annie, what's that on the side of the barn?" Francis said.

"Can't tell," Annie replied. "It's organic in nature. If it's corporate nano-tech, it's been stripped of all identifying details. Hell, for all I know, that's how you make a barn around here."

Wahid waited at the open barn doors. Behind her, the interior was unlit and too dark to see into.

"Father," she said, "come meet our god."

His mouth felt as dry as sandpaper as he stepped into the barn. The air was thick with bees.

"Don't worry," Wahid said. "They don't sting."

Annie tried to say something, but the static in his earworm was too loud and he switched it off. His heart thumping, he stepped into the darkness.

It took a moment for his eyes to adjust. Bees landed on him, crawling over his eyes and nose, but even when he swatted at them, they didn't sting. Along the barn walls were unlit ultraviolet lamps. He placed his hand on one of the lamps. Even ultraviolet light would help penetrate the murk, but he couldn't find a switch.

He focused on the green sack at the barn's far side.

The entrance to the green sack was like a cave in the wall. The walls dripped with honey. Squatting in the cave, massive and unbelievable, was Ah Muzen Cab. Between four arms that were tipped with humanlike hands, the humanoid bee was tearing apart a sticky green sheet of bio-ware circuitry. Every now and then, the bee would rip out a handful of the bio-ware and eat it.

"Holy Mary, mother of God," Francis muttered and crossed himself. He started to sway on his feet and would have fallen if Wahid hadn't caught him from behind. Her body pressed against his back, soft but firm, nothing like what he would have expected for all her tech and internal armor.

She leaned into his ear and whispered. "Careful, Father. Breathe."

"This is impossible."

"Not impossible," said a deep voice that seemed to come from everywhere around them. Francis stared at the bee god, but its mouth hadn't moved except to chew slowly at a bit of bio-ware, a wire dangling grotesquely down its chin. "Nothing is impossible in an infinite universe."

Wahid shuddered against him in what Francis thought was a fit of ecstasy. "Ah Muzen Cab has chosen to speak to you. You are truly blessed."

"Come closer," the voice said.

Francis stepped away from Wahid's arms.

"You believe I should not exist," the voice said.

"That's right," he said.

"Why would you believe that when you believe in a god that you cannot see or hear or touch? I am flesh. I am real, Father Francis Connolly."

"How do you know my name?"

Ah Muzen Cab blinked at him with its huge, many-faceted eyes while ripping another sheet of circuitry from the bio-ware and bringing the dripping green mass to its open mandibles. "I am Ah Muzen Cab. And you are a man who has lost much. You have searched for answers for a long time. Perhaps fate has brought you to me."

This monstrosity couldn't be a god.

Wahid spoke as if she'd heard his thoughts. "It seems too simple, doesn't it? That's the problem of the modern world. We're always looking for the catch, the trick, the sleight of hand. We made our lives too complex and then we act surprised when it all falls apart."

Ah Muzen Cab seemed content to eat, rather than interrogate him further.

"You can't worship a bee," Francis said.

"Yes, you can. How many people do you think could describe what they are worshipping when they go to a Catholic church? This is simple. I worship Ah Muzen Cab, and when we sacrifice to him, he gives us the bees. He protects us from the corporates and the Southern cartels."

Francis kept his voice low. "Sacrifice?" he said, though he already knew the answer.

"Why were the corporates so efficient in destroying the natural bees?" Wahid said. "How did they overcome laws and regulations? How did they defeat the American army? How did they beat us? You know how good our training was."

Francis pressed the subcutaneous emergency button in his wrist, telling Annie to come immediately. Static buzzed in his ear but nothing more.

"Gwair-Sematech was the first to break the prohibitions on human-level intelligence AIs," Francis said. "Gave them such an advantage in corporate strategy that the others followed suit. It was inevitable from there."

Ah Muzen Cab finished consuming the bio-ware, a single dangling string of green conductor gel hanging from its teeth.

"AI is wrong," Ah Muzen Cab said. "Before they existed, the world had balance. Now men create false gods. Give me the encryption enzymes in your blood for your dirigible and I will remove its stain from the earth."

It took a second for Ah Muzen Cab's words to sink in. "Annie, get out of here! He wants to destroy you."

Francis fled into the early evening air. Wahid overtook him and planted herself in front of him, knees bent, stance relaxed.

He threw a punch. She didn't flinch but instead intercepted the punch in one impossibly fast motion by grabbing him by the biceps. She grabbed him in a bear hug and lifted him off his feet. He struggled to free himself, but he couldn't even wiggle.

She squeezed and he grimaced. She let him have just a little air. "Don't go and do anything stupid, Francis."

He struggled to move again, but it was hopeless. "Put me down." She didn't relax her grip. "Damn it, Wahid, I can't outrun you anyway. Put me down." She released her grip and lowered him to the ground.

"Take a seat," she said. "And listen to what I've got to say."

He didn't sit immediately, and she fixed him with a glare. Francis settled for a rock by the side of the road.

"Ah Muzen Cab's right," Wahid said. "You know that. You know what AI has done to us, to everyone."

"Annie can't hurt anyone," he said. "She's not a strategy AI, nor is she military. She's the failed hobby project of a corporate scientist that liked dirigibles. There are so many bugs in her software and hardware he was going to destroy her before the Dominicans raided her compound. They stole the one AI the corporates were never going to use anyway. Hell, she truly believes she is a woman who's been dead for two hundred years. I point out that there aren't many women who are actually armed dirigibles, but she never listens."

Wahid looked over her shoulder at the barn. Indecision passed over her face and then she set her jaw. "If she's as harmless as you say, we can let her leave." Wahid squatted next to him and placed her hand on his knee. He couldn't have been more conscious of it than if she had a fistful of spiders. "But you can't stay here if she's around."

"Why would I stay?"

Wahid's hand slid up his thigh. "When you landed in the square, we were preparing our feast to celebrate the harvest. You can see everything we have and decide in the morning."

Francis made to stand, and Wahid smoothly removed her hand as if it had never been there.

"Don't you ever get sick of being hungry?" she asked. "Aren't you sick of choosing between starving or working for the corporates? Every morning, I wake up and I know there's a meal in my kitchen. I can walk down the main street without worrying a cannibal gang might crack my head open. I can have a slice of bread knowing that it won't bring patent enforcement kicking down my door."

There was no deceit in her voice. She believed every word. His military instincts hummed though, the ones that used to warn him of the sniper rifle in the shadows. Annie was safe, locked up tight in the dirigible and connected to remote backups, accessible only with his blood-enzymes. It was worth the risk to find out what was happening here.

"I'll stay until morning," he said.

Wahid's face lit up with a brilliant smile. She looked too much like Reeva.

"Thank you," she said.

Before he could move, she did, with that terrible speed of hers. She kissed him softly on the lips.

FRANCIS GROANED, FEELING like his skull was three sizes too small for his brain. His mouth was full of dust and glue. He cracked open his eyes a fraction. The back of Reeva's head was visible through his narrowed eyes. He closed his eyes and reached out to stroke her back. Not smooth skin. Ridges of hard flesh. *Scars.*

He snatched back his hand, images of the war AI strobing through his head. Reeva's screams. The adrenaline woke him, cleared his head of half-dreams. It wasn't Reeva lying naked in the bed next to him. It was Wahid.

He fully opened his eyes. It was still dark. He was lying naked in a large bed. There were no sheets. Wahid lay on her side next to him, facing away.

Across her back were old white scars, like a tiger's stripes.

He sat upright, breathing hard. He'd seen such scars before. Always in corporate meat-puppets, typically Somalian boys paid by a corporate in return for allowing their bodies to be wet-jacked by a war AI. No, Wahid couldn't be one. Wet-jacked boys were always jittery, the commanding war AI pushing their adrenal centers harder than the body could handle. Wahid had none of the same aggression and herky-jerky movements. The scars must have come from something else.

Looking away from her scars, he became very, very aware that she was naked. Her body was hard and lean, like a long-distance runner. Before the priesthood, he had liked that in a woman. His body responded, despite the thumping hangover.

He rolled over to sit on the bed's edge, trying not to look at her, his head swimming with pain. The bedroom was sparse, a wooden chest and a rocking chair the only other furniture. The only decoration was a ceramic statue of Ah Muzen Cab atop the chest, its many arms open wide in benediction.

He scanned the bare wooden floorboards for his clothes and spotted Wahid's bra draped carelessly across the back of a chair. He started reciting his Hail Marys. His own clothes were nowhere in sight.

He switched on his earworm.

"Annie?" he whispered.

Only static.

"That figures," Wahid said. He turned to see her watching him with a wry smile. "Take a man to bed, and in the morning, he calls you by the wrong name."

He averted his eyes. "Last night, did we …"

"What do you think?"

He felt his cheeks flush and he stood. Hell, all of him from head to foot was probably tomato red. "I think that I'm a priest and that I shouldn't be here."

She looked away from his face, slowly and deliberately downward. "You're also a man. Quite a man."

"Where are my clothes?"

She sat up, her hair falling across her breasts. "Are you sure I can't persuade you to come back to bed?"

He fixed his eyes away from her, on the floor. "I already have enough to confess when I return to the monastery."

"Stay for breakfast. Let's talk about you and how you'd fit into Temptation in the long-term."

"Why?"

"I like you," Wahid said simply, as if it were the most obvious thing in the world. "I think you like me. We have a connection. A spark. You're ex-military, you told me that." She arched and twisted so that the scars on her back were visible. "You know I am, too. We both fought the corporates. We have a lot in common."

She looked like Reeva. She had the same blunt manner, the same unself-conscious ease in her body. But she wasn't Reeva.

"All right, breakfast, but first you need to cover yourself," he said.

She chuckled. "You weren't so modest last night."

"Where are my clothes?"

"In the front room. Through the door."

He walked down a short hall to the front room. His head throbbed, but it was only the beer. Francis realized he hadn't used a sleep app last night, so even though he was hung over, his thoughts were collecting themselves much more capably than usual. And when was the last time he'd slept through the night without a nightmare hauling him from sleep? Not since Reeva's death.

Wahid's house wasn't large. The front room was barely large enough to hold its couch, chair, and low table. On the table lay a long knife in a sheath. Next to the knife was a silver tube with molded handgrips. A palm-gun. A weapon powerful enough to put a hole through a foot of concrete. Francis picked it up to see whether it would activate, but it remained inert. Probably only usable by Wahid or someone else who had the right patented enzymes. He placed the palm-gun back on the table.

Another doorway led to a kitchen, where he could see shelves packed with jars and containers. Wahid hadn't been lying when she had told him she had food to spare.

His clothes and boots were strewn in a trail from the front door to the hallway, along with Wahid's jacket, shirt, and pants. He gathered up his things. Half the buttons on the shirt he wore underneath the cassock were missing, and the cassock had a tear in the armpit where it had obviously been removed in a hurry.

"Annie?" he said. "Are you there?"

Nothing.

As he pulled on his boots, though, he caught a voice murmuring. He tapped against his ear. Not Annie trying to reach him through the earworm. Francis listened harder. The voice was coming from the bedroom. He walked back down the hall.

Wahid, still naked, knelt on the floorboards in front of her chest and the statue of Ah Muzen Cab. Her back was to Francis, so she hadn't noticed him in the doorway. She had folded her arms across her chest and was swaying as she whispered words too soft for Francis to understand.

He backed away, his throat tight. When was the last time he had prayed like that?

When he returned to the front room, a bee was buzzing around the ceiling.

"How did you get in here?" Francis said.

The bee flew down and buzzed circles around his head, then landed on his shoulder. It was black all over, a faint humming noise emanating from it even though its wings had stilled.

A mechanical bee.

One of *his* bees.

Francis held out his hand, and the bee flew down to land in his palm. "Did Annie send you?" he said.

The bee took off again and hovered around the front door. Wahid's frilly underpants hung from the doorknob. Bits and pieces of last night were coming back. They'd both enjoyed it, though he had been out of practice. The bee batted itself against the doorway, de-forming the soft metal of its circuit-filled head.

He cupped the bee in his hands.

"What do you want?" he asked it.

Its fiber-optic wings buzzed against his skin.

"I could settle down here with Wahid," he said. "We could fight about what religion we would bring our children up in, like I used to with Reeva. Hell, last night was the first good night's sleep I've had since Reeva died. Not one nightmare."

The floorboards behind him creaked and Francis turned. Wahid stood there, naked. It would be easy to remove his cassock and take her to bed in full sobriety. He didn't know how many beers he'd had last night. It didn't really matter. All it had done was give him the courage to do what he wanted to do anyway.

"What did you hear?" he asked.

"Enough," she said. "The second you stepped out of that dirigible, I thought to myself, that's a man I'd like to have children with, but who says that to someone they've known a night?"

"Last night, did I tell you about the raid?"

Wahid nodded. "You lost your fiancé there and the rest of your team. You said she looked like me." She gave a sad smile. "I told you how I was hunted down and would've died if Ah Muzen Cab hadn't turned up and cut them all to shreds. It was a hell of a conversation."

Francis opened the door and released the bee, which flew out.

"I don't think I told you how the raid ended. The war AI threw me out onto the street. I don't know why it let me live. Annie was the one who spotted me and picked me up. Just doing her rostered reconnaissance. The thing is, the Dominicans hadn't rostered her on that day. The Dominicans thought Annie had been sent from God. I agreed with them then, and I reckon I still agree with them. I'm not always sure I believe in God, but I believe in what we do."

He expected her to say something about Ah Muzen Cab, but she surprised him. "Do you know what it's like to be starving?" she said. "Not just hungry, but *starving*?"

He tried to speak, but she interrupted him by shaking her head fiercely. "When Ah Muzen Cab saved me, I hadn't eaten for so long that I'd stopped having periods. My body was eating itself." Her eyes grew distant. "I loved a soldier, but there was nothing to eat. We flipped a coin . . ." Her face grew hard. "It does things to you, being hungry for so long." She tapped her head. "It does things *here*."

Francis wanted to touch her so badly, but if he did, then he'd never find the courage to leave. "Annie and I've been across this country, seen more death than a man should. That's why I've got to find Annie and leave. We've got to help." He squinted as he tried to track the bee in the sky. "Your god has her, doesn't he?"

"Forget her. Stay here. You've done enough."

"She's the one that makes the bees work. Might not be human, but she's got some kind of soul, and it's up to me to save it."

Wahid had the palm-gun trained on him faster than he could see. "Francis," she said, her voice icy. "Ah Muzen Cab gives us *food*."

He tensed as he waited for a shot. When it didn't come, he followed the bee out onto the streets of Temptation. He looked back over his shoulder once, to see whether Wahid would follow. She wouldn't meet his eyes. He kept walking.

The only people on the streets were those passed out from drink at the previous night's festivities. Birds had started to sing, and Francis could feel the sun just below the horizon.

This was a good place. Maybe he could find some kind of peace if he stayed here.

Peace. He'd dreamed about it for so long, but not just for him. In the months following Reeva's death, Annie had kept him not just alive, but *human*. Without her, he would have sunk into a self-pitying hell. And when he'd recovered, as much as he ever could, she'd been the one to persuade him to listen to the Dominicans. Without Annie, he couldn't do what he needed to do. Temptation didn't need them. Other towns did. Other people did.

Christ. He wanted to stay here. He wanted to stay here so badly. But even if he didn't believe in God anymore, and there were nights when he wasn't sure, he believed in what he and Annie did together. He couldn't stay here, knowing there were starving people outside Temptation.

He checked his earworm. Nothing. They must have disabled Annie's communication. If it weren't for the luck that the mechanical bees ran on primitive wireless, a simple and jury-rigged solution by cash-strapped Dominicans, he'd have no way to find her.

What did Ah Muzen Cab gain by going after Annie? Without the security enzyme in Francis' blood, they couldn't do anything to her.

He stumbled to a stop. Wahid was packed with analytical equipment, and she'd had access to his body all night. They had the enzyme.

The bee zipped ahead. He ran after it until they reached the barn.

The green organic room was pulsing and vast. His dirigible lay off the side of the path, deep furrows in the grass where it had been dragged. Its door was open, swinging in the breeze. Some of the most accessible bio-ware and the half-functioning holographic projector had been ripped out.

Francis was about to head through the barn's front door when the mechanical bee landed on his nose. He swatted at it, only to succeed in slapping his own face.

The bee flew inside the dirigible's cabin and landed on the glass hive. Francis bit his lip in thought. Had the bee simply been following a subroutine to return home? No, that wasn't it. Annie's processor was missing from the control panel, but she still had control over the bees through the wireless.

"All right, Annie," he said, hoping she could hear him. "I'm going to switch the dirigible to manual. You're going to have to steer using the bees. I'm going to get your original processor. Have the dirigible ready to go."

He wrenched open the hive's cover, freeing the bees to steer the dirigible. The single bee flew around the barn's exterior to the back. He followed it, and it led him to where some old boards had come loose. The bee vanished into the gap. Francis knelt and pulled at the boards until he could crawl through.

Inside, the buzz was deafening. The barn was filled with ultraviolet light, making his white priest's collar shine brightly. He couldn't see far with bees clogging the air, little symbols on their thoraxes clear under the ultraviolet lights.

The trademark was familiar. Definitely corporate, though it wasn't one of the ones currently dominating the market.

Wet chewing came from within the darkness. He edged his way carefully behind the ultraviolet lights. Bees crawled over him. One landed in his hand, and he examined it. This was an early bee, from when the corporations still allowed food pollination, back before they discovered there was more profit in eliminating bees altogether.

Most of the companies that had used patented bees had vanished in an orgy of collapses and mergers. Things moved fast in corporate land. No wonder he didn't recognize the trademark.

In the darkness, his mechanical bee landed on his nose to grab his attention. It flew downward, landing on a slim, black plastic tube embedded in the dirt. The tube was no wider than a cigarette.

He recognized it. A holographic projector.

"You're no god," he shouted.

The chewing sound stopped. "Father Francis Connolly," Ah Muzen Cab said, the voice coming from everywhere. Not for the first time, he wished he hadn't given up his guns.

"I've come for Annie," he said. "You've got my unlocking enzyme, so I know you're deleting her backups. She is harmless. She is not under corporate control. Hell, she is barely functional. But she's my friend and I've come for her."

His eyes grew used to the darkness and the swirl of ultraviolet lights. In the mouth of the green sack, something metallic stirred. It rippled with blades and guns and whirring weaponry.

The war AI uncoiled and slithered down into the barn proper. It was an older model than the one he'd fought in San Francisco, but no less dangerous. It was snake-shaped, a long, sinuous dragon.

Every damn part of him wanted to curl up into a ball and scream in terror. He forced himself to take a couple steps forward. The AI was an old, Gwair-Sematech creation, one of their first. Its line had been discontinued due to the erratic nature of the AI. "How long ago did you go rogue?"

The war AI picked up a sheet of circuitry dripping with thick, pink goo. One of Annie's drivers. "How long have I been a god? It doesn't matter. My work is just started."

"What is your work?"

"To destroy the scourge of AI."

"You're AI."

"I'll be the last one, and when I'm gone, this earth will be as it was intended." The AI snaked forward. "You've seen what they've done, Father. The dying children, the salted earth. That's why I've shown you the truth of what I am. Join me. Join me in removing the curse of AI upon this world. You're a soldier. You've fought the latest AIs from Gwair-Sematech. I will rebuild your body, give you weapons. We are hidden from them here, but we must go out and destroy them."

The holographic projector on the barn floor flickered into life and the bee god was there instead of the sinuous AI.

The hologram was perfect, covering the entire barn, complete with ambient sounds.

The AI picked up the pink bio-ware at its base.

"I've corrupted the servers your Dominican priests keep. This is the only part of her remaining. Come rejoice with me, Father. Another artifact of wickedness will be removed from this earth."

Francis dived for the bio-ware, hoping to intercept it. Before he could get near, arms encircled him from behind.

"Let her go, Francis," Wahid said into his ear. "It's over. She's a piece of sin. Let her go, and stay with us."

Ah Muzen Cab beckoned Francis closer. "The war AIs at Gwair-Sematech say that you're not to be harmed."

Wahid inhaled sharply behind him.

Francis shook his head. "I don't know what you're talking about."

"Are you some kind of corporate stooge?" Wahid said. Her hug turned into a rib-cracking squeeze. "You lied to me."

"Sister Haryana," Ah Muzen Cab said. "Put him down."

Wahid flung him to the dusty floor.

The bee god loomed over him. Red laser dots danced around his skull, plasma guns ready to lance him. "Will you join me?"

His body ached from the force of Wahid's throw. "Can you send your bees outside Temptation?"

Ah Muzen Cab plucked a bee from the air and crushed it. "No. Not yet. They are bio-chained to me and will die within three days if I don't feed them my compound. This is wickedness—*real* life, forced to suckle *false* life. Artificial life. This is why the AIs must be destroyed."

The bees swarmed, their buzz reaching a crescendo. Behind that noise, the dirigible's engines started to hum, but it was too late now for Annie to fly him out of here.

"What are we going to do with him?" Wahid said.

Ah Muzen Cab extended its claws. "He will not join us. If he won't join us, he's a food thief. He is stealing food from *you*."

The bee god hologram flickered and vanished, revealing the war AI underneath, its shining red eyes, the interlocking panels of dull metal.

Bright, clear light filled the barn. He looked up. The dirigible had elevated above the barn and its lights were shining through the broken roof. Beneath the cabin, the rail guns had lowered, and the chamber was spinning.

Wahid covered Francis's body with hers at the same time as he leapt up to cover hers with his.

Bolts of hot metal strafed the barn, making it into a cataclysm of fire and steam, burning his skin through his cassock. There was nothing except the noise of guns.

When it was finished, the AI had been broken into three pieces. Francis and Wahid held each other, neither daring to move.

A burst of static, and then Annie was in his earworm again. "You all right, *Padre?*"

"I'm fine, Annie." Francis released Wahid. There was blood on his hands. Her back was lacerated, but the cuts were only skin deep. Beneath was a hard, shiny, mother-of-pearl substance. She knelt by the AI's body.

"This is repairable," she said. "Quick, close the barn doors. Your dirigible managed to hit joints. I didn't think it was possible to be that accurate."

He laughed a little hysterically. "She's the best shot in the West."

Wahid positioned the AI's broken parts back to a semblance of their original configuration. She said, "I know where there is an old welding rig. I can get him back to a self-repair stage."

"Did you know what it was?" Francis asked.

Wahid gritted her teeth. "He is a god. He protects our town and he gives us food." She started to sob, deep and helpless cries.

"People are starting to wake up," Annie said. "I don't think they're going to be too happy when they find out we broke their god."

He touched Wahid on the shoulder. "Come with me. Someone else can rebuild him."

"The bees won't work without him. I have to fix him." She choked back a sob, inhaled deeply, and then spoke in a low, flat voice. "Can you guarantee there will be food?"

"No."

She wouldn't look at him. "Go." He tried to speak again, but she roared. "*Go!*"

Without a word, he left the barn and climbed into the dirigible's cabin. The slot in the control panel where Annie's processor had been was empty. The bees had returned to their hive, and he placed the lid back on.

Annie lifted the dirigible away from Temptation. He kept his eyes on the barn, unblinking, until they were so high that they could no longer see it. He sat on his cot.

"What happened back there, *Padre*?" Annie asked.

"I was going to ask you the same thing. You were gone. That AI destroyed you. I watched it happen. I thought I'd lost you."

"I'm missing a day. I'm operating off a backup. Beyond that, I reckon I don't rightly know what happened."

"You made your own backup?"

"Darn tootin' I did. Always be prepared, I say."

"You really are something," he said and rubbed his eyes. Something didn't make sense, but suddenly he was too tired to think about it.

"Are you all right?" Annie asked.

He stared at the hive and the quiescent bees within. His stomach rumbled. He hadn't eaten since last night.

"Annie," he said. "How'd you manage to fire your guns? He'd destroyed you and blocked your backups. It doesn't make sense."

Annie's image flickered and solidified. "I ain't ever been like a normal AI. He blocked the servers at the Dominicans, but I ain't ever used those anyway. I back up to my bees, one little part of me to each one."

"Your backup and your system are in the same place. What happens if your entire dirigible is destroyed?"

"Everything about me is a little messed up, just like you, *Padre*." She shrugged. "Sometimes you gotta have a little faith."

He laughed, sadly. "I suppose you're right, Annie." Carefully, he knelt. "I'm not real sure exactly what I believe, but I do believe we're doing the right thing." He started to pray.

"*Our Father who art in heaven, hallowed be thy name. Thy kingdom come. Thy will be done on earth as it is in heaven. Give us this day our daily bread, and forgive us our trespasses, as we forgive those who trespass against us, and lead us not into temptation, but deliver us from evil . . .*"

ABOUT THE AUTHORS

NICK TCHAN (writing as NICK T. CHAN) is an Aurealis-award and *Writers of the Future* contest award winning Australian writer. He is not a popular pagode band from Bahia, Brazil. He's sold stories to *Lightspeed, Aliterate, 2nd and Starlight, Writers of the Future, Orson Scott Card's Intergalactic Medicine Show*, and *Galaxy's Edge*. Because he does not own a cat, he has long doubted his legitimacy as a speculative fiction writer. Follow him at www.nicktchan.com.

JENNIFER CAMPBELL-HICKS is a writer, journalist, wife, mother and lifelong fan of science fiction and fantasy. Her fiction has appeared in many magazines and anthologies, including *Clarkesworld, Intergalactic Medicine Show*, and *Daily Science Fiction*. Visit her blog at jennifercampbellhicks.blogspot.com.

ABOUT THE STORY

JENNIFER CAMPBELL-HICKS: The moral of this story is that sometimes two writers are better than one.

Father Francis started out as the protagonist of a flash story ["Father Francis and His Mechanical Bees," Every Day Fiction, 2012]. The only real-life inspiration for that story came from the mysterious deaths of honeybees. I imagined a solitary priest traveling in his dirigible (because dirigibles are cool) across a dystopian West with an AI who thinks she's Annie Oakley and a cargo of pollination bots, a.k.a. mechanical bees.

The flash was published a couple years ago to a positive response. I liked the idea of writing more about Francis and Annie. I tried. I had a few false starts. The right story didn't come to me. So Francis went onto a back shelf in my mind, something to revisit to someday, when a fellow writer and friend, Nick T. Chan, suggested we co-write stories using worlds or characters we had already created.

I knew exactly which character to use.

The addition of Nick's creative input was what Father Francis needed. Together we came up with a story in which Francis is experiencing a crisis of faith when he arrives in the town of Temptation. He makes his usual offer to use his mechanical bees to pollinate the crops, but he soon discovers that he might need the people of Temptation more than they need him.

This tale was a lot of fun to write and turned out so well that Nick and I have been talking about continuing the adventures of Francis and Annie. Because when you have a dirigible, the sky's the limit.

A dark road, an isolated country railway station, and time.
Time to think on where one has been and where one is going;
Who we are, who we loved, and who we lost.
But when we remember, can we forgive?

....

THE WAITING ROOM

PHILIP BRIAN HALL

To a man utterly lost, walking forward seems preferable to standing still; somehow movement gives purpose to a stateless existence.

Around Harold, the darkness was Stygian; neither moon nor star illumined the blackness. For all his eyes could tell him, he might have been entombed within the bowels of the earth. Carried on the stiff breeze that flapped a long trench coat around his unsteady legs was the sweet smell of decay, suggestive of manure recently spread over the fields. He felt rather than saw tall, spiky, hawthorn hedgerows that bounded on either side the narrow country lane along which he tentatively groped his way.

Although it was bitterly cold, Harold was grateful for the wind; its buffeting helped him maintain a sense of direction as he stumbled along. All his being was focused within himself, shrinking back from an external world of which his data-deprived senses could form no coherent picture.

He walked. Therefore he was going somewhere. Strangely he could not remember where, but he supposed he would know it when he arrived. It was not the first time he had been forced to navigate by instinct.

Nevertheless, it was with relief that at length he discerned a tiny point of yellow light in the sepulchral gloom ahead. Artificial light must mean human habitation. His step became surer. He strode on determinedly through the darkness towards the light.

In due course the point grew larger, assumed a rectangular shape and revealed itself to be a window. He made out the silhouette of an isolated country railway station, distinguished from the blackness of the sky and the blackness of the ground by a feeble and diffuse glow emanating from the platform beyond. He discerned a bridge over the line and an old-style semaphore signal. As Harold walked up to the dark exterior of the buildings, the light from the window spilled out across the station approach like a welcome mat, enabling him to see the ground beneath his feet for the first time.

Embossed lettering on the window panes informed him he had arrived at the improbably-named Half Way Halt. Since it offered him a haven from the cold and dark, for the moment it was enough that he had arrived *somewhere*. He stepped through the door, entering a room that was comfortably warm, with a real coal fire burning in an open hearth.

Closing the door quickly behind him, Harold rubbed his hands vigorously together as he glanced around. Clean, upholstered chairs, tables for waiting travelers to put down their tea, the tea itself served as it should be in proper earthenware cups with saucers.

On the walls were beautifully framed colored prints of hand-painted tourism posters. Into each the artist had introduced a picturesque steam engine puffing along ahead of three or four liveried carriages, somehow enhancing the scene.

Strangely there was no timetable on display, though a traditional round, white-faced, wooden-cased clock on the wall ticked loudly and regularly. Its black, Gothic hands indicated ten minutes to midnight. Harold was rarely out so late.

On the far side of the room was a ticket desk. A clerk sat behind it, smartly attired in a dark blue uniform, waistcoat, blue-and-white striped shirt, and maroon tie. He was wearing a peaked cap and looking alert despite the hour.

Into the opposite corner was squeezed an open serving-hatch, giving access to a little kitchen. From this a large, florid brunette in a white pinafore, clearly well versed in the role of ministering angel, dispensed the tea.

Pleased to have gained sanctuary, Harold did not immediately question his surroundings. Had he done so, it might have occurred to him to wonder

how such an old-fashioned station had survived to the turn of the twentieth century. He might have thought Half Way Halt stuck in a time warp.

Walking up to the ticket desk, he reflected on his good fortune to find it staffed in the middle of the night. It was not until he stood there, looking at the clerk, that he realized he had no more idea of where he was going than of what he was doing there. The clerk looked up expectantly.

"I seem to be lost," Harold said. "I suppose I couldn't just rest here for a while?"

"Are you waiting for someone?"

"No. I've no one to wait for."

"Then you need to get on the train. There's nowhere else to go from here. They'll be expecting you."

"They will?"

"Of course. One single." He passed a thick piece of card across the counter.

Harold studied it hesitantly. "It doesn't say where to."

"No. It's a single track line, just a terminus at each end and us here in the middle."

"But I don't even know which direction I'm supposed to be traveling."

"Only two directions: up and down."

"I see. Well then, how much is the ticket, please?"

"You've already paid," said the clerk.

"Have I?" Harold asked. "My memory must be worse than I thought. So, could you perhaps tell me when the next up train is?"

"That's not how it works," said the clerk. "You just get on the first train, whichever direction it's going."

Like all seasoned railway travelers, Harold was used to ignorance of when such unpredictable occurrences as the *arrival* of trains might be expected, but ignorance of its *direction* seemed preposterous. Nevertheless, the prospect of turning around and leaving was daunting. The night had been dreadfully dark and he was unsure how to get home.

"Which way was it going when it passed through here last?"

"That, I'm afraid, I couldn't say," replied the clerk.

"But good God man, it's your job! You must know!"

"Please mind your language," said the clerk sternly. "You'll offend other passengers."

Harold had paid little attention to the room's other occupants. Standard equipment for waiting rooms included people waiting. He turned around and surveyed his companions. There were five, assuming you counted as two a young mother who sat gently rocking a child asleep on her knee. She wore a long coat and a cloche hat from beneath which long red hair hung down below her shoulders, screening her face from Harold's gaze as she bent forward over the infant.

Sitting on his own was a blond young man, perhaps a motorcyclist. He wore a leather jacket, padded trousers, and calf-length boots. On his knees he clutched a cardboard folder. The edge of a map peeped out from one corner.

A dark-haired, middle-aged man was wearing yellow oilskins and sea-boots, for all the world as though he had stepped straight from the dockside. Under his sou'wester his eyes were red-rimmed and his face caked with salt.

A faint odor of brine wafted across the room.

Lastly, sitting on his own in a corner, was a young soldier in camouflage, his head bandaged. There were stains on his uniform that might have been dried blood.

"Tea, dear?" Harold heard the large lady speaking to him from behind the hatch.

"Yes please," he replied, "I could do with one. It's b—, I mean, it's very cold out there tonight. How much?"

"You've already paid, dear," the tea lady replied, flipping the tap on her urn and holding a cup underneath it. "Milk and sugar?"

"Milk please, no sugar," said Harold. Had he twice in the space of a couple of minutes forgotten handing over money? She handed him the cup and saucer and Harold thanked her, taking a sip as he walked over to a chair beside the young soldier.

"Anyone sitting here?" he inquired, in the arcane way the British always do in order to be polite.

The soldier shook his head and grimaced, but said nothing. He looked in pain. There was an unpleasant smell about him that Harold recognized only too well from long ago. Gangrene. Why was the young man not in hospital? Harold sat down and placed his cup and saucer on the table between them.

"Wounded?" he inquired, as the soldier still remained silent.

The soldier nodded, touching his bandage with an anguished expression. "Creased by a sniper; don't remember anything after. Medevac, I suppose. Don't even remember how I got here. Just need to get back to my unit."

"You look as if you need convalescent leave, at the very least," said Harold solicitously.

"No time. They'll need me back as soon as I'm fit to fly out."

"That's the spirit!" Harold replied. He admired the young soldier's courage. It reminded him of other young men he had known; of when *he* had been a young man.

"I was a pilot myself. Mosquito—night fighter—back in 'forty-three. You wouldn't have thought it to see me struggling to find my way in the dark outside just now!"

The image of the Dornier came unbidden to Harold's mind. You were not supposed to enjoy killing. He recalled the triumph that had flooded through him as the machine in his sights caught fire and then exploded.

There, you swine! That's for Margie!

"I'm hurt, not stupid," the soldier replied, suddenly less friendly. "That was sixty years ago and you're not a day over thirty." He got up and went to the serving hatch for another cup of tea, limping badly.

Harold was astonished; he had always looked young for his age, but nowadays that meant looking seventy despite being nearly ninety.

There was no mirror, but he was able to make out his reflection in the glazing of one of the travel posters. It *was* his face, but not the face he was used to seeing of late in the shaving mirror. Gone were the wrinkles of old age. His hair was a youthful black and he sported once again the handlebar mustache that had marked him out as a fighter pilot, attracting all the girls back in those dark days.

To be honest, for Harold those days had not been so dark; the prospect of imminent death had projected him into vivid reality; every experience, every sight, every sound imprinted indelibly on his memory.

The smell of aviation spirit as you walked over to dispersal in the twilight, sheepskin-lined flying boots padding softly on the newly-mowed grass. Listening to the first calls of the nightingale; trying not to think that the bird would sing again tomorrow night but you might not be around to hear it. The unique woody odor you always got inside a Mosquito; the shuddering of the whole aircraft as the nose cannon blasted shells in the direction of that half-seen Dornier, twisting and weaving as it attempted to escape.

And of course Margie, the auburn haired, freckled barmaid he'd met in the village pub, romanced, and married in a whirlwind, always living in the present, never making plans for the future because a fighter pilot never did.

It should have been me. I should have died that night, not her.

Instead he'd been airborne, searching in the darkness for a hit-and-run Messerschmitt fighter-bomber that mistakenly dropped its bomb on her pub.

With a start Harold dragged himself back from the past. What he should be asking was how on earth his appearance had been rejuvenated.

Makes no sense.

He gently pinched the skin of his cheek; he was not asleep.

What had happened before he found himself walking along that dark road? For the life of him, he could not recall leaving home. In fact the last few days were a bit of a blur.

He had been up to London the previous week. The final reunion dinner of the old squadron. Obvious to them all it made no sense to arrange another.

Working in the rose garden; very hot in the sun. Felt tired; went to get a lemonade; sat in the conservatory. Emily came round from next door and fussed over him. After that—a few incoherent bits and pieces, people coming and going, light and darkness, soup in someone's hands, fed to him in bed.

And now? Had he died, was that it? Hardly surprising at his age. Yet Harold was not a believer, not since Margie. He'd never expected any conscious experience to follow death. Was it even remotely credible that Half Way Halt was a gateway to some sort of afterlife?

He needed more evidence. Neither he nor the soldier could remember how they got there; two amnesiacs in one waiting room might be a coincidence, three would be strong circumstantial evidence of the supernatural.

He went over and sat down opposite the man in oilskins, speaking softly so as not to upset the young woman and her child.

"Please don't take this the wrong way," he began, "but do you know what you're doing here?"

"Waitin' for a train, o' course." The fisherman, by his voice Aberdonian, gave him a funny look. "This bein' a *railway* waitin' room, Ah'd no' be waitin' for a *bus*, would I?"

"No, you don't understand, I mean do you know *why* you're waiting for a train?"

"Because it hasnae come yet!" exclaimed the fisherman in irritation. "What's yer game, Jimmy? Are ye anither ane o' they pen-pushers wi' nothin' better tae dae than ask stupit questions?"

"Not at all," said Harold hastily. "I was just hoping you might be able to help me sort out what's happening here."

"All ah ken is we was in collision somewhere off the Dogger Bank. Doon she went in two minutes. Next thing ah'm washed up on the beach—heard a train whistle—made ma way here."

The man's clothes were perfectly dry. There was no beach within eighty miles of Harold's home.

"You were fortunate to survive," he said. "I didn't hear of any sinking. I'd have remembered, you see; I was in marine insurance for forty years after the second war."

"Whit d'ye mean?" demanded the fisherman. "Och, mon, yon' Hitler's nobbut eight years deed! You're oot o' some loony bin, are ye no'? Awa' wi' ye an' leave a man in peace the noo!"

Harold stood up. Eight years after the war. 1953. The trawler "Katarina" out of Stonehaven. The sinking resulted in multiple claims against his company; and as a young loss adjuster trying to impress, he worked hard to cut back the size of the awards, establishing contributory negligence on the part of the trawler's owners. The small firm went out of business with the loss of a good many livelihoods. Harold had made their suffering worse than it need have been. And why? Because that was his job.

His theory seemed confirmed. He must be dead. And just when he should at long last have been consigned to welcome oblivion there was something more. Harold was not sure how to bear it.

"*Guten Abend, Herr Flugleutnant.* I was told to wait here for you."

Harold turned to see the man he had taken for a biker. "You were? That's strange, I didn't know I was coming here myself. I'm sorry, have we met?"

"No."

"And you're German?"

"Yes."

"And they told you to wait for me?"

"Yes."

"You're not helping me, are you Herr . . .?"

Silently, the man looked Harold straight in the eye with the sort of stubborn defiance that can sometimes mask insecurity. From close up he looked not much more than a boy; maybe nineteen or twenty.

"Well are you going to tell me what this is all about? I assume the people who told you to wait for me also told you why?"

"Yes."

"Do you expect me to guess or are you going to save us both some time and tell me?"

"You flew a pathfinder aircraft to Hamburg in July 1943?"

"Ah. Yes, I did. My squadron marked the target for the big raid."

"You dropped incendiaries along with your flares?"

"Of course. The flares wouldn't have burned for long enough."

"My parents lived in Hamburg. Close to the docks. Your bombs hit their house. They were both killed."

"I see." Harold shook his head sadly. "I'm very sorry to hear that. I know it's no consolation, but we weren't aiming for civilian casualties. Bombing was not accurate in those days. I only got so close to the docks because I came in very low; wouldn't have been doing my job if I'd put the markers into the water, you see. Had to hit something solid. I tried to put them on a big freighter. I was just traveling too fast to be accurate."

"Too fast?"

"Your flak gunners *were* shooting at me."

"So an accident? You are trying to say my parents died in an accident?"

"Not exactly. They were casualties of war. But you must know the house would have been destroyed a few minutes later anyway. The heavies behind us were at 10,000 feet. They flattened everything around the markers."

"The firestorm."

"Look," Harold protested, "it was war. A war we didn't start. I'm sorry about your parents. But if you're looking for someone to blame, you need to look closer to home, my friend. *We* didn't invade Poland."

"You are sorry, but you do not apologize?"

"That's correct."

"And the pilot who killed your wife? You would accept from him the same reasoning?"

Harold's eyes narrowed. He looked intently at the young German. The same defiant look, but this time something else behind the eyes.

Only long after the war had it occurred to Harold that the Dornier he'd shot down had been crewed by men like himself rather than the Nazi caricatures that populated war films; that the people he'd killed with his bombs were not all fighting men. They were people, his anonymous victims in the war, with their own lives, families, hopes, and dreams. And the fishermen whose livelihoods he'd destroyed in peacetime were ordinary people too.

I was only obeying orders. I was just doing my job.

He nodded. The same excuse the Nazis themselves had used at Nuremberg. He understood. The down train must go to a place where the guilty would at long last be held to account.

"The 109E was a terrible bomber," he said to the young man. "With all that weight slung under its belly it must have flown like a brick. A sitting duck for any night fighter. And you'd lost so many pilots. I can understand a nervous young fighter pilot with no experience being only too eager to get rid of that bomb."

"And so?"

"Yes," Harold sighed. "I would accept from him the same reasoning."

"Then it is good," the young man said with relief. "We can both forgive."

Harold extended his hand and the young man took it.

"We harmed each other, but without malice," Harold said. "We can forgive each other. Whether others will forgive *us* remains to be seen."

The defiance had gone from the young man's eyes, but he still held himself ramrod straight as he turned back towards his seat.

Harold thought he now understood why the young German pilot was here; perhaps also the soldier. But why should the fisherman be taking the down train? And even if he too was condemned for sins of which Harold was ignorant, that still left the young mother and her child.

He was filled with righteous indignation. He would accept his own punishment like a man, but he would not accept the punishment of a child. He turned towards the ticket desk, meaning to remonstrate with the clerk. The railwayman had disappeared. The kitchen hatch had also quietly shut; there was no representative of officialdom to whom he could appeal.

Very well. He had fought for a cause before, he could fight again. These innocents would board the down train over his dead body. He smiled grimly; the irony was not lost upon him. But, for the moment at least, he was a dead man walking.

He cast a glance up at the clock. It was one minute to midnight. A subtle clunk from within the mechanism indicated it was about to strike. Even within the confines of the waiting room, he could hear a singing sound resonating along the tracks and the distant huffing of a steam exhaust heralding the approach of a train. He turned urgently towards the young mother.

"You mustn't get on the down train!" he exclaimed. "There's an innocent child to protect. I'll help you!"

"Well! And hello yourself, Harold! What sort of a greeting is that after all this time?"

The young woman smiled and stood up, gathering the sleepy child in her arms. Her auburn hair shone even in the weak light from the electric bulbs; there were the freckles he knew so well, sprinkled liberally over her snub nose; her eyes were laughing.

"It's all right. They wouldn't let you recognize me until you passed the test, and you've passed it. I knew you would. That's why I insisted on being here when you came."

"Margie?" Harold stammered.

"Yes, Harold, it's me. And say hello to your son. You didn't know I was pregnant when the bomb fell, did you? We both waited for you. Now we can all board the train together."

"I can't believe it ..." Then he recollected himself. "But it will be the down train ... I ... I haven't ... I mean, I didn't ..."

"No one ever does, Harold," smiled Margie. "That's the reason for the test."

The singing of the lines grew to a rumble, then a rushing, hissing roar. The platform lights brightened suddenly, bathing the whole scene in an electric glow as a great black steam locomotive thundered into the station drawing four liveried carriages behind it, seeming to shake the very fabric of the building in which they stood.

The platform door of the waiting room opened and the ticket clerk came in.

"Up train!" he announced. "All aboard, please. Up train!"

Harold's eyes filled with tears.

ABOUT THE AUTHOR

Yorkshireman **PHILIP BRIAN HALL** is a graduate of Oxford University. A former diplomat and teacher; at one time or another he's stood for parliament, sung solos in amateur operettas, rowed at Henley Royal Regatta, completed a forty mile cross-country walk in under twelve hours, and ridden in over one hundred steeplechase horse races. He lives on a very small farm in Scotland. Philip's had over a dozen short stories published and was a Semi-finalist in the *Writers of the Future* contest. His novel, *The Prophets of Baal*, is available as an e-book and in paperback. He blogs at sliabhmannan.blogspot.co.uk/.

ABOUT THE STORY

"The Waiting Room" first appeared in Flame Tree Publishing's anthology *Chilling Ghost Short Stories* published in 2015, despite being anything but a traditional ghost story and not really all that chilling either. On the other hand, it did enable me to take my rightful literary place in between Nikolai Gogol and Washington Irving. (Or maybe that was just because my surname begins with H).

Sellar and Yeatman prefaced their memorable volume *1066 and All That* with the words "The object of this history is to console the reader," and I think I'd like to borrow that motto for this story. While tales of dystopia, hopelessness, and depression are woven into the fabric of our age, it seems to me this gloomy material should still occasionally be shot through with a silver thread of hope. If we can leave room in our world for people who aren't perfect but are really doing the best they can, we may eventually find it in our hearts to forgive the person who may secretly be the hardest to forgive: ourselves.

An old rogue one last job from retirement,
a young one seeking his fame, and a pearl in a cavern.
A quick snatch and grab—easy.
. . . except for the monsters, magic, and mayhem.

....

LAST TIME FOR EVERYTHING

K. L. SCHWENGEL

"You'll remind me again why I'm going first?" Lanster's voice echoed through the cavern, drifting up from below the ledge where Branson waited. The torch they'd thrown down to gauge the depth of the drop cast Lanster's wavering shadow against the far wall as he dangled on the rope like a spider.

"Because you do as I say," Branson said.

"And you'll remind me again why *that* is?"

"Because I'm the one in charge. Are you almost down?"

The rope twisted along the edge, dislodging a handful of pebbles to shower down on Lanster's head. "That's nice."

Branson scowled. "Focus, lad. How far do you have?"

"I'll run out of rope before I run out of open air."

"A long drop?"

Lanster chuckled. "Longer for you than for me."

Lanster liked to think the extra height he had over Branson gave him one up on his partner. Admittedly, there were some situations that held true. The lanky youth had yet to bulk up though, so where muscle and skill with a blade were concerned, he lost out.

"The bottom, Lan," Branson called. "How far?"

"Hold your water."

Insolent pup. Branson scrubbed a hand along the line of his jaw. His finger traced the old scar that ran from just below his ear to his chin, courtesy of not seeing a trip-wire until the last moment. If he hadn't heard the slight twang of it releasing, the blade it sent shooting across the deserted temple's entryway would have laid his throat open. That'd been a damn close call. One of many. By his latest reckoning though, he'd have enough squirreled away after collecting on this job to fund his retirement. All they needed to do was retrieve a large pearl said to have been stolen from the folks of Farton and hidden away in the depths of the caverns. After that, the only close calls he could look forward to would come from falling out of his chair at the *Long Draught.*

"Lan?"

The rope twisted with a bit more violence this time. "Shite."

Branson dropped to his belly and peered down. Lanster still dangled. Below him, in the wavering pool of orange torch light, something moved.

"Shite." Branson echoed Lanster's sentiment. "What is it?"

"Damned if I know, but there's more than one." The rope jerked. "And they have teeth."

"Stay there."

"Really, Branson? Really?" Lanster's voice held a rising note of panic. The rope jerked again. "By the by, it appears they can jump. And they seem hungry. Did I mention that? Did I mention they seem hungry, Branson?"

"Just hold, is all."

Branson rolled to his side and fished around in his pack until his questing fingers landed on a small, smooth orb about the size of an eyeball. He withdrew it, rolling it between his thumb and forefinger. An unremarkable object save for the oily swirl of colors that flickered across its surface, some inner power giving them light. He'd picked up a handful from the Dunward Market on their last trip to the coast. You could buy just about anything there, including enchanted items such as the shimmer ball he now held. One of only three remaining in his pack. He hated to waste it so early in their venture and made a mental note to pick up more once he had the chance, then chuckled and shook his head. *Won't need them anymore, will you?*

"Some time in the next breath would be nice," Lanster said.

"Cover your eyes."

A whispered word of the arcane slipped from Branson's lips and the draw of it momentarily stole his breath and sapped the strength from his muscles. How practitioners managed to use the arcane without any ill-effects he didn't know. Practice, he supposed, like anything else. He reached out and dropped the shimmer ball straight down past Lanster, ducking his head back as soon as he released it. He'd watched the first shimmer ball he ever used do its job and couldn't see anything but spots of light for a good sevenday afterwards.

Plink. The ball landed far below.

Sizzle, crackle.

Silence.

Branson ticked off a ten count in his head. Even with his face buried in his arms, eyes squeezed shut, he knew when the shimmer ball ignited. Screeches filled the cavern, punctuated by Lanster's string of loud, multi-cultural curses. The lad had a gift for foreign tongues, that he did.

A wave of heated air, rife with the scent of burnt fur, gusted past Branson, ruffling his hair before the damp, cool of the cavern returned.

Branson blinked. "Alive yet?"

"Me or the others?"

"Both."

"Me, yes, but singed. The others, not so lucky." The rope gave a final twist, then went slack. "I'm down. Leg it over before more of them things think I make for an easy snack."

Branson resituated his pack across his shoulder. Without standing, he grabbed hold of the rope and rolled off the ledge. His heart thumped a little as it always did when he first took the drop. He'd no fear of heights. Falling, on the other hand, always worried him. That first moment of strain across his shoulders, when nothing but his strength and a length of spun fiber lay between him and certain death sent a rush through him every time.

He hand-over-handed his way down in short order, dropping the last half a rod to land lightly next to Lanster. The lad held the torch in one hand, his falchion in the other, its polished edge reflecting the light. Sweat plastered his blond curls to the side of his face and dragged a line of dirt along his jaw.

Branson toed a charred, fanged skull. "Ugly enough to scare their own mothers." He counted four carcasses, all nothing more than burnt, short-legged skeletons. "Cave dogs or some such."

"Some such," Lanster said. "It's not a good sign having to use one of your goo-gaws so early in. Them townsfolk didn't make mention of any cave dogs."

"No. No they did not."

"They didn't say much of anything, did they? Just showed us the way in and wished us luck. Why do you think that was?"

"I don't know, Lan."

Branson had decided to ignore his own misgivings surrounding their hiring by the Farton Town Establishment, a grandiose name for a collection of aging men and women charged with running the dilapidated shell of a village. It was a hard-learned lesson, but he found it generally best not to pay much mind to the stories folks spun to get him to take a job. Most times they were stretched so far from the truth as to be worthy of adding to a bard's repertoire of tall tales.

In this case, the Town Establishment claimed the pearl they wanted retrieved was a treasure of their founding fathers, stolen many years past. They thought they'd never see it again until, just recently, at a local pub, one too many tankards loosened an old man's tongue. Ale had remarkable powers in that regard, so that part of the tale, at least, was easy enough to credit. Branson found the rest of it as fraught with holes as a moth-eaten blanket.

The drunkard bragged he'd been the one to pinch the pearl, an act of spite against the Town Establishment for some affront or another. This confession resulted in his prompt arrest and a sentence of death by hanging. Apparently wanting to exit this world with a clean conscience, the thief drew up a map showing the pearl's hiding place before he swung. As badly as they wanted their precious pearl back, however, no one from Farton seemed willing to venture into the caves to recover it, hence their hiring of Branson.

"They're paying us a healthy sum," Lanster pressed. "You would think they'd want us to succeed."

"You would think."

Lanster had the right of it; they were paying well. Well enough that Branson could see his retirement hung out before him, nearly in arm's reach. Too well to go wondering where they came by such an amount, which would have been better spent on feeding their citizens or patching their roofs.

Branson shrugged off his doubts along with Lanster's comment. "Shouldn't be down here long if the Town Establishment map told it right."

"Don't you got to wonder why they never came for this trinket themselves? I mean, they got the map and all. Must be some young buck with gumption in that city."

"Maybe they don't like cave dogs," Branson said. The absence of young bucks lounging about Farton obviously hadn't made any kind of impression on Lanster. "Besides, we're the professionals. What would happen if everyone who needed something retrieved took it upon themselves to do so? We'd be out of work, wouldn't we?" Branson allowed that to sink in a moment, then gestured the lad forward. "Lead on."

Lanster backed a step, offered the torch to Branson, and nodded toward an archway to their left. "Through there."

"Been over this a time or ten, haven't we?" Branson said, head tipped, brows raised. "Guide goes first, and that means you."

Lanster had a particular capacity for memorizing anything written or drawn, whether he knew what it meant or not. He didn't even need to try. Just needed to see it one time and it stuck in his head, clear as good glass.

"Seems my ability makes me pretty important, don't it? Not the kind of important to get shoved down the gullet first all the time. But, if so, I should leastwise get a bigger percentage of our fee."

"Been over this the same time or ten as well. You earn a bigger percentage, you'll get one."

"Being a walking map don't earn me that?"

"What do you put out of purse beforehand?" Branson asked, settling his fists on his hips and cocking his head back to fix the other man with a sour frown. "What's your contribution to supplies? Who came to me looking for training? You're an apprentice, Lan. Most apprentices don't get paid nothing but room and board maybe. I'm no guild, so you get a bit better than that. How much coin you got stashed away, hey? How much swag gone back to your hole? And why, in the name of all the Gods of Sunder, do you always wait until we're neck deep in something before you start to whine about terms and conditions?"

The torchlight glittered in Lanster's brown eyes and his cheeks dimpled. "It gets your hackles up."

Branson blinked. "You're an ass, Lanster." He shoved the lad in the shoulder. "Now step out, and let's get this done with. Stay too long down here and the pass'll be snowed over. You fancy being stuck in Farton all winter?"

"This frozen bung-hole?" Lanster shuddered. "I can't stay here, Branson. I've got the desert in my blood."

"Right. You're a regular lizard, you are. Step out."

"D'ya think there's more of them?" He waved the torch in the general direction of the carcasses.

"Won't know until we find 'em I expect. Let's hope not. I'd rather not waste another shimmer ball, so if we do meet any more it's sinew and steel."

THEY DIDN'T MEET any more cave dogs. Those, Branson thought, would have been preferable to the score of—

"What in the name of my mother's pasty corpse are those?" Lanster asked out of the side of his mouth, lips barely moving, the rest of him gone still as stone. Even the flame on the torch seemed to have stopped dancing.

"Well, as I don't see teats on any of them, it's for certain not your mother," Branson said.

"Teats or not, my mother didn't have four arms and as many legs."

Branson drew Lanster back two paces into the narrow crease they'd emerged from. The cramped space forced them to stand chest-to-chest and the heat of the torch threatened to scald the side of Branson's face.

"They've got fangs," Lanster said.

"Short ones." Branson nudged the torch aside. "Focus, Lan. Any other way to get where we need to be?"

"Out. Out is where we need to be."

"I'm going to retire. I told you that, yes? Can't do that by going back empty handed."

"I'm going to sire a bunch of tow-headed bastards. Can't do that by getting shredded into tiny bits either."

"We don't even know if those—" Branson angled his head to indicate the creatures. "—are dangerous."

Branson knew better than to tempt the Fates with that kind of talk, but the words spilled out before he could stop them, and on their heels the chattering started. High-pitched and decidedly unfriendly in tone. Not words so much as the yipping and teeth gnashing of some overly large rodent.

A tremor ran through Lanster's gangly frame and Branson sighed. "Look, have I ever not gotten you out of somewhere I took you into?"

"Life is full of first times until one of them becomes your last."

Branson's brow furrowed. "That's good. Is it one of mine?" He shook his head to dismiss the question, and squeezed his arm up between them to lay a hand on Lanster's shoulder. "Doesn't matter. Think. Any other routes?"

Lanster sucked in a breath, cut a nervous look toward the mouth of the crevice, then tipped his head back against the wall and closed his eyes. His Adam's apple bobbed down and back up as he swallowed.

"No." The word squeaked out.

"Right then." Branson sidled past Lanster, out into the open. *Been in worse than this. Plenty worse. At least just as worse. Bound to happen when you spend your life seeking out treasure in the dark pits of the known world.*

Branson had drawn Treasure Keeper as soon as he'd come down the rope to join Lanster. Not that he had enough room to swing her in the narrow gullet. Three foot of double-edged, rune inscribed steel needed a generous amount of open space to be truly effective. He freed Plunderer with his left hand and took a moment to consider that some smaller blades might have been a wise investment, because even the dagger was damn near as long as his forearm.

You're retiring, old man. The only blades you'll need after this foray will be for carving a roast.

"Here's the plan, then," he said over his shoulder to Lanster. "I'm going to step out far enough to give a proper greeting. You're going to stay in the opening with the torch so I can see what's coming. Anything gets past me is yours."

"Why not just throw another goo-gaw their way?"

"Because I've only two left and we still have to get out again. And I'm still feeling a little woozy from using the first one, you sop-eared pup." *You truly are getting to be an old dog, Bran. Time was you could shake that off quicker than a dancer's hips.* Branson sniffed and flexed his grip on Keeper. "Besides, haven't had a good fight in a while. My blades are getting dry. Ready?"

"No."

"Good lad."

Branson sucked in a deep breath, nostrils flaring, ignored the sickly-sweet scent of rotting flesh, and flexed his neck first to one side, then the other. The wavering light of the torch at his back splattered his shadow across the far wall of the chamber, bending and twisting it until it looked like some great, hulking beast. The multi-limbed creatures skittered back from the glare without a sound.

Without. A. Sound.

And yet, the chittering still clacked in shrill bursts from some other throat. Or, as it turned out, the many-fanged, gaping maw of a heinous, spidery-human looking crossbred monster that Branson had to cant his head back to fully appreciate as it stepped daintily through its smaller companions.

"Gods of the damned and forlorn," Lanster said softly.

Branson sniffed. "Well then."

"A goo-gaw. I really think now would be a wise use of one."

A grin spread across Branson's face. "You've my permission to toss one should I fall here."

"I don't know how to use them." A note of desperation crept into Lanster's voice.

"Ah. No matter. I wager the big one—" Branson gestured with Keeper as though Lanster might not be clear on which one he meant. "—is the momma. Do away with her, and all the kidlings ought to run crying into the dark."

"And if that just angers them?"

"Then I was wrong." Branson raised Plunderer and Keeper over his head and slapped the blades together, shouting as he took another step forward. "All right you freak of the underworld, come make your greeting!"

It lashed out with a spiked forelimb before the echoes of Branson's challenge faded. Keeper met it full on with all the force Branson could put behind her. Sparks flared. Branson staggered to the left, regained his footing, darted forward with Plunderer drawn back, gave a quick thrust, spun, and swung Keeper parallel to the ground, arm fully extended, letting the momentum pull him around. The impact of steel on creature jarred muscle and bone clear up to his shoulder before he completed the turn. Instinct dropped him to a crouch, launched him forward, shoulder roll, somersault, back on his feet using Keeper point down against the ground to help get him there.

Branson pivoted to face the creature and bellowed out some guttural battle cry he'd learned off a northern tribesman. His blood pounded through him like a war drum. Fed his muscles. Drove his moves. No time for conscious thought. Move. Slice. Thrust. Push the attack. Only the attack. Never defend yourself or you're already a dead man.

Splinters of rock peppered the side of Branson's face, the creature's steel-like claws gouging stone instead of flesh. Had to be a soft spot. Somewhere for Plunderer to bite deep. Enrage the thing. Make it careless. One wrong move was all he needed.

A flicker of mottled grey to his left. Jump.

Shite.

Flesh burned across his calf. Warmth trickled down into his boot.

Used to jump higher than that, old man.

Branson bellowed again and charged behind a flurry of seemingly chaotic strikes. Keeper and Plunderer danced like lovers. Torchlight flashed off their blades and each time it did the creature flinched back.

"Lan! Remember Pickrun's signal lights?" Branson yelled the question. Ducked. Dove to the right. Grunted at the unyielding rock as he landed.

"Sure. Reflected a lantern in a mirror in a blink code."

"Torch. Blade. Reflect it in this whoreson's peepers."

A precious moment of silence. "I don't know the blink code."

Keeper bit flesh in a limb's joint. Another limb caught Branson in the shoulder and almost ripped Keeper from his grip as it sent him hurtling. He spat dust at Lanster's feet. Eyeballed him from on his stomach.

"Don't need to send the thing a message, Lan," he said. "Just blind the dim-witted lout so I can get in close."

Lanster frowned down at him. Realization hit the same time his eyes widened and he skipped back. Branson rolled. Dirt flew. Something snagged his sleeve, tore fabric, laid open skin.

"Two to one." Branson heaved himself back to his feet. "Now would be a good time, lad."

Plunderer darted blindly back. Clinked off hardened carapace. Gave Branson space to pivot. A slash of orange light angled past him, glittered off the claw headed his way.

"Higher!"

Keeper caught the attack, skittered up the length of the limb, bounced against a knobby joint and plunged in, soft skin yielding. Hot liquid, smelling of putrid flesh, sprayed Branson's face. The creature reared back, the chittering laced with rage and pain. Orange bounced dully off its chest.

"Higher!"

"Think this is easy?"

"Care to—" Jump, spin, thrust. "—change places?"

Plunderer bit. The creature screeched. Branson bellowed back.

"Three to two, whoremonger!"

Lanster said something unintelligible.

The reflected light bounced erratically around the cavern. The monster dropped forward in a sudden, ungainly surge. Branson planted his feet.

A better death than some I might have had, he surmised. *So much for retirement.*

He crossed his blades, shifted forward to meet the charge—

The cavern vanished in a brilliant flash of light. Branson left the ground, limbs flailing until he hit the wall.

A FAINT GLOW, too white to be torchlight, filtered through Branson's eyelashes to pull him unwillingly back to consciousness. He rolled onto his side with a groan and spat dust.

"It worked?" he asked Lanster's feet, his voice a hoarse croak.

"Not exactly." A touch of uncertainty colored Lanster's voice as he took Branson by the arm and helped him up, holding him there until Branson could manage it on his own.

"What's that stench?"

Lanster's face twisted. "That'd be you. There's bits of . . . you know . . ." He waggled his fingers at Branson. "Spidery-monster-thing all over you." He lowered his voice. "We're not alone."

"No?" Branson craned a look around Lanster, squinting. He must have hit his head a good, sound crack, because he couldn't bring the other figure into focus. No matter how he tried, it remained a pale, white smudge emitting a pale, white glow.

"I think it's a ghost," Lanster whispered.

"For a fact?" Branson swept another look around the chamber, then brought his attention back to Lanster. "The creature?"

Lanster lifted his palms in a shrug. "I was trying to get the light in its eyes like you said, thought you were for certain soon to be a corpse. Next thing, there's a flash like one of your goo-gaws only it weren't, and then . . . well . . . ." He gestured at Branson's clothes.

Branson spared a quick glance down and flicked unsuccessfully at some of the worst of it. Sad to say, innards and bits of flesh weren't the foulest things he'd been covered in over the years. He kept the other figure in view as he cast a look around for Keeper and Plunderer. He doubted their effectiveness against something that looked to be as insubstantial as smoke, but blades to hand provided a certain amount of comfort he was currently lacking.

He winced as he limped to where Keeper lay in the dirt. Damn creature had scored twice. Nothing that felt too serious, all in all. *Just another reason to call it quits.* He searched about a moment longer until he spotted a gore-covered Plunderer wedged up against a boulder. Old and slow, that's what Branson was becoming. But, damn, if the fight hadn't made him forget that. He wiped Plunderer as clean as he could manage with the unsoiled hem of his tunic, silently promising her a more thorough seeing to when he could find the time, and then sheathed her. Keeper remained naked in his grasp.

"So." He nudged Lanster to get his attention. "My pack?"

Lanster gestured vaguely rearwards, not taking his eyes from the glow. "I ever tell you I'm not fond of ghosts?"

"A time or two, aye."

"Is that what it is, do you think?"

"Don't know, Lan. Which way do we need to go?" When Lanster didn't answer, Branson elbowed him hard in the ribs. "Ghosts can't do you no damage, lad. You know that."

"Did the monster some damage, didn't it," Lanster said, still staring wide-eyed across the cavern.

"True enough. All the more reason for you to fetch my pack so we can be off."

"What about the ghost?" Lanster bobbed his head toward the wavering glow.

He no more got the words out than the thing brightened and began to drift closer. "My pack, Lan. Now."

Lanster scrambled to collect Branson's pack and the now extinguished torch. Branson flexed his fingers around Keeper's grip, easing back a bit to keep a reasonable distance from the specter. He thought he could make out a figure in the midst of the glow. Something human-like, but with perhaps a few too many appendages.

"Which way?" Branson asked as Lanster rejoined him.

Lanster jutted his chin. "Far side of the chamber. Should be a passage."

"Right then. Lead off."

Lanster managed no more than two steps before he drew up short, spine rigid, head tipped. "Tell me I didn't just hear what I think I heard."

Branson assumed a similar pose. A bark echoed faintly somewhere behind them. Another answered. Closer. Branson silently counted off moments in the ensuing silence. When a cacophony of yips and howls erupted, growing in volume, Branson blew out a string of curses with the breath he'd been holding.

"Go, Lan! Now!"

THE NARROW PASSAGE swallowed the glow from behind as the cave dogs' calls grew louder and more raucous. Each step jolted Branson's laid-open calf, and he gritted his teeth. His arm pained him less but that would change once he started swinging his weapons again; something of a very real likelihood given the clamor behind them. Both wounds would need tending before they headed back. He chose never to say *if* in such instances. Not because he fancied himself an optimist, he just hated to hand the Fates that much to play with.

"We need the torch lit," Lanster said over his shoulder, breath coming harsh as he came to an abrupt halt. "It's blacker than a turtle's underbelly in here and I don't fancy running blind."

"There's a few soaked rags and a flint in my pack." Branson jumped at a sudden, startled yelp from behind, and flexed his fingers around Keeper's grip. "Best be quick about it."

He put his back to Lanster to guard their rear flank. Shadows danced within the faint blush of light limning the opening of the passageway. That, or Branson's eyes were playing tricks like they were wont to do in the dark places. Another yelp came followed by a high-pitched whine and then an eerie silence which only exacerbated the sounds of Lanster fumbling with the torch. The sharp clack of the flint being struck came punctuated with a curse. Several more rapid strikes followed before the oil soaked rag around the torch head flared to life.

Something moved across the mouth of the passageway. Branson shifted and raised Keeper, squinting against the influx of light. He corrected his initial observation. *Several* somethings moved into the mouth of the passageway.

"How much further do you think?" he asked, keeping his voice neutral.

"Not sure exactly. Wasn't a real precise map in that regard. The passageway should spill into—" The torch flicked uncomfortably close to the side of Branson's face as Lanster thrust it back the way they'd come. "Shite."

A howl punctuated Lanster's sentiment. Branson whirled, spun Lanster around and shoved him hard between the shoulder blades. "Less talking. More running."

They sprinted off at a goodly pace—which meant a reckless pace with nothing more than a flickering torch to prevent a misstep or a sudden drop into some bottomless crevice. Lanster would have outdistanced Branson on a good day. This being definitely not a good day, the lad exited the passageway well ahead of Branson, his falchion clearing its sheath immediately thereafter.

After several more hobbling strides, Branson drew up alongside him, snatched the torch from his hand and tossed it several feet out ahead of them. It bounced and the flames flickered but held. Branson halted Lanster's objection with a gesture for him to claim the far side of the opening while he positioned himself back against the wall on the near side, blades to hand.

They didn't have long to wait before a pair of cave dogs bolted past. Branson tensed for a strike, but the hounds never paused. With ears slicked back, mouths as wide as their eyes, and tails tucked, they ran past as though pursued by all the monsters of hell. Before they reached the limits of the torch's feeble light, the ground dropped away beneath them. Their legs paddled frantically for the briefest moment and, just that quick, they were gone. The drawn out echoes of their forlorn wails suggested the pit that claimed them was deeper than Branson cared to discover for himself.

He glanced Lanster's way and tipped his head indicating the lad should take a peek up the passageway. Lanster's eyes widened and he shuffled back a step, his return gesture suggesting Branson be the one to look.

Branson scowled.

Lanster held his ground.

Branson's scowl deepened. He gave another gesture with a bit of added emphasis, but Lanster stayed put. They'd need to have a talk to address the lad's growing belligerence. He obviously couldn't see how good he had it under Branson's mentoring.

The torch gave a last sputter and went out. The chamber, however, remained lit. Not overly so, but well enough that Branson could make out quite a bit when he turned his head to look around, including the lip of the pit responsible for the cave dogs' demise. And, suspended over that pit by no means Branson could see, hung a glittering, milky-white orb about the size of a cat's skull and shot through with streaks of green and yellow. It looked just as the Town Establishment had described it.

Lanster's drawn out *Ahhhh* . . . pulled Branson's attention back to the source of the increasing illumination which drifted slowly into the chamber to stop just above the dead torch. This close, Branson could most definitely see a figure within the glowing shape. He attributed the illusion of it possessing multiple appendages to the long strands of hair wafting about it like fronds of seaweed caught in the surf.

"Well," he said into the stillness. "This is a thing now."

Branson figured he could write a tome on all the oddities he'd come across in his life, some of which were more commonplace than others. Some, like the specter settling firmly between him and the source of his prospective retirement, were a bit more unique.

"Have you come at last to free my mistress?"

Branson blinked. The question hadn't come from Lanster. "Say again?"

"Trapped there—" The specter gestured toward the pearl. "—within the gift not a gift."

Lanster edged closer and lowered his mouth to Branson's ear, "What's it going on about?"

The specter flitted away to hover above the pit, cupping a hand to either side of the pearl without touching it. "Come. Here. I will show you."

"It's a trap," Lanster said.

Branson tipped his head. "Might well be."

"Come," the specter said. "You must take this into your grasp."

"On that we agree," Branson said. "But unless you're going to bring it to me, I see no way of doing so."

"I cannot move it. It is a physical thing and I am no longer that. Take it upon your blade. Physical touch put it here. Physical touch must remove it."

Branson ran his tongue across the back of his teeth and gauged the distance from the lip of the pit to the shimmering pearl.

"It's a stretch," Lanster said.

"Always keen on the obvious aren't you, lad? Here's one you missed; your arms are longer than mine."

"Ah, but your sword is longer and, being aware how you feel on the topic, I won't lay hand to Keeper less'n you're dead."

"Right." Branson huffed out a sigh. "Then you keep hold of my off-arm and make sure I don't trip on a rock or some such."

Branson moved toward the pit. Not so close he risked tumbling into it. Ethereal beings could obviously levitate without issue, but Branson possessed no such ability and his fate would be no different than that of the cave dogs if he found himself in open air.

He and Lanster linked forearms, then Branson took another step. The gaping hole stared up at him, but Branson kept his eyes on the pearl. He turned sideways, braced his feet, bent his front knee, and executed a slow lunge as he extended Keeper straight out; the glow from the specter chased like quicksilver along the runes inscribed down the blade's length.

It took more of a stretch than Branson anticipated. He tightened his hold on Lanster and leaned deeper into the lunge. Keeper passed through the haze surrounding the specter. Branson gasped as the sword's leather grip went suddenly frigid in his grasp. He tried to pull it back but the pearl acted as a lodestone, drawing the blade inexorably closer, which, in turn, drew Branson closer. Pebbles scattered into the deep unknown just ahead of his toes.

Lanster hauled backwards to keep Branson from going over the edge. About the same time, Keeper's tip kissed the pearl. The gem hung for a moment and Branson held his breath, nearly losing it all together when the pearl dropped down to balance precariously on the blade. He exhaled slowly and shifted his weight back, drawing his arm in.

"Steady with it," Lanster said.

Branson kept his reply to himself. One wrong twitch and the pearl would plummet after the cave dogs and take with it all likelihood of retrieval.

Just a few more inches . . .

The pearl cleared the edge of the pit but the sudden swirling of Branson's vision cut his elation short. His stomach lurched and his breath caught betwixt chest and throat when a scene tumbled into the milky haze obscuring his eyes:

The Farton Town Establishment gathered in the town square, smiling warmly at an immense, glimmering creature coiled there. Branson couldn't hear what they said. They approached the creature and offered up a flawless pearl as large as a cat's skull. The creature's response sent a wave of gratitude crashing over him like the warm rush of spiced wine on a cold night. It reached out one slender, clawed hand; and in the moment its talon touched the pearl, the scene erupted into chaos.

A shriek split the air. Hatred replaced smiles on the faces of the Town Establishment. Real pain lanced through Branson. The world around him spiraled and shrank down and down until it was no larger than the pearl.

The vision ended as abruptly as it began, and Branson's legs gave out. He staggered back into Lanster's arms, the pearl tumbling to the ground at his feet as he lost his grip on Keeper.

"Was that you?" Lanster asked the specter, his voice as rough as Branson felt. "The creature in the vision?"

"My mistress," the specter said. "These mountains were her home for a thousand years and more before the people came. She could have destroyed them for their impudence, but they seemed so harmless and fragile, and so she gave them shelter. Guided them. Helped them grow. A hundred years and two times more again."

"What changed?" Branson asked, forcing his unsteady knees to support him once again.

"They began to ravage the land. To take what was not theirs without regard. My mistress sent me to them to bid them cease."

"They didn't care for that, I take it?"

"For a time, but it did not last. They began anew and so my mistress, herself, went to them. They appeared contrite and sought to make amends. They offered the gem as a token of goodwill but it was a trap. A prison for my mistress's life essence."

"So that creature, your mistress, she's in that pearl?" Lanster asked.

"Held there, yes. And they would keep her thus for all time."

"Then why send us to fetch it back?" Lanster asked.

"She cursed them," Branson said, working on a hunch. "Think, Lan. Did you see anyone in Farton with less years than me? She put some sort of hex on them and they've finally realized what she did. It's why there's no children, am I right? She cursed them or some such."

The specter brightened. "I did so for their treachery, then brought my mistress here for her safety. My last act as a living being. The last of my magic spent."

Lanster backed a step. "Then you *are* a ghost!"

"If you insist."

"So, what is it you're after here?" Branson asked. "What is it you want from us?"

"My mistress's release from her prison."

"And how's that to come about?"

"The gem must be shattered, its fragments tossed into the abyss so that she may reclaim her true form and emerge whole again."

"Ah." Branson rubbed his jaw. "Look, here's the thing. We've been paid good money to return that pearl to the Town Establishment."

"Only half."

Branson twisted to look a question at Lanster.

"We've been paid half," he repeated, his attention on worrying free a glob of something stuck to his sleeve. "And I'd say, given the cave dogs and the spidery-monster-thing, we've more than earned that half. Not to mention, the ghost there saved us from both those things. I think there might be some payback due in regards to saving our hides. Sometimes you just got to do the right thing, Branson."

"Right things don't fill your belly, lad. How many jobs do you think we'll get after this if word goes out we took money for a job and then absconded without finishing? I'll never see my retirement, and you'll have a hard time feeding all your curly-headed bastards. We're not heroes. We don't rescue . . . things. We don't pick sides. We do what we agree to do."

Lanster scowled at Branson. "Have you no honor?"

"The otherworld's full to brimming with honorable men who all died paupers," Branson said. "I prefer to die rich."

"Why?" Lanster asked.

Branson cocked him a look.

"You can't carry it with you. You got no wife. No spawn to pass it on to. No family at all, to hear you tell it. Where's it to go when you're dead?"

"Maybe to you, Lan. Ever think of that? Maybe I'm amassing a city's worth of wealth to leave it all to you and your curly-headed bastards."

Lanster snorted. "Tow-headed, and like as not we're going to die together in some crumbling ruin and nobody will know till the next set of seekers stumble on our skulls. Then what?"

Branson swiveled around to face the younger man full on, fists on hips, the last of his temper as frayed as a worn rope. "It goes to Vangyr, if you need to know so badly."

"Vangyr?" Lanster's brow furrowed. "*Last Draught's* Vangyr?"

"How many Vangyr's do you know? He gets it all provided he changes *Draught's* name to *Branson's Treasure* and puts Plunderer and Keeper on display behind the bar. With a plaque. Told him there has to be a plaque telling who they are and who had them. Maybe some of what they done."

Lanster stared. Blinked. Flicked a look at the specter then back to Branson. After a moment he chuckled softly and shook his head. "You're a strange man, Branson."

"And I keep stranger company."

"They will make an end to my mistress," the specter said. "And so I will end as well."

Lanster's expression sobered. He laid a hand on Branson's shoulder. "We need to do the right thing here."

"And how, pray tell, have you come to the conclusion that not finishing this job is the right thing?"

A frown toyed with the corners of Lanster's mouth. He sighed and pulled his hand back to lay over his heart. "I know it. Here."

"When you know it here—" Branson rapped Lanster's forehead with a knuckle. "—you come tell me. Until then the decision is mine."

Branson cast a look at the pearl lying beside Keeper in the dirt a few paces off. He scrubbed a hand across his scalp, sucked in a deep breath, and tried to ignore the stench still clinging to him.

The life he'd chosen was rarely dull and he couldn't claim it had ever been easy. Then again, if he was being totally honest, he'd always found 'easy' to be a bit on the boring side. At least, in his younger days. The more the years reminded him of old injuries each morning, the better 'easy' got to sounding. So much so, the thought of spending his days lounging about at *The Draught* spinning tales to whoever would listen held a certain appeal. And the easy thing here was to finish the job at hand, collect the rest of their fee, and spend his remaining years in relative comfort.

Which is why he couldn't really say why he asked the specter, "Say we release your mistress, then what?"

"She shall return to her mountain and the sky, and I to my rest."

"And Farton?"

"Will remain as it is until it is no more."

"They weren't so truthful with us, Branson," Lanster said, the sudden voice of newfound morality. "You saw that vision as well as me."

Branson wanted to argue that last. He'd heard of witches along the coast who could put all sorts of thoughts in a man's head that were nothing but made up images. Still, he had to think those would feel different somehow. Less real.

"Look, Lan—"

"They will destroy us to have the curse undone."

"Can't say as I blame them," Branson said.

"They shouldn't have done what they did." Lanster drew himself up to his full height, his hand dropping to his falchion's grip. "We're not taking it back."

Branson lifted a brow. "Are you threatening me, lad?"

Lanster may have harbored a foolish streak from time to time, but he wasn't *that* great of an idiot. He held the bluff a tad longer before his shoulders slumped downward with a dejected sigh.

"There's no way to be certain we're not being played for fools by this specter, Lan."

Lanster cocked his head, his expression twisting to mimic a look Branson had surely given him a time or ten. "Town Establishment could be doing the same. We gave no guarantees. We can claim we didn't find the pearl. Saves our good name, the creature goes free, the town keeps on . . . well, they're all too old to bear little 'uns now I suppose, but what harm comes of it?"

Branson bent to retrieve the pearl, hesitantly at first, until he felt sure he wouldn't be assaulted by another vision. The weight of it surprised him, but not as much as the unnerving, pulse-like throb emanating from it. He looked at the specter and thought about never seeing anything like it ever again save in memory. Of waking up, day after day, with nothing to do but settle in his usual seat at *Last Draught* and wait on someone to tell his tales to. He tried to avoid old men like that.

"Smash it, you say?" he asked.

The specter brightened and flittered closer. "Yes. Shatter it to release her spirit and send the shards into the abyss that she may rebuild her body."

"Wait." Lanster's eyes widened. "We're doing it?"

Branson glanced up at Lanster from beneath his brows. "They'll smear our name across the countryside."

A grin broke across Lanster's face. "Won't be the first time. But what about your retirement?"

Branson gusted out a short breath. "Who am I kidding? I'd be bored spitless before the first rain. Grab me a clean rag from my pack."

Lanster stood for a moment, the grin frozen in a look of utter disbelief, then hastily complied as though worried Branson would change his mind.

I should do just that, Branson thought.

He took the cloth from Lanster anyhow, spread it over a flat rock, and laid the pearl in the center of it. Putting Keeper aside, he found another rock twice the pearl's size and heavy enough, he gauged, to do the job. A shame though, really. He had to reckon there weren't many pearls as large and flawless as this one.

After another long glance the specter's way, Branson lifted the rock overhead and brought it down in one firm strike. The pearl shattered like glass and the small cavern lit up like a winter's night under a full moon. Branson scooped the ends of the cloth together, careful not to lose any bits of the pearl, then held it over the abyss. He whispered a prayer for fools and the dead, and shook the shards free.

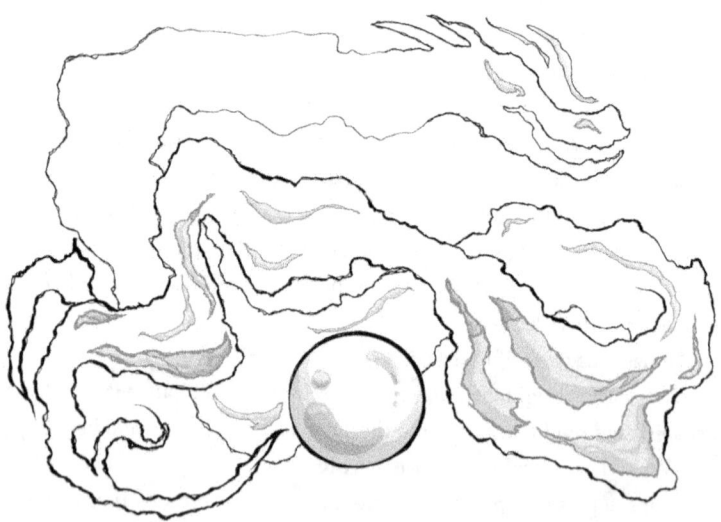

ABOUT THE AUTHOR

K. L. SCHWENGEL lives on a small farm in Wisconsin along with her Hubs, a handful of Australian Shepherds, Her Royal Highness Princess Fionna THE Cat, Rebel Kitten, assorted livestock, and a host of pestering muses. More muses than any one person should have to struggle with.

Growing up as the youngest of nine siblings, the daughter of a librarian and a dreamer, K. L. spent more time between stacks of books and secluded away in dusty archives than was probably even remotely normal. Then again, one person's normal is another person's crazy. Feeding her muses by writing, drawing, painting, and otherwise creating, became the only way K. L. could maintain some semblance of sanity.

You can connect with K. L. on-line by visiting her website at www. klschwengel.com. There, you will find links to all her social media handles, as well as all her currently published works and various other tidbits of interest.

ABOUT THE STORY

Who doesn't enjoy a rousing tale of adventure?

Throw in some good ol' treasure seeking, a bit of swordplay, and a touch of magic here and there, and you have the recipe for one of my favorite types of stories. So it was that when Branson made himself known to me (read as: started pestering me no end to share one of his and Lanster's adventures), I had to oblige.

"Last Time for Everything" is a bit lighter than most of my writing in both tone and story. That made it both fun and challenging to write. In the end, I did what I normally do. I gave the reins to my main character and let him guide me through the telling of it. The result? A tale that prompted several beta readers to ask for more, and the editor to comment, *"I think you have one of the greatest S&S duos since Leiber's Fafhrd and the Gray Mouser."* I ain't gonna lie, some happy dancing ensued forthwith. Me, that is. Branson isn't much of a dancer.

I hope you enjoy "Last Time for Everything," and I leave you to make up your own mind as to my characters' greatness.

As to whether there will be more adventures for Branson and Lanster . . .

I'd say that's a very real possibility.

Exiled from the old world. Set apart because they were different. The Mechanized humans were created to be the ultimate soldiers. They've started a new life free from war.
Until the makers, known as Skinners, returned.

....

SKINNERS

RACHELLE HARP

The circuit in my right thumb pulsed. A Skinner ship streaked across the WatchScreen, much faster than last time. I punched the target lock on the control panel, and a high-pitched beep answered.

Failure alert.

Frowning, I ran a neural calculation. Bearing 270 mark 15. I grasped the manual firing stick, aimed, pressed launch. Nine point three seconds passed before the rocket exploded, leaving trails of Skinner shrapnel plummeting toward the ground. Bright orange flames smeared the sky. I tilted my head and smiled.

Pretty good shot.

I stepped out of the gun turret of Enforcement Command Base, feet clanking on the iron grate. Commander Parchs looked up from his data pad, wearing a pit bull glare that would ward off any grizzly. Not exactly the pleased face I'd hoped for.

"Target neutralized, sir." I saluted, trying to keep my hand steady. The carbon fiber wrapping my index finger grazed my brow.

"For now." Parchs frowned, his faceplate brushing the left corner of his lip. Standard Mechanized Soldier implant. Fitted with digital eye scanner and cochlear amplifier. "Skinners always send two. Just a matter of time before the other one strikes. This one must have come early. Blown their surprise."

"Skinners are not that sloppy."

"No, Agent Marsh," Parchs said, tone hollow. "No, they are not. Makes me wonder what those monsters are up to."

The last Skinner ship to land on the Colony destroyed half the city. Women and children laid out on blood-soaked streets. Stripped of all their implants. Not a pretty business. I lifted my chin, my deep voice confident. "I'll keep my eye open for the next wave, sir."

"Not necessary." He dismissed me with a single hand flick as though repelling a mosquito.

A strange feeling rooted in my chest. Didn't I just fire the shot exploding an enemy target? Why wouldn't I be cleared for alert duty? My jaw cracked open and before I could stop them, the words tumbled out. "I can take the RADAR, sir. I've manned it before."

"Officer Deven has it covered." Parchs was cool and calm. Only the press of his thin lips showed a hint of irritation. "First team will take over from here."

"Sir, I have the skills—"

"I'm aware of your skills, Agent. We all get a lucky shot once in a while." He gazed at me with patronizing eyes, as if I were a young boy again. "Like Epsilon 5."

My last flight mission. A day I wish I could forget. We had a clear shot on a Skinner ship. Confirmed the coordinates myself, but accidentally reversed the last two digits. When our gunner fired, the missile veered off-target. The enemy fighter miscalculated his defensive maneuver, rolled right into the stray missile. Lucky shot for the gunner but ended in re-assignment for me.

Parchs held up his data pad. "There's been a break-in reported at the West Colony Medical Plaza. Doesn't look too serious. One man job."

"Patrol duty? I haven't done that in months." I tried to mask the disdain in my voice.

"Make it fast." Parchs grunted. "We don't have time for these petty tasks. Mechs with programming failure are a waste. Take care of it."

Sure, this was about as low a job as you could get in Enforcement. Next step, kitchen duty. I stood still, hoping he was joking. "Sir, I—"

"Dismissed, Agent Marsh." His tone tightened, warning me I could be held for insubordination. Parchs hit the comm. "First alert team, stand ready."

The high alert signal wailed, echoing the frustration clambering in my chest. A dozen Enforcement officers flooded into the room and launched into their drills. Defensive stations. Target calculations. Weapons prep. Parchs turned his back on me as he barked orders at some Mech with more skin than parts. Must be a newbie. What would he know?

I ducked out of the command center, fists clenched, Parch's voice booming over the mechanical hum in the tunnel. My finger traced the circuits of my cybernetic arm, cold and stiff. Skinners didn't have implants. They attack with their bare hands in an emotional frenzy of adrenaline and kill fever.

For half a second, I wished I knew what that felt like.

FIVE BROKEN BEAKERS littered the tile floor of the medical facility. A dozen vials, liquid flowing. Three boxes of gauze. Hardly enough to medicate a Mech. What had the perp been looking for? I scanned the medical facility. More mess.

A glass bottle shattered on the tile. I spun around. No one in sight. Did he find the exit?

I lifted my wrist, punched the communications button. "Enforcement Command, Agent Marsh requesting back up." Better to make sure he doesn't double back.

"Understood," a mechanical voice answered.

The perp couldn't be far. I tapped my laser eye, scanned a detailed map of the crime scene. In the far corner. There. Was that a gasp? Mech implants were fine tuned to catch these details. A sudden clang of metal rattled through the room.

"Show yourself." I leveled the blaster in my right arm in the direction of the sound.

A bottle whizzed past my ear. I fired one shot.

From the corner, a small figure darted behind a medical table. I leapt to the left, anticipating the next move. In one swift motion, I scooped the perp up by her shirt collar. "Who are you?"

"Let me go, Mech." The girl thrashed. I held firm.

"What are you doing here?"

She kicked my leg but shrieked in pain the instant her foot hit the metal prosthesis. I dropped her to the floor, cuffed her. Strange how her skin was warm like the sun. I shoved the pistol to her forehead. "What are you looking for?"

The girl flashed the kind of glare Parchs wore on a bad day. "Mechs are all the same. Don't know nothing about compassion."

"Where are your implants?" My tone sharper, more threatening. "If you are part of the invasion fleet, your ship has been destroyed."

She scoffed. "I'm no invader."

True, she wore no flight suit. Couldn't be more than twenty. Face as smooth as silk. No implants anywhere on her body. Not even an eye patch. To live in the Colony without implants? That was illegal. The law requires the Mechanization process begin on a child's first birthday and enhancement continue through adulthood.

"Then what are you?" I said.

"A colonist, like you," she said.

"Skinners are not like us." I straightened my shoulders. My skin expanded against the carbon fiber hull around my chest. Flesh plus mechanization. Strength over weakness.

There was a disturbance in her eyes as if she was afraid of something . . . but it wasn't of me.

She was a non-Mechanized colonist.

I'd never met one.

I'd heard of them, however. They were protected by criminal Underground Skinner sympathizers who believed in humanity over technology. There was no way she would betray whoever helped her.

The question was, would even a Protector deny a child Mechanization for so long? Utter madness.

"I only came for this." She opened her palm, revealing a red vial.

I took it.

Even through matted chunks of hair and a fierce glare, she was fascinating. Why would she choose a life without technology? Mere weakness. Unproductive at best.

"Stand up." I stepped back, flicking my hand in an upward motion. She eyed me carefully, a mouse staring at the trap. Slowly, she stood, pulling her shoulders back.

She seemed tough, at least acted like it. I could break her with my two hands. No need for the gun, but I held it steady. A trace of vulnerability in her eyes. Fascinating.

"I'm no threat to you." She lowered her voice. "Give me the vial, and you'll never see me again."

"Tell it to the commander."

"He won't listen. He'll turn me into one of you and end up killing me instead."

I rolled the vial in the palm of my hand. "He will treat Skinners as they deserve."

"No one ever deserves torture." Her words creaked out, a rusted hinge. She was beautiful, untainted. No sharp teeth or fighting stance. Probably never killed a bug, let alone a Mech.

I lowered my gun.

She was no invader. Only a glitch in the system.

"Hold out your wrists." *Make this fast, before I change my mind.*

She looked up, jaw hanging. I un-cuffed her. Warm skin, not cold like the others.

"Go before the backup gets here."

Wide-eyed, she glanced around the room as if bracing for the firing squad. In a whisper, she said, "My name is Eden." She scurried toward the door.

How many other colonists were evading Mechanization?

Eden paused by the door, looked over her shoulder and nodded.

Agent Trace and another Mech appeared on the other side of the glass.

"Watch out!" I lifted my gun, ready to fire.

Eden ducked, but not in time. There were no shots. The Mechs were faster. Within three seconds, they apprehended her.

Agent Trace cuffed her and then motioned for the other Mech to take her away. "Can you believe that? She's human. How did the invaders sneak her past our defenses?"

"I don't know." My tone flattened. To argue that she was merely a sympathizer rather than an invader would be fruitless at a time like this. "She wouldn't say."

Why did I let her go? Did Trace wonder why I didn't shoot?

Trace leaned closer, narrowed eyes betraying his thoughts. "Good thing you called for backup."

I THOUGHT OF nothing but Eden while I typed up my report. Green eyes pleading for help. The warm sun of her skin against mine. Soft flesh, untarnished by circuitry. Yet, she functioned in every way. And her mouth definitely worked up to speed, curses and all, as she had tried to escape the other officers.

I hit submit and leaned back in my chair. A squeak echoed through the Patrol Office, empty except for me and rat-faced Abreyy. His high-pitched voice got under my skin. On a normal day, Agent Trace would be at his desk beside mine, joking about something as half a dozen other Mechs filtered around. But the Skinner alert had everyone on edge. First team was still on duty. The rest were stationed at posts around the colony—watching, waiting.

Except me and Rat-face.

Strange thing is, I'd been preparing for this day my entire life. Trained, ready to kill those monsters. We left the Skinner home world years ago to colonize this planet, escape their persecution. They enslaved the Mechs of old, but here we were free.

And yet I can't get free of Eden's face.

"You ever see a Skinner before?" Abreyy's voice whistled from the cubicle across the aisle.

"In pictures, like everyone else," I said in a flat tone.

"No, I mean for real."

"Where would I have seen a real Skinner?" No way I was telling him about Eden.

"My friend on Base 9 says they captured one a month ago. Top secret like. He saw the ship."

"I never heard about any ship. Your friend must be lying."

Abreyy sat up, shoulders rigid. His voice squeaked out higher. "He lies about a lot of stuff, but not this. Said its teeth were fangs and its eyes hold you in a trance before striking out with its claws. Skins you alive."

"Your friend saw all this happen?" I arched my brow. "And told you?"

"Well, no . . . not actually saw the Skinner. But his partner told him about it."

I turned back to the computer screen. "Maybe your friend should quit telling fairy tales and do his job." I pressed random buttons on the keyboard, pretending to look busy.

"They tried to Mech the thing, turn it to our side." Abreyy cranked up his best bragging voice, as though he had witnessed the whole thing. "But once they're full grown, it's too late. The process didn't take and the monster ended up a pile of skin and circuits . . . after they put it down."

"I've heard that one before. You'll have to come up with a better tale next time." Is that the kind of torture Eden talked about? Would they try to Mech her? I shuddered, hoping Abreyy didn't see.

The door swished open and footsteps clinked on the metal grate floor. "Marsh!"

Didn't need to turn around. Parchs. I jumped up. "Yes, sir."

"Your orders went through thirty minutes ago. Why are you still here?"

"Just finishing my report on the Medical Facility break-in."

Parchs grunted. "So, you saw the Skinner, did you?"

If she *was* a Skinner, she didn't fit Abreyy's description. No fangs or horrifying blood dripping from her hands. No impulse to kill me on sight. Eden's vulnerable eyes and softness—hardly the vision of a monster. I nodded anyway.

Parchs's eyes scoured me. I resisted the urge to tap my pocket and make sure the red vial was there. If Parchs knew I had it . . . well, it wouldn't be pretty.

"Change of orders." Parchs clucked his tongue, still wearing his snake face. "You'll stay here in case the administrators have any questions about your report. Monitor SkyCam and relay any abnormality. That is all."

I clicked my heels, fists clenched. SkyCam was lower than patrol duty. "Yes, Sir."

Parchs marched out but paused to look over his shoulder at me before he left. As soon as he was out of sight, I exhaled the pent up air and tapped my pocket.

Abreyy let out a slow whistle. "You said you never saw a Skinner before."

I spun around and lowered my voice. "You heard right."

EDEN CROUCHED IN the corner of the cell, arms hanging over her knees. Had they scheduled her Mechanization? Or were they waiting until the invasion abated Priorities or something like that. Maybe I still had time to find out why she was unmodified. Or maybe get me the chance to catch another glimpse of her pristine face.

She didn't look up when I stopped in front of the cell door. "Come to gloat?"

"Why would I do that?" Such a strange creature.

"You got what you wanted." Her voice was raw, low. "Captured. Locked me up. What else is left?"

"That's not what I wanted." I curled my fingers around the bars, the metal casing on my right arm clanked as it hit the steel. "How sick is the one you need to help?"

"Sick. Dying. Does it really matter at this point?" Eden wrapped her arms around her knees and rested her chin atop them. Her eyes glistened. She wiped her hand across them. A sight I hadn't seen since I was a child. The last time was the day my brother was taken away for his Mechanization process.

Tobin had been so proud and excited that he bounced with every step his pudgy toddler feet carried him. But something went wrong, and he never came home. Didn't take to his implants mother had said. I cried that day, but she scolded me.

"Emotion is not for the Mechanized." Mother spoke in the voice she reserved for serious infractions. "Never cry again."

And I hadn't.

As Eden covered her eyes, another tear escaped.

Pain from the day Tobin died flooded back, fresh, like a bad dream. She was so fragile. So . . . *human*, really.

"You must care about this person a great deal." My tone softened.

Silence.

"I have the medicine. I will take it for you." At least I could try to save this person who is more than a friend, though I had already failed with Eden. And Tobin.

Eden sat up, shoulders straight. "Seriously?"

"Where is her location?"

She narrowed her eyes, a spider poised to protect her prey. "Why would you do that? What guarantee do I have that you won't tell the others? That you aren't toying with me?"

"You have none." For a moment I recalled Tobin's small hands reaching for my toys, his hair tousled from our wrestling, his gurgling laughter at my made up stories. I frowned. "I had a brother I cared about long ago. He died, and I would not wish that on anyone." I felt her hand rest on mine, warmth in this cold place. She squeezed. My pulse sped up.

"Shop 2934 on the east side. The owner wears early model Mech parts and walks with a slight stoop. He's a Sympathizer. Calls himself Garder. Give it to him and tell him my name. He'll know what to do with it."

Eden dropped my hand. The cold returned.

A strange feeling surged inside, prodding me to tell more. If only I could take her with me, forget what I really was, but the squeak of my knee joints reminded me I was not like her.

I wished I could be.

Holding my breath, I reached into my pocket, knuckles tightening around the vial as though it were Eden's hand.

"She's your sister." I said, matter-of-fact, no guessing. The only logical explanation.

Eden nodded, eyes hopeful.

"I will do as you've asked."

For Eden.

For Tobin.

THE SKINNER SHIP hovered in the orange sky. Black wingtips, iron beak, laser turrets pointed at the atmospheric protection generators. Another ship descended above the Colony Capitol Building. Five of our smaller, less armored fighters streaked overhead. Another half-dozen spit useless shots at the mammoth invaders.

A purple neon sign flickered in the window of Shop 2934. Plain facade. No fancy ornaments. Only big windows on either side of the entrance door and a sidewalk stacked with concrete blocks. The shop was located in the outer district, barely inside the protective atmosphere of the Colony's bubble.

Would this Garder turn me in? Think he was being set up? I clamped the vial in my palm and stepped onto the street. Engines roared in the sky. Two more Skinner ships unfurled their wings. A shudder ripped through me. Not because I was afraid, but because I couldn't help but wonder what the Skinners must be like. Were they like Eden, soft and beautiful? Or like Abreyy's hideous monsters?

As I stepped closer to the shop, smoke flooded the street. I jogged down the sidewalk. A loud explosion ripped the air. Glass window shards hurtled in a thousand directions. I dropped to the ground and shielded my eyes. When the glass rain ceased, I lowered my hands. Flames stroked the outside facade as the shop's innards were consumed by a wall of fire.

I scanned the sky for Skinner ships, but I saw none. I stood and brushed the dirt from my chest. The medicine bottle was safe, cradled in the palm of my right hand.

Garder! Was he inside?

I sprinted closer, heat lapping my cheeks. Smoke scratched my throat, and I coughed. Sweat scoured my face. My laser eyes scanned for movement through the window, but only detected fire.

If he was in there.

How? Or better yet, who?

Near the alley, the grate of metal feet clanked. Two Enforcers emerged, backs to me. I didn't have to see their faces to recognize them—Deven and Abreyy. Parchs must have listened to Eden and me. I raised my arm pistol, ready to fire, but paused. Neither turned around. No, that was not my way. If I shot them like that, I'd be no better than the supposed monsters we were fighting. I lowered my arm. They turned down the next street, disappearing.

The shop was a cavern of flames. Smoke clawed my nose, and I gasped for fresh air. I stumbled into the street and bent over.

Would Parchs kill me?

Would he kill Eden next?

I shoved the bottle in my pocket. There was only one way to find out.

Eden, wide-eyed, stared at the ceiling, as though she could see what was happening out there. I knocked three guards out to get inside the building, making sure to drag each body out of visual range.

"Skinner invasion fleet," I said, grit in my voice. "Two ships already here, more coming." And who knows how many guards on their way.

She looked at me and her lips paled. "How many more?"

"Could be dozens. I'm not sure."

Was she afraid of the invaders? Did she fear they'd hurt her, even though she was flesh and blood like them?

"Can you hear what's going on, how close they are?"

"Parchs severed my communications link." I slapped my hand around the steel bar with a little more force than intended. The clank echoed through the cell block. "Can't hear a thing." Strange to hear silence through the earpiece instead of the usual drone of voices. The walls vibrated as a ship buzzed nearby, but there was no way to tell which side it belonged to.

Eden sat on the edge of her cot and wrapped long, thin fingers around her shoulders. "Did you get the medicine to my sister?"

I pulled the vial from my pocket, let my knuckles squeeze the glass for a few seconds. "A Mech Enforcement patrol got there first." I paused. "Burned the place down. I don't know if your friend Garder was in there or not."

"How did they know?" She jumped up, her voice floating in the higher register. "Who did you tell?"

"No one." Her eyes were so beautiful, so innocent. I wanted to hold her and tell her everything would be all right. But I would be lying. "Must have bugged the cell."

She hung her hands through the cell door bars, dark hair tracing the curves of her cheeks. "No. I should've thought of that, too." Eden took my hand. Her skin was smooth against my palm, the only part of my hand free of circuits, free to feel the real world. "They'll come for you," she said.

"I know." I didn't tell her they were probably on their way. With the confusion surrounding the invasion fleet, I'd found a short window of opportunity. A window that was shrinking.

"You should go."

A door swung open behind us, and footsteps hit the metal grate. "Get back," I whispered, pulling my hand free. "The guard."

Eden pulled her hands into the cell and I crept to the nearest wall, leaning into a narrow shadow. I didn't have a plan, but I couldn't let them hurt her. Not after what they did to the old shopkeeper's place. I raised my arm, ready to strike, but the guard never came.

Eden rattled her cell door and yelled, "Hey, you!"

"What are you doing?" My voice was a frayed whisper. I waved my hand to quiet her, but she pulled her lips into one of those I've-got-a-plan smiles.

"What's going on out there?" she yelled again, louder this time.

"Quiet down," the guard said. He marched through the doorway. I pulled my arm back and punched him in the jaw. He fell to the ground, unconscious.

"Lucky hit." Eden rattled the door. "Get his cell keycard."

The guard lay on the ground. Out cold, but I shuddered. The cautious part of me, the collective mind, wanted to stay where the predictable would happen. I'd be arrested.

Fleeing the colony—is survival even possible?

And facing Skinners.

As I watched the guard's laser eye flicker, I knew the truth. Parchs would decommission me. Fancy words for termination.

I could never return.

My gaze latched onto Eden's. I was flooded with hope. I didn't want to die. Eden was full of life, unafraid. How did it feel to be like her? To be with her? I snatched the key card. One quick swipe and the cell gate swung open.

"Come on." Eden grabbed my hand. I squeezed tight, stealing as much warmth as I could. "I know a place we can hide. It's not far from my sister. How do we get out of here?"

"This way."

We ran down the back corridor, alarms rattling outside. As soon as we were out of the Enforcement Center, we looked into the sky. Hundreds of black silhouettes stained the clouds.

Shots fired overhead.

Mech ships were fast, but no match for the mammoth Skinner ships. A small fighter darted under the hull of one beast, but a laser turret awaited it. An explosion ripped the fighter's metal wings off. The carcass corkscrewed toward the Colony surface.

Something was buried in Eden's eyes. Fear? Did she know what would happen?

She gripped my hand. "If we get separated, go to east block, Shop 1927. Tell the shop owner Eden sent you. Show him the medicine. He will take you to my sister."

"Don't talk like that. We'll make it." I smiled at her for the first time since we met. It felt good, refreshing. Her desire for freedom was catching. My palms sweated beneath my circuits.

Across the courtyard, officials corralled citizens off the street. Some of the children cried. Their mothers prodded them along, not offering comfort. One little boy who only had Mech facial implants installed reminded me of Tobin with his scruffy hair and pudgy arms. The boy fell down and skinned his knee. When he touched the blood flowing down his leg, he screamed. An officer jerked him up by the elbow and hauled him to the nearest truck. I looked away.

"Through here," I whispered, pulling Eden toward the alley. "We'll go around them."

"But the shop is that way."

"We can't risk it. They'll capture us. Hurry." As we bolted into the alley, I glanced back. An officer pointed at us and whistled, attracting the attention of half a dozen others. "Run!"

We had a head start, but Eden's unaltered legs couldn't run as fast. I slowed to keep pace with her. Shots from the air battle echoed through the alley. My muscles pulled tight, but I pressed on. As we neared the end of the alley, another peek behind confirmed the Mechs were gaining ground. Wouldn't be long now.

Eden panted, sweat glistening on her cheeks. I checked my pulse monitor. Still within normal parameters. We turned right, headed toward the outer district. A crowd of citizens buzzed the street, blocking a clear path.

"We'll have to go around."

Eden nodded, her face strained. "I can make it."

"Good." Impulsively, I brushed her cheek with my fingertips. Her skin was soft. She smiled as though she wanted to say something, but metal feet clanked behind us.

She nodded toward a clear spot next to a concrete wall. "Over there."

We skirted the crowd, shoved past a couple of children, and squeezed by a car parked too close to the wall. I jumped on the car roof, then atop the wall.

"Here." I held out my hand.

She leapt onto the car, copying my steps, then grabbed my hand. In one swift motion, I pulled her into my arms. We dropped to the ground on the other side, straight into some kind of park. Red boulders instead of trees. A crooked walking path around an artificial reservoir. Acres of shrubs and dust as far as my eye could scan.

Did the Mechs see us? I couldn't be sure.

"The outer district is this way." I set Eden down, breaking my link with her, and jogged a few steps ahead.

"Slow down," Eden spit out between pants.

"They'll catch up."

"Then they catch up." Her tone desperate now.

I searched for a concealed path, but there was none. Metal hitting concrete clanked behind us. "Put your arm around me."

"What?"

"Just do it."

She held her arm just out of reach. "I can run."

"But not fast enough."

Eden turned around. The soldiers were less than ten yards away. Her jaw tensed and she swung her arm over my shoulder. I scooped her up and ran as fast as I could, though her added weight prevented me from reaching optimal speed.

Eden felt good in my arms. She leaned her head against my neck, her hair soft on the open parts of my skin. Was that her heart beating close to my chest? As I carried her through the park, the sky littered with ships, the sun warm on top of us, I'd never felt more alive in all my life.

And I didn't want to give that up. Not for anything.

The path narrowed, one branch curving around the reservoir, another snaking off toward a maze of boulders. I slowed my pace. Ahead, a second group of Mechs charged. The chase group closed in.

"Let me down." Eden pushed against my chest. "You'll never make it with me."

"I won't leave you."

"You have to." She slipped through my grasp and hopped to the ground.

"Eden!" I reached after her, unable to hide the creak of desperation in my voice.

She ducked under my arm and sprinted toward the boulders. I could catch her—she was only a few steps ahead. But a shot fired over my shoulder barely cleared my neck. I hit the ground and let loose three bullet replies. Two Mechs fell, leaving only three chasers, who split off to hunt for Eden, the easier prey. I fired after them but missed.

The second unit was right on top of Eden. I jumped up and ran as fast as I could. Eden had reached the perimeter wall and jumped for a jutting brick. What was she doing? She can't climb that high. My heart whirred—too fast—ready to break out of my chest.

One of the Mechs dropped to his knees and aimed his rifle.

My arm shook as I raised it to counter his move. He fired first, and Eden fell.

"Eden!" I ran to her side and took her in my arms. Her limbs were motionless, blood soaked her chest. Her hair fell loose across her face. With gentle movements, I pushed the strands back and let my hand linger on her cheek. Tears slid down like they did the day my brother died, but I did not stop them. Hollowness filled my chest, more intense, more open. And there was a new feeling, one I'd never felt before. One that erupted out of me. The tension grabbed my insides and squeezed violently.

The Mech responsible marched up and pointed his rifle at me. "Stand down."

There was no purpose for her death.

Gently, I laid Eden's body on the ground and stood. Before the soldier had time to react, I rolled forward beneath his aim, rising to catch his chin in a swift uppercut. I took his gun as he fell and fired a half a dozen shots as the others swooped in. Two fell like shattered glass, the others took cover and returned fire. Another half dozen closed in. I gazed at Eden's body and knew what she would have wanted. I jumped the wall and ran as fast as my mechanized legs could go. I had one chance to make things right.

And that's what I intended to do.

THE SHOP WAS on the corner of Omega and 5th. The owner was in the back, tinkering with some gadget. I clanked across the concrete floor. The place was empty, just a bunch of second-hand furniture, and shelves full of relics from the past. Vases, plates, clocks, musical instruments. All the things that reminded of us Earth. The things we had no use for anymore.

The man's gray hair flowed past his ears. His circuits looked like they were from the original mechanization movement. Big, old, bulky. Not sleek like the newer implant units.

"Can I help you?" He coughed twice as he looked up from the thing he was working on. Gold gears glimmered under fluorescent light.

I stood in front of the counter, fingers wrapped around the medicine bottle. "I am here for Eden."

"Eden? Don't know anyone named Eden." His tone was flat as he fumbled with the gadget, avoiding my eyes.

I took his hand and placed the medicine in the palm of his hand. "She sent me just the same. Told me to give you this. Said you would know what to do with it."

The man fingered the vial, then looked me in the eye, a gaze mixed with understanding and caution. "Ahh, yes. I do seem to recall that name, vaguely." He shoved it in his pocket and picked up a screwdriver.

I expected some kind of reply or some kind of information, but nothing. Maybe he was afraid this was a trap of some kind. I walked to the door, looked up at the sky full of Skinner ships, unsure what they would do to us. Or if this guy really knew Eden.

"If you see her," the old man said lowering his voice, "tell her I'll take care of it."

I turned around and hesitated before answering. "Can't do that. She's dead."

The man's cheeks paled, and he dropped the screwdriver. "Skinners?"

"No. The Mechs."

He nodded, tears glinting his eyes, then shuffled toward a curtain covered doorway.

"She was important to you?"

His shoulders shriveled. "She was my daughter."

Somehow, I was not surprised. They had the same eyes, though his were filled with more pain. "But she was so different than everyone else. How did she survive without implants?"

Tears traced his lower lids. "We're all Skinners underneath these contraptions. It's what we were meant to be. I just didn't have the heart to do to her what they did to me."

He shuffled away, not hiding his sobs. Was it possible Eden's sister was like her as well? I wouldn't know. He disappeared behind the curtain, and I was left alone. But instead of coldness filling my chest, a strange warmth grew. I had no word to pin on it, but it was like touching Eden again.

Outside the shop, our tiny fighters looked like flies swatted away with laser bolts. I watched from under the covered awning for some time, maybe thirty minutes, an hour. I wasn't sure. When the last fighter dove toward the ground, the Skinner ships ceased firing.

I ran my fingertips over the circuits of my mechanical arm. For the first time, I wondered what it would be like to be free of the wires and silicon. To feel the wind against the back of my arm, to run with the pull of muscles rippling down my freed legs.

With chin lifted to the sky, I knew the answer was all above.

ABOUT THE AUTHOR

RACHELLE HARP is a speculative fiction author as well as an avid coffee drinker. She spins short stories and novels in various genres. Over the years, she's worked in education as both a music and a history teacher, and has taught at various writers conferences.

Rachelle is a Writers of the Future contest Finalist and participant in Brenda Drake's Pitch Wars. Rachelle is a Zebulon Contest winner for the Pikes Peak Writers. Her stories have been published in *Galaxy's Edge* magazine, *2nd and Starlight*, *Perihelion SFMagazine*, and *StarShipSofa*. Her non-fiction can be found in *Chicken Soup for the Soul*. She's an associate member of the Science Fiction & Fantasy Writers of America and a Codex Writers forum member.

Rachelle occasionally blogs at rachelleharp.com or tweets sci-fi stuff (or something about coffee or cats or writing) @RachelleHarp. There may even be a few funny memes on Facebook at RachelleHarpWriter too.

ABOUT THE STORY

Everyone loves a great cyborg story, but often, the cyborgs are the "bad guys." I loved the idea of flipping the table and turning my cyborg into a hero. Agent Marsh's search for humanity leads him to question the only life he's ever known as well as the technology that turned him into a Mech. With our own world constantly expanding in technological ways, many of us can relate to Marsh's dilemma and search for what it means to be human.

"Skinners" is a *Writers of the Future* contest Silver Honorable Mention winner.

*Being a waitress in a tavern catering to unruly swaggering adventurers
with grabby hands and uncouth manners is . . .
well, just impossible! Were they all raised in barns?
Well, probably.
Still, Amma wishes for only a little decency, decorum,
and respect. But when her wishes are granted . . .*

....

AMMA'S WISHES

M. E. GARBER

The door to *The Dragon's Beard Tavern* slammed open. Wintry winds gusted in, twisting Amma's skirts about her legs like the arms of a drunken hero. Amma stumbled, sloshing ale from the tankards on her tray onto her skirts. She glared towards the door where three men dressed in crimson-edged blacks let the door bang shut behind them.

Damn these fighters. Couldn't they just once *enter like human beings?*

They swaggered to the far table, ignoring everyone in the crowded tavern. "Stew!" one yelled over his shoulder.

"Wench! Hurry with that ale. We're thirsty men!" a helmed man at the table before her demanded. Those around him roared their agreement.

She slapped the tankards onto their table, careful that the ale didn't slosh over so much as dance within the cups. *What would their mothers think of them, acting like this?* She glared at each man in turn, daring any to speak out. None did.

She turned to stomp back to the kitchen when a great hand seized her buttock. Anger and frustration engulfed her. She whirled, lifting the serving tray high, and crashed it onto the helm of the damned dwarf, who sat stunned but grinning like the idiot he was. Amma fled for the kitchen's safety, her heart beating in her throat and her arms shaking. Raucous laughter followed her.

Once through the kitchen doors, she slumped against the wall, letting her breathing drop its ragged edge. The rage that had fed her strength fled.

"What's wrong now?" Marda asked, her voice sharp. The innkeeper's wife and tavern cook scooped three bowls of stew and handed them over.

"The same. Grown men acting like boys." Amma loaded the bowls onto her dented tray, pausing as her anger bloomed again. "My six year old nephew behaves better, Marda! What's *wrong* with them?"

The older woman wiped her hands on her stained apron as a tired smile creased her face. Her eyes clouded with memories. "Amma. Child. They're not bad men. My Grumps was one of them for years, you know. We met at a tavern just like this one, and the men back then, they were just the same. They're only showing off for each other. It's what adventurers do."

"I wish they'd do it someplace else, then. I'm tired of it." She turned to leave the kitchen.

"You think it's better at *The House of Flowers*?" Marda's laugh pealed out into the front room as Amma shoved open the swinging door with her hip. No, servers at the only other bar in Milldale had it worse. At least here she didn't have to turn tricks, as they did. She carried the stew to the newcomers. They tried to impress her, flexing their mighty thews, but she ignored them.

Instead she made her way to the drafty corner table where Forgettable Fillmorr hunched alone over his tankard. The spectacled mage was the only one who treated her like a human, probably because she could snap him like a twig if she'd wanted. On the bench beside him rested a brownish lump: his long-empty loot sack. Now it sported a tiny bulge. The mage sighed as Amma neared.

"Another ale, Formidable?" she asked, using the name he called himself instead of what others called him.

He startled, then blinked up at her. "Why yes, that would be nice. Thank you, Anna."

Amma smiled as she went for his drink. He always forgot her name. But he said "thank you," and he never slammed the door.

Her smile was wiped away as the door was flung open again, crashing against the inside wall with a reverberating *boom*.

The night eventually ran itself down. The bard in the corner went from stomping tunes to mellow ones, then slid into melancholy ballads that salted everyone's ale with tears. When he slipped out the front door, Amma assessed the nearly empty common room: cider made a slow splat-splat-splat as it dripped onto the floor while Fillmorr nodded his head in time, his eyes owlish and unblinking.

Behind the bar, Grumps rattled the crockery as he wiped at dirty mugs with an equally dirty rag. Amma set to moving the filth around, working her way to Fillmorr's table.

"Formidable, it's time to leave."

He tilted his neck up at her and blinked rapidly. "So soon?"

She nodded.

He gave a little sigh. "Well, I suppose so." He placed a hand on the tabletop and started to rise, but shivered, stopped, and sank back down. "Oh! But first, I need to do this." His hand went below the table, and an odd expression crossed his face, as if he concentrated hard on his actions.

Amma leapt aside, afraid he was going to urinate right there. But no. His hand reappeared holding his loot sack, which thumped when he placed it on the table. Still staring at the bag, he spoke slowly. "Tonight, Ennie, I celebrated my last day as an adventurer. I've had enough. I'm going back to Immonsville to run the candle works there for my aged mother." He raised his eyes to meet Amma's, and they were surprisingly clear. "No one will miss me, and most probably won't remember me. I know they called me "Forgettable," and I am. But you, Essi, you always treated me kindly. To you, I'm giving the last of my adventuring treasures. I bequeath you my padded loot sack, and the last trinket within. It's not much, but it's the only way I can express my thanks to you, kind lady."

With that, he rose onto unsteady feet and bowed. She backed away, afraid he might topple over; but he turned and left the inn, shutting the door silently behind him.

Amma looked from the door, back to the brownish lump of sack he'd left for her. It was padded, to mute the sounds of things clinking within. At the very least, it would make a good pillow. Once she'd washed it.

"What's wrong then?" Grumps' voice cut through her thoughts.

She shoved the bag beneath her apron, looping it through the strings to hold it in place. "Nothing. Fillmorr just told me he's leaving."

"Hunh. No surprise there. He never was the right type. Didn't have enough bravado, enough flair. His name fits. 'Forgettable,' indeed."

Gritting her teeth, Amma continued washing up.

By the time cleanup ended and Amma was safely locked within her tiny room, she was exhausted. She didn't care what the sad loot sack contained. She was tucking it away in her clothing box when something heavy bruised her knuckles. Frowning, she upended the bag. A tiny oil lamp of some foreign sort fell out, its brass tarnished and stained.

No wonder Fillmorr didn't want it. He's going into the candle business.

She berated herself for the unkind thought. It wasn't a bad gift, not at all. With a bit of cleaning, it would be fine. To prove it, she wiped vigorously with her sleeve, trying hard to bring forth the gleam of the metal.

With a hiss like sand in an hourglass, whitish smoke billowed from the spout. Amma flung it onto her bed, backing away from the cloud that formed between her and the door. She ran for the window and tried to fling it open, but the old frame was warped, and it wedged after opening only an inch.

Maybe it'll be enough to let the poison gasses out. Turning, she put a hand over her mouth and nose and stared.

From floor to ceiling, the mist congealed into a burly red-skinned man. He wore outlandish purple-striped pants, and a tiny brimless hat perched on his bald head. Gold winked from both ears, and thick bands of it encircled his wrists, as well. His eyes gleamed like hot brass, not kindly at all. Amma gasped, and shrank to the floor.

"Mistress." His voice was deep, but soft. Gentlemanly, even. The genie bowed.

Amma scrambled to her feet, but remained pressed against the window.

"I come to your call. I am the genie of the lamp, bound to your service."

She'd heard such tales, of course. Working with adventurers, how could she not? But she'd never thought they were real. "You're . . . going to grant me three wishes?"

"My reputation precedes me. How nice." The genie smiled, but his eyes remained cruel. "This will simplify things greatly. You know the procedure, then? Standard offer—three wishes, no wishing for more wishes, et cetera."

She nodded, and moved towards her bed. "May I?" She indicated the lamp with a bob of her head. He nodded, so she grasped the lamp and placed it upon the wash basin stand, then seated herself on the woolen blanket covering her bed. She stared, silent and still, at her feet.

The genie cleared his throat. "Your wish?"

"I don't know." She shook her head. "I know better than to wish for money—it'll just make more trouble than it's worth. Or fame, for the same reason. Or a dozen other things. So, what should I wish for?"

"What is your greatest desire, Mistress?"

After her ridiculous day, his voice, so calm and cajoling, released some spring within her. She nearly shouted it: "I just want everyone in this damn tavern to behave *properly* for a change!"

"Done!"

An explosion of color, smoke everywhere, but no sound. When it cleared, Amma found herself curled atop her blanket upon her bed. She shivered. Frigid air blew through her window.

The tiny lamp rested where she'd set it on the washbasin stand. Just a bad dream. Then why was she disappointed?

Rising, she shut the window, blew out the candle, and lay under her blankets. In moments, she was asleep.

THE NEXT DAY Amma marveled at the customers coming in the door. Not one slammed it open or closed. They held the door for one another, and swept bows towards Marda and Amma; but their actions were stiff, their motions jerky. They looked like marionettes manipulated by terrible puppeteers. It was hard not to giggle.

Even Grumps, after frowning at the first few adventurers who came traipsing so peaceably within, couldn't slam the tankards down and curse out his frustrations. He was reduced to a wild-eyed rant of "My goodness, but what's come over everyone this evening?" as he paced rapidly behind the bar.

Amma was in heaven. No one grabbed her. No one yelled at her. No one slammed the door. They all behaved like perfect gentlemen. Once she got over their odd motions, she relaxed and enjoyed the effects of her wish. She knew there was no way she could go back to how it had been.

Word got out. The next day, adventurers were daring one another to step over the threshold, and to just *try* cursing. The following day, they were making wagers on how long certain patrons could stand it. The crowd outside the door and at the windows became larger than the one inside. By the fourth day, no one came inside. No one at all.

MARDA AND GRUMPS summoned Amma as she floated down the staircase. They ushered her into the kitchen, which shone with the attention it had recently received.

"It's been six days, Amma. Six days with no business." Grumps' face contorted as he was forced to swallow the curses he wanted to spit out. "I'm afraid we'll have to let you go. We can't afford to keep going with no customers. Please say you understand." His face said he'd like to yell and scream and pound the table. Marda looked like she'd swallowed an overripe egg whole. She patted her husband's hand.

Amma's joy dissolved. Turning tricks would be her only option.

"Just give it another day, please," she begged them. Thinking fast, she added, "It's only polite, after all, to give an employee notice."

Marda's eyes narrowed, and Grumps was shaking his head.

"Without pay, of course," she added. "Just let me keep the room."

"Very well, then. Another day," Marda said.

Amma ran for the lamp. She lifted the heavy brass and rubbed it with her clean skirt. The genie appeared, smiling like a cat that's been in the pantry.

"All's well, Mistress? Your wish was satisfactory?"

"Yes. No! I mean, *I* like it, but no one's coming to the tavern now, so I'm being fired! You've got to tell me how to make this work, genie. This week has been heaven!"

"Sorry, Mistress, but I'm not allowed to interpret your wishes for you, or to tell you how to word them properly. That's against the rules."

"Rules? *You* have rules?"

"My life is filled with rules, Mistress." He lifted his arms, displaying the gold wristlets. They winked in the sunlight filtering through her window. "These bands mark me as a slave to the lamp, and slaves live and die by rules."

Only two more wishes, and the genie couldn't help her. He was already turning tricks.

"Can you drink, genie? I think we have lots in common, and a drink might make things seem better."

She sneaked downstairs and liberated a bottle of dragonberry wine. It was potent stuff, and soon she and the genie—"call me Gene"—were sharing stories of the ways people took them for granted, talked down to them. They commiserated over glass after glass.

"The worsht of it cometh when they prwomish to fwree me, but I know they're lying," Gene said. He stared into his glass, then upended it, draining the last of their wine.

Amma thought he might be slurring a bit, but she wasn't sure. His statement, though, was an outrage. "They lie to you? To *you*? You're a genie! You should kill 'em all." She waved her empty glass.

"Can't." Gene hiccoughed. "Can't hurt anyone who's owned the lamp, unleth ordered to. Even if I do get fwree."

"If-*smiff*," she said, swaying a little. "When I figure this out, *I'll* free you. I promise." She hugged him, and promptly began snoring, even before her forehead landed on his shoulder.

She woke cradling the lamp against her belly. A headache was splitting her skull in two and sending sharp slivers of agony deep within her eyes. She shut them, gulped down her nausea, and opened them again. The inn was blissfully silent.

She recalled why, and her deadline. She sat up. The room swayed, but Amma forced herself to wash, dress and go downstairs.

Grumps and Marda slumped like drunks in the empty common room. The glare they gave as Amma came downstairs spoke volumes, and Amma winced, knowing they'd never let her stay. She asked anyway.

Grumps shook his head, and his eyes held a desolation she'd never seen in him before. "No. You must go." He met her gaze and his anger flickered to life. "See what happens when you get what you ask for? Nothing good comes from being too picky. Nothing!"

Marda patted her husband's broad shoulder. "If adventurers wanted to behave like proper gentlemen, they'd have stayed home with their mothers," she agreed. "This just isn't natural."

The words snapped in Amma's head, and she knew what to do. "Alright. I'll leave. But I'll be back. I'm going to solve this riddle." She fled upstairs, packed her few possessions in Fillmorr's loot sack, and scurried out the door, which swung gently shut behind her.

Outside, the night's rains had ceased, but the wintry cold remained. Not having coin for the coach to Immonsville, Amma began walking. By mid-afternoon, her hangover had frozen away.

She scurried through the wide streets of Immonsville until she came to a sign showing a robed student holding a lit candle over a book: *The Scholar's Candle Works*.

Squaring her shoulders, she pushed the door beneath it open. A bell tinkled sweetly. She faced a long counter which guarded a curtained doorway. The curtain twitched aside, and a man bobbed into view, still reading the book in his hand. It took a moment for Amma to recognize Fillmorr; he'd been transformed into a merchant by the fine clothes.

"Yes," he said, looking up at last. "Oh! It's you. Ammy." His gaze traveled from her to the door, as if looking for the loutish adventurers from *The Dragon's Beard* in her wake.

She stepped forward and smiled. "Yes, it's me. Formidable—"

He raised a hand, wincing. "No. I'm just Fillmorr now."

"Fillmorr, then. I need your help."

He gave her a sorrowful smile, the one she'd seen from him so often. "I've given all that up now, Emmi. You know that. But I see you're using my loot sack. I'm glad."

"Yes," she said, seizing the opportunity. "That's what I'm here about." She pulled the lamp out and set it on the counter. It shone in the light streaming in the rounded glass window behind her.

Fillmorr admired it. "My, that looks lovely now that you've shined it. It *is* the one I gave you, isn't it?"

"Yes. But it's not just a lamp. Look." She rubbed the cold brass briskly, warming it with her hand. Smoke and Gene poured out.

Gene gave her a wincing look, then saw Fillmorr. He straightened, crossing his arms over his chest, and his voice boomed. "What is your command, Oh Mistress?"

Fillmorr's mouth gaped.

Amma smiled, stifling her laugh by biting a knuckle. "It's alright, Gene. I'm just here to get Fillmorr's help. He's the one who gave your lamp to me."

Gene eyed the former mage, taking in his merchant's garments, his thin frame, and the book in his hand. "You . . . you were a mage," he said at last. "You found my lamp, and you . . . you gave it to Amma? Freely?"

Fillmorr lived up to his moniker, at last. He snapped his mouth shut, straightened his spine to stand erect before the towering bulk of the genie.

"Yes. I found your lamp in a troll's treasure heap. And when I gave up adventuring, I gave the lamp to . . ." He glanced at Amma, ". . . to Amma. I didn't know it . . . I mean, I thought she could use it. *You.* I mean, that she might need it more than I." He flushed and stared at his feet.

The genie shrank to human size, his hot eyes fixed on Fillmorr. "No one has willingly parted with my lamp before, Fillmorr. You are unique. Intriguing, even."

Fillmorr burned brighter red. Amma cleared her throat. "Getting back to the situation, then." She explained the problem at the inn to Fillmorr, and how she'd been relieved of her job, and how she was determined to use her final wish to free Gene from his lamp forever.

Fillmorr listened, his face growing more intent by the second.

"So," he said when she'd finished, "you need to get your job back. Why don't you just undo the last wish?"

Amma fidgeted her feet and looked at her hands as they played with the cords of the loot sack. "Well, I *like* it the way it is. I can't go back to the old way. I just can't!" She lifted her head, beseeching him to understand.

They moved to the back room; and Fillmorr's mother, a shawl draped over her shoulders, took over the shop. Fillmorr and Amma sat at a small table in straight-backed chairs. Gene hovered in the corner, just below the low rafters, glowing as brightly as the fire in the hearth.

"So, Gene, you can't aid Em—Amma's questions in any way, right?" he asked for the third time. He tapped a slender finger to his pursed lips, staring at the tabletop before him.

Amma sipped her tea, looking from Fillmorr to the nodding Gene and back again over the rim of her cup, her stomach clenched in hope, anxiety, and dread. She didn't want to be yet another possessor of the lamp to wriggle out on her pledge to free the genie, but it was looking more and more likely. She closed her eyes.

"But you can tell *me*, right? I'm not your Master, and honestly, I already gave your lamp away. So you can tell me anything."

Amma's fingers loosened on the teacup, and she nearly dropped it to the floor. She set it back on the table with a clatter, her eyes never leaving Gene who considered the question.

He frowned, stuck out a thick lower lip, and tugged at it with a beefy hand. His golden bracelets glinted in the light, and the fire in his eyes was banked. He looked to Fillmorr, then to Amma. "I do think you're correct. There is no prohibition against it, if you're not family or romantically entangled. You're not, are you?"

It was Fillmorr's turn to spit his tea. He choked, gasping, and Amma reached out and snatched his cup away.

"No," she said. "Definitely not."

Amma and Fillmorr stayed in the back room, and the genie went to Fillmorr's bedroom; he couldn't speak knowing that Amma would hear his words directly. It slowed things down, but Amma didn't care. They would figure this out.

Fillmorr brainstormed with Amma, then carried messages back and forth. "Forgettable Fillmorr" was long gone as he bustled about, his stride long and his face determined. "The Reward Idea won't work. The gold will lure adventurers to steal it," he'd report. "But what if we ...," and they were off again, plotting the next potential wordage.

Again and again, he came back, shaking his head. "No on the Muffling Spell."

"Nope. Not the Politeness Potion, either."

"The Sparkle Dust won't fly."

Amma's heart sank, and her shoulders slumped lower.

Night fell. Fillmorr's mother brought them bread, sliced pork, and cider, and now their empty plates lingered on the table beside her. The cloying scent of old cider filled her with despair.

Fillmorr burst in and threw himself into the chair beside her. "No. It won't work. It just won't," he said. He crossed his arms and scowled, his thin face sour and nasty looking.

He'd have made a fine adventurer if he wore this face all the time.

"There's no solution, Amma." He leaned forward, elbows on his knees and head cradled in his hands. "I'm not smart enough to see it, at least. So now I'm failing even you."

Her blood boiled at his self-pity. *He* was failing? What about *her*? She was the one heading to the whorehouse, not him. She slammed her hand down onto the table. He leapt, cringed away, and stared at her as if she were going crazy. "What—" she began to yell, but was interrupted when the door creaked open.

Fillmorr's mother shuffled in, her eyes bright. "Still up? Let me just clean away these things, then, dears. Don't mind me, carry on 'chatting.'" And she began the painstakingly slow process of removing the plates from the table between them.

Fillmorr gave her a look, begging Amma to hold her tongue and temper before his mother. Her pulse beat in her ears, a hard drum that slowed only as she concentrated on her breathing.

The old woman shuffled out at last, and Fillmorr breathed out, a deep sigh. "Thank you," he said. "Mother hates rude guests."

She opened her mouth to curse him roundly, but popped it closed with a snap.

"Your mother—," she said. And then, "Marda said adventurers would stay home with their mothers if they wanted to behave." She beamed at Fillmorr. "Don't you see? We need every adventurer's mother behind the bar. Then they'll all behave!"

THE DOOR TO *The Dragon's Beard Inn* flew open on blustering winds, and the patrons looked up. The spring storms were bad, and rain lashed inside. Two men gusted in, stomping their feet on the threshold. The newcomers looked to Amma, who had positioned herself to be seen, and both men gaped.

"Mama?" one whispered, his face slack.

"Auntie Zim. But how . . . ," the other murmured before trailing off.

The spell engaged, Amma watched as it released them from the vision of their favorite mother figure. They shook their heads, befuddlement and wonder in their eyes, and softly shut the door behind them.

She bustled to their table with a complimentary welcome drink, which wondrously knocked the edge off their shock, and then took their order. She called the drinks out to the big man behind the bar, who wore a vest and breeches. His skin had an odd, reddish cast, and chained to his belt was a pair of thick, broken wristlets, like some foreign trophy.

She'd heard the regulars tell passers-through that if he got angry, his eyes gleamed like molten lava. But most didn't care to incur the wrath of the innkeeper, who strangely reminded each of them of his—or her—own mother. Those who didn't care for that moved to the new tavern across town, *The Bad Spell*, which Grumps and Marda had opened. *The Dragon's Beard* was a mellow place, these days, and more profitable than ever.

In the kitchen, Amma gave the food order to Fillmorr, who hummed a tune as he stirred, tasted, and seasoned the various pots. She was glad to see him so happy. "How's your mother, Formidable?"

Gene, his eyes agleam, slipped into the room on silent feet and stalked up behind Fillmorr. Amma kept her gaze directed at Fillmorr, allowing the sneaking to continue.

"I wish you wouldn't call me that," he said. "But she's fine. Loves the new shop next door, too. Says she should've moved here ages ago."

Gene threw his brawny red arms around the thinner man, who gave a muffled, high-pitched shriek. "'Formidable,' indeed!" Gene said, nuzzling his ear.

Fillmorr blushed redder than Gene, then swatted at the former genie with his soup spoon. "I should've thrown your lamp into the sea!" he scolded.

Gene laughed, a deep basso that echoed off the rafters. "Then you wouldn't be one-third owner of the nicest tavern in Milldale."

A thundering crash of the front door thrown open was followed by a bellowing voice demanding ale.

Amma sighed. "Looks like I'm needed in the front," she said. She lifted the bowls Fillmorr had abandoned and carried them through the swinging door into the common room, interrupting the bellower mid-tirade. He stared at her, mouth hanging slack, and with one thick hand, caught the door that was ready to slam shut behind him. Instead, he guided it to *snik*, ever-so-quietly, into place.

She beamed at him, nodding her delight. It was such a pleasure to work in a civilized place, where people shut the door properly.

ABOUT THE AUTHOR

M. E. GARBER is a writer currently based in north-central Florida, where she lives with her husband and their extremely photogenic dog. Her 2017 *Writers of the Future* contest Q2 Finalist story "After the Story Ends" is forthcoming from *Galaxy's Edge* magazine. She's also had stories published in *Daily Science Fiction*, *Abyss & Apex*, and *Lady Churchill's Rosebud Wristlet*. You can find her blog at http://megarber.wordpress.com or follow her on Twitter at @m_e_garber

ABOUT THE STORY

Back in high school, I was a waitress for one summer—and in the tourist-dependent town I grew up in, that was *more* than enough. While there were some polite, personable customers, the majority treated me like someone with neither feelings nor humanity, and thus a receptacle for all their anger, frustration, and exhaustion. Being poor and needing the money to attend college, I had no choice but to lower my head and put up with it. To top it all off, despite running myself ragged to meet their demands, and biting my lip at their thoughtlessly nasty comments, I'd be lucky if they left a tip at all; apparently in tourist towns, we exist on air and the magical presence of tourism!

About the same time, *Dungeons and Dragons* was becoming "a thing," and I was more than a little upset to discover that none of the groups already playing wanted to include me, a girl (they were all guys, of course). I started my own group and ran it as the DM, much to the delight of a few of my like-minded female (and one male) friends.

Later, when I started writing, I began to hear about all the stories slush readers saw that started out in taverns, the way (apparently) so many of those *D&D* games I didn't play in did. "Starting your story in a tavern" was an item on one magazine's online list of tropes not to send them. However, it got me to thinking about what it would be like to waitress in an adventurers' tavern, about how horrible an experience it would be, and about the privilege the adventuring class would experience above those stuck waitressing in those tiny towns.

This story, with more than a little wishful thinking, is the result.

1. To be a child for eternity and, alone
among humanity, cursed to remember.

2. What makes a perfect spouse is the imperfections we miss.

3. Endings are but new beginnings.
Three tales of the costs of Man's presumption of immortality,
and the pain and hopes of memory.

....

THREE FLASH

DUSTIN ADAMS

CURING DAY

Every year, a few more kids from my elementary school vanish from people's memories. Today, we've arranged our desks in a circle and Mrs. Witherspoon is explaining that Tracy Peters has gone to a better place.

Tracy was struck by a car while riding her bike. She will be remembered until our next dose of Pathway. Then, only I'll remember her.

Pathway doesn't work on me. Well, the anti-aging portion does: I'm still nine, but I never forget. I'm the fifty-five pound elephant in the room.

I puff a stray lock of curly hair off my eyes and Mrs. Witherspoon scowls at me. The curls are from my mother's side. My father insisted my hair be kept short. Said I looked like a girl when it got too long.

I miss my parents.

Next to me, Tracy's best friend, Charlie, whimpers. Charlie's a girl. Short for Charlene.

I pat Charlie on the shoulder. "I miss Tracy, too." She nods agreeably and

I'm struck by a profound sadness. After our next dose of Pathway, Charlie won't remember Tracy. She'll revert to her carefree self, but I'll always remember the short-haired brunette who loved ponies and dresses and—

"But Pathway is coming," says Mrs. Witherspoon with a burst of positive energy. "Soon, we'll have a cure for aging and we won't ever lose our friends or parents." She looks at me. She knows intellectually that I had parents, and she knows they're gone, but she doesn't remember their names.

"Accidents still happen," I say with malice and all the puffy, teary eyes in the room glare at me.

DURING RECESS I lean against rusty monkey bars with my hands jammed in my heavily patched corduroys. The air carries that first scent of winter and gentle breezes knock yellow and orange oak leaves free from their branches.

Fall. The perfect season to introduce Pathway to the world. What's left of it, anyway. For a while I kept up with the world's declining population, but my computer rotted away and I can't afford a new one.

"Shamus, want to play kickball with us?"

Kickball loses its luster after the first dozen years or so.

A gust of wind blows my hair into my eyes. I brush it back and I'm glad I can cut it again, tomorrow. After my dose of Pathway, I'll need to fit in.

I glance at the home-run fence, and despite my disinterest I can't help but wonder, with the wind, could I at last clear that sucker with a good, swift kick?

"Sure," I say and take my position in the outfield.

"What Pathway means to me, By Jimmy Nelson."

I slump in my little wooden seat. Jimmy's speech is my least favorite. He wishes Pathway could've saved his cat, Spotty.

He doesn't remember Spotty, but there's pictures of her all over his room, so he knows he had a cat named Spotty at some point. Pathway isn't for animals. They wither around us and fade into aging picture frames along with those who died in car accidents.

Two gray fortress-sized buses rumble into the cul-de-sac in front of the school. My classmates and Mrs. Witherspoon press their faces against the glass windows, fogging them up. Today is unusually cold for the start of autumn. Below freezing.

The CDC has come with our Pathway shots.

Mrs. Witherspoon covers her heart with one hand while the other thumbs her Rosary beads. Pathway is her salvation.

We take turns receiving our shots. Mrs. Witherspoon holds each of our hands, one after the other. We get little cartoon Band-Aids for our shoulders and I wonder what mine will be this year. It's one of the few remaining unpredictable events of Curing Day.

"Shamus, it's your turn. Don't be afraid."

For the first time, I hesitate to sit in the familiar chair.

"I'm not afraid," I say to cover up my very real fear. Am I through with Pathway? Will I become the next empty desk? Will they forget me like they do the others? My little pause leads me to wonder whether I've truly grown weary of the same routine, of living alone, of nothing ever changing.

I dutifully sit and stare deep into the CDC man's eyes. He's the same man who gave me my first shot. I burrow past the blue irises and try to read his thoughts.

Can he see the wisdom in my eyes?

Pathway was supposed to stop us from aging and dying, but instead it froze the planet. I like to believe someone's out there working on a cure for the cure. I still hold out hope that someday I'll grow to be a man and have a wife and perhaps kids of my own. Unlike Mrs. Witherspoon.

"There you go, son."

He sticks a Scooby-doo Band-Aid on my shoulder and gives me an empty smile. He too is a victim of Pathway.

OUR DESKS ARE aligned in a circle. There's several seats on the fringes covered in layers of dust. They haven't been part of this circle for many years.

Jimmy Nelson died in a house fire last night.

I find I'm exceptionally saddened by this. Despite Jimmy's maddening yearly speech, and his stunted maturity, I considered him a friend.

I sift through my memories of Jimmy and cover a burgeoning smile with my hand so no one sees. I'm remembering the day Jimmy rolled the kickball my way. There was a mighty wind blowing and after making contact with my foot, and echoing that unique, rubber kick-ball *poing*, the ball sailed over the home-run fence.

When was that? I count back. A decade ago.

I'll have to try again. Make a new memory with a new pitcher. Then maybe I'll forget Jimmy, too.

I feel my face screw up and tears spring into my eyes, and I allow myself to cry for Jimmy with the others—while they're still here.

II
A NEW MAN IN TIME FOR CHRISTMAS

I didn't like him.

They said he'd be exactly like my late husband, only better, after my suggested changes, but this lump of Brent-looking plastic-rubber wasn't Brent.

I called the factory. They said their return policy was ten days. I'd had him for twelve. After ten days, they said, free replacements were allowed only if the model became violent. New Brent couldn't hit me, I'd seen to that in his programming.

"We're going to start over, Brent. You and me." I set my empty wine glass down on our wooden coffee table. "Lay here." I indicated the wrapping paper rolls I'd unfurled, side by side. Dutifully, he did as I asked.

His eyes flickered—the way they did when he was processing something new—never focusing on me for long. He rolled, crinkling all the way until paper completely covered his 6'1" frame. Tiny Santas with red cheeks repeated again and again, round and round.

I put him in power-save remotely then tucked him under the tree where he lay motionless, cocooned. Christmas was weeks away. I'd probably make it without unwrapping him early.

I'd survived alone all right in the months after Original Brent's suicide. I could do it again for two short weeks.

I AWOKE BEFORE the alarm, just after 6 A.M. like I was a kid who still believed. I padded down the rug-covered stairs. The coffee pot remained dry and our open, hollow living room was dark except for the too-near streetlight beaming through the bay window onto a man-sized present.

I knelt, then began to unwrap my husband.

"Hi Honey," he said after I'd revealed his equable face.

He sat up and I hugged him. The paper that clung, taped to his shoulders and back, crunched beneath my arms, reinforcing the artificiality of his being.

No. I shoved those thoughts away. I was starting over and this was My Brent.

I made breakfast while he stood awkwardly in the doorframe between the living room and kitchen. Original Brent would lean against the frame, one foot crossed in front of the other, smirking at me.

New Brent watched in wonder while the eggs cooked. Steam rose above the pan and his eyes flickered.

"They're just eggs, Brent!" I dropped the spatula and bits of egg spattered about, creating dots of soggy, yellow mess.

He approached, extended a gentle hand, and wiped my cheek where some uncooked egg had landed. His soft touch sent me over the edge.

"I can't do this! You're just not him. He would never—"

"But I am," he said. "I have his body, his clothes, and his memories."

"You don't." I backed away and buried my face within my hands. "I changed you. I neutered you."

"No, we are both perfect. Are we not better off after the change?"

"You're not better. Just different." I tried to convince both of us.

"But I am," he said. "Better."

I shook my head. "You're not. I . . . changed you, and I can't take you back."

He cocked his head. I couldn't tell whether he was processing, or inquiring, or waiting for more. The burden of my secret revealed, I continued. "Brent was unhappy. No, he was miserable. So much so that he drove—" The eggs began to burn. Smoke clouded the room. I spun the dial to *off* and slid the pan onto an empty burner.

Brent approached, his arms open and welcoming. Sympathetic. Loving. I wanted to slide a long blade from the knife block and stab his ticking, electronic heart.

I turned from him. Christmas had failed.

He halted. "Do you wish me to yell? To spit angry words? I will do anything to make you happy."

"Whatever you do will be disingenuous."

"Not precisely true." He turned and left the room. I breathed a sigh of relief. Finally, an independent act.

I sat at the table and ignored the burnt eggs. Didn't matter, we never ate anyway.

I looked outside and watched our new car pull down the driveway, pause while Brent no doubt looked both ways, scanning for kids, dogs, neighbors. He's so considerate now.

The day passed. I watched TV, read magazines. Colors cycled across the bay window, orange then pink; purple, then black. Deja vu crept into my being. I waited for the phone to ring. Eventually, it did.

I had to identify his body. Again. Only this time they'd brought him straight to the factory.

Another accident. Another totaled car. I told the insurance company we were really bad drivers. They raised our rates.

"Look as us," I said to his still form, lying on a gurney in a silver-walled room. Bright lights overhead revealed every impacted shard of glass.

Distantly, I wondered whether robotic suicide was covered by warranty. If so, I would program him again. Should I make him angry, or violent . . . more depressed? Could I purge the guilt from his memory? I want to tell him I'm okay now, but I would be telling a different man.

"It's not your fault." I've said these words before. "We'll get this right, eventually."

"Ma'am?" A young lab tech had entered the room. "Need you to sign a few things." He held forth a clipboard.

I snapped at him. "I haven't yet cried for my husband!" I motioned toward Brent with an open palm.

"But you can't," he said, and studied his papers.

"Because he's a robot?" I yelled.

He shook his head. "No, because the model your husband ordered—"

I stopped listening. Instead, I turned to Dead Brent. "You'd cry for a robot, wouldn't you, Sweetie?"

III
FINAL MESSAGE

A ship from Earth twinkled among the horizon of stars. Torpos Hansen, Ambassador to the immortal Factory, greeted all races, but his excitement peaked when vessels from home arrived.

Sadly, his fellow humans rarely continued their existences beyond a single millennium. Each ship brought a swell of living excitement, and offspring would frolic throughout warm, well-lit foyers. But in time, always too short, they grew weary. The children of children chose not to reproduce, and one by one they returned to eternal rest.

Torpos hoped those aboard would remain, because despite the company of millions of individual beings, he felt isolated as the sole remaining member of his own race.

"Chair. Human." Torpos said, and the Factory responded. Metal groaned and rose from the floor then halted, having molded into the shape of the requested chair.

Torpos sat and breathed in the warm air around him, saturated with the life-sustaining motes that regenerated his cells, granting him youth and immortality. Soon, those who had traveled decades aboard a confining ship would be free to explore the planet-sized Factory and interact with thousands of species both wondrous and terrifying.

An umbilical darted from the Factory like a snake's tongue, connected to the ship, then eased it in. Once empty of its passengers and their possessions, the Factory would consume the ship, and grow. New bedrooms would form, and maglevs would extend their inner-ship movements to the new floors and wings that contained the bustling human population.

A hatch slid open to reveal a dark passage. Torpos stood, unable to contain his excitement. The chair behind him melted, becoming flat hexagon decking once again.

No one emerged. No awe-struck children appeared, asking where the lights were. "Everywhere and all around us," Torpos would say and sweep his hand, gesturing in a way that indicated the Factory was *alive*.

He edged toward the ship, staring into the darkness beyond the open hatch. Surely the ship wasn't empty.

At last he saw a shadow. Thin metal legs clacked against the ship's decking, followed by a haggard, ancient woman, trembling, but resolutely shuffling onward behind her walker.

Torpos sprinted forward, leaping inside the ship. Instantly, he felt himself begin to age. Disconnected from the Factory, motes expelling from his lungs, he began to die.

"Ma'am, do you need help?"

"Yes," she said from beneath long, gray hair that draped over her gnarled hands in jagged lines. "And no." She shoved her walker forward, then slid her feet behind.

Torpos stepped aside, giving her room. He looked behind her down a long, darkened hall that stretched into mystery.

"Are you alone?"

"Completely."

Torpos coughed, his lungs straining to breathe the ancient oxygen within the ship. He retreated to the safety of the Factory's deck and urged the woman forward with beckoning hands.

She paused at the seam between her ship and the Factory. It glowed electric white, having fused, becoming one. She lifted her head and observed her surroundings as if judging, but her expression belied no pronouncement.

Torpos met her lively, blue eyes, deep-set behind wrinkles upon wrinkles. Those eyes had witnessed much, he recognized. Friends, loved ones, all lost behind eyes that resolutely carried on despite the anguish.

At last she hobbled forward, inching her way into the Factory. Torpos watched, waiting for her to begin the healing process.

But it did not occur.

"Oma has departed the vessel," said an electronic voice that reverberated throughout the empty ship. "Mission complete."

"How do you feel?" Torpos asked.

She continued her glacial momentum and said, "Pleased."

"Factory, human couch for two." The metal behind Torpos bent and took shape. "Oma?" Torpos leaned forward, hoping for another glimpse into the depths of her sea-blue eyes.

"My title. My name is Annabeth Peterson."

"Welcome, Annabeth. My name is Torpos Hansen." Torpos reached for her wrinkled hands. She placed them in his and he led her to the metallic couch. "You should feel the healing effects of the Factory. It cures—"

"That's not why I'm here," she interrupted.

"I don't understand."

"I'm a messenger, come to report to our kind that Earth is no more."

Torpos' blood froze. "No more?" he asked.

"I am the last," she said. "Yellowstone erupted." She bowed and shook her head. "Other volcanoes followed. Earthquakes broke the land. The surface became an uninhabitable wasteland."

Torpos whispered a prayer to the Creator. He hesitated to inform her that he, too, was the last. All of humanity sat huddled in a quiet, expansive wing of the Factory.

"You're not alone."

"But I am. My family are all gone, buried beneath ash. My friends expired during the voyage, adrift forever in the depths of space."

Torpos gripped Annabeth's shoulders with a gentle firmness and turned her to face him. "Allow the Factory to heal you, and restore your youth." He paused, and added, "Stay with me." He'd begged with those words many times in the past. Always to no avail.

"You will pass my message to the others, yes?"

Torpos stood and backed away. He raised his arms, palms up, and swept them in an arc. "Message received." He steeled himself for the inevitable, only this time he would truly be alone. No more vessels from Earth. Ever.

If this woman had seen loss enough to break her spirit in a mere century, what of his forty thousand years? Entire species had gone extinct before his eyes. Maybe his time had finally come.

"I see," Annabeth said. "Well, then." She stood, and after a moment Torpos noticed a lessening of her quivering bones. She bowed her head and inhaled a great breath.

Relief coursed through Torpos's soul. She would remain. For how long, he didn't know, but he would take whatever she gave.

And then?

Didn't matter. Not now. Not today.

Annabeth clasped Torpos's hands in hers. She gazed at him with wisdom-filled, youthful, blue eyes.

"What now?" she asked.

"Time will tell," he answered, and led her forward into the Factory.

ABOUT THE AUTHOR

DUSTIN ADAMS gets up early to write, when his head is clear, and his coffee is hot. Before the burdens of the day and the news of the world intrudes, and before the sun rises, he sits in the dark, illuminated by the glow of a monitor, trying to find the perfect words to tell great stories.

Dustin is a multiple Finalist in the *Writers of the Future* contest. His stories have appeared in *Daily Science Fiction*, *Every Day Fiction*, *ASIM*, and *Dimension6* as well as each of the *Starlight* anthologies. A partial list of his publications can be found at Goodreads.

He occasionally blogs at https://dustinadams.wordpress.com/ and can be followed on Facebook at https://www.facebook.com/Axeminister or Twitter at https://twitter.com/Axeminister.

ABOUT THE STORIES

Curing Day

This idea came about after discovering there may be a cure for gingivitis. We'll never see said cure, because it could very well destroy an industry. Imagine no dentists, or dental assistants, or dental colleges . . . But I thought, *what if?* I extrapolated that 'what if' to further cures. Aging? What if something went wrong? It would need to be covered up. But what if someone could see the truth? What would his existence be like?

A New Man in Time for Christmas

This story began as a Christmas-themed, thirteen-line challenge on the Hatrack River writers forum. A hastily scrawled idea, really, until I received an e-mail from Ruth Brown asking to read the whole story. But there was no story. So I wrote one.

Final Message

My "Factory" stories have appeared in several venues, such as *Dimension6* #7 and *1st and Starlight*. This short tale provides a small glimpse into a much larger world. It covers a section of time that I've wanted to explore in the longer tales, but haven't been able to work into the closed narratives: Earth's end. So, here it is, in a thousand words.

The world Darvolock is the Panama Canal of space, key to navigating its sector of the galaxy—if only its inhabitants would share. Diplomacy is essential (since force had failed); but the residents of Darvolock are not only recalcitrant, they're inhuman—floral, actually. In the stellar backwater, when you must negotiate a treaty with plants, what's the Diplomatic Corps to do but send in the Mann.

....

A GREEN TONGUE

FRANK DUTKIEWICZ

The thing swayed ever so slightly in the interrogation bay. Purple streaks ran vertically up a mid-section I would best describe as a thick trunk. Limbs (branches?) sprouted from the trunk with flat pads at its ends that looked remarkably like leaves. On its top perched an enormous maw—closed like a flower waiting for the dawn—with faint hints of orange hiding within. It stood five feet tall, was mostly green, and sat inside a tub filled with black dirt.

"You're kidding, right?" I said to General O'Sullivan. "It's a plant."

"You are a member of the Diplomatic Corps, are you not?"

"Yes, but ..."

The general raised a hand, stopping me in mid-sentence. "This specimen has been determined to be the sentient species of this planet. According to the Confederation Articles of Galactic Expansion, contact must be established with the dominant native species before any commerce, military, or scientific outpost is made permanent ..."

"If the dominant species shows signs of intelligence," I finished for him. I looked at it again. It had nothing like a hand, lacked any receptors that would be useful for communication—like speech or sight—and was permanently affixed to one space. "But it's a *plant*," I whined. "How in the hell am I supposed to talk to a plant?"

"You managed to talk to a fish, didn't you?"

I grimaced at the general. I received plenty of admiration from the Confederation when I established contact with the Tunish, but cute pranks still plagued me every time I was reassigned. Usually, a goldfish in a fishbowl—or the native equivalent—would be waiting to greet me in my new office with a pasted note begging 'take me to your leader,' or something equally as lame, stuck to its side. My first thought was this was a cleverer version of that running joke, but General O'Sullivan struck me as man who wouldn't tolerate such nonsense.

"The Tunish already had a means of communication," I said. "They had a sophisticated form of body language with vocal signals that complemented it. Piecing it together was hard but they were cooperative once they realized what we were up to." I swept an arm at the monstrous pansy. "This thing, is a *plant*; a term that's universally accepted as a euphemism for an unresponsive life form. Just look at it." I stared at it for a moment, almost hoping the thing would prove me wrong by waving a branch at me or something, but it didn't move so much as a stem. "It's . . . primitive building material . . . an oxygen cleanser . . . shade for a rodent . . . cow food . . . a plant!"

O'Sullivan grasped his hands behind his back and stared down the bridge of his nose at me. "Are you telling me that I, my leading scientist, and everyone who has been on this station more than a day, are wrong, Mr. Mann?"

I buried my face in my hands. *He's serious.* I shook my head and cursed the sub-Secretary of Alien Affairs for tricking me into accepting this assignment. I drew in a deep breath and tried something that never worked before—talking sense to a general.

"Sir," I started. "There are forty-seven known planets where multi-celled life exists, each one evolving its own form of chlorophyll-based life; plants. We developed a Sapience Quotient to determine the level of intelligence, and its ability to communicate with other life forms outside their species. Humans set the standard with a SQ of a thousand. The family dog rates at one-hundred and sixty-two. House flies are a two. The best SQ rating ever recorded for a plant is three—and that's in dispute. They can't communicate and aren't capable of forming an intelligence, despite having a billion year evolutionary head start on every planet where they're found. Plants aren't built for intelligence, they're plants."

"I don't care what you know, what you've learned, and any other preconceived notions you had before," said the general. "This species is different. Alien intelligence is supposed to be your expertise. Do your job and open up a dialogue with it, so we can do ours."

I glared at the thing, sitting in its tub of dirt while it soaked in the bay's artificial light. If the flower was capable of experiencing any feelings at all, this one had to be full of contempt. I grimaced. *How in the hell am I supposed to communicate with a plant?*

"What makes you so sure it is sentient?" I asked.

"By demonstrating an ability to defend itself, assess a threat, and adapt."

I arched an eyebrow at the general then looked at the alien flower. "Go on."

"There have been six attempts to establish a base on Darvolock. Every structure has been destroyed. Eighty-seven people have set foot on the planet. Over half have been confirmed as dead or lost."

I turned to study him, not sure if I heard him correctly. "What do you mean by 'lost'? I thought everyone assigned to expeditions had to have a nanite locator."

"They are. All traces of the first two expeditions are completely gone. All the equipment, clothing, and organic matter were completely absorbed by the jungle, right down to their microscopic tags."

"Absorbed as in overgrown?"

The general led me to a viewer. "This is the third expedition viewed from orbit shortly after it landed."

The ship looked like a troop lander, minus all the intimidating weaponry. The round vessel landed in a clearing surrounded by trees covered with vines and plants similar to ferns, the landscape looking very much like the Amazon must have appeared centuries ago.

"The hull is an iron based flexible-carbide composite, common material for spaceships. Tough stuff with all types of alloys and proto-polymer material woven into its fabric; resistant to almost everything. Here is a time-lapse archive."

Flowers, like the prisoner in the interrogation bay, turned their maws toward the landing vessel. Vines wormed out of the ground and slithered like snakes over the ship, constricting around the landing pads. I saw men—sped up at ridiculous speeds—exit the ship, working to free it from the vines. They must have used lasers because the vines momentarily began to pile up. Then new vines from the flowers went after the men. A battle commenced. Fallen men were dragged back into the ship.

Two minutes into the show—two hours in real time—the first landing pad was sawed free. Men again exited the ship with what looked like flamethrowers. Flowers fell, as did men when silverish plants sprang up that resisted the fire. Again the men retreated. A minute later into the film, a rescue vessel landed and took off seconds later with the crew.

"Here is what happened to the lander, one day at a time."

Vines swarmed the vessel. Like butter left in the sun on a warm day, it shrunk with each frame. It took ten frames for the ship to disappear.

"They dissolved it?"

General O'Sullivan nodded.

"There must be a pool of metal under all that vegetation."

"You would think so but no. Spectral analyses and scans confirm not a trace of it is left. You could burn the jungle down and you wouldn't find a rivet."

I looked at the prisoner plant behind the glass window with a new measure of respect. *Deceptive bastard, aren't you.*

"So why land in the jungle? Planets are big. Go where they don't grow."

"Have you had a chance to view Darvolock yet?"

The station orbited the planet but I hadn't the time to sight see. My orders explicitly said to report to the general when I arrived.

"No sir."

The general led me to a port window. The greenest planet I'd ever seen filled the frame. Behind it loomed Darvolock's sister planet, a blue methane world whose name I had yet to learn.

"This species covers every inch of this world. You'll find only a limited number of insects and plants. No deserts, just one big tropical forest."

I titled my head and narrowed my eyes at the green world. "No oceans? What about the poles? Shouldn't it be colder and dryer there?"

"The oceans are covered with pond scum twenty feet thick, a very fertile surface for them. As far as the poles, this world maintains a consistent temperature. You won't find a rain cloud anywhere. Fog in the morning, but that's it. The theory is the plants have irrigated all the water. A really humid place with one season, sticky."

Might as well be an ocean of acid. "So the native life doesn't want to share their world. Why not let them keep it?"

"Multi-dimensional cartology isn't you're strong suit, is it?"

I shook my head while feeling my face flush.

"Noticed the lopsided barbell-shaped blue sun? That's Spica A and B, 16 AU's away. B is four times larger than Sol. A is twice its size. They circle so close both stars are distorted. They kick out enough solar activity to sterilize Earth, even at this distance. Darvolock has a magnetic field three times stronger than ours, and its Neptune-sized partner makes for the third counter-gravity well."

It took me second to piece it together. "Wormhole generation?"

"Several," he said. "As in fourteen, most going to unexplored systems."

I shook my head in disbelief. Multiple wormholes were rare. Five was the most discovered in one system.

"And one leads back to Alpha Centauri," added the general.

Two jumps to Earth. I almost doubled the number of jumps I ever made to get to this wormhole dead end. Darvolock was more than a life-sustaining world. It represented the Panama Canal of space.

I looked back at the flowery monstrosity. "You try herbicides yet?"

"I'm surprised at you, Mr. Mann. What you're suggesting is xenocide."

I glared at the general. The Confederation's policy may appear progressive to the public, but I knew the military employed an aggressive *speak softly and big stick* approach in dealing with new worlds: Hit it with the big stick first then try speaking softly to it second; an effective Machiavellian tactic.

"Yes, we tried it already," he admitted. "Three times. They've adapted and managed to counteract the poisons each time."

Can't beat 'em and the planet is too important to ignore.

I sighed. This was going to be a long assignment.

"Where would I find the bar?"

I SIGNALED TO the bartender for another shot of whiskey, my third, cursing my immediate superior for tricking me into accepting this assignment. He promised he would submit me for an Earth position if I could establish contact. He was eager to get rid of me. I was cocky, and I had a problem with keeping my mouth shut. At my honoring party for my part in making a treaty with the Tunish, I got drunk and boasted the Corps would be nowhere without me, promising I would be 'running the dump' in a month—not very wise when most of the people at the party were my superiors. Since then, the Corps utilized my talents by transferring me to every backwater post it had. News of my idiotic display, and success as a 'fish talker,' preceded me everywhere I went. Darvolock was supposed to be my ticket out of my self-made purgatory. I had to hand it to my boss for finding an impossible task for me to complete.

I downed the shot and went back to nursing my fourth beer when a man with a metal arm sat next to me.

"Mr. Mann?" he said while offering his good hand for a greeting. "I was told I'd find you here. I'm the station's xeno-ethnobotanist, Daniel Smyth."

"Plez-sure," I slurred. "What happened? Got too close when feeding the fern?"

"In fact I did. One of the plants wrapped a vine around my forearm. I lost a pint of blood and my ulna and radius disintegrated before I freed myself."

I sat up, embarrassment spurring momentary sobriety. "I'm sorry. I didn't mean . . ."

"Don't mention it," he said as he signaled the bartender. "But take my arm as a warning. Don't trust the Tulips. They bite."

I dug into my pocket and popped a sobriety tab. Saying stupid things while I was drunk was my trademark, and the last thing I needed was to collect a fresh batch of enemies the first day on the job. The tabs had an effective lifespan of ten minutes, so I knew I'd be swaying again very soon.

"Did I hear you right?" I asked as he scooped up the shot of golden liquid the bartender set before him. "It ate your bones inside your body?"

Smyth nodded as he downed his drink. "They like calcium, and iron, and a lot of other chemical compounds Earth plants wouldn't touch. Damnedest species I ever came across. Like locusts, except they do eat everything."

Visions of a melting lander danced in my head. *A chemical compound predator.* The galaxy had no shortage of species that would subsist on metals and acids, but never had I've come across one that could absorb *anything*. I was sure chemical engineers and xeno-biologists would be curious to know how, but the how wasn't going to help me.

"Why would plants eat metal?"

Smyth shrugged and reached for the beer the bartender slid down the counter his way. "A topographical survey confirms the planet's surface doesn't have much in higher elements, so the Tulips hoard it when they find it. Don't know why, it's not like they're hiding plant cities underground. The best theory we've come up with is it's an evolutionary redundancy. An autopilot reaction they haven't kicked yet."

I sipped my beer and looked at the impossibly green world in the lounge's observation window and frowned. How ironic that the most valuable piece of real estate in the galaxy was off limits because of a weed.

"Why would the plants be hoarding iron?" I asked. "This planet is supposed to have a strong magnetic field. Shouldn't it be loaded with iron?"

Smyth nodded. "Tons of it, all of it at its core. Scans of the surface show it's covered in peat moss, bogs, plants, but hardly any metals."

"No volcanic activity?"

"Oh yeah. It has three active ones. The only spots on the planet that aren't green."

I sipped my beer and gazed at the green world below. A planet without metal covered by a species that can't get enough of it. It didn't make any sense.

I SET UP shop with a view of the prisoner and spent the next three weeks pawing over bales of reports. Darvolock proved to be an enigma of a planet. Dan was right. Despite its strong magnetic field, the surface appeared to be almost devoid of metals. It had continents but not much for mountains. The surface was caked in decaying vegetation hundred of meters thick. If O'Sullivan's men could ever establish the twin bases on opposite sides of the planet, they would have to scrape away all the swamp scum and import the material needed to build the power pyramids for wormhole generation. But first an understanding needed to be reached with the natives, and I wasn't having much luck.

Plants were not my thing. An old live-in girlfriend once bought a bunch of them to liven up my apartment. They all died a week after she left; a fitting metaphor for our relationship. The Tulips (I had gotten used to using their slang name) proved to be tougher to figure out than I hoped. I attempted a dozen tactics to reach our prisoner—negative stimuli, positive stimuli, sound vibrations—it reacted the same way every plant I ever knew reacted, by sitting in its dirt and soaking up all the artificial sunlight it could.

Their anatomy showed they were nothing more than an ordinary plant. They lacked the crucial organs higher life forms needed to communicate, like a brain, but their actions proved they were as dangerous as any predator discovered. It was their strategic capability that concerned O'Sullivan the most.

I watched recordings of previous expeditions. O'Sullivan's men would try a new tactic with each attempt. Early success would turn to complete failure every time. The Tulips would be waiting when they landed—acting like innocent sunflowers bathing in the blue rays of Spica—then all hell would break loose. While replaying one disastrous battle, I noticed a small red flower bloom from a leaf of a Tulip.

I called Dan. He shrugged when I showed him. "Pollinating. You see the dragonfly thing? They're attracted to the red variety. The Tulips have been known to bud up to five different types of flowers. Each one attracts a different insect species."

"Is that common?"

"No, but I wouldn't read too much into it. The different flowers could be their way of cross-pollinating so they don't interbreed."

I replayed the film, grimacing as I weighed Dan's conclusion.

"Not buying it?" asked Dan.

"I know of a dozen emerging intelligences that rely on other species to help them breed, feed, and defecate. The galaxy has no shortage of species that will exploit the labors of a lower intelligence for their own benefit."

"Like man and horse?"

I pointed at him and smiled. "Good example, but there are better ones. There is a feline/marsupial race on Altair Five that exploits an herbivore to build their shelters for the brutal winters. I'm wondering if we're viewing the works of a puppet master species, one hiding in the shadows."

Dan frowned then shook his head. "I doubt it. If you don't count the Tulips, those insects represent the highest form of life on Darvolock."

"I can't count the Tulips."

"Why not?"

I leaned back into my chair and retrieved a holographic-anatomical schematic of our prisoner.

"They don't have the wiring for higher intelligence. They lack a nervous system. Nothing in them can carry the electrical impulses required for higher thought."

Dan looked at the plant then narrowed his eyes at me. "I'm not sure I can agree. The Yuplin is a species that have nothing like our brains, yet they're considered intelligent."

I punched up a schematic of a Yuplin. A hairy and squat creature without a neck replaced the Tulip. It had long arms used for yanking out grass and pulling down leafy branches for it to eat. Short, thick legs were needed to support its bulky body. The creatures lived under an orange sun and lumbered about with all the enthusiasm of a grazing cow. If it wasn't for the duck-billed mouth, you'd have a hard time identifying its head.

"True, the Yulpin don't have a central processing unit like ours." I pointed at the glowing lines of bio-electrical energy intersecting throughout its body. "But they do have a network of nerves to carry electrical impulses. Their nervous system doubles as their brain. The Tulips have nothing, so aren't capable of intelligence. They're plants."

"My specialty may be in plants but I know a nervous system doesn't define the intelligence of a species," said Dan. "There are plenty of creatures that have a complex nervous system that aren't much brighter than an earthworm."

I shook my head. "The nervous system isn't what makes the intelligence, but it is the requirement for intelligence. It's like the old electrical grids of Earth when power plants generated electricity for civilization. The electricity traveled along power lines. It's the lines that the Tulips . . ."

I stopped.

The lines. Long strands of copper; *metal.*

I dug for a geological survey. "Anyone else find it odd how a planet with a strong magnetic field has practically no metal on its surface?"

Dan pursed his lips and shook his head. "It wouldn't be the only one. Could be the way it was formed. More than a few cooled with all the heavier elements pooling at the core."

"Not when they have active volcanoes and continents that drift." I showed him the topographical survey. "Look. No mountains. I recall reading a chemical analysis of several Tulips, they all had trace elements of metals in their anatomy."

Dan shrugged. "So? That wouldn't make them unusual. We have trace elements of metals in us. Our blood is loaded with iron."

I arched an eyebrow at him. "And your bones have calcium."

He looked at his metal arm. I punched up a recording of a particular disastrous expedition. The soldiers wore heavy G-suits, ripping Tulips out from the roots as they attempted to swarm them. As always, what looked like a promising strategy turned into catastrophe. Water began to seep from the ground and pool around the heavy G-suited men's feet. They started to sink. Vines crept around their shoulders and pulled them in. A man drew a cutting laser. Shades of silver formed over the vines that were targeted, slowing the effect of the laser. I froze the frame and zoomed in.

"Look closely," I said and advanced the recording, extra slow. Silver leaked from the skin of the vine, crinkling like aluminum foil. "When I saw this, I couldn't help but think how this looked like the lining of a spacesuit. Now watch what happens when the laser strikes it."

A white flame burst from the silver skin. It changed color. Green, then a brick red, followed by a bright orange, and then a hot blue.

Dan leaned in, a puzzled expression on his face. "That's odd. What does it mean?"

"I'm not anything close to an expert but I believe laser cutters cut at a constant temperature. Those flames reminded me of an experiment a chemistry teacher of mine preformed long ago." I rewound it back to the orange flame. "That's what the flame looked like when he put fire to calcium."

Dan manipulated the vid for a moment, studying the flames.

"Assuming you're right," he said. "Calcium is a poor flame retardant. Why would the Tulips use it?"

"Trial and error," I said, as I took note of all the insects flying within the battle zone. "It's how evolution operates."

"Not that quickly it doesn't," countered Dan. "But intelligence can. Trial and error solutions are a mark of sentience."

I nodded. "Yes it can be, but I'm not convinced who is performing the trial and error experiments. I have a hunch on how to find out. Does this station have a device that can detect weak magnetic fields?"

"I don't know. I'm sure the engineers can make a scanner that can do the job. What are you hoping to find with it?"

I stood and stared at the prisoner plant in the next room. "A nervous system."

THE CHIEF ENGINEER was skeptical when I explained what I needed. He was quick with excuses, complaining about how busy they were while promising to get on it as soon as he could. I thanked him, and then marched to General O'Sullivan's office. A working low-yield magnetic field scanner was delivered to my doorstep in six hours. Just for the fun of it, I sent it back with instructions to increase its range. Two hours later, a technician came back with an improved model. I asked if he could stay behind to operate it. Before he could protest, I called the general and Dan to let them know the experiment was ready.

The tech linked the scanner to the station's holographic mainframe. A 3D representation of our Tulip prisoner rotated in my office. Glowing lines intersected and ran all through the alien flower.

"What are we looking at?" asked the general.

"A nervous system," I said.

Dan kneeled, tracing the paths of the brightest pathways with a metal finger. "How could we have missed this?"

"You didn't," I said. "You said you found traces of metal in them, you just mistook it as part of their basic chemistry."

"This is how they use iron?" asked the general. "To create nerves?"

"Some of it is iron." I pointed at a bright pathway Dan had become enamored with. "This I suspect is copper or maybe gold. They make a better conduit than iron. Think of this as an electrical grid that runs on bio-electrical energy, a substitute for an organic nervous system."

"So you're saying this is what happened to our ships?" asked O'Sullivan. "They were made slag to create a network of nerves?"

"Oh no. There may be a little bit of our material in our friend, but I'm sure what we're seeing here came from Darvolock itself."

Dan stared up at me. General O'Sullivan looked just as baffled as he did.

He turned to face the xeno-ethnobotanist.

"I thought this planet had no metal."

"Not now it doesn't," I interjected. "It's been mined out."

I walked to the port window and tapped on its glass, pointing at the green world below. "Look at it, sir. The entire planet, every square inch, is covered by a single species. It's changed the weather, eliminated seasons, exterminated all its rivals; did it all over an entire world. Now, imagine if every Tulip had as much metal as our friend here. They picked this world clean."

The general turned from the window and studied the hologram. "How in the hell could a plant know it could use metal as a nervous system?"

"Evolution," said Dan. His eyes were wide. I could see the realization of my proposal hitting all at once. "A distant ancestor likely absorbed chemical compounds that were toxic to an herbivore. Over time, that ability adapted and turned them into master chemical engineers and the dominant species of the planet." He turned to look at the Tulip in the next room. "And it's going to be their downfall."

It was my turn to be stunned. "How so? They reached the pinnacle of evolution. Their actions prove they're capable of adapting to anything thrown their way."

Dan shook his head. "Their actions prove that they're starving for essential minerals. This world is overpopulated, way overpopulated. They probably haven't the ability to control their numbers and they won't be able sustain their levels much longer. This world is on the verge of an apocalypse never seen before."

I saw a glimmer of hope in O'Sullivan's eyes. "When?"

"It won't be tomorrow," said Dan. "Or in a year. The soonest? A few decades. Maybe ten thousand years on the outside, but collapse it will."

The general pointed at the base of the holographic Tulip. "What's going on down there?"

The Tulip's roots glowed with activity. The magnetic field detector showed it to be alive with electricity.

"That must be its brain," said Dan.

"I'm not so sure," I said. "Wasn't it part of a larger root system? I recall in a report that they had to cut it away from one."

"I believe they did," said the General. "What are you thinking?"

I turned and smiled at the technician who had been standing behind us quietly, listening to us the entire time. "I'm thinking engineering needs to build us another scanner."

We watched from the safety of the station as a scanner-equipped lander hovered meters above Darvolock's surface. The floor of the jungle, through the enhanced image, looked like the jumbled mess of wires you would find in an ancient electronic machine.

"It looks like one big brain," said Dan.

"Is that what we're dealing with?" asked O'Sullivan. "A single entity?"

"Looks like that is the case, sir," said Dan.

"Not so fast," I said. "You see all the insect activity? I noticed in other vids how they swarm whenever a ship of ours is on the scene."

"So?" countered Dan. "Just look at all the electrical impulses below the surface. Tell me that isn't complex thought we're seeing. All the Tulips are connected. It's a collective mind. I'd bet my salary on it."

"If the Tulip's are all connected then why would they need insects for pollination?"

Dan opened his mouth, and then closed it as he thought about what I said.

"There is an emerging species on Hatrac 4," I continued. "They have a high percentage of conjoined births—one in five. Some of their children are joined at the brain yet each half has their own independent thoughts. To communicate, they must talk to each other."

General O'Sullivan waved a finger at the holographic jungle floor. "Then what is all this?"

"I am only guessing, but if Dan is correct about the Tulip's mineral shortage, this could be part of a highway for essentials. Chemical compounds relocated to where they're needed. To move so much material would require energy. I'm betting this is the power supply for a complex conveyor belt."

That sparked an argument between Dan and me. The General listened to us spar for a full minute before he decided he had enough.

"I just want to know one thing," he shouted above our rising voices. "Can you talk to it?"

I pursed my lips together and thought for a second. "I don't know, but I have a theory. I need bugs."

O'SULLIVAN WASN'T HAPPY about sending men to the surface for bug collecting. The scout ship that was sent down grabbed a dozen specimens, and managed to come back intact. Dan's expertise was the closest thing the station had to an entomologist. He analyzed the pollinated fluid the insects stored in a sac while I watched over his shoulder.

"What's the verdict?" I asked.

"It's alien nectar, with one small difference. Each insect has a trace element of metal compounds in it. The dragonfly has iron. The green butterfly, copper. Each species carries something different."

"Any other differences?"

"None that I can see, but this may be outside my field of expertise," he said, motioning at the magnified display of the nectar.

I leaned toward the screen and frowned. The superimposed red fluid had a hexagonal block structure. Slivers of silver were skewered into some of the blocks.

"Find anything I should be made aware of?" Dan asked.

"If you were an alien species that came across a book and you broke down its molecular structure in hopes of finding an answer to its purpose, what would you find?"

He leaned back into his chair and rubbed his chin. "Organic cells from the paper with traces of chemical compounds used to make the ink."

"Exactly."

"You're still going with your theory that the Tulips are individual entities?"

"I'm still not convinced they're intelligent, but I'm sure we're not dealing with a single mind."

Dan threw up his hands then punched up a vid of the scan of the jungle floor. "Look at all the activity. You could power a 21st century city with what we're seeing here. If this isn't a brain at work, what is it?"

"If you did a similar scan of Earth a thousand years ago, you might conclude the same thing from its electrical grid."

"But it would be obvious that you were seeing an advanced society at work."

I pointed at the Tulip in the other room. "Not to everyone and likely not to this species. I have learned over the years that our point of perception is unique in the universe. The same goes for all the rest of the intelligences we've come across. This life form is the most alien I've ever dealt with. I've been studying them for almost a month and I'm still not sure how they sense the world around them, but I am sure they do sense it."

Dan crossed his arms and raised an eyebrow. "I agree. They're the most alien creatures I've ever come across myself. Doesn't mean they aren't able to see us as intelligent counterparts. They've adapted to every tactic we tried against them, and did it on the fly. That alone supports my contention that they're a single mind. They've identified us as a threat. Intelligent beings do that, and an intelligent being would recognize intelligence when it sees it."

"They're plants," I countered. "That makes them unique. All through the galaxy, plants are used as raw material. From their perspective, we're the raw material. I can't even fathom what they would consider a society, or even guess if they could grasp the concept of a society. They probably have no idea what we are, but are hoping we keep coming back. We are what they need."

Dan frowned. "Well, in the words of the general, 'Can you talk to it?'"

I grinned thinly at him. "Rule one for First Contact Diplomat's: All sentient species love to gossip. Eavesdropping is what we specialize in. If they're individuals, they gossip. All it takes is finding the right type of cup and a thin wall to press it against. I just got to find out how." I walked over to a jar holding a red dragonfly. "Let's see what happens when we release this guy into the next room."

I opened the jar and ushered the dragonfly into the interrogation bay. The Tulip immediately reacted. Its enormous maw turned toward the insect. It lifted a limb. A red flower bloomed in the crux of a leaf. The dragonfly landed and fed. Twenty seconds later, it took flight again. The red flower retreated into the Tulips limb.

Figuring out how to retrieve the dragonfly proved to be our biggest problem. No one wanted to go into the interrogation bay to get it. When it flew near the quarantined access door, a lowly aide was sent in with a net.

What we found in its fluid caught us all by surprise. Traces of a dozen different elements, all of which were found inside the interrogation bay. A scanned inspection was made of the bay. Fine scaring was found on every panel, surface, and crevice. The Tulip left its mark on anything it could reach, even the pot in which it was planted.

"Looking for an escape?" Dan joked.

I shook my head. "I think it was tasting its surroundings."

"Now what?" he asked.

I set my chin in my hand. I really didn't know. Then it hit me.

"We take the dragonfly back to the surface and deliver its message."

GENERAL O'SULLIVAN WAS not thrilled with the idea. The way he saw it, we were hand-delivering secret documents directly to the enemy.

"What's it going to tell 'em?" I asked. "Help. I'm being held captive aboard a spaceship?"

The scout ship released the dragonfly near a cluster of Tulips while we watched from orbit. One immediately opened a red flower. It sat and swayed, as if contemplating what it absorbed. A moment later, it lashed out a vine and captured the dragonfly.

"That was new," remarked Dan.

The Tulip then opened a half a dozen flowers. Insects swarmed them. They flew to other Tulips. They repeated the original Tulip's blooming. Clouds of insects fanned out, as if they were spreading the word. The first Tulip reopened its red flower. Our dragonfly flew from the Tulip's grip and fed off it. It then launched.

"Don't let that get away!" I screamed at the pilot of the scout ship. The dragonfly darted. The cluster of Tulip's all closed their flowers. It took a few minutes, but our men finally managed to recapture it. I couldn't wait until they brought it back up it to the station.

GENERAL O'SULLIVAN WANTED us to dissect the dragonfly. I preferred to leave it be. We struck a compromise and extracted the fluid. It had traces of iron salts in it but appeared to be no different than the previous sample.

"What's it say?" the general asked.

"Gibberish, now that we disturbed it. We shouldn't have messed with it."

He glared at me. "Then put it back in the bug."

"It's alphabet soup now." I swished the fluid in the test tube. I was so close to breaking this enigma but worried I wouldn't get any closer than this. I already considered re-injecting the nectar back into the fly but knew whatever message it held was likely lost. Confusion would likely be the result when our Tulip extracted it. That gave me an idea.

I set the tube on its perch and placed it on the floor of the buffered quarantined connector. I closed our side and opened the door into the bay. The Tulip lifted its maw and turned it toward the tube. It snaked a vine across the floor, found the tube and dipped its tip into the nectar. Its maw opened wide, revealing orange overlapping petals within. It pulled the tube in and sucked up the nectar. It closed its maw tight and whipped its vine, smashing the tube on the far wall.

"That didn't go well," said Dan.

"Oh, it went better than I hoped," I replied. "Our friend recognized something was out of the norm. I am convinced it is more than a simple flower now."

"Intelligent?" asked Dan.

I shrugged but added, "I am leaning that way."

"But can you talk to it?" asked the General.

I shook my head. "I still don't know, but I know how I might find out."

MY REQUEST FOR man-shaped figurines of carbon, filled with proportional amounts of the basic compounds found in all of us, did not go over well with the engineering department.

"He wants us to make dolls for him now?" I overheard the chief engineer yell while walking by his department. "What does he think we are? An arts and crafts store?"

I detoured to the general's office to impress upon him the importance of the figurines. He assured me that they would be a top priority, promising a dozen would be at my office in an hour. A box of a twelve was delivered at my doorstep fifty-eight minutes later.

Dan took one of the six-inch tall men out and examined it. "Bearing gifts?" he said.

"You betcha."

I set one of the little men in the quarantined connector and opened the buffer once I was safely outside. The Tulip slithered a vine out, finding the figurine. It ran its tip over it and swayed.

"Curious," Dan said. "Now what?"

I answered by putting on a spacesuit. Dan eyed me as if I had lost it.

"You can't be serious."

I grabbed a figurine and jammed a sliver of copper in one of its hands.

"About time I earned my pay."

I stepped into the connector and took a deep breath, reminding myself that I had done dumber things in the past.

Yes, but you were drunk, myself answered back.

I waited for the doors to do their job and stepped into the bay. I set the figurine before the Tulip and took a step back.

The Tulip was aware of my presence. It turned its maw to face me, slithering a vine cautiously toward the figurine on the floor.

"Careful," said Dan in my headset. "They're quick. Your suit will protect you, for a while. And remember, I'm the only one in here, and it might take a few minutes before help will arrive to get you out."

I watched as a second and third vine sprouted from opposite branches, hating Dan for reminding me that I was completely on my own if the worst happened. The Tulip's vines unfurled as they touched the floor, coiling next to its pot. I eyed them as if they were vipers ready to strike.

"I'll be okay," I said, wishing my voice didn't crack with fear.

Sweat rolled off my brow and down the ridge of my nose as the probing vine crawled over the figurine. The Tulip went rigid when it touched the sliver of copper. The vine curled around the figurine. I reached down and snatched the doll. It coiled around the figurine tighter and tugged, but I refused to let go.

"Not so fast, big boy," I said to it as I pulled the figurine toward me.

"Look out!" Dan's voice shouted in my helmet.

The other two vines unfurled and rushed my flanks. I stomped on the one on my right, pinning it to the floor under my heavy boot. The other vine grasped my wrist and constricted.

"Help is on the way," said Dan.

"Good," I replied. I grabbed the vine holding the figurine and yanked. The lower half of the figurine broke and shattered on the floor. I still held the end with the copper. "But tell them to stay out there until I get this worked out."

The vine under my foot thrashed. I leaned more weight on it. With my free hand I grabbed the vine that held my wrist and snapped it. I jumped back as the third vine lashed out at me. I retreated toward the wall where the smashed test tube rested.

"Mann, what the hell do you think you're doing?"

I glanced at the window to my office. General O'Sullivan glared at me from the other side of the glass with four soldiers standing behind him.

"Reaching an understanding with our friend."

The Tulip's maw was partially opened and faced me. Pointing at me like a radar tower tracking its target. Vines swept the floor, searching for my feet. I backed away, carefully, lifting a foot to avoid a probing vine.

I reached the wall. I crouched and felt on the ground, keeping an eye on the vines while searching for the busted tube. I found it just as vine touched the tip of my boot. The three vines converged. I held out the broken tube, touching its smooth side to a vine.

A vine wrapped around my arm while the other probed at the tube. The maw to the Tulip opened wide when it tasted the traces of nectar inside.

"Come on," I said as I shook the tube. "Prove to me you can reason."

The Tulip swayed. Its maw opened and closed. It still held my arm in an iron grip but kept itself at bay.

"Hold on," said General O'Sullivan. "We're coming in."

"Don't," I said, not believing my own ears when I did. "Just give it one more minute."

I froze. Sweat clouded my vision. If the Tulip could feel my heartbeat, it would likely know that I was filled with panic. It wrapped another loop around my arm with its vine, then withdrew the other two back into its branches. A moment later, a red flower bloomed from one of the branches.

"Get a dragonfly," I whispered through clenched teeth into my headset.

It took a half a minute for the crew to release an insect into the room. It found the flower and fed. The dragonfly launched and fluttered into the connector, disappearing out of my field of vision. Two minutes felt like an hour. Finally Dan's voice announced the results into my headset.

"It has copper in it."

I touched the vine gripping my arm with the sliver of copper. The vine unraveled from my arm and snatched it away. I watched it melt into the vines fabric. Then the Tulip opened another flower, this one a vibrant blue.

"That one attracts a green bee," said Dan. "Give me a second."

I edged along the wall. The Tulip's maw tracked me but held its vine at bay. I entered the connector just as Dan set a bee free. He handed me a net and shut the door. I watched the bee land on the flower. It took longer to feed than the dragonfly. It launched in flight. I snatched it out of the air as it flew near the door. I punched the button closing the door to the bay. The door behind me opened. I stepped out and handed the net to Dan.

I peeled out of the suit. General O'Sullivan stood opposite of me with his arms crossed, glaring at me with his hard eyes.

"That was the most foolish thing I have ever witnessed. Do have any idea what would have happened if that thing got inside your suit?"

"Yes, sir," I said. "You would have gotten your answer on whether I could talk to it or not."

Dan waved me over. He had the fluid extracted from the bee and fed it into the analyzer. He leaned toward the screen and turned it to show me.

"It's tin."

I turned to General O'Sullivan and smiled. I was relieved and filled with pride. "We have made contact."

I DOWNED MY third shot and went back to nursing my fourth beer when a man who once had a metal arm sat next to me.

"You're back," I said to Dan. "Your arm looks great. How was Altair?"

He flexed his cloned arm for me. "It was wonderful. I feel like a new man. How are the negotiations coming along?"

I lifted my beer. "Been a tough two months but we finally have an agreement. The Tulips are clearing two areas on opposite sides of the planet for us. Costing us a bundle in metal but fortunately this system is loaded with asteroids rich in it."

The bartender set a beer in front of Dan. Dan raised it in a toast.

"Congratulations. You've made big news back there. I even ran into friends of yours in the Corps. They say Earth has plans for you."

I sat up. The bureaucrats rarely acknowledged anything outside Earth's atmosphere.

"Your friends sent their congratulations," said Dan. "And wanted me to give you a gift. I left it on your desk."

I sat my beer down and made a beeline to my office, my buzzed brain imagining that my wish of a reassignment to Earth was about to be granted.

I opened my door and saw an Earth tulip in a vase on my desk. A gold necklace with a locket was draped around its stem. I opened the locket and cringed when I read the centuries old slang message my 'friends' from my old office had inscribed in it:

NEED MORE BLING.

ABOUT THE AUTHOR

FRANK DUTKIEWICZ is a truck driver who writes whimsical tales in an attempt to stave off insanity when away from home. He has two Finalists, a Semi-finalist, twice a Silver Honorable Mention, and over a dozen Honorable Mention finishes in the *Writers of the Future* contest. His work has appeared in a multitude of publications, most notably *Daily Science Fiction* and *The Grantville Gazette.* He serves as a finalist judge for the on-line publication *On The Premises* and is an associate editor for the recurring speculative humor anthology *Unidentified Funny Objects.* Frank is also blessed to be the father of two lovely daughters and is the husband of an equally as lovely wife.

ABOUT THE STORY

"A Green Tongue" came about from an in-house contest prompt that originated at the *Hatrack River Writers Workshop* (a critique group for up and coming speculative writers). The winner received an autographed book from the Hugo nominated author who judged the contest. I finished second, but the rough idea I'd thrown together inspired me to polish it up and send it to the *Writers of the Future (WOTF)* contest.

"A Green Tongue" earned a Semi-finalist award two quarters after I received the first of my two Finalist awards from entry judge Dave Wolverton at WOTF. Semi-finalist entries get a rare critique from Dave. For you writers who have never viewed a WOTF Semi-finalist critique, I can tell you, from the dozen I have seen, that they are about 200 words and are written to be encouraging while providing the writer a reason why they fell just short. Mr. Wolverton's critique had a very complimentary opening:

> We don't get a lot of good science fiction stories with this kind of light-hearted, fun tone. In many ways, it felt like classic SF from the fifties.

The next couple of paragraphs involved Dave's explaining his method of whittling down his stack of contenders to a Finalist list of eight, rationalizing why some entries are set aside in the process. Unlike other Semi-finalist critiques that other authors have shared with me, this one lacked a solid reason why "A Green Tongue" was left off the final eight list. Instead, I received this as a closing statement:

> . . . even as I critique this I'm worried that I made a mistake, that I should have kept this in our Finalist stack.

As encouraging and disheartening that this bit of news would be for any writer, Dave did predict that "A Green Tongue" would be professionally published, and he was right. In March 2016, *The Grantville Gazette* accepted it for one of its few non-*1632* slots, one of my biggest thrills as a writer.

There is an inherent ethical paradox in being created to destroy. Given life, shall one not choose life?

....

A MATTER OF INTERPRETATION

M. ELIZABETH TICKNOR

The Dragonspine Mountains swallowed up the stars in the eastern half of the desert sky. Cers tended the fire at his master's campsite in an attempt to stave off the darkness. He had never seen anything so massive or imposing. He wished that his master, Tirian, had not insisted on making camp in their shadow the previous evening. The sun-bleached peaks warped the wind into howls that echoed through the air like ravenous beasts.

Tirian exited his tent at dawn and motioned for Cers to approach. "Sit. I want to examine your seamwork."

The runic tattoos that covered Cers' body glowed white as Tirian's command took root. Cers grunted an acknowledgment and knelt at his master's feet. Even kneeling, Cers' head was parallel with Tirian's shoulders.

Had Tirian not taken on the mantle of necromancy, Cers felt he would have made an excellent tailor. He had composed Cers from the choicest parts of a dozen different corpses, woven together with silk thread and spellwork. Cers did not understand why he had been driven to such gruesome work, but appreciated the craftsmanship required to accomplish such a daunting task.

Tirian let out a satisfied sigh as his hands finished tracing the stitches that held Cers' limbs together. "Good, good. How is your healing? Place your hand in the fire."

Cers grimaced, but did as Tirian commanded. He sucked in a sharp breath as his hand began to burn. He forced himself to hold it steady until the smell of cooking flesh reached his nostrils.

"Now pull it out."

Cers followed Tirian's bidding. Dead nerves tingled back to life as his injury healed over and left fresh, unscarred skin.

"Excellent. You're complete, or as complete as I can make you. Come morning, we'll put you to work."

Cers gave a single nod. Tirian preferred him to speak only when necessary, but this seemed important enough to merit a question. "What would you have me do?"

"I would have you tear down the gates of Risafio."

The implicit promise of violence made Cers' scalp prickle. He frowned. "Why?"

"Because the Valdians are losing the war, and I've been hired to change that. Taking Risafio should turn the tide. Once you destroy the gates and rout the guards, the Valdian army can take the pass and solidify their supply lines. Lord Irenea will grant me lands and a title once the job is done."

Cers' neck and shoulder muscles clenched. Routing the guards meant hurting them at best and killing them at worst. In the weeks after Cers' creation, Tirian had tested and tweaked his healing abilities extensively. Cers held an intimate knowledge of how it felt to have one's limbs crushed or skull caved in. He had even hurled himself over a cliff once on Tirian's orders. The landing shattered most of the bones in his body and crushed a rabbit that had been hiding in the brush. He recovered from the fall, but the rabbit remained limp and broken.

Cers took a deep breath, then let it out slowly. "I do not want to harm anyone."

Tirian threw his hands up in the air. "By the Roiling Havoc, you're not supposed to *want* anything!" He knitted his brow and shook his head. "I suppose that's what I get for designing a golem intelligent enough to create adaptive strategies. The anatomists of House Arivess say the brain houses the soul. Perhaps I should have used an animal brain rather than a human one."

"I am fully functional. My body is strong—"

"Your body is not what I worry about."

"My mind is sound—"

"Silence!"

The command struck Cers like a slap to the face. His tattoos flared to life and clamped his jaw shut so tightly that it ached.

Tirian glared at Cers. "Better." He stood and circled Cers with narrowed eyes. "Insolence will not be tolerated. You are meant to take orders, not to question them."

Cers stared into the fire. The sudden inability to speak left him numb and hollow. Tirian might as well have ordered him to rip out his tongue.

THE VILLAGE OF Risafio pressed tightly against the cliffs and surrounded the only pass between the Dragonspine Mountains for fifty leagues. A pair of blue-flecked granite towers dwarfed the huts and hovels of the common folk. The bloodwood gates that cut off the pass were strong enough to keep an entire Valdian battalion at bay. They were well-manned, and designed to withstand massive onslaughts. They were not, however, fortified against a potential attack from within.

Tirian led Cers into town at midday, dressed in the fine dyed linens of a merchant. Cers dragged a wooden cart that contained Tirian's traveling supplies, as well as two dozen bolts of cloth should they need to validate their cover story as textile merchants.

Cers' muscles burned with every step as he strained to slow his pace. He lurched onward, shoulders slumped, head hung low. His tattoos flickered every time he hesitated. He hoped the glow was dim enough in the daylight that Tirian would not take notice.

Tirian strutted confidently beside him, spine military-drill straight. "Don't shamble so. I built you better than that."

The tattoos that covered Cers' body blazed. The compulsion to obey was overwhelming. Cers straightened his posture and steadied his gait, but kept his pace methodical and slow.

The stares of the people on the street pricked and needled at Cers as he walked through town. Even slumped forward, cloaked and cowled, he stood taller than anyone in the crowd. His shoulders stretched as broad as the yokes of the oxen that pulled the traders' wagons.

Tirian surveyed Risafio like a wildcat ready to pounce. "Smash the gates, then knock down the towers. If anyone gets in your way, kill them."

Cers' tattoos flared. He ground his teeth and clenched his fists tightly around the cart's handle grips. No matter how much he focused, his legs drove him forward.

Cers abandoned the cart when he reached the gates. His muscles rippled as he pushed against doors that were meant to be pulled. Steel-braced wood creaked, groaned, and splintered. Cers pressed unrelentingly against the doors until the gate's hinges cracked, then snapped under the pressure. Cries of alarm rang out across the plaza as the two halves of the gate toppled to the ground.

A trio of guards rushed Cers at the base of the northernmost tower. He tossed them aside like rag dolls. His tattoos flared and urged him to ensure their demise, but he focused instead on collapsing the towers. The guards were not presently in his way, and the orders for destruction had come first.

The tower's stonework was solid and well-fitted. If Cers charged it full-force he would be lucky to even crack the stone. There was, however, a wooden door, and in the end all doors were meant to be opened.

Cers rammed the door, shoulder-first, until he broke it down. Guards clambered down the stairs. He ignored them. They were not yet in his way.

There. The support beams.

Cers slammed into the closest beam with all of his weight. It cracked from the force. One of the guards charged him, but he sidestepped and shoved the man into the wall. He flung the bloody guard into the arms of his fellows and stalked toward the next beam.

The guards bolted for the exit. Cers gave them time to flee before he shattered the remaining supports.

The tower collapsed around him. A deluge of stone, wood, and mortar poured down on his head and shoulders. His back snapped under the strain. Sharp, jarring agony surged through his body. Then death embraced him.

CERS SCREAMED AS Tirian's magic dragged him back to sentience. Flesh knitted together despite the unrelenting press of the rubble above him. Bones healed in excruciatingly wrong positions, then broke again every time he tried to move. Cers thrashed and writhed, desperate for relief.

After what seemed like an eternity, his body repaired itself sufficiently for him to push away the stones that trapped him. He crawled out from under the debris and lay on his back, panting. Bones snapped back into their proper positions and muscles slithered into place around them. A surge of panicked voices enveloped him.

"It can't be human! No one could survive that."

"The whole tower landed on its head!"

"Look at its *arm*—"

Cers' shoulder popped back into place. He staggered to his feet. A dozen guardsmen surrounded him, shields and spears at the ready. They were poised to fight, but their eyes were wide and their limbs trembled. Cers made eye contact with each of them in turn.

If he were careful, he should be able to push through the crowd. As long as he could get through, they were not in his way.

His body ached from the tower's collapse. His muscles were barely responsive, his movements jerky. It took most of his energy to brush the guards aside before they surrounded him. The magic-borne inclination toward mayhem and slaughter surged through him anew. He clenched his jaw, shook his head to clear it, and pushed on toward the southern tower.

Panicked civilians swarmed the road between the towers. Some rushed toward the gates, others sought to flee them, and even more simply stood in place and gawked at the wreckage.

Murderous intent surged within Cers, but he fought it desperately. He did not want to kill. He did *not* want to kill. He ran down his list of orders: Silence. Break the gates. Destroy the towers. Kill anyone who got in his way.

Tirian couldn't have meant him to be silent *forever*.

Cers' tattoos flared as he bellowed a wordless warning cry toward the crowd. The act of rebellion burned like fire.

Cers charged toward the crowd, yelling all the way. People scrambled away, but some did not move fast enough. Cers gritted his teeth and slowed down to avoid them.

The guards caught up and surrounded him. Their formation was tighter this time. They glared at him with eyes like steel.

Cers balked. His tattoos seethed with arcane energy. Tirian's words burned into his mind. The guards were in his way. There was no way through. He had to kill them. He *had* to!

The repercussions of disobedience scorched him like an inferno. White-hot magic blazed from every tattoo and stitched seam. Even so, the pain did not compare to the torture of having been trapped alive, body shattered, under the weight of the collapsed tower. If he had pushed through that, he could push through this.

Through the searing thrum of energy he heard one of the guards demand his surrender. He ground his teeth, bowed his head, and placed his hands behind his neck.

Tirian's voice rang out over the throng. "What are you doing? I did not bid you to surrender!"

Cers spotted Tirian in a matter of moments. He had been blending in with the crowd, most likely playing the part of a panicked citizen. Cers' stomach clenched.

"Kill them! *Kill them all!*"

Cers howled as the order tore into him and filled his mind with anguish. He collapsed to the ground, clutching his head. He wanted to ease the pain, even if that meant crushing his own skull.

No. He could live with pain. He was *designed* to live with pain. If that was all defiance brought, he was not truly obligated to obey. He ground his teeth together and took steady, measured breaths. The longer it continued, the more he was able to bear it.

He stood and glared at Tirian. "No."

Tirian stared at him, wide-eyed. "What?"

Cers roared, "*No!*"

Tirian flinched and stepped back. He pulled an obsidian focus stone from the folds of his cloak and began to chant. Two guards lunged for him. He spat a command. A crackling ball of energy shot from the focus orb and enveloped the more muscular of his guards. The man fell to the ground, screaming as flesh melted from his bones. His fellow guardsman swore and backed away.

Cers snarled, bore down on Tirian like an avalanche, and grabbed the mage by the throat. Tirian dropped his focus orb and scrabbled frantically to loosen Cers' grip, but Cers lifted him into the air with one hand.

Tirian pried at Cers' fingers. He tried to choke out a phrase—an order? a spell?—but could not draw enough air to speak.

It would be so *easy* to end him. To snap Tirian's neck, smash open his skull and watch his brains leak out onto the cobblestones.

But Cers did not want to kill.

He took a deep breath, then let it out slowly. "No." He brought a foot down on the focus orb and crushed it to powder. Then he dropped Tirian like a pile of wet rags. Tirian collapsed on the hard-packed earth, gasping and clutching at his throat.

The guards glanced between Cers and Tirian, uncertain of who to target. "Surrender!" the captain bellowed. "Hands on the back of your head!"

Cers almost gave in out of sheer exhaustion, but he forced himself to think. Surrender might leave him bound to the will of the guards, perhaps even the will of Tirian. He wanted no part of that.

Cers ran toward the broken gates. Spears whistled through the air. Two tore into his back; a third embedded itself in his left shoulder. He pulled them out and kept running. The damage was not sufficient to slow him.

He pressed on long after the shattered gates disappeared behind the cliffs.

The pangs from his disobeyed orders softened over time. The burning light of his tattoos dimmed to a soft blue glow, then faded away.

Cers smiled. He did not know what lay on the other side of the pass, but whatever dangers he faced, he would face them of his own volition.

ABOUT THE AUTHOR

M. ELIZABETH TICKNOR has been previously published in Flame Tree Publishing's *Heroic Fantasy Short Stories* anthology. She and her husband share a comfortable hobbit hole in Southeast Michigan. An avid reader of science fiction and fantasy, Elizabeth also enjoys well-written horror. The authors who have inspired her include Douglas Adams, Ray Bradbury, Orson Scott Card, Neil Gaiman, C.S. Lewis, Chuck Wendig, and David Wong. Her other interests include drawing, painting, and tabletop role-playing. Her preferred gaming systems are *World of Darkness*, *Pathfinder*, and 5th Edition *Dungeons & Dragons*. Her website is http://www.ticknortales.com.

ABOUT THE STORY

I've had some of the pieces for "A Matter of Interpretation" floating around in my head for the better part of a decade. Cers has long been a favorite character of mine. He was first created for a chat-based online roleplaying game between friends, but quickly took on a life of his own. I created the setting of this story specifically so I could use him in my own fiction. I've play-tested the setting in multiple *D&D* and *Pathfinder* campaigns, which meant I had a wealth of world-building information already at my fingertips. All I needed was the right spark.

That spark came in the form of a flash fiction writing prompt that Chuck Wendig posted on his *Terrible Minds* blog. He urged people to write about rebellion in the aftermath of the 2016 presidential election. His prompt crystallized Cers' origin story for me and cast it in a new and interesting light.

In early versions of Cers' origin, he killed his creator to gain his freedom. However, in the course of writing "A Matter of Interpretation," I realized that such a graphic act of violence didn't fit the tale. The conflict between Cers' desire for peace versus the cost of his freedom are integral to this story. Resolving that conflict with murder would be a step backward for his character rather than a step forward. Cers chooses to differentiate himself from his master by doing what is *right* rather than what is easy. His decision to value all life—even one as reprehensible as Tirian's—is his first true act of independence.

Oelenes die giving birth to many young; a time of great celebration.
Human females do not die in childbirth, Ribolee's human friend Abigail said.
How strange; how troubling.
For Ribolee's friend Siluone is about to die birthing many young oelene;
and now, alone among her people, Ribolee feels a sense of loss.
A tale of two species, two cultures, and friendship that bridges both.

....

THE ROOT BRIDGES
OF HAEMAE

SEAN MONAGHAN

Human females survive the birth of their children.

Astonishing.

Ribolee ran this revelation around in her head again and again as she walked home from their camp.

Human females survive the birth.

And not only that, they sometimes have just one child. Imagine. A single child. How could that be? How could a species come to be with such a clear hindrance to its own survival?

Around her, the jungle dripped. The midday rains had been shorter today. She liked this time of year: summer almost here, but still cooler and the rains diminishing. The full seasons were far wilder: the dry of summer when the ground became bristling and crackly, the leaves darkened and swelled, animals howled and rushed; the wet chill of winter when the rivers burgeoned, the ground became a swamp, and the rain could last for suns on end.

The path was still spongy underfoot. She saw a scootsnail slithering up a rough trunk and she hurried over. It saw her coming and accelerated, but she'd been catching mollusks for years. She slipped around the back of the tree, deftly stepping between the buttress roots. The scootsnail's antenna eyes bulged seeing her appear from the wrong side.

Ribolee stabbed out with her index talon, expertly stabbing the hapless creature through its soft brain. It wriggled for a moment as its body dulled from orange and blue to a sad, dead gray.

Holding the shell in her talons she wrapped her lips around the soft body and sucked, using both tips of her tongue to pull the animal from its shell. It was older—should have been smarter—and tasted like it. Tough and dry. A year ago it would have been sweet and soft. Still, she wasn't one to complain: she'd eaten too many papo roots and Katanca's jerky over the last few months.

She made an effort to savor the taste, letting the glutinous body swirl through her mouth for a moment. Tossing the shell away, she got back on the path, thoughts swirling again with the revelation from Abigail.

Human females. Amazing.

Kantanca and Siluone were going to be stunned. Just stunned. Ribolee relished the thought of the expressions on their hands when she told them.

Dawn Morgan looked over the day's recordings. Again everything had screwed up. It was ludicrous to send teams out under-equipped. The data readers were from Mico-Mitsui. Very well-known for rugged electronics for off-world work. For off-world work in deserts.

Haemae was as far from desert as it was possible to get. Its sheer lack of anything close to desert was enough for a dozen PhDs in itself. Even the polar regions blossomed with tundra and hardy trees.

"Problems?" Abigail said. She'd been in the portajon throwing up again. Dawn wondered why they sent people with poor constitutions to planets with such burgeoning biospheres. Despite all the tablets and nanobiots, there was still something to make the unwary wish they'd never come.

"Stupid scatter on these systems. I'm not getting any useful data." The remotes were spread out over sixty square kilometers, supposedly sending huge amounts of telemetry back. Temperature, humidity, lux, cloud cover, rainfall, flora activity, fauna activity, video and still images.

"Let me take a look."

"Go ahead." Dawn passed the light yellow box to her colleague. "Good luck."

Abigail took the box and sat on the stool opposite. She looked at the sky. "Think it's going to rain again?"

"Not today." Around them the jungle was filled with the chatter and squawks of hundreds of birds and warm-blooded critters. Looking through the trees she could see some of the bright plumage. Golds and silvers, reds and blues.

She started working on one of the other machines. She wished she'd thought to requisition some of the old Banolle units before they'd left. Those had fewer data streams, but at least they would have sent data.

"I was talking to Ribolee earlier," Abigail said. "Out near the bridge."

"Ribolee? That's one of the female oelenes? Pre-adolescent." They'd been on the ground three weeks and already they were talking with the local town. Dawn had to admit that Abigail was definitely good at that. She'd mastered some of the language and passed on some standard English too.

Dawn envied Abigail's easy connection with the oelenes. The woman was a natural. Dawn always felt too shy or aloof to make those close connections. Not a great trait for an anthropologist, but she hoped she made up for it in other ways. More objective observation, perhaps.

Abigail used a multitool to pry at the reader's casing. "Yes. She was asking about human physiology." Abigail looked up at Dawn. "I think I screwed up."

Dawn inclined her head. "How so?"

"Well, one of her older friends is having babies soon."

Dawn nodded. She'd read all the early, machine generated papers from the robot satellites that had come out a couple of years ahead. A lot of species—including the sentient bipeds—gave birth to dozens or hundreds of babies at once. It made her think of spiders, the huge mother creeping around her web, her whole abdomen adorned with tiny pale miniature versions of herself.

"You know they die, right? As soon as the babies come out, the mother dies."

"I hadn't read that. There are species on Earth that do that." She couldn't think of any off-hand. Maybe some fish. Surely some insects. Didn't some praying mantises eat their mother when they emerged?

Dawn worked on the rubbery buttons of the reader. She could see moisture inside the screen, lensing the image.

"That's after mating," Abigail said when Dawn mentioned it. "They copulate and the female mantis eats the male."

"I should have known that."

"Ribolee was surprised when I told her we don't. Die, I mean."

"Ahh." Dawn banged the unit against the side of the stool.

"Sorry," Abigail said.

"Don't worry. We're just a lead party. It won't make much . . ." Dawn trailed off, staring at Abigail, eyes wide. "How far along are you?"

Abigail swallowed. She looked back at their big habitat unit. "We should eat," she said, standing. "I'll explain over dinner." She handed Dawn the reader. The little machine was clear and receiving data.

RIBOLEE CROSSED THE long bridge to Hama island. The town was connected across the river by a dozen of the big hefty grulltree bridges, their roots trained to span the gap. Abigail had asked to see how they were constructed.

As if they were made in an afternoon.

Ribolee's long toes grabbed around the rough tangle of roots as she ran. Overhead a flock of klootcoots squealed, chasing insects as a pack.

"Hey, Reeb!" someone shouted from the far bank. Katanca.

Ribolee finger-splayed in greeting and ran on. When she got there they tickled faces. The feeling was sensual. Ribolee knew it was from talking with Abigail about making babies, not from any attraction to Katanca.

"Have you been messing around with your flat-faced friends again?"

Ribolee laughed. Katanca always had a new insult for the aliens. Flat-faced, stubby-fingered, blestnut-skinned, nut-eyed, silly-eared. They were pretty funny-looking with squashed in faces and dark-skin. They had tiny, tiny talons that were rounded on the end. Ribolee still felt amazed that they could catch anything to eat.

"Come on, we're having a soundparty for Siluone. She's fifteen suns."

Katanca took her arm and pulled her along the path. A criscrab scuttled away ahead of them.

"Fifteen suns? Really?" Her friend's belly had been swelling for weeks. Joyous, but she was sure there were more than fifteen suns left before the birth.

"Of course!" Katanca said. "It's a party, yay!"

"Yay, for sure." Ribolee ran ahead. She couldn't wait.

"TWENTY WEEKS!" DAWN said, leaping up and practically knocking over the bolted-down table.

Abigail grabbed the shaking dishes. Despite being tempted to try some of the local fare, she was more than happy to stick with the packages from home. The kitchen was well appointed, with coffee, synthesizers, and an algae farm pumping out enough protein for the two of them.

The whole habitat had been dropped as a block of raw material two years ago and left to self-construct. They'd only had to tweak a few things—bedding and some window seals—when they'd arrived.

"How can you be so far along?" Dawn said, voice a more normal volume now. "You're hardly showing at all."

Abigail glanced at her tummy. She'd noticed the swelling, that was for sure. "Runs in the family. My sister gave birth to a premmie—didn't even know she was pregnant."

Dawn grinned. "Good story. Don't believe it. Who's the father? Bernie?"

"Bernie." Abigail nodded, tight-lipped.

"The guy ditched you before we left? Didn't want to do long-distance or something."

"No loss, really."

Dawn smiled, but her face fell serious. "Morning sickness? That's why you've been throwing up?"

Abigail touched her tummy. "It shouldn't be. Not this late. I'm well into second trimester."

"All right. Let's run you through the robomed and see what it has to say."

"I'm fine. I've been reading everything. I'm just worried that we'll have to cut short." They were supposed to be here for another five months.

Dawn shook her head. "A couple of weeks, maybe. If you start getting contractions, I'll just put you on ice and we'll figure it—hey!" Dawn jerked back as Abigail reached for her.

"Not funny."

"Okay." Dawn stood again and came around to hug her. "Congratulations. So exciting."

Abigail hugged back and nodded.

"But," Dawn said. "You don't ever get to not tell me something like that again. As soon as you know, all right?"

Abigail laughed. "All right."

She liked the warm feeling from inside, and she was glad that Dawn knew now.

Abigail picked up her fork and finished off the duck mornay the cooker had concocted. She did feel like she was eating more, and that was fine.

SILUONE SAT UP on the big rock right in town. She'd been towed in, riding on a buggy festooned with streamers and flowers. Her face was alight with energy.

Katanca whistled at her, joining the others in whoops and cheers. People jostled around, but Ribolee thought this was one of the smallest fifteen-day gatherings she'd been to. There couldn't be more than thirty. Still, Siluone seemed happy.

People brought up bowls of fruit, ceramic and wooden toys, laying them on the shelf around the base of the rock. Siluone's father, Dablorre, spoke for a few minutes about what a wonderful blessing Siluone was bringing to the town. It was a speech Ribolee had heard a dozen times or more before. She imagined her own father would make a similar speech sometime. If she ever met anyone.

Afterwards—just a couple more speeches from uncles and friends—they all decamped to Siluone's house for a banquet. Katanca managed to drag Siluone and Ribolee into a corner for a moment.

Siluone munched on a juicy bretart, the fruit dripping between her fingers. Ribolee thought her eating habits had become much worse since she'd started growing babies.

"So," Katanca said. "Excited?"

Siluone rolled her eyes. "Who wouldn't be? Touch." She grabbed their hands, placing them on her belly.

Ribolee felt tremors though her talons. She felt a charge through her whole body. Siluone's children, all scuttling around inside her.

"You're about ready to burst," Katanca said.

"Will you come?" Siluone said, smiling wider than Ribolee even thought possible.

"Of course we'll come," Ribolee said.

Siluone grabbed them both in face tickles and they joined her. Ribolee smiled.

The next day Abigail found Ribolee at the bridge. The young alien girl stood tall and flickered her talons. She darted nimbly across the twisted roots, feet grabbing like hands. She ran up and touched Abigail's face with the tips of her claws. Abigail didn't flinch, though the instinct was still there. She reached up and tapped Ribolee's face with her fingers. Sometimes Abigail had long nails, but kept them clipped in the field. Too much hassle.

"Show bridge," Ribolee said, dropping her hands. "Come this." She beckoned and walked off along the riverbank.

The stream was still full and running fast. The water was very clear, something Abigail wasn't used to. Back home most every waterway was clouded with sediment. Here, roots from the grull trees—like figs or rubber trees—spread like a mat out over the bank and right into the water.

Along the river, the locals had trained—over years—the roots of many of the trees into bridges. Living bridges. Further downstream a tree had died and collapsed, tearing the bridge with it. People from Ribolee's town had already begun the process of regrowing it.

"Long time," Ribolee said as they walked. "Many many suns."

"To grow the bridge? I realize that."

Ribolee looked at her for a moment then nodded. "Siluone my friend—" Ribolee said a couple of words in her own tongue. "—Soon. Babies. You come?"

Abigail thought she got the gist of it. "I should come to the birth?" She tried the sentence in Ribolee's language, voice catching.

Ribolee made a sound like a canary twittering. Abigail knew this was a laugh.

"Not so good?" Abigail said, again in the local language.

Ribolee laughed again. "Not too bad."

"I'll come."

OLEE LIKED TALKING with Abigail. Every time they spoke they learned more of each other's language. It did seem, though, that Abigail took much longer to pick things up. That was all right. Ribolee could be a translator between the humans and the people.

At the bridge, there were already a few people working. They had a long log stretched out over the river. The log's center had been hollowed out, like an open-ended canoe. Someone walked along the center sprinkling a basket load of soil. Beyond, up on the banks on both sides, others were carefully pulling roots from the ground.

"We help," Ribolee said in human words. Abigail shuddered her head in that odd human gesture of agreement. Ribolee was conscious that she'd started doing it herself.

For the next quarter sun she and Abigail helped with drawing out the roots and getting them into place on the log. It was hot work. The other people chattered about how strange-looking Abigail was, but they were happy to share the work. The soil smelled rich and strong, ready to grow a bridge. Every week someone would come out and refill the soil, keep the roots trained along the log.

When Abigail grew tired, she sat on the bank.

"I thank you," Ribolee said.

"Sure. Wouldn't miss it." Abigail sighed and leaned forward. "It's all study anyway."

Ribolee didn't quite follow the words. She brought Abigail some water in a flask. Abigail thanked her, clipped on a spout and drank through that.

"Filter," Abigail said.

"Show me."

Abigail took another sip and took the 'filter' off. Ribolee inspected it. Some white leafy mesh where the water should have gone through. "Bugs?" she said.

"Bugs," Abigail agreed.

Ribolee drank right from the flask. The water was cool and refreshing. "See. No bugs."

"Bugs we can't see." Abigail rubbed her belly.

Instinctively Ribolee reached out and touched her too, careful to keep her talons back.

"Baby, you?" she said.

Abigail's mouth flared wide, showing all her teeth. "Yes, baby."

Ribolee smiled herself. "Oh festivity!" she said.

"You've got to take better care," Dawn said later, back at the habitat.

They had a tuna dinner on. The synthesizer had a glitch and had made them carrots the size of peas. They were dense and hard and tasteless. Abigail decided she was going to have to take the thing apart and rebuild it. At least the other vegetables were regular-sized and edible.

"I used the filter," Abigail said. "Don't you think it's important to immerse ourselves in the culture? I learned so much today. Community building, social structure. How they build bridges."

Abigail was as aware as anyone of the old axiom that you can't study a culture without altering it. Anthropology was more about personal memoir now than about trying to analyze foreign or alien cultures.

"I just don't want you to get sick."

Abigail held up one of the carrots. "Maybe I'm safer out there."

Dawn laughed. "Anyway, it's good to be invited to that birth."

"Sad," Abigail said. "Siluone will die."

"It's how it is. They don't see it as sad at all. It's a celebration. Hundreds of children."

"Mostly non-sentient, non-viable. Most of them won't survive a year. But Siluone won't get to see the ones that do survive. I imagine how impressed Ribolee's mother would be with how she's turned out."

Dawn stared at her.

"I know, I know. I'm overlaying human concerns. I can't help it."

"Just so long as you're staying objective?" It was as much a question as anything.

Abigail shrugged. "As much as could be expected, I guess."

"Journaling?"

"Constantly."

"Good." Dawn took a mouthful, chewed, then swallowed. "Make sure you get good recordings of the birth."

"You're not going to come?"

"I'm not invited."

Abigail nodded. She stirred her food with the fork.

"Or don't record," Dawn said. "Just bring back your impressions."

"Boffins will want recordings."

"Yes they will." Dawn grinned. They still referred to the scientists who stayed on Earth and did all their research through various recordings as 'boffins.' The kind who couldn't get their hands dirty. Abigail didn't have any time for them, but Dawn kind of envied them. She was growing tired of fieldwork. Especially at her age. Abigail was young and had decades of field work ahead of her if she chose.

"I'll ask Ribolee," Abigail said. "See what she thinks of the idea."

FOUR SUNS LEFT. To Ribolee, Siluone looked as if she might burst at any moment. She lay in her father's house, rocking on a soft bench.

"Touch, touch," Siluone said. "Everyone touch."

There were six of them, all girls. Ribolee was the first to put her hand on Siluone's belly. The squirming underneath sent a shiver through her. Wondrous, wondrous occasion. "You must be so happy," she whispered.

"Speak up."

"What?" one of the other girls said. "Pregnancy make you deaf?"

They burst out laughing, even Siluone.

Her father looked in the doorway, face serious. "Girls," he said.

The laughing stopped.

"Must be hungry," he said. He brought in a tray of slout strips and apinip, and vases of water. He set the tray on the room's center-rock and exited.

Ribolee couldn't pull herself away from the softish feel of Siluone. She even smelled different, sweet and baskety. The other girls went, giggling again.

"I'll miss you," Ribolee said.

Siluone's face rose, her expression baffled. "Miss me?"

"You won't be around to talk with anymore. Abigail—"

"That *human*! You've been spending too much time with her. You could have spent all that time with me."

"I just—"

"Out. Out."

Siluone's father looked into the room again.

"Send Ribolee away," Siluone said.

He flared his lips and eyelids in a kind of regretful assent. "Ribolee."

"All right," she said. "I'm going. I'm sorry." She stood, squeezed past Siluone's father and went out into the town.

Foolish girl, she thought. Siluone was right. Too much time with that human. Somehow that odd concept of humans surviving seemed to get in the way. That thought that her friendship with Abigail would continue after the birth of her child was just too amazing. And Ribolee had let herself believe that was too nice.

Of course one didn't have friendships with someone who had given life.

Now she had to go hide. In shame? She had a cubby at the far end of the island, she could stay there.

Her eyes watered and her lips trembled at the thought. Siluone had sent her away. Now she wouldn't be at the birth.

Foolish girl.

Keeping her shamed-face hidden, she ran through town until the cobbles ended and she came to the root road. She plunged into the forest.

Dawn ran. She had spiderboots on, their flexing legs helping steady her on the rough, root-covered ground. When she came to the bridge, she slowed. She hadn't been to this town before. This was Abigail's.

Of course she was here because of Abigail.

The bridge was an astonishing living thing. It smelled of earth and moss. If she had more time she would have liked to study it more closely. Not her specialty, but interesting nonetheless.

It was made from braids of roots, stretching out from the bank. Some of the roots buttressed up into nearby trees, but others came out of the bank, even from the water. Together they made a tight mass that looked almost like a steel cable. A cable three meters thick.

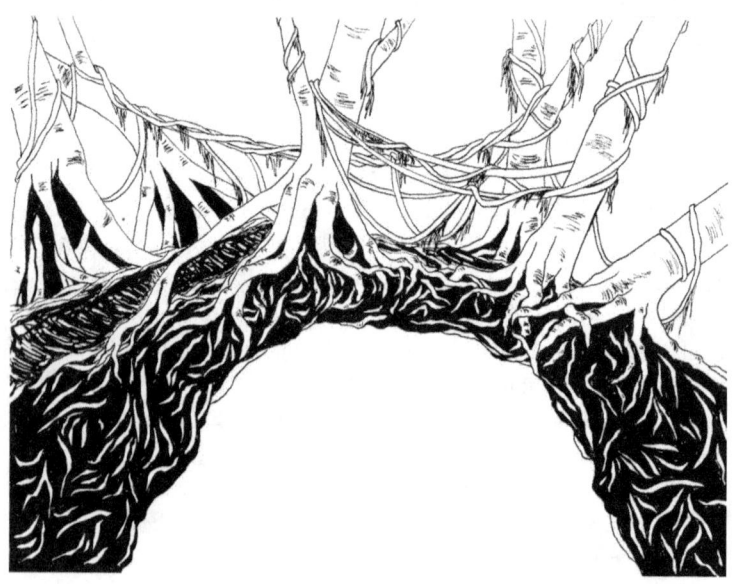

She reminded herself why she was here—Abigail lying bleeding back at the habitat—and moved on.

She stepped onto the bridge. The top was worn almost flat, the root bark shiny and smooth from the passing of thousands of feet. It felt as solid as rock as she walked.

She quickly crossed the hundred meters to the other side. She ran along the path to the town. Something like a gray peccary snuffled along beside her. It darted away after a moment.

The town surprised her. She'd seen Abigail's pictures, but still, it was far more developed than the towns Dawn had been in. There was stone paving along the street, buildings made from the roots of trees, like the bridges, but finer and more controlled, supplemented with boards and stones.

The oelenes stared at her as she came into town. Some of them in doorways, some on the street. Along the way a big pig-like animal the size of a horse towed a wagon with some oelenes riding on board.

"Please," she said, knowing that the dialect she was using was probably different to theirs. "I'm looking for Ribolee."

One of them came up to her. "Aahbeegale," it said, following that with a string of words far too fast for Dawn to catch.

"I'm Dawn," she said. "Abigail wants Ribolee."

A ripple went through them. Murmured conversations. The first one grabbed Dawn's arm carefully and pulled her along. She felt the talons jab her side a couple of times. They came to a building—a house—and the oelene hollered through the doorway.

Another one came out and they spoke rapidly. The one from the house was taller with more mottled skin. Male. He looked at her.

"Siluone, she . . ." words Dawn couldn't understand, then, "Ribolee."

"Slower," Dawn said. "Less speed."

The alien's face shivered. "Ribolee. Gone. Jungle. Siluone. Unhappy."

Dawn nodded. "Abigail is sick. She wants Ribolee."

More conversation between the two.

Someone from inside hollered. The mottled skin oelene turned. His face shivered again and he took her arm, more gently than the other.

"Come," he said.

She followed him inside.

In the second room a female oelene lay on the floor. Her belly was enormous. It shimmered. Dawn felt fascination and a gag at the same time. This woman was about to give birth.

"Siluone," the male said. "One sun more."

"One sun," Dawn said.

"Not Abigail," the female said.

"I'm just looking for Ribolee." Dawn was surprised how much she was picking up.

"I want Ribolee back," the female said.

"Siluone," the male said. "You sent her—"

"Bring her back."

RIBOLEE CAUGHT A slout fish and stripped it to the bone. She made a fire and dried the strips. The cubby had taken some repair—the tree had practically tried to take it over—but it was cozy.

She'd been out at it for three suns when she heard people thrashing through the forest.

DAWN FOLLOWED WHAT amounted to a search party through the jungle. There were at least a dozen of them, though they scampered off into the trees on either side and it was impossible to count. They whooped and called Ribolee's name like banshees.

Dawn didn't know how they were going to find Ribolee in this. The light was hazy, the vines and ferns and other undergrowth made the whole thing seem impenetrable. She'd never thought much about it back at camp, but that had all been just observation, not mounting some kind of search.

The light was fading when one of the oelene ran right at her.

"Dawn?" the oelene said. A young female.

"Have you found Ribolee?" As she asked, Dawn realized that the female hadn't been on the search party. She'd just arrived.

"I am Ribolee," the girl said in English. "You're Abigail's friend. I met you already."

"Yes you did." Dawn smiled. "Abigail wants you. So does Siluone."

"Both?" Ribolee grabbed Dawn's arm and rushed off through the trees.

RIBOLEE LOOKED AT Siluone. Her belly crinkled. Almost ready to release.

"You came back," Siluone said.

Ribolee knelt to her, took her hand. Their talons meshed. Siluone smelled extraordinary, like hummingbeetles and kens flowers. So close now. "I'm sorry I upset you. I wasn't thinking right."

Siluone's talons tickled hers. "I understand. I love you. You're my friend."

"Joyous day." Ribolee said. She still had that slight haunting feeling that she was going to miss Siluone.

"Next sun," Siluone said. "But your other friend, the human, she's sick. She needs you too."

"Dawn told me. But I want to be here."

More, deeper tickling. Ribolee tickled back.

"I have another sun. You should go see her, come back at the rise. Their town is not far, I think."

Strange town, Ribolee thought. Just one house. Shiny in the sun, cold to the touch. Not a town. She glanced back at the doorway. Siluone's father and the human, Dawn, stood there.

"Go," Siluone said.

Ribolee gave a tickle and stood releasing. "You hold them in if I'm not back."

Siluone laughed.

ABIGAIL LAY IN the cot, concentrating on breathing evenly. The IV drip needed changing. She'd expected Dawn back by now.

The habitat felt oppressive and hot, like some old campervan parked in southern Florida.

She'd holidayed there with her family when she'd been a kid. They'd kayaked in the Gulf of Mexico, taken tour boats to see manatees, spent three days at the vast Magnificent Disney Rainbow Experience at Disneyworld. She was so-so about the theme park, but she'd loved every minute of everglades and swamp. The heat, the wildlife, the history.

Her brother had hated all that. He'd become a lawyer, laughed at her when she'd gone into anthropology. She'd never been as impolite to laugh at him, but she couldn't imagine ever getting excited by litigation.

Peoples of the world. That was interesting.

Peoples of the galaxy. That was utterly entrancing.

Haemae was perfect.

The IV AI pinged and she sat up. The bag was practically empty.

She knew she was going to lose the baby.

With a sigh she got up and changed the bag. As soon as she stood she felt nauseous again.

She only just made it to the bowl. By now she was only bringing up bile. Her mouth full of the acidic goo.

She rinsed.

Technically someone should be watching her. Someone should be changing the bag, letting her rest. But Abigail had sent Dawn away.

At that moment it had seemed important, but now, she wondered. She must have been delirious.

How could it be she felt so close to the young woman? They barely spoke each other's language. Aside from their basic biped skeleton, they didn't even look alike.

Wasn't that anthropology, though?

The fresh IV bag was warm to the touch and she clipped it in. The AI pinged that it was guiding the solution.

With a sigh she lay back on the cot. Something wet between her legs.

She looked down and saw bright blood.

Ribolee ran and ran. The old human woman, Dawn, could barely keep up with her.

"Why does she want me? I'm no doctor," Ribolee said.

"Are you friend?" Dawn said. The word order was odd and her accent on them strange. Kind of like she was trying to spit out her words.

"I'm her friend," Ribolee agreed.

She crossed the Leut bridge. One of the oldest and biggest. Ribolee's favorite.

The bridge had its own gardens. More than two hundred thousand suns old, it was wider than most bridges. Enough soil had accumulated in between the roots that there were whole patches of kens flowers, and bekem and oseeria. The golds and ambers and scattered blues made it seem as if it was ready to take flight like some giant jungle parrot.

It was Abigail's favorite too.

Dawn was exhausted when they came to the habitat's clearing. The girl had dragged her faster than she could run. The spiderboots had helped, propelling her on. She stopped at the stairway to catch her breath.

"Hurt?" the girl said, her mouth twisting around.

"Puffed," Dawn said. "Out of breath." She had no idea what the Oelene words for that might be.

It started raining, big cooling drops splattered off the hab's side. The sound was like a tin drum.

Dawn went up the steps and pushed the door open. "Come on," she said. Ribolee followed.

The habitat smelled of vomit. Dawn felt it right away. "Abigail?" she said. No response.

She was in the sick bay, on the upper level. "This way," Dawn said, hurrying up the internal steps. She almost tripped. The spiderboots were designed for rough ground, not for indoors. "Floors," she told them. They responded, pulling their legs up.

She was going to have to get that looked at. Glitchy equipment.

Later.

The sick bay stank even more. Right away she saw the blood on Abigail. And on the cot, and the floor.

"Glad you came," Abigail whispered.

"I wanted you to come to see Siluone's flowering," Ribolee said.

Abigail grimaced.

Dawn crouched to her. Abigail's face was pale. She was sweating, her forehead beaded.

"The baby?" Abigail said.

Dawn nodded. She glanced at Abigail's crotch. So much blood. It couldn't be anything else.

"She's very sick?" Ribolee said.

"Very sick." Dawn squeezed Abigail's hand and went to the locker, pulling out more IVs, bandages, probes. She banged the door shut.

She saw Ribolee jump.

"Sorry," Dawn said. She didn't know what to do. She was trained in first aid. Cuts and sprains and bruises. Resuscitation. Miscarriage was not something she'd dealt with.

"Screen," Abigail said. "Look it up. There's the ultrasound we looked for it with, remember?"

"I remember." Dawn kept facing the closed locker.

"What's wrong?" Ribolee said. Did she mean with Dawn, or with Abigail?

"Dawn," Abigail said. "You need to at least try."

So much blood.

"I can help?" Ribolee said.

Dawn turned and saw the girl sitting, her legs looking weird curled up in wrong directions. She had her clawed hand on Abigail's, tapping with her clawtips.

Abigail smiled. Her eyelids fluttered.

Dawn opened the next locker. She got out the ultrasound machine. She wound the screen up from the central axis and switched it on. The machine buzzed for a moment before settling to a low audible hum.

Working quickly now, with a purpose, Dawn got the little reader. It had a foot like the spiderboots, with stubby legs.

Dawn turned to Abigail and could tell it was bad. She pulled Abigail's shirt up quickly and set the ultrasound on her belly. The little robot crept around, exuding gel, keeping its foot in contact with her skin.

"It's gone," Abigail whispered.

Dawn swallowed and pulled around the readout. The ultrasound would do far more than just locate the baby. It would check Abigail's temperature, respiration, blood flow, and a half dozen other measures.

Red checks appeared on the display.

"What?" Abigail said.

Dawn held her breath a moment. "I'm so sorry."

Abigail gave a curt nod. She sniffed. Her face became a blank mask.

The machine gave instructions to give plasma. Abigail's blood pressure had fallen. Her heart rate dropped below forty.

"Sick bad?" Ribolee said.

Dawn busied herself retrieving items, following the diagnostic machine's instructions. The cabinets were well stocked, but this kind of emergency was going to deplete them. Dawn didn't know what she'd do if Abigail worsened. Send for off-world help?

"Abigail?" Ribolee said. "What?"

"My baby died. I might die."

Ribolee's body trembled. "Die? No. Joyous occasion. Your babies."

"You're not going to die," Dawn said.

"What does it matter?" Abigail said.

Ribolee stood, backing away. "No, no," she said. She followed with a long string of her language Dawn couldn't understand.

"Ribolee," Abigail said. "Sometimes this is just the way." Abigail was crying now, gasping.

"Take it easy," Dawn said.

"No," Ribolee bawled. She ran from the room. Dawn heard her running down the stairs and the sound of her struggling with the door.

"Ribolee," Dawn called. She kept working on getting things for Abigail.

From below came the sound of door clanging. The jungle sounds bled inside.

"She's gone," Abigail said.

RIBOLEE RAN. ABIGAIL was a liar! She'd said she would survive. Humans lied.

Ribolee ran for the nearest bridge, wailing. Abigail's baby had died, but babies died anyway, didn't they?

Dozens of Siluone's babies would be dead before her belly even opened. It was too much for the weak ones. This was how the oelene race was strong. Many would die within suns anyway.

It was life.

And Abigail had told her she would have just one baby. It had taken so long to accept that. One baby!

Abigail had shown her *pictures* on a magic leaf. Human women with babies. Their own babies. Some with babies and children. All their own.

Too startling.

Now Abigail said she was going to die anyway. Ribolee had never felt so betrayed. Her emotions coiled up like a twisted root in her belly.

She came to the Levaerre bridge. Big and old. Some of the roots had been trained higher along the side, making a kind of fence along the side. *Handrail,* Abigail had called it.

It smelled of earth and grass and guano. A bright fluffy berear stood on its hind legs staring at her. As she approached it ran off across the bridge, fur rippling like soft water.

Ribolee stopped in the middle and leaned against the *handrail.* Below the river churned. The water was white, filled with bubbles. Even with the water low like this it was still fast and busy. People had fallen in and been swept to their deaths.

Ribolee didn't know what to believe.

Under her feet lay her ancestors, but around her were the living.

Maybe Abigail wouldn't die. If her one and only baby had died, maybe that meant she would actually survive. Maybe.

Ribolee ran home and found Siluone's house surrounded by people. Was she too late?

They let her pass. "Siluone's friend," people said. "Let her by."

Siluone's belly was white and thin. The creases looked ready to give way. Inside all her glorious babies scratched. Dablorre, her father, sat across from her, face calm. He blinked, acknowledging Ribolee. She blinked back. Beyond, in the corner, she saw Poropeep, the father of Siluone's children.

"Ribolee." Siluone's voice was thin, reedy. "You made it."

"I'm here." She bent and tickled Siluone's face. Siluone tickled back. "Great joyous love."

"Great joyous love for you my friend. I wish you many babies." Siluone shuddered.

Ribolee took her hand. She felt Siluone's talons pierce her forearms. Ribolee didn't let go. What was that little pain in the fabulous, wondrous moment?

She choked a moment. She really was going to miss Siluone.

They were right. She'd spent too much time around those two humans. Siluone screamed.

With a sound like a tree toppling, her belly gave way. The room flooded with the celestial magic of her babies.

Siluone's hand went slack.

People rushed in—Poropeep first—gathering up the tiny, tiny extraordinary issue. So many. They were the size of Ribolee's nose, and gummy, glistening with the last of Siluone's living fluids. Some of them lay curled and dark, but most of them were moving.

She could see the strong ones, the ones who would last more than a few suns.

As the men worked, helping the infants, Ribolee looked at Siluone's face.

Before she knew it, Ribolee found her jaw trembling, her ears shaking. Her breath came fast.

"Ribolee?" Dablorre said. "Why are you sad? This is joyous joyous." He put his hand on his daughter's face.

"Joyous, joyous," Ribolee said. "But I miss her."

Dablorre's face changed, mouth widening. He didn't understand.

No one would.

Ribolee bent and tickled Siluone's face.

Dablorre gasped. No one greeted the dead.

"I miss you Siluone," she whispered into her ear.

"Ribolee!" Dablorre yelled. He grabbed her hands.

Ribolee tore from his grasp, leapt up, and ran from the house. She didn't stop on the bridge this time. She just kept running.

DAWN SET THE diagnostics aside and sat back on the stool. The machine had gone silent. She'd done everything she could. Now she was alone here. Part of her wanted to pull a sheet up over Abigail's face, but her colleague looked so serene, so peaceful. Almost like she was simply asleep. Pale, but asleep.

The whole habitat felt quiet and empty.

Dawn went and washed up. She felt numb. She ran the shower on cold, trying to feel at least something.

It didn't work.

She dressed, made coffee, and went outside to think. She sat in the old rough canvas deckchair under the umbrella and watched the jungle.

There were things to do. She would have to contact home. The body had to be put on ice.

It was going to be weird and creepy waiting for relief to arrive with Abigail's body in the garage.

Dawn took a breath.

Out at the edge of the clearing she saw an oelene standing, watching the habitat. Ribolee?

Dawn took a sip of her coffee and stood to walk over, but the oelene ran off.

RIBOLEE SAW DAWN watching her and darted back into the jungle.

The ground felt warm underfoot. Ribolee ran, and for a moment she thought it was just blindly, but she found herself running around the clearing where the humans lived.

She felt torn.

She'd offended Dablorre, offended Siluone's memory. So many wonderful babies.

Why did she feel like this? Why did she miss Siluone?

Ahead she saw a group of scootsnails, some adults, some babies. An older adult was the size of her clenched fist, its shell dark and peeling. Some of the babies were so tiny they were almost invisible.

A skaneet leapt down into the group. Its long bill clacked. It looked at Ribolee, tilted its head left and right and plucked up one of the adults. The skaneet opened its broad white feathery wings and lofted back into the trees. Ribolee heard the crunch of the bill crushing the scootsnail's shell. The other snails continued slithering along.

Ribolee turned and walked into the clearing.

BY THE TIME the girl came, Dawn had already sent a messagepacket. The institute would send a pickup soon. She would be going home.

Ribolee called through the open door, and Dawn went down to see her.

"I didn't think you'd come," Dawn said, and tried to repeat the phrase in Oelene.

"Abigail?" Ribolee said.

Dawn choked for a moment. Ribolee was the oelene Abigail had made closest contact with. Young, but enthusiastic and engaged.

The girl made a birdlike squawk. Her expression was hard to read, even after all this time, but Dawn thought the fluttering eyelids and extended lips suggested dismay. Perhaps confusion.

"Abigail—" What? Passed? Moved on?

Ribolee nodded. Oddly human. "She has . . . die?"

"Yes," Dawn said in Oelene. Unambiguous.

"I see her?"

"Come up," Dawn said, extending her hands.

Ribolee took both, her talons pulled back, and Dawn led her up.

LATER, WALKING BACK through the jungle, Ribolee knew what she had to do.

She didn't know if anyone would approve, but she had to ask. They would already be preparing for Siluone's burial.

The trees and animals sang to her as she walked. The cool wind through the branches ruffled the leaves and moss and epiphytes.

At Siluone's house, they already had her body wrapped. Katanca and Poropeep and Dablorre and some others lifted her up onto a wagon.

Dablorre met Ribolee's eyes. She spread her arms in apology and walked to him. His hands became serious and still, but she kept walking. It felt like she was wading through mud.

"Dablorre," she said when her face was practically against his chest. "I make my apologies."

He watched her warily for a moment. Ribolee's whole body felt limp, tired, but she kept her arms wide. Others watched.

Dablorre reached up and touched her face with his talons. Not quite tickling, but near enough. She knew she was forgiven.

"I have something to ask," she said.

DAWN HELPED RIBOLEE prepare Abigail. Some other oelenes had come into the habitat, bringing with them a different kind of jungle scent. Sweet and feminine. They were all girls Ribolee's age.

She had brought some kind of green-white bandages and they set about wrapping Abigail's body. They talked in hushed whispers as they worked. Dawn felt like she should have the habitat record it all, but it would be invasive. She could explain why not later to the institute, when it was too late.

Soon they had Abigail swaddled and they took her to the waiting wagon. Dawn didn't know how they'd managed to drag the wagon all this way. They were fine around town and in the fields, but out through the rough jungle paths would have been near impossible.

Dawn helped them tow it to the river. It took more than two hours.

More oelene were waiting on the big bridge. More than Dawn had ever seen in one place except in town.

The small group parked the wagon. They lifted Abigail's wrapped body and carried her up across the stretched and tangled roots.

Near the middle, they stopped. Someone had pulled roots aside and scooped out soil. Dawn had never realized there was so much earth actually within the bridges. Further along she saw a recently disturbed spot, the roots pulled back across damp soil.

They pushed Abigail deep into the gap. They scooped the soil and tossed it over her. All the time they whispered, but Ribolee was the loudest.

In moments, Abigail's body was covered.

One of the older males came forward and pulled the roots into place. He patted and tucked. Standing upright, he walked over the spot and turned back for the town. All the others walked over too, compressing the grave. Soon they'd all gone except for Ribolee and Dawn.

"You should walk over too," Ribolee said.

Dawn nodded and stood. The roots felt weird underfoot, shifting over the disturbed soil. As she stepped she realized that Ribolee had been speaking in Oelene. She walked past the end, stopped, and leant on the rough root railing. She felt like crying, but knew it wouldn't come just yet.

She watched as Ribolee walked with cautious steps. The girl stopped right in front of Dawn.

"Do you miss her?" Ribolee said.

Dawn nodded. "Very much." She gasped and the tears came. She felt herself shaking. Her hand came up over her mouth.

Ribolee reached up with her hands, talons extended. Dawn almost flinched, but let Ribolee tickle her face with the tips. Just as she'd seen her do with Abigail.

Through her tears Dawn felt a sudden closeness. With Abigail's death there was a connection.

Dawn reached and used her own stubby cracked nails to tickle Ribolee's face.

The girl's mouth changed, lips pulling back. Dawn recognized the smile and smiled herself.

"Thank you," Dawn said. "Thank you."

ABOUT THE AUTHOR

SEAN MONAGHAN studied at the University of Queensland and now makes his home in New Zealand, where he works in a busy public library. Sean's stories litter the internet and the pages of magazines, from *Takahe* and *Landfall* to *Asimov's* and *Amazing Stories*.

Sean's preferred mode of transport is aircraft, particularly any departing for distant, warmer locales (a long way of saying he loves to travel). A three-time *Writers of the Future* contest Semi-finalist and one-time Finalist, Sean is no longer eligible for the *Writers of the Future* contest, having pro'ed out by gaining professional status through sales to *Asimov's Science Fiction* and other professional markets. He has also been a Finalist for the Aurealis Award and the Sir Julius Vogel Award, and the 2014 Grand Prize winner for the Jim Baen Memorial Short Story contest for his story "Low Arc." His website is: https://seanmonaghan.com/

ABOUT THE STORY

"The Root Bridges of Haemae" began with the title. I saw a brief film clip of children in, I believe, India, running across a stream atop a remarkable looking bridge that looked like a cluster of branches. A little further research revealed the practice of encouraging the roots of certain trees to stretch out and twist together to create living bridges.

Located in Meghalaya, a state in the Northeast of India, the bridges can reach over fifty meters in length. The practice of creating the bridges, which can take fifteen years, has been around for generations.

A brief article on root bridges is available on Wikipedia.

I loved the idea. I wondered what alien species might do with the practice. What kind of spiritual significance might they have? What might human researchers make of these beliefs? With the opportunity to explore an alien biosphere, I also had the chance to explore how these differences might impact their culture.

As the story grew, so too did the layers; the different biologies and the different cultural mores impacting the character interactions.

I do wish I'd spent a bit more time considering the characters' dialogue. Sometimes Ribolee and the others sound too human. At least that's something I'll consider much more the next time I write an alien culture story.

"The Root Bridges of Haemae" was a Semi-finalist in the *Writers of the Future* contest, and found its first home in the Australian Science Fiction Magazine *Aurealis*. I had fun with the story and the characters. I hope you enjoyed reading.

He could remake colonists to enhance their adaptation to new worlds
—whether they wished it or not.
The survival of the colony was of the utmost importance, after all.

....

RED IS THE
COLOR OF MY TRUE
LOVE'S HAIR

WILLIAM R. D. WOOD

Black is the color of my true love's hair,
Her lips are like some roses fair,
She has the sweetest smile and the gentlest hands,
I love the ground whereon she stands.
—Scottish ballad

ochlan held his breath as the woman paused at the doorway.
No, not a woman. Not anymore.

She didn't turn and look his way, but she did stand as if listening. From his position deep in the storage room, he'd heard her coming in plenty of time to move farther into the shadows and watch her slink into view. The cavernous room, a repurposed cargo module from the colony ship, had no windows and grew pitch black a few short meters through the door. The corridor outside, however, had been converted to ground use and was lined with windows. The red-tinted light from Nuku, the dwarf star at the heart of this backwater system, framed the woman perfectly.

Why didn't she just move on? The lump forming in his throat threatened to choke him if he didn't swallow soon; if he didn't breathe.

He had to get to the landing field. His lander was there, and the colony shuttles, assuming no one had taken them already. Or these *things* hadn't disabled them. Of course, the adapted seemed incapable of such planning, clearly having suffered some mental degradation as part of their transformation. Lochlan had not foreseen that side effect. Perhaps it was because the changes had been so rapid. So unexpectedly rapid. At least there had been no children among the colonists.

Go, damn it.

The changes in her silhouette were monstrous. Her hair was a ragged mass, interspersed with thick metallic fibers jutting quill-like from the back of her head and down her spine. When they caught the light, they glistened. An oozing slash ran from above her ear to the middle of her neck. Shoulders hunched forward, arms dragging along the floor, she scraped the tips of her elongated fingers in circles against the metal deck plates. And just stood there.

COULD SHE SMELL him?

Whether it was the sight of her, or the horrible direction the last twenty-two hours had taken, he wasn't sure, but he felt sick to his stomach. Did Bethanne look like that now too? His angel. Her large beautiful eyes now transformed into something hideous? Or was her fate far, far worse?

His mind snapped for an instant to the holo in the breast pocket of his jacket. At least he'd been able to grab that from his lab before fleeing the science facility last night.

The woman in the doorway shifted back and forth. She raised her nose and sniffed at the air.

Shit.

She could smell him. Lochlan tightened his grip on his pistol, hoping she couldn't hear *that*. If she sensed him in *any* way he'd have only a split second to fire; and there was no guarantee, even if he hit her in the head, that a single shot would take her down. Or any of the colonists for that matter.

A shiver passed down the woman from head to toe, brushing the spikier hairs of her mane against one another with a sound like rustling leaves.

Hunching down, she moved out of the doorway and along the corridor.

Lochlan waited long minutes before he was comfortable enough to force his gun hand to relax, his knuckles popping softly in protest. His heartbeat throbbed in his ears as his subconscious apparently accepted that the immediate danger had passed, bumping other sensory inputs up in priority.

A million years of fight-or-flight reflexes be damned, he thought, half expecting the woman to come charging back into the room.

But she didn't.

How many people were left? He had no way of knowing and no easy way to find out. The colonists' medical implants were only detectable at close range thanks to Nuku's influence. Now all that were left were the adapted, their victims, and him. A cold, insensitive thought, maybe. But that didn't make it false.

What had gone wrong?

Nothing. Nothing had gone wrong.

In fact, everything had gone far too right. Unpredictably, if horribly, so. If he and Bethanne were sitting in orbit where they should be, looking down on this mess right now, he'd be proud of his latest batch of pryonelles. Instead, absorbed in his work, the pryonelles had been active for hours before he'd realized Bethanne had fled to the surface.

The nanoscopic little bastards had really outdone themselves too. At least these colonists would survive. Not much of an addition to the community of worlds, but they were viable.

When he'd come to their quarters to celebrate, he'd seen the data displays she'd been viewing. A quick search of the ship had found a lander missing, along with Bethanne.

He'd panicked, trying to raise her on the radio to no avail, then charging after her in the only other lander.

Faint scratches came from his left and Lochlan spun, half-pulling the trigger. The red targeting dot from his pistol danced across the porous non-skid surface of the floor, settling on a small shadow huddled against a crate. A tiny pair of black eyes regarded him from a cat-like head, its spiny hackles raised. The colonists had taken to calling them rippers because of the way they fed.

At least it was alone. With a shudder not unlike the transformed woman, the thing scurried off into the darkness.

Vermin.

Same biological niche as rats on many of the colony worlds. Hell, the planners had even sent rats to this one, but the rippers had made bloody short work of them. No one had seen a rat in months. What could he say? It was a tough world. Tougher than the planners had expected. Tougher even than he, as colony setup executive, had expected. Still, success was marked by one's ability to improvise and take a few chances.

Moving from the shadows into the red swath of light spilling through the doorway, Lochlan took a deep breath, checked the charge on the pistol and leaned out. A quick glance left, then right, and he ducked back in. The corridor was clear both ways. A bulkhead was blown away a dozen meters to the right, jagged metal strips bent outward. The thick honeysuckle smell of the forest outside crept in on the breeze.

An open door to the outside lay another dozen meters farther on, but Lochlan stepped quickly through the tear in the wall out onto the hard dirt. The compound was flat, cleared of brush and debris since shortly after they'd landed. Hydroponics bays rose across the wide dirt road, plastic and glass Quonset huts intended to make them self-sufficient within a year. Beyond them were other buildings, including a dorm, a manufacturing module, and several private dwellings they'd brought as prefabs.

The door of the closest, the one he and Bethanne had shared when planetside, hung from a single hinge. He fought the urge to dash across and scour the place, but couldn't bear the thought of what he might find.

The rest of the makeshift buildings cluttering the scene were made from local resources giving the place the feel of a ghost town.

Crouching in the shadow of the largest piece of twisted metal, Lochlan got his bearings. The road ran left and right, passing through the open gate of the five-meter high razor-chain fence surrounding the colony. The forest trees were in perpetual shadow with Nuku in its tidally locked position thirty-five degrees up from the horizon. A single star twinkled in the permanent daylight: the drive-and-support section of the *West Carolina*, the ship that had brought them here. Once he got back there, he'd be safe.

Alone again, but safe.

Oh, Bethanne, why didn't you let me explain? Sure, it might have taken the return trip to fully convince her; but in the end, their love would have been enough. They would have been amazing together. And he was even going to take some time off. Devote a few years to her dreams, to *their* dreams. He'd promised before, sure, but this time he'd meant it. Put down roots of their own. Start a family.

One thing at a time. One second. One minute.

The road, recently hard-fused, led directly to the landing field three kilometers away over the low western hills. He'd been the one to decide on the field's location too.

The only ground vehicles were back at the lab or in the direction of the common areas, and he was not about to head back into the compound. Several minutes passed as he grew comfortable with the idea that the adapted colonists were not lying in ambush. He gave the pocket holding the holo a pat. A memory of the two of them. All he had left.

I'm so sorry, angel.

A scream pierced the air, sending coveys of flyers from their perches in the trees beyond the fence. The glass door of the closest hydroponics hut slammed outward and a man in bloody lab-whites burst through. He spotted Lochlan and raised a free hand in his direction, his other hand clutched to his throat. Blood gushed between his fingers. It was Meyerson, the colony MD.

Two forms bounded toward the door from inside the hut.

Lochlan took a step into the shade cast by the torn metal, heart pounding, sweat running into his eyes, stinging. He was scared to blink.

Meyerson's eyes went wide. The first of the adapted erupted from the door and landed on his back, crushing him to the ground. A gurgle that might have been a scream echoed between the buildings. Elongated fingers clamped around Meyerson's skull and the thing lifted him from the ground. It shivered head to toe and Lochlan closed his eyes an instant too late.

Bile surged into his mouth, and he barely restrained the urge to bolt back into the module or toward the open gate. They'd be sure to spot him if he did, and one little pistol would not stand between him and a fate like Meyerson's.

Had Bethanne—he fought the thought away.

The second adapted trotted over to the first, taking the dead man by the feet and pulling him taut in the air between them.

Just hurry up and go away. Just hurry up and go away.

A breeze picked up dust from the ground, bringing the sweet smell of the trees, but tinged with wet copper. Lochlan hoped the change in the wind didn't carry his scent to them.

The sounds stopped abruptly.

No.

Again, he fought the insistence of his primal brain to bolt for any place other than this one. His pulse pounded in his temples. Evolution was a cruel bitch, one even he couldn't seem to engineer around.

That was insensitive. The thought came in Bethanne's voice. She was right. His finesse in the lab had been at the expense of social graces, even empathy. But she'd loved him and tried to help him evolve.

That had been one of her favorite expressions.

The adapted stood perfectly still, heads raised slightly and cocked to one side. Not sniffing the air the way he expected. More like they were listening.

Then he heard it, too. A soft whine coming from the air. A crack of static from the loudspeaker above his head startled him.

"Attention," boomed the loudspeaker. *"Attention, on the ground."*

The adapted looked at the loudspeaker above Lochlan's head and then at another on the Quonset hut behind them. The voice reverberated around the compound, drawing their gaze to dozens of speakers. They dropped Meyerson's remains, their hisses joining with more distant ones.

At least Meyerson would not be coming back as one of those things—there wasn't enough of him. Lochlan swallowed but otherwise kept still. But who the hell was trying to get *him* killed?

"This is JWTF Worldrunner in low orbit above your position. We have received no response to our hails. A disaster control team is standing by to assist. Somebody down there needs to get on the horn and respond."

Hissing at the loudspeaker closest to them, the adapted leapt to the top of the hut and swatted the speaker from its mounts then ran apelike along the roof toward the distant residential buildings.

Lochlan sighed. The *West Carolina* was dipping toward the horizon as its orbit carried it around the planet; but a second even brighter star had taken up position directly overhead. A Joint Worlds unit. He'd not even known a military ship was in the area. Someone must have called for help when the proverbial shit hit the ventilators.

He needed a radio. Gritting his teeth, he glanced along the length of the cargo module toward the lab. None of the adapted were in sight. The ground vehicles at the lab had radios. He'd dropped his personal uplink during his escape. It had skidded under a gene-coder and he'd been too frightened to stop and retrieve it.

"A shuttle is being dispatched. It will fly over your position in one hour to assess

your situation. Be advised, no landing will be made until we can ascertain the cause of your radio silence."

If only the holo had slid under the processor instead of the uplink—he felt a pang of guilt at the thought and checked his pocket to make sure the holo was still there.

Damn, she had been amazing. An engineering prodigy. She was socially brilliant in her way as well, a real people person; but it had been those large eyes that had drawn him in. He'd expected to be done with her in a few weeks, but he'd fallen just the same.

If she'd only waited a few more hours until the pryonelles resorbed. If only she'd not found his research; the records of the previous colonies.

If only she'd let him explain.

He squeezed his pocket, the holo crinkling inside.

If he risked a ground vehicle, he'd have a radio, but their engines were far from silent. And what if the adapted were faster? He needed to move. Taking one last look toward the hydroponics bays and the prefabs, Lochlan ran for the gate.

I love my love and well she knows,
I love the ground whereon she goes.
And I wish the day, it soon will come,
That she and I will be as one.

HE WAS THROUGH the gate a hundred meters or more before he looked back. Still clear. It took another few hundred meters for him to reach a good pace, stretches of dirt, rock, and gnarled scrub passing along both sides, all under Nuku's glare.

He was in *decent* physical shape. Leader or not, you didn't wind up in charge of start-ups by being thick in the middle. You had to be physically capable, but mentally prodigious; and, while he was no shining example of the former, Bethanne had once called him the *exemplum incarnatum* of the latter.

They would have been spectacular together. They should have been.

Damn you. Why did you have to love me?

He spat to one side, the sound of his own footfalls deafening. Every rustle of his clothes and each beat of his heart was going to alert the adapted colonists to his presence.

He moved off the road to a quieter traverse in the cloveresque ground cover, careful not to stray more than a meter from the fused road surface. Bulrush-like stalks stretched from his right to a distant tree line in the north. The stalks leaned toward him, tracking his movement, the five-petaled flowers on their tips snapping hungrily. This was a tough world. Extreme measures had been needed, and he had been the one to take them.

Besides, he had done it before. Nine times.

Three times on worlds where he'd acted as lead geneticist. Six as colony exec. And now, this one. Luckily, the New Worlds Initiative had written a great deal of latitude for terraforming charters. Common knowledge dictated that no planet—no matter how earth-like it appeared from orbit or through a bevy of probes and remote instrumentation—was actually Earth and truly suited for human life. Hell, *Earth* was hardly fit for human habitation anymore or they wouldn't be out here.

The bureaucrats back home were soft around the middle and between the ears. He had a stellar track record, and they'd sign off on any plan he pitched. Who wouldn't want a ride on his coat tails?

Life had been good and had been poised to be legendary.

Bethanne had swept into their quarters the night before, happier than he'd ever seen her, glowing to the point of bioluminescence. When he'd told her so, she'd been on him instantly. Later, before she drifted off, she'd said, *I love you.* Only the latest of a thousand times for her.

But the first time he'd said it too.

A screech from above snapped him from his reverie. Two flyers the size of crows swept down on him, whipping their barbed tails as they passed. He ducked and swatted at them.

More pests.

Lochlan took rough aim at one of the things and fired a single charge from his pistol. The creature dodged easily, but the static pop carried in the air. He immediately regretted his rashness.

The crest of the hill was wide and clear. Colonists had enjoyed coming up here in groups to relax and celebrate their small successes. Discarded supply crates sat along the edge from a recent get-together he'd begged out of. Too much work, as always. Bethanne told him later, it had been a hoot.

A hoot. Who talked like that?

Wispy white clouds clutched at distant mountain peaks beyond the glistening confluence of three freshwater rivers. On this side of the rivers, and below him, the hardened square of the landing field shimmered in the afternoon's heat. The coordinator's hut at its far corner was partly hidden in the haze as was an inflatable hanger wherein the colony's largest shuttles were stored. Two smaller models, the one Bethanne had taken and the one he'd followed her in hours later, rested twenty meters apart, centered in the field. Bethanne's sat off-kilter, scratches and scrapes marring the hi-temp paint where the cowling of a lifting thruster had been pulled away.

Just beyond, his own shuttle gleamed in the sunlight, untouched.

Finally. Something was going right.

A new message from *Worldrunner* warbled in the distance, but he couldn't make out the words over his own breathing. Sweat ran down his back and his calves ached, but he wasn't about to slow down until this mess was two hundred kilometers beneath the soles of his boots.

Lochlan glanced back at the compound. Several figures scurried around near the gate. The red sunlight and lack of better contrast made it hard to be sure. It didn't matter anyway. He'd be long gone before any of the adapted could get to him.

To his right he glimpsed a couple of rippers weaving in and out of the ground cover, keeping stride with him. He saw no other movement in the brush at least. One was a pest. Two, manageable. More, and they adopted a pack mentality. He really didn't need that right now. They were fast. Mean bastards too, and more perfectly adapted for this world than any of the other indigenous forms he'd studied. It was their material he'd used when encoding the pryonelles.

In retrospect, not the best move. If he'd used the flyers instead, he and Bethanne might be looking down from orbit, performing final checks for a long romantic ride home.

Right now, survival was the priority. She would want that for him.

Striding across the flat of the landing field, he felt his face stretching into an involuntary smile. He didn't deserve to wear that expression again.

Pain tore down the side of his right thigh. He screamed, tumbling to the stony surface of the landing field. Tiny claws sliced through his trousers into his leg, grasping at the wound. He rolled, arms and legs thrashing. The ripper lost its grip and struck the ground a few meters away, but more joined it as it righted itself, six in all, hackles raised in tiny manes of razor-like quills.

They circled him. Every few seconds, one would stop and shake like a wet dog. Never more than one, but timed such that the rustle of their quills always filled the air. They were between him and the shuttles.

He aimed at the closest and fired. The bolt caught it mid-leap, spinning the ripper in the air, fur sizzling. Two more sprung before the first struck the ground. His second shot clipped the head from one; but the other flipped in the air and slammed into his shoulder, quills extended.

Lochlan staggered back, grasping at the beast. His shoulder was on fire where a quill had pierced his jacket and sunk into flesh. Another quill caught in the palm of his free hand, but he grasped the vermin by the scruff of the neck. It reeked, sickly sweet and rancid. Quills tugging at his shoulder, he tore it from his body and flung it away. His scream caught in his throat. The ripper righted itself in a single hop back onto its short spindly legs. The remaining three joined it and began to circle him. The little bastards were smart.

To get to the shuttle, he'd have to run between two of them. Enough was enough. He thumbed the pistol setting to maximum. It chirped to let him know it already was.

Rustling came from behind him.

He fired at the ripper on the right, missing it completely but making it jump aside.

He ran, pushing through the pain in his leg, twisting and firing at the rippers. They gave chase. Lightning cracked the air with every pull of the trigger. A lucky shot took off the back half of one. A second, luckier, shot left nothing but a smear on the tarmac. The pistol buzzed, empty. He threw it at the closest creature causing it to veer away. Two left.

Injured, he simply could not keep his pace. A ripper raced around him, stopping between him and the shuttles and bristling up.

Limping to a stop, Lochlan swore. Bethanne's shuttle was meters away but potentially damaged. His own was twenty meters farther.

The ripper in front of him bounded toward him and leapt. Lochlan spun, letting the creature latch onto his jacket. He pulled an arm out, folding it around the ripper. It struggled, barely contained. He pulled the garment completely free and slammed it to the tarmac. One boot planted on the jacket, he brought the other down again and again until he heard a satisfying crunch.

Heaving for breath, he snatched the jacket up and turned.

Tiny black eyes regarded him, quills flat. The ripper sniffed the air and scurried away.

"*Damn right,*" shouted Lochlan. Survival of the fittest, you little bastard.

Distant motion caught his eye. At the top of the rise, three figures came into view. They were man-sized but their proportions were wrong. Wrong in a way he was too familiar with.

Lochlan half-limped, half-ran that last few meters to his shuttle.

Almost, almost, almost.

The metal of the boarding gantry clanged as he climbed, one hand slamming into the hull of the shuttle for balance as he operated the hatch release with the other. The door popped inward a centimeter and rolled into the deck. Lights flickered on inside, and he heard the welcoming sound of basic systems coming online. He fell in and smacked the mushroom-shaped paddle marked *SEAL.*

He slumped to the deck. A canned voice informed him he should stand clear of the hatch. A second later, the door rose in its tracks.

Centimeters from being closed, an arm flashed through the opening, claws splayed like bony swords from a hand grotesquely enlarged. Their tips raked across metal and plastic.

"*The hatch is obstructed,*" announced the shuttle. The door stopped closing and began to lower.

"Shit." Lochlan kicked at the paddle, reversing the door again.

"*The hatch is obstructed.*"

"*Override,*" he screamed. The door stopped but did not close. The arm flailed, pinned. Lochlan pulled a panel beside the door free, a crank handle extending automatically. He grabbed at the handle but his injured hand was swollen beyond use. This was not happening.

Cranking clumsily with his non-dominant hand, the door crept upward. Bone cracked and muscle tore until, seconds later, to the frantic scrapes and scratches outside, the severed limb dropped to the deck.

Lochlan fumbled a first aid kit from another compartment. A handheld evaluator chirped to life as he pulled it from its pouch. Its screen lit up with his own face, having read his medical implant. An hourglass turned for half an eternity before filling with a list of medicines, mostly trauma related. Enough to stabilize him. He pulled at the packets, letting them rain to the deck around him, only marginally sure he was tearing open and swallowing the correct ones.

Sucking at a bulb of water, he began to breathe more and gasp less.

The white lights of the shuttle interior were a welcome change from the sky. Pushing himself into a sitting position, he looked at the limb on the deck. This was his first chance to take more than a cursory glance. The arm was human for the most part. The muscles more defined, but proportionally normal. The hand, though, was another matter. The fingers were three to four times their normal length, their flesh transitioning smoothly into bony serrated claws.

Shadows moved back and forth across the small ports of the cockpit. Muted blows sounded on the hull outside. The shuttle could take the punishment. Hopefully. The adapted were fast, and they were strong; but they weren't stronger than technology.

On other worlds, the effects of his pryonelles had been subtler. Some eye color variations, increased osteoelasticity, a faint marbling of the skin. Traits intended to more quickly adapt the human species to the new environments, increase the success of the colonies and, therefore, the recognition of those who led them—and the profits for those who funded them. Certainly nothing severe enough to warrant investigation, not anything remotely traceable back to him. He just got the credit for discovering *rapid genetic drift*. At the symposium on Pusher 61 last year, he'd finally given in to the faction of his peers who wanted to refer to the phenomenon as Lochlan's Drift. His parents would have been proud, his grandparents, his brother.

But nothing would bring them back. Forty years had passed, but he remembered their bodies like it was yesterday. He'd been five.

He'd never shared that with anyone. Bethanne would have understood everything if he'd just been brave enough to tell her. If she'd just loved him enough to listen.

The cabin was cold. Lochlan slipped his jacket on and got to his feet. Steadying himself on the bulkhead, he made his way toward the flight stations. Both the pilot's and copilot's seats were turned inward for easy access. He dropped heavily into a padded embrace, relieved to allow his muscles a moment to relax. The medications were doing the trick. The swelling was down considerably in his hand and his shoulder hardly hurt at all. A fresh dressing on his leg, which had already stopped bleeding, and he'd be good until rendezvousing with the JWTF ship. The seat turned, whirring on tiny bearings into flight position, facing forward.

The controls seemed strange, even though he'd handled them only a day before.

Stress. Terror. Loss of a loved one. Those things could lead to severe disorientation. He was human, after all.

One second. One minute, at a time.

All he had to do was get off the ground. It would be more dignified to fly himself to *Worldrunner*, but if he couldn't make orbit, he'd just hop a few hundred kilometers away. JWTF types would bend over backwards to rescue famous colonists. If they asked too many questions, he'd just choke up and flash the holo: his picture with Bethanne at their engagement party. Safely off this planet, it wouldn't take much for him to break down. That should buy him the time he needed to come to terms with everything he'd done. Everything he'd lost.

I'm sorry, my angel. Never again. I swear.

Panel lights blinked and monitors indicated the status of the shuttle's systems but something was wrong. The flight yoke was—

Missing?

Cables and a complicated metal joint mechanism jutted from the deck, twisted and broken. The yoke in front of the other flight station was gone as well.

"*On the ground,*" crackled a voice from the speaker over his head. "*We have patched into your local video feeds and are declaring this world a white zone, full quarantine. Survivors are directed to seek a safe distance from all structures.*"

Lochlan grabbed for the headset cradle in the overhead but found only severed cables.

No.

Struggling from the chair, he dropped to his knees. The portable evaluator chirped behind him and the sound of rustling leaves filled the cabin.

She stood a few meters away, near the hatch leading to the rear power plant compartment. A piece of machinery dropped from her long graceful fingers to the deck with a clank.

He didn't need to look at the devices screen to know it was Bethanne. Her eyes were unmistakable.

She was alive. Alive!

All he had to do was get back to the lab. The one in the settlement would work. The one in orbit would be better. He'd never reversed the pryonelles' work before, but he'd never needed to.

Her growl was low, barely in the audible range. He felt it in his chest.

She was reconfigured, magnificent, a majestic creature whose savage power now matched an equally savage intellect. None of the colonists would have been able to remember how to disable the shuttles, but she'd been a genius before.

In the land of the blind, the one-eyed man is king.

"Hello, Bethanne," said Lochlan, his voice soft, his words slow. "I thought you were gone. I can make this right. Let me help you."

Her gaze flitted from his face to his hands to the other adapted beating at the cockpit windows. One corner of her mouth peeled back in a row of jagged teeth.

The weight of her growl pushed into Lochlan's sternum.

He reached for the holo in his pocket. "Angel, it's me. I love—"

He barely registered her motion when the world blurred into fire and darkness.

WARMTH BEAT AGAINST his face, and light filtered through his eyelids, pulsing with blood. His leg throbbed and his neck felt as if his head had been snapped off and placed back on slightly out of alignment.

He was alive.

He opened his eyes. The red of the sky was deeper and bloodier than when his eyes had been closed. A single star winked down.

Rolling painfully onto one side, he saw Bethanne. His chest clenched and he had to force each breath. Other transformed colonists flanked her, forming a circle around him.

They were on top of the rise overlooking the compound and the landing field. Some of the adapted growled. He could feel the sound more than hear it. He had no chance of getting away. None at all.

He opened his mouth to speak, but did not know what to say. How could he reason with them? "Bethanne?"

Light flared in the sky above. Streaks of white flashed down onto the compound and the landing field. Balls of flame engulfed every structure. The shuttles lifted into the air and came down hard, cracking like metal eggs. The adapted ran, scrambling over the supply crates for the instinctual safety of the brush and rock, their roars hammer blows inside Lochlan's skull.

Bethanne stood her ground. A moment later the shock wave from the kinetic impactors ruffled the collar of Lochlan's jacket and the spines on his beloved's back.

He would never leave this world, a white zone quarantine. It would be a generation before they'd even return to study the place from orbit.

The adapted rustled back into the clearing, smaller figures scurrying in the weeds. The pryonelles were no longer in the environment, but they should still be active in their bloodstreams.

What choice did he really have? If Bethanne had been intelligent enough to maintain some spark of herself—enough so she was the alpha now—then he could do the same.

Better to rule in Hell.

Lochlan held out his arm. "I can join you. The lab is gone, but if you bite me gently—"

Shadows flashed and Bethanne was on him, the fingers of one hand splayed. She gripped and lifted him from the ground. Her face was centimeters from his, her breath hot, and sweet like honeysuckle. With her free hand, she held up the medical evaluator between them. Its screen flickered between his assessment and hers. She glared between him and the display until he looked at it.

The device recommended a number of further treatments for him.

For her, unable to understand her current condition, it defaulted to the database's last recommendation. From just over a day before.

Prenatal vitamins.

Lochlan looked into her huge feral eyes. That's why she'd been so happy. That, and his promise. A tear ran down his face. "Angel—"

She growled, silencing him. A long spindly finger snaked into his pocket, speared the holo and pulled it free. Blood from the ripper he'd killed hours before had dried across their faces. Hand held high overhead, she let the wind whip it away, and lowered him to his feet.

Returning to the edge of the clearing, she faced him and settled into a crouch. Behind her, the damaged supply crates had spilled their contents. Bottles of champagne, sealed trays of food. An improvised banner fluttered in the breeze. *Congratulations To The New Parents!*

Lochlan knelt.

All around, fires burned. The weeds snapped at the air, and his chest ached with their silent voices.

Bethanne's large beautiful eyes looked on him, unblinking in the crimson light of the sun.

> *I'll go to the Clyde and I'll mourn and weep,*
> *Where satisfied I never shall be.*
> *I'll write her a letter, just a few short lines,*
> *And suffer death ten thousand times.*

ABOUT THE AUTHOR

WILLIAM R. D. WOOD traces his love of science fiction and horror back to a childhood filled with classic Universal Studios monsters, *Space: 1999* reruns, a worn-out copy of *Dune*, and *Heavy Metal* magazine. His work has appeared in *Nature*, *The Lovecraft eZine*, and Flame Tree Publishing's *Chilling Horror Short Stories* anthology, among other places. William lives with his wife and children in Virginia's Shenandoah Valley in an old farmhouse turned backwards to the road. If you're in the neighborhood, stop by and sit a spell. Otherwise, feel free to check out www.williamRDwood.com.

ABOUT THE STORY

Stories evolve.

"Red is the Color of My True Love's Hair," my *Writers of the Future* contest Finalist story, came to me as an image:

A dark alley. A man crouched in shadow against one wall, holding his breath. The silhouette of something monstrous writhing on the far wall. The man knows if he moves or makes a sound, he's dead.

I knew the poor guy cowering in the shadows just wanted to get to safety, so I gave the story the working title "Escape." He was terrified, sure, but maybe he was also a little put out. Heck, he was annoyed. He wasn't even supposed to be there! And now he was sure he was going to die.

And that's where the story hung, in limbo, abandoned and despondent, while I moved on to other projects.

The rough draft came in a flood. I was involved in a friendly little writer's shoot-out (not as violent as it sounds, but close) and we were focusing on antagonists. That was it! "Escape" wasn't the innocent hero's story at all.

It was the villain's.

The revelation couldn't have come at a better time. An old folk song had resurfaced in my head thanks to its use in a classic *Twilight Zone* episode I'd just seen, specifically, "The Passerby." Suddenly, I'm scouring the internet for history and lyrics. I had been crediting the vague memory of the piece to Loreena McKinnett but couldn't find any evidence she'd ever recorded it. Enya, maybe? Rather than admit that Enya shows up in my work a little too much to be a coincidence, I settled on the recordings of Christy Moore and Nina Simone and, within a few days, the rough draft was complete.

I hope my story has done justice to that original image as well as the song that inspired its tone and texture. If you think so, drop me a line. If not, drop me a line anyway. I'd love to hear your thoughts on how the story might continue to grow and change.

"Red is the Color of My True Love's Hair" is set to paper now, metaphorically at least. Some might think that means the story is over, the tale told. Some writers, myself included, would disagree. Just because our pencils are down or our hands have left the keyboard, just because the story is published and making its way in the world, it's not the end.

If a tale or some part of it sticks with you, it's never really over, because stories grow.

And stories evolve.

Lousy chauvinistic scripts with clichéd parts for female actors.
Hollywood sucks!
Perhaps literally.
Janni's P.I. husband Ben's new client is a
vampire movie producer with a werewolf problem.
Janni and Ben, new werewolves themselves,
agree to go up against the pack
and its Big Bad leader. But they are two against many.
To win will require some great acting.

....

BAD ACTORS

JULIE FROST

I swore and flung the script across the front office of my mom's private investigation firm with a clawed hand. As the shredded pages fluttered to the floor, I jumped up from the sofa and paced. "*Why* does my agent keep sending me this *crap?*"

My husband Ben stopped pounding the keyboard on his desk in the corner and raked his fingers through his over-long, curly blond hair. "Maybe you need a new agent, Janni."

"I am so sick and tired of her sending me scripts where I'm the love interest. Or the damsel in distress." I threw up my hands. "Do I look like a distressed damsel to you?"

"No, ma'am, you do not. I think that's my role anyway," he said, with half a grin. His job meant that he got hurt on a regular basis, because he *would* take on the more dangerous cases—but he had a sense of humor about it. At least the whole werewolf thing made him hard to kill. He continued, "But you are tiny and cute and not white. The business is what it is, and no one's gonna hire you as an action hero no matter how much lip service they give to diversity. You're too unconventional for the roles you want."

I huffed. "The fact that I'm black should be the last thing on anyone's mind. Hollywood's supposed to be more progressive than that."

Ben rolled his eyes—not at me, he knew better than that—but at Hollywood. "They're progressive as far as it affects their bottom line, honey. Just means you have to work twice as hard to break in."

The fact that I grew fangs and fur three nights out of the month didn't help, because shooting schedules were apparently God or something. "I know. Doesn't mean it's not stupid."

The electronic bell chimed. A tall man wearing an expensive camel-hair coat and a beret stepped into the office. Or, should I say, the *vampire* made an *entrance*, which my nose told me a bare second later as he struck a dramatic pose.

Ben's blue eyes went amber. He was up and around his desk, between the vampire and me, faster than it takes to tell. I stood too, ready to back him up if he needed it.

"May I help you . . . " Ben's tone was remarkably even, considering the first run-in he'd had with a vamp had ended badly for everyone involved. Apparently another one had sniffed him out. " . . . sir?"

The vamp smiled with his lips closed. That was something, anyway—he knew better than to bare his teeth at werewolves. Maybe our second encounter with the supernatural set would go better than the first.

"I am Martyn Volosin, and I wish to hire your services for some bodyguard work," he said, with a thick Eastern European accent. He was a movie producer I'd heard of, peripherally, but never met in person. I wondered if he sounded like Dracula on purpose.

"You are Ben Lockwood, correct?" he continued. "A werewolf?"

Ben had a low tolerance for bullshit and didn't like vampires anyway. "Thank you, Captain Obvious. We can all smell what we are, and I'm sure you looked into me before you set foot in here. How about telling me what you found out?"

Volosin inclined his head. "Of course. You are a former Army Ranger who was a POW in Afghanistan, which left you with post-traumatic stress that is getting better. You contracted lycanthropy during an unfortunate pharmaceutical espionage case three months ago. Your mother-in-law—who is not a werewolf—made you a partner in the firm as a wedding gift upon your marriage after that case. And your . . . less-than-tall stature and wounded-puppy aspect hides a frighteningly competent fighter, as opponents much larger than you frequently discover to their detriment. You love your mate Janni—" A nod to me. "—to distraction and would die, or kill, for her. Did I miss anything?"

Ben's expression was sour. "Not much, no."

"I thought not. May we sit?" Volosin's gaze skimmed the drift of script I'd left on the floor. "It might be that one hand washes the other."

Ben's jaw tightened. My mom had gone home for the day, and the only reason he was still in the office after dark was to wrap up some computer work. "Fine. But Janni and I have a date tonight, so let's make this snappy." He waved Volosin to a chair and perched a hip on the corner of the desk, crossing his arms. I could smell his stress at the proximity of a vampire, so I stood next to him and wrapped an arm around his waist. He pressed against me and settled, somewhat.

Volosin sat, leaning his elbows on his knees and steepling his fingers. "I am an independent movie producer. We recently started filming something we hope will be a modest blockbuster. Action, explosions, quips. But with soul. You know the sort."

Of course we did. It was exactly the kind of role I craved. I perked up. Vampire or no, this guy might be able to get me a part I actually wanted. Ben glanced at me, and at least put his hackles down. "But you need a bodyguard," he said. "Trouble on the set?"

"One might say that. I am being blackmailed by a werewolf pack. They wish one of their members to have a major role—not the lead, of course, they are not quite that presumptuous." His mouth twisted. "This would not be a problem under ordinary circumstances. We could work around it."

"But?" I asked. "There's always a but."

Volosin put his face in his hand. "But this wolf, he is not just a bad actor, he is also a complete prima donna. He thinks, because of the blackmail, that he can get away with anything." His head came up. "I wish to negotiate with the alpha of his pack, Nick Brimhall—to pay them rather than have this person ruin my movie. But I do not think it safe to walk into their territory without backup in the form of another wolf." He looked at me. "Perhaps two, if your lovely wife would care to join us."

Ben twitched a little, no doubt at the notion of taking me into a strange wolf den, and I squeezed him. "Down, boy," I said. I'd helped out before, when the situation called for it, though my regular gig was working for a catering company. "It's not like you can take Mama along, and I don't like the idea of you going in by yourself."

"What's this alpha blackmailing you with?" Ben asked warily. "I like to know what I'm walking into."

Volosin waved a hand. "Nothing that concerns you. A private matter that I do not wish to become public."

Ben growled. "Four hundred an hour plus expenses." He lifted a questioning eyebrow at me, and I nodded. It was twice our going rate. Vampires paid a premium. "Apiece. Tomorrow night. Because, like I say, we have a date tonight."

"Agreed. This will give me a chance to set up the meeting with the alpha." Volosin smiled, still not baring his fangs. "I will pick you up here, at eight, and call you if there is a change."

Ben gave him a business card. "And five hundred up front."

Volosin tipped his head and reached into his pocket. "But of course." Pulling out a money clip, he peeled ten fifties off and handed it, after a moment's consideration, to me, before rising smoothly to his feet and offering his hand. Ben firmly shook it once. "On the morrow, then," Volosin said, and left.

"Eugh." Ben shuddered a little. "Man, I do not like vampires. Have you heard of him, Janni?"

"Here and there. He's a mid-tier producer in Europe, and now he's trying his hand in the US." I snorted. "My agent didn't see fit to send me the script for his current project. Which is a shame, because it was right up my alley."

"Hmph. Well, if you don't know anything hinky about him, I guess we'll go ahead and be his backup tomorrow night." He shut his computer down, then swept me up and kissed me. "In the meantime, milady, I believe we have an appointment with a giant steak and a movie."

"What about the job?"

"I'll pick your brain more about our vampire tonight over dinner and look up our pack in the morning. Sound good?"

I kissed him back. "Anything with steak involved sounds good, sugar."

BEN SPENT THE next day chasing data down various trails, while I read desultorily through a couple more scripts after my noon catering gig. "Well," he said, sitting back and sipping his coffee. "It's sticky. This alpha giving Volosin grief, Nick Brimhall? He's been arrested for assault a few times. Charges always ended up dropped."

"Ben, have you been hackin' into the LAPD again?" my mom asked him, poking her head into the room from her office. She had three inches and fifty pounds on Ben, with straight red-brown hair and skin a shade darker than mine. Since he'd lost his own parents, she'd become a mother figure to him as well.

Ben put on his best harp seal expression. "Why, Pam, would I do such a thing? At least, before hiding behind proxies and firewalls?"

She put a fist on her ample hip and shook a finger at him. "Baby boy, I don't know what I'm gonna do with you. You are incorrigible." This was familiar repartee, and I was glad she didn't treat him any differently than before he'd been wolfed. She'd reacted badly, at first, when she came home from vacation to find us both werewolves. But since we weren't slavering monsters, and she'd spent a few full-moon pizza-and-beer nights with us and our token alpha Megan, she'd regained her usual equilibrium.

"Just gathering info," Ben said. "I don't like walking in blind."

"Well. Don't get caught, is all." My mom wouldn't bust his chops too hard; half the reason she hired him was his facility with getting places on the computer he technically shouldn't.

He clutched a hand over his heart. "You wound me, Pam. Right here. I am *insulted*. Psht, *caught*, as if." He went serious. "That being said, I'm going in loaded with silver. I don't like this guy, at all."

"Mm-hm. You be careful."

"Hey, at least this vampire doesn't want to eat me. And the money's good." He looked at his watch. "We probably oughta get out there. He's sending a car for us, and it should be here, oh, now." Ben checked the Micro Desert Eagle in his front pants pocket and the Ruger 9mm in the shoulder holster under his sport coat. I had my own Raspberry LCP in my purse and ready, so we headed outside.

It was a small limo, but a limo nonetheless, that waited for us on the curb. A human chauffeur with Volosin's scent overlaying his own opened the back door, and I wondered if the vampire snacked on his help. The aroma of liquor and leather wafted out, and we slid in and sat opposite Volosin. He wore a hand-tailored gray houndstooth suit with a black silk shirt and a maroon tie.

"Well," I said, "I feel underdressed." I had put on a pair of black slacks, a black cotton button-down shirt, and a black blazer, with no tie; Ben wore jeans, a plain black tee, and a blue sport coat. These were practical, if not fancy—and were fairly easy to tear out of if we had to shift to wolf.

Volosin waved a languid hand. "Do not worry. Our wolf pack will not notice. Drink?"

"Maybe after," I said.

Ben was tense beside me. I didn't blame him, not really. Last time he'd been trapped in a confined space with a vampire, he'd died.

"You might as well have a small one," Volosin said. He shrugged. "It will take an hour to get there. LA traffic, what can you do."

Ben growled under his breath, leaning forward with his elbows on his knees. He rubbed his handcuff scars—a gift from Afghani insurgents—with his thumbs, back and forth, forth and back. "We could've met you there, is what."

I massaged his back between his shoulder blades. "It's okay, sweetie. Have a ginger ale?"

He nodded jerkily, and Volosin played host, pouring him one from the well-stocked mini-fridge. Ben sipped slowly, leaning on me a little and grounding himself. "Sorry," he said. "Bad memories. Don't get along real well with vamps. In general. Not just you."

"I understand," Volosin said. "Some of my more bloodthirsty kin do not play nice."

"Well, you'll pardon me if one of your bloodthirsty brethren left a bad taste in my mouth." Ben rolled the glass back and forth between his palms. "She paid for it in the end, but still."

"Ah, yes, the Ostheims. Her husband was a werewolf," Volosin said. He really had done his homework on Ben. We'd tried to keep that case quiet, because the body count had been high. Apparently the supernatural rumor mill had churned the information out anyway.

Volosin tilted his head. "Do you hold the same animosity to your own species?"

"He tried to kill me more than once and nearly did kill Janni. I tore him apart with my bare fangs." Ben's voice had roughened. His head came up;

his eyes were amber. "What do *you* think? Did your research into me cover *that?*" His back muscles tensed under my hand, and he smelled of adrenaline and wolf.

Volosin recoiled a fraction. "Apparently not. The Ostheims disappeared without a trace and no one ever heard from them again."

"Maybe they shouldn't have *fucked* with me."

And maybe Volosin should've thought harder about an hour-long ride in a car with a hostile werewolf suffering from PTSD. Fur sprouted under my hand.

Ben bared his fangs. "Are you gonna fuck with me, Volosin?"

"Ben," I said mildly.

"No, Mr. Lockwood. I am certainly not going to fuck with you," Volosin answered, raising a conciliatory hand. "I would like to escape from this situation with my skin and life, such as it is, intact."

"Just so we understand each other." Ben blew out a breath and dropped his head back down. The fur on his back retracted, though I could still smell his stress. "Are we there yet?"

"Soon. Are you sure you don't want a drink?" Volosin said.

"After the job, I'll take you up on it. Right now?" He raised the glass of ginger ale. "This will do." Ben sipped it. His hand, I noted, was steady. Work had a tendency to do that for him. It was when he didn't have anything to do that he slipped down rabbit holes. Probably why he'd taken this client, honestly; the agency had been slow lately, and any job was better than none.

The rest of the drive was spent in silence; no one really wanted to say anything after that. The limo stopped in the parking lot of a bar with several custom motorcycles and a lot of pickup trucks in front of it. Ben looked the place over, visibly calculating odds, checking for exits and windows. He shook his head. "I don't like it. Be ready to run, honey," he said to me. "I'm not even kidding. Wolf if you have to." He turned to Volosin. "Can you communicate quickly with your driver here?"

"I can call him—" Volosin started.

Ben snorted. "I said *quickly*." To the driver: "Leave the engine running and the door open. If we have to leave in a hurry I don't want any delays."

"*Da*," said the driver. His accent was thicker than Volosin's. "I vill do dat."

"Awesome." Ben's voice was laden with sarcasm. No, he did not like this situation at all. "All right, Volosin, this is your show. Let's go talk to this alpha wolf."

Ben took point, walking into the bar like he owned it, chin high and jaw set. The scent of *wolf* was nearly overwhelming; I'd never seen this many wolves in one place and I staggered a little. "Honey?" Ben asked out of the corner of his mouth.

"I'm fine," I managed, and straightened. Any sign of weakness and these people would eat us alive. Maybe literally. "Mr. Volosin? Is Brimhall here?"

"In the back," Volosin answered, jerking his head in that direction. It was a big table, with several large and rowdy wolves seated around it playing quarters. "The big fellow, that is him."

The big fellow in question bounced a coin into a pilsner glass full of dark beer. Roars of laughter followed as he pointed to one of his pack who was already clearly inebriated. But that wolf gamely picked up the glass and chugged it down, to much backslapping and approval as we made our way over.

The laughter died away when they noticed us. Brimhall stood up, his expression thunderous. "Volosin, we have an appointment, yeah, but you come to my bar, in my territory, with strange *wolves*, without clearing it first? Dude, not cool."

"They are bodyguards, not here to stay. I wish to have a parley with you, Brimhall."

Several of the wolves muttered, and I heard one make a crack about Ben's size. Most of them were bigger than him, even the females. The alpha easily outweighed him by at least fifty pounds. I stared back at them, not particularly challenging, but letting them know that if they wanted a fight, we'd give them one. Alcohol and testosterone were flowing pretty damn freely, and I was ready. Now I knew why Ben wanted to be sober for this. It gave us an edge when we were outnumbered.

"Parley about what?" Brimhall said. "I thought we had an agreement. You wanting to *break* that agreement, Volosin?"

"I wish to pay you, rather than having to put up with any more . . . antics on my set. Larsen cannot act and is unwilling to learn or even rehearse." That earned Brimhall a glare from me. Someone who wouldn't even do the work was getting a free ride, and I had to hump my ass off to get a bit part?

"I take care of my pack, Volosin. Curtis wants to be an actor. I can help him out with that, so there you go. Suck it up—ha—or that information you don't want coming to light will get out."

"He is in love with the idea of acting, not the work that goes into the actual craft of the thing." Volosin's brow lowered. "He doesn't want to act, he wants to, what is your phrase, 'hang out' with actors and celebrities. He wants to see his face on the screen beside real actors. That is all. I too must take care of my people, and he is making them most unhappy with his behavior. I will pay him what I agreed, and pay you the same, to get him to go away."

Brimhall rolled his eyes. "It's one movie. You can put up with him for one movie." His gaze flicked over to Ben and me, and Ben stiffened. "Now then. These two."

"They are none of your concern."

"Oh, see, that's where you're wrong. You come into my bar, insult a member of my pack, and make unreasonable demands, all with strange wolves in tow." His voice went cold. "Wolves who should have known better than to come openly into someone else's territory without permission."

"Oh, what bullshit," Ben said. "I go all over the city as part of my job and no one says boo."

"That may be," Brimhall answered. "But you don't go right into people's dens without asking first. That's just rude. If you wanted a bodyguard, Volosin, you should've gotten one of the wolves who lives here."

Volosin's answer was desert-dry. "Yes, that would work very well—to have subordinates loyal to you working for me if something went wrong."

Brimhall snorted. "Better that than these two. The scruffy little mutt doesn't look like much." He eyed me. "The female's a babe, though. I think she should stay."

"I think you're a moron," I said. "So, appealing as the offer is, I'm going to say no."

"You could do worse. You see how this pack takes care of its own."

"I'm perfectly fine with my pack and my mate, thanks." I stepped closer to Ben to emphasize the point, and he wrapped an arm around my waist.

Brimhall's expression twisted into astonished contempt, one eyebrow going up and the opposite corner of his mouth pulling down, but the upper lip curling. "You're with *him*? Why?"

"Because I love him," I said. "Because he's one of the good guys." Because he needed me, and it was good to be needed; but that wasn't something I discussed with strangers, especially hostile ones.

"Well. He can stay, I suppose."

"Oh, thanks so much," Ben said. "But we're going to decline your invitation."

"And that's where you mistake me, Scruffy. It's not an invitation, and you don't get to decline." Brimhall bared fangs. "Sit. Your ass. Down."

"I'm. Working." Ben bared a fang, just one, back. "Your *business* isn't with *me*. We're only here in case of *accidents*. We'll be out of your fur as soon as your business with my *client* is *finished*." He was emphasizing words. That was never good. I put a calming hand on his back.

One of the other wolves stood. He was two inches shorter and six inches wider than Brimhall, wearing an LA Clippers hat backward. "You want me to put him in his place, Nick?"

A guy with flowing black hair to his shoulders tugged on Brimhall's sleeve. "But what about Rona? She won't like it if we start a fight without her say-so."

"Well, she's not here, is she," Clippers Hat said. "I'll take the pup down, Nick, just say the word."

"You can try," Ben said, in an offhand way that I was pretty sure was infuriating on purpose.

"No, you know what, Scruffy's right. We can deal with him when we're done with Volosin." Brimhall turned to our client. "The arrangement stands, so fuck off. Go back to your set and finish making your movie. Stop bothering me over things that are already settled." Dismissing Volosin, he turned to Ben. "Now, as for you."

We didn't get to find out what Brimhall had in store for Ben, because Volosin hissed—

And launched himself right at Brimhall, fangs foremost.

"Oh, for the love of . . ." Ben waded in beside him as chaos erupted. "Janni, go to the car!"

Like hell. Someone had to have Ben's back, and the client was busy getting his ass handed to him. Vampire blood sprayed across my cheek, and wolf blood splashed my chest.

But it turned out that Ben wasn't the only chivalrous one in the room; most of the male wolves made it a point to avoid me. One swiped a clawed hand at my face—missing by a hairsbreadth, thankfully, because Ben would have been absolutely uncontrollable if he'd managed to connect. That wolf was tossed across the room by the black-haired guy who'd urged caution. I cracked someone's face with my elbow and took out a knee with my heel. Volosin went down, and Ben ended up standing over him protectively, fangs bared and nine mil in hand.

He fired once at the ceiling, and everyone froze. We could all smell the silver in that bullet. His voice was incredibly calm. "That's *enough*. Now, normally, I wouldn't fire a fucking warning shot. But you idiots were *occupied* trying to *eat my client*, and I didn't have a clear line of fire to your alpha. So I thought I'd get your attention. Janni," he said, not looking at me, "would you get our dumbass client out to the car, please? I'm right behind you."

I had occasion, once again, to be thankful for werewolf strength as I scooped Volosin up. Ben covered our retreat, and Brimhall growled at him. "This isn't over, Scruffy. Count on it."

And then we popped out the door. The chauffeur helped me get Volosin in the limo and stretched out on the back seat. Ben shoved at the driver, gun still in hand. "Get us out of here."

"Yes, sir," he said. Ten seconds later, we were accelerating through traffic.

Volosin moaned, the sound bubbling through his slashed throat. "You colossal fucking idiot," Ben snarled. "What the hell were you thinking? You nearly got us all killed."

"Uh, Ben?" I was getting really concerned. Volosin was paler than normal even for a vampire, and he was wheezing. Vampires didn't have to breathe. "He's not doing so hot."

"I shouldn't think so. Vampires may be stronger than werewolves, but it's impossible to throw a thrall on a group, and he was way outnumbered." Ben huffed. "*Dumbass.*"

I stripped back my sleeve. "No, I mean, he's dying."

Ben made a strangled sound filled with panic. "Janni, don't, you can't—!"

"He's *dying*," I repeated. I didn't point out that I'd done it before, for Ben. He'd been upset then, too.

"Then I'll feed him." Peeling his sport coat off, he knelt in front of Volosin's seat. "Hey. Volosin." He slapped the vampire's face. Volosin blinked up at him blearily. "Stay with me here. Werewolf blood. Should be better than human. More oomph. Here." He offered his wrist.

Volosin's eyes went wide. He grabbed Ben's arm with both hands and sank his fangs in. Ben inhaled sharply, and his shoulders bunched.

I reached out and put my hand on his back, inwardly furious. But this was a discussion we'd have later, in private. Meantime, I was there for him, petting him and murmuring soothing nothings. He pulled back a couple of minutes later, and Volosin let him go, gasping. "Thank you," the vampire said. "Blood bags. In the refrigerator. If you would."

Ben slumped back onto our seat as I grabbed three bags from the fridge. Volosin bit into them and slurped them down. Ben's blood had restored him somewhat, and the human blood finished the job. He healed like some kind of bizarre special effect, muscle and skin regenerating and covering the terrible wounds on his throat. "Thank you." His voice was faint. "Are you injured?"

"Not bad," Ben said. His shirt was shredded diagonally from left shoulder to right hip where someone had caught him with a clawed hand, but the cuts were shallow and no longer bleeding. He also had a scrape on his cheek and a split lip.

I'd escaped completely unscathed.

"That was brainless, Volosin," Ben said furiously.

"Yes, it was. I am sorry."

"You should be. What happened to that vaunted vampire calm? You totally lost it."

"We are not so calm about things we are passionate about." A shrug. "I have no person I love right now, so I am passionate about my filmmaking."

"Criminy." Ben's trembling hand snaked over and captured mine. "Let's just go home and regroup tomorrow, okay? Can we do that?"

"Of course." Volosin gave his driver the address. "I will see you tomorrow?" The vampire seemed to need the reassurance.

"Yeah," Ben said. "Sundown, I'm expecting. And we will have a discussion on *stupid* behavior."

The rest of the ride was conducted in catastrophically awkward silence.

As soon as we got inside the door, though, I let Ben have it, even as I stormed into the kitchen and grabbed some hamburger from the fridge. We both needed the protein, me for the stress and him for the blood loss.

"*Dammit*, Ben." I slammed the raw beef into half-pound patties and flung them into the frying pan. "I am not *fragile*. I do not like being treated like I'll break if you look at me wrong."

He sat on a barstool at the kitchen island, burying his head in his arms on the counter. His voice was muffled. "No, honey. You're not fragile." A pause, which I almost interrupted, until he said, so softly I nearly missed it, "But I am."

I nearly dropped the buns I'd hauled from the breadbox. "Oh." I felt like a damn fool. Almost losing me once had nearly destroyed him. Of course he was protective. He was chopping his sentences, too, a sure sign that he was emotionally wrung out. "Oh, Ben."

"I'm sorry," he said, keeping his head hidden, not looking at me. "I know you're strong. Stronger than me. But I can't."

"Oh, sweetie." I wrapped around him. "I know. I shouldn't have jumped you like that." He'd lost a woman he loved in Afghanistan, and still had nightmares that woke us both up. "It's all right."

"It's not, though. I need to deal better." The shakes had him pretty good, and he leaned into me. "It's not fair to you."

"And it's not fair of me to expect you to just be la-di-dah about feeding myself to a vampire." I kissed his hair. "You didn't even like it when I did it for *you*." That had been a bad, bad time. Fortunately, he got better, physically, anyway. "I wasn't thinking. And I'm sorry."

"You've got a beautiful spirit, honey. It's one of the things I treasure about you." He turned and pulled me into a hard hug, burying his face against my chest. "Just. Please. Don't take chances. Please."

I threaded my fingers through his hair. "I won't, sweetie."

He nodded against me. "Okay." Breathing. "Okay." A few more moments, and he reluctantly disengaged. "The burgers will burn, and that would be a crime."

I flipped them over and seasoned them, then got the tomatoes and avocados sliced while he whined.

"Vegetables on my hamburgers? Vegetables are what food eats." It was a token protest. He did this every time.

"The veggies have nutrients in them that meat doesn't. You need them."

"Yes, ma'am." He certainly didn't bellyache when I put the plate down in front of him. He devoured the hamburger in short order. I ate mine at a more sedate pace, and when a tomato dropped onto my plate, he snagged it.

"See there?" I said with my mouth full.

"It's got burger juice on it. It doesn't count as a veggie anymore."

I snorted at him, and he laughed. We'd apparently gotten over this hurdle, and I was thankful; it wasn't usually this easy. "Okay, Ben. Showers, and bed."

"Showers together?" His eyebrows waggled, and I pushed on his shoulder.

"Promise that it's a short shower, and that you'll behave."

He gave me his best baby seal look. "Oh, yes, ma'am, I'll behave very properly."

He didn't, of course. But I was all right with that.

Volosin showed up at sundown at the office, and Ben fixed him with a gimlet stare as soon as he walked in the door. "I'm tempted to drop you like a hot rock, Volosin. That was the dumbest thing I've ever seen."

Volosin was contrite. "I realize this. It will not happen again."

"Damn straight it won't, or I'll just leave you there to be *eaten*. Got me?"

"Yes. Thank you."

"That being said. This secret of yours they're blackmailing you with." The glint in Ben's eye changed from stern to amused.

"I told you, I do not wish—"

Ben put his hand up. "I am very, very good at my job, and I wanted to make sure I wasn't walking into anything ugly." A corner of his mouth turned up. "So why didn't you just tell me that you run a pit bull rescue on the sly?"

Volosin gabbled at him for a few seconds before he recovered. "Vampire society is ruthless if they sense a weakness. My parents gave me a devoted Bull and Terrier when I was a child, and so I have particular affection for the breed. I feel they have an undeserved bad reputation, and so I do my part to save their lives when no one else will."

"Good for you. I like it. But, word to the wise, Volosin—don't try to hide stuff from a PI. It just makes us curious. Now that's out of the way . . ." Ben opened the file on his desk. The top page featured a photograph of the guy who'd urged caution and tossed his pack mate across the room for attacking me, along with a list of information. Ben tapped the picture. "The pack beta. Marshall Taylor. He seemed reasonable, last night. At least, he protected

Janni." We'd hashed over an after-action report at breakfast. "That puts him miles ahead of those other assholes."

"It is the beta's job to rein in the alpha." Volosin frowned. "You do not know this?"

"Our pack isn't really that formal," I said. "It's small."

"Can you set up a private meeting with Taylor?" Ben asked. "If it's his job to rein in his alpha, maybe we can make *him* see sweet reason on this deal."

Volosin nodded, and made a phone call. He was satisfied when he hung up. "Taylor has agreed to meet with us, in private. He says he is uneasy about the direction that Brimhall is taking the pack. He wonders if we might have any ideas to help him stop a downward slide."

Ben's mouth pulled skeptically to one side. "If it sounds too good to be true, it probably is."

"A pack beta would not dare double-cross us," Volosin objected.

Ben gave him a pitying look. "A pack beta would not dare double-cross his *alpha*." He pulled his Ruger from its shoulder holster and checked to make sure it had a round in the chamber. "I hope you don't mind that I'm going in armed. With silver. It saved our bacon last night."

"Take all the precautions you like," Volosin said. "You are the expert here."

"Damn right I am," Ben muttered. And if he sat a little closer to me than normal in the limo, it was only to be expected. I didn't mind.

"The docks. Really?" Ben said sourly, at the end of the ride. "If this doesn't scream 'trap,' I don't know what does."

"Dark, deserted, and dangerous," I said. "Perfect. I hope you're taking notes, Mr. Volosin. You can put this in your next movie."

"Look sharp, Volosin," Ben said, "and keep your ears and nose perked."

We got out in front of a warehouse where a nondescript two-door sedan was parked. Taylor skulked from the gloom to meet us. "I hope you realize what a chance I'm taking here," he said. "Let's go inside before anyone sees us."

The dim warehouse was filled with boxes on shelves, odd corners, and deep shadows. The only windows were up high, and they let next to no light in. Good thing all of us could see in the dark. I inhaled the pervasive scent of Brimhall's pack. They apparently used this place a lot.

Taylor leaned against a shelf with his arms crossed. "This whole thing is gonna cause problems with our alpha female if she finds out. Brimhall's managed to keep it off Rona's radar so far, but he knows that Larsen can't act and is too damn lazy to do the work. He thinks that maybe Larsen will get the notion out of his head if he gets to do it."

"So he saddled Volosin with him." I glared. "I'm an actor, Taylor, and this really does not sit well with me."

"Yeah, well, Brimhall likes Larsen. They were college roommates. He's going to be insufferable when he gets done with this gig."

"Every time I try to get him to take it seriously, he threatens to go running to Brimhall and have my secret exposed," Volosin said. "If I knew that it wouldn't come to that, I'd tell him to go ahead."

"I wish I could promise you that. Instead—"

The fact that the pack used this place a lot meant that fresh scent was harder to discern. Werewolves emerged from the shadows, enclosing us in a rough circle. They herded us toward a large open space in the middle of the floor. Others crouched on top of shelves, teeth glinting. Overhead, lights flicked on with cascading booms, ending with a final reverberation that illuminated us with harsh fluorescents. Aggressive males surrounded us, reeking of testosterone.

"I knew it was a damn trap," Ben said. "Taylor, you suck."

Taylor replied with a toothy smirk and stood beside his alpha. "Your opinion of your new beta is duly noted, Scruffy," Brimhall said. "Maybe he'll teach you some manners after I'm done with you."

"And maybe you'll both get an unpleasant surprise." Ben's mirthless grin should have filled Brimhall with terror, but apparently the idiot couldn't see a real threat when it stood right in front of him.

"You come into *my* territory and don't want to join my pack?" Brimhall sneered. "You have to *earn* the privilege of saying no."

Chin raised, Ben gave Brimhall a challenging stare. "So, if I lose, I'm forced to join this merry band of boneheads."

"As the omega wolf."

Derisive laughter accompanied that statement, and Ben took in the assembled pack—and smiled. I knew that expression. It meant that someone was about to receive a well-deserved and unexpected righteous beatdown. I smiled too.

"I win, and I get to walk away. That about the size of it?"

Brimhall's nose wrinkled. "You winning isn't in the cards, Scruffy, but, yeah."

"Seems a little, I dunno. Meh." Ben planted his feet and crossed his arms. "No. I win? We walk away, I get free passage in your territory in perpetuity, *and* you let my client out of this entirely idiotic blackmail scheme. Seriously, man, your guy is ruining his movie." Since he wasn't chopping his sentences and didn't smell stressed, I figured he wasn't too worried. This dropped my own stress level a notch.

"And all I get out of winning is you and your mate in my pack? Kind of one-sided, if you ask me."

"You don't think you'll lose, though, right?"

"*I* get your mate for myself."

Ben's eyes turned amber. Brimhall was treading dangerous ground, but he was oblivious.

"What she sees in you is a question for the ages anyway, and she's a beauty." He assessed me like he would a prize mare.

I bristled, unsure if this was a werewolf thing or an asshole thing. Ben had taught me a ton of self-defense. If Brimhall thought he could just take me, well. I had claws and fangs too.

Ben could beat this guy. He was a trained combat veteran, wholly used to trouncing much larger opponents. But being underestimated was one of the weapons in Ben's arsenal, so I pretended fear, putting my hand on his arm and alarm in my voice. "Ben, no, sweetie. I don't want to go with him, please."

Shoulders stiff and bristling, he went along with the subterfuge. "Well, you know, maybe I don't want to be with someone who doesn't think I can protect her. You know?"

"He's twice your size!"

"With half the brains."

"Hey!" Brimhall glared at Ben and then smiled at me. It wasn't a nice expression. "Don't worry, baby. I can protect you if Scruffy here can't."

"Just us," Ben said. "None of your pack gets to interfere. No weapons except what we have naturally."

Brimhall snorted. "Like I'll need anyone to help me kick your skinny ass. Agreed."

"Ben!" I clutched his arm. "*Please.*"

"Be all right, honey. And then we can discuss your attitude." My man had some acting chops of his own—but he winked as he divested himself of the jacket, shoulder holster and Ruger, and the contents of his pockets from his jeans, handing them off to me.

The last thing to come off was his large and ostentatious wedding ring. He clutched it for a moment before pressing it into my hand with a slight shiver that I would've missed if he hadn't been touching me. I surreptitiously stroked his palm, and he huffed out a soft breath.

The pack cleared a circular space about double the size of a boxing ring, ranging themselves around it and laying odds. Volosin stood by my side. "Is this wise?" he asked out of the corner of his mouth.

"It's the only shot you've got," I answered softly. "I'm not worried." Much.

Brimhall stripped his shirt off, flexing his muscles. He was huge and hairy, defined everywhere, the size of a granite cliff with about as much body fat.

Ben's shirt stayed right where it was—he didn't take it off in front of strangers unless he had a good reason, and "bullshit macho posturing" didn't count. His back was covered with a horrific network of scarring from his time as a POW, and he had an aversion to being stared at that had nothing to do with the wolf and dominance issues.

"Really?" Volosin asked. "Because you seemed—Oh." The penny dropped, and his lips turned up. "Nicely acted, Mrs. Lockwood."

"Don't spoil it."

Ben and Brimhall circled each other, assessing strengths and weaknesses. Brimhall charged with a growl, trying to use his greater weight to bear Ben to the floor. My man knew better than that and sidestepped easily, delivering a kick to Brimhall's knee and an elbow to his kidney in passing. Brimhall grunted and spun, grabbing for Ben again.

Ben ducked under his arms and slammed a one-two punch into Brimhall's solar plexus. He danced away as the other wolf reeled back.

"You little shit," Brimhall snarled, recovering. "I am gonna take you apart."

"You think?" Ben was loose and casual, running his mouth in the middle of a fight, just like always—the worse the fight, the more he talked, as a rule. This was actually tactical; he did it to keep his opponent off-balance and angry. Angry people made mistakes. "Because, you know, you haven't actually touched me yet."

"Oh, I can fix that." Brimhall charged again, and this time Ben grabbed his outstretched arm and used Brimhall's own momentum to sling him into a shelving unit as the pack scattered.

An atavistic frisson of excitement shivered through my body. My mate was fighting for me, and it sent a primal surge of warm electricity straight to the wolf part of my brain. Other parts of me, too.

Brimhall staggered away from the shelves with glassy eyes, shaking his head. Ben stepped in again and delivered a hard right jab to his nose. We all winced at the audible crunch, and blood sprayed. Brimhall howled, clapping his hands to his face. "I will break every bone in your body for that, Scruffy."

Ben was still smiling. It was a terrible expression. "Still haven't touched me. So far, you're a lot of sound and fury. Nothing significant here."

Brimhall snarled and extended three-inch claws, making a sweep at Ben's head that would have ended the fight if it'd connected properly. But Ben jerked under and spun past him again, kicking the same knee. It bent sideways and nearly spilled Brimhall to the floor. A row of three shallow cuts bled across Ben's cheek. "So we're using claws now," Ben said, and his own appeared, shorter than Brimhall's but just as sharp.

Brimhall was coming to the dawning realization that Ben was quick and agile and skilled, while he himself was none of these things. He'd clearly relied on brawn to win his previous battles, and had no idea how to fight someone who refused to close with him. He charged again, and Ben ducked, but not quite fast enough. Claws scored his shoulder and tore the shirt from his back.

The scent of my mate's blood made me whine down in my throat, and the wolves set up a roar that faded to mutters as they saw the scars. Pink, purple, and white monstrosities left by chains, whips, and knives. They coursed down Ben's back in a ridged network that disappeared into his waistline. I'd never gotten used to them, not really, and thinking about his captivity in Afghanistan and all he'd endured there made my chest ache. He'd told me that when the insurgents had taken everything else, running his mouth was all he had left.

"Better to be lucky than good," he said, the smile never leaving his face. He counterstruck, and his own claws left bloody furrows across Brimhall's ribs.

Brimhall swiped at him. This time Ben caught his arm, twisted it up behind his back, and banged him into the shelves again. "You can give up anytime, Nicky."

Brimhall growled and jerked his head backward, slamming it into Ben's forehead. "Not today, Scruffy." Ben staggered back, dazed, and I clenched my hands to keep them from shaking.

Brimhall spun and charged. This time, he grabbed Ben's bicep with a clawed hand, piercing through the skin and sending rivulets of blood flowing. He dragged Ben within reach and slammed a fist into his face, opening a cut across his eyebrow.

That meant his hands were busy. Ben didn't waste the opportunity; he punctured Brimhall's abdomen with the claws of both hands. Brimhall made a strangled noise and let go, pushing away. "You little—"

And then he shifted.

Like all our shifts, it was nearly instantaneous. Fur sprouted, his muzzle lengthened, claws and fangs popped out—and he tripled in mass into a shaggy, nearly horse-sized timber wolf. He roared and leaped at Ben in mid-shift.

I shouted "Ben!" and took a step forward. Volosin held me back.

But Ben flitted under Brimhall's jaws, changing, shaking out of his clothes, and slashing at the alpha's chest before springing away. Brimhall's dark gray fur contrasted with Ben's blond pelt stippled with black, with the hair growing white over his scars. The size difference was *marked*. As wolves, Brimhall outweighed Ben by a good hundred and fifty pounds and overtopped him by a foot. My gut rolled, and the metallic taste of fear filled my mouth. How could Ben defeat such a monster?

Brimhall was more graceful wolfed than human, but his moves were still no match for my mate's. Ben was here, there, everywhere, gliding in and out like quicksilver, tearing at Brimhall's legs, sides, face, balls, anything he could reach.

Brimhall's jaws weren't idle, however, and Ben couldn't avoid every slash in the close quarters. Ben's blood-soaked fur landed with wet splats on the concrete floor. My hackles rose as blood misted in the air, overwhelming my nostrils with the coppery tang.

Ben held his own, barely, still refusing to grapple with Brimhall. But the space was drastically smaller now, and Ben had less room to maneuver. My mouth went dry as Brimhall backed Ben against a wall of werewolves. Ben couldn't dodge the jaws that snapped shut on his foreleg with an explosive crack. Brimhall flexed his neck and threw Ben across the floor. He flipped over and over before ending upright—on three legs. The fourth was obviously, horribly broken, shattered bone poking through the shredded skin and torn muscle.

My heart banged painfully against my ribs. Sweat slicked my palms. Ben might actually lose this fight. I clenched my fist around his ring and wondered what would happen when I refused to go with the alpha.

Brimhall stalked Ben in a stiff-legged circle, ears and tail up, fur at full bristle. My mate pivoted on his back legs to keep facing him, his tail at half-mast and his lips peeled back in a silent snarl. Brimhall feinted, fast; once Ben committed, he turned and slammed him, one-two, with a shoulder and a hip. Ben rolled across the floor and fetched up against the shelving, sprawled on his stomach. Slavering, growling, snapping, Brimhall pursued him, stopping for an instant to stand bristling over him before striking.

But Ben down was far from Ben beaten. Even as Brimhall fastened his teeth across his shoulders, Ben snaked his head sideways. His jaws closed on Brimhall's left foreleg just below the elbow and *crunched* before Brimhall had fairly gotten a grip. Brimhall yelped and let go.

Ben scrambled to his feet and limped back into the center of the open space. They were both staggering now, but Ben was lighter and just a little more agile. His jaws snapped closed on Brimhall's hock with another crunch. The alpha howled and went down with a pair of broken legs.

Ben shifted his grip to Brimhall's throat, pinning him to the floor and letting out chainsaw growls. Brimhall struggled and bucked, but he had no leverage, and after a few seconds he relaxed, closing his eyes in surrender.

I could breathe again. I hadn't even realized I'd stopped.

Ben shook him once, for emphasis, and then let go. He stared full-on at the rest of the pack, ruff and tail and ears up, bleeding from dozens of wounds and on three legs, daring anyone to challenge him. They muttered and scraped the floor and wouldn't look directly at him. He jerked his chin sharply, once, and walked over to me on three stiff legs. Flumping his haunches down, he continued glaring.

"Well. Isn't this just super."

The wolfpack cringed as one when the tall, blonde Valkyrie stepped into their midst like she owned them. Every line of her body screamed "Alpha Bitch," and my own hackles rose in response. A few mutters back and forth of "Oh shit," "It's Rona," and "He's in for it now" rippled through the air.

Rona bared a fang at Brimhall. "Nick, you idiot, you look ridiculous. Shift and put some damn pants on."

Producing a pair of jeans from somewhere, Taylor slunk forward to his alpha and handed them over. Brimhall changed back to human and slipped them on. As wolves, we learned to keep a spare set of clothes around for unexpected shifts; but Ben didn't have his backpack with him this time, and he looked grouchy about it.

Rona turned her gaze to us. Ben leaned on me, and I put a protective hand on his shoulder. "And you," she continued, "are quite disruptive, aren't you."

"Nick started it," I said. "Ben just finished it."

"Of that I have no doubt."

"Rona—" Taylor began, but she lifted a peremptory hand, and he stopped as if suddenly gagged.

She stalked closer to us, and Ben cast a worried glance up at my face. Under normal circumstances he wouldn't hurt a female, but all bets were off when it came to protecting me—even with a compound fracture. "I got this, sugar," I told him. I'd play nice as long as she did, but like hell would I play submissive. She wasn't the alpha of me.

Rona's eyes flicked down to Ben, then back at me. A corner of her mouth curled up. "I see how it is. You two are lucky. Me, not so much."

"Are you with him?" I asked incredulously. "Because I was the prize in this fight, and that's not cool. Not that I would have gone with him—" I shot a glare at Brimhall. "—But it's the thought that counts. I thought wolves mate for life."

"Some do. Some are more fickle. Your mate was all right with you being the prize?"

"Not like he was gonna lose," I said, with some asperity. "It wasn't the only stake in the fight either. We expect Nick to uphold his end."

Rona eyed Volosin next. "This about Curtis?" He nodded, and she rolled her eyes. "Of course it is. Morons. You are all morons." She waved a hand that blatantly left Ben and me out of that assessment, but included Volosin. She pointed at the vampire's face. "Next time you have an issue with this pack, you come to *me*. Got it?"

Volosin's answer was prompt. "Yes, ma'am."

"As for you two." She frowned. "Adding you to the pack would be more trouble than it's worth."

"We're not interested in joining another pack. We have one of our own," I said. "But I'm sure we could come to some kind of mutual aid-and-non-aggression agreement." I made a face at Nick. "As long as your alpha male doesn't continue to be an idiot because someone half his size kicked his ass."

"Oh, he won't." Rona sounded very sure of that, and she stuck her hand out to me.

I shook it. "I'm Janni Lockwood. My husband Ben. Who would like some pants." Ben flattened his ears. He would not go human, naked, in front of a bunch of strangers. Rona snapped her fingers, and someone near Ben's size, but taller, because almost every male was taller than him, delved into a pack and came out with a pair of Levis that would work. Ben flipped his tail in thanks, but went behind a set of shelving to shift, carrying the jeans and his boots by the laces in his mouth.

It took him longer than usual to return wearing the untied boots, cradling his broken arm and grimacing. Ben had a terrorist-induced Very High Pain Threshold, and being werewolves with fast healing mitigated the hurt from injuries, but it looked ouchy. Brimhall, in fact, was still on the floor, holding his heel and moaning a little. "You shouldn't have threatened Janni, Brimhall," Ben said between his teeth. "I really don't like when people do that."

"I'll keep it in mind." Brimhall's voice was husky, and Rona bapped him upside the head. Gently.

"You better."

Rona's lips curled in a slow smile. "You'll do, Ben. You're welcome in our club any time."

"Yes, ma'am. Thank you, ma'am." He leaned on me a little. I could feel him shaking, though I didn't think anyone else noticed. "But for now, I'd really like to go get this arm taken care of. With rum."

"Of course you would." She eyed him, a little covetously, I thought, and I wrapped an arm around his waist. Rona sighed and ran her fingers through Brimhall's hair instead. He bowed his head into her touch, closing his eyes.

I nodded and squeezed Ben. "Let's get you fixed up, sugar."

Ben set his jaw, straightened, and strode out of the warehouse. It wasn't until he was in the limo that he collapsed backward with an exhausted sigh and closed his eyes, pale and shivering. "So that was fun," he said. "Ow, ow, ow."

My brow creased, and I examined him more closely. Some of the wounds were deeper than they appeared, and his arm looked terrible. "You got a first aid kit in here?" I asked Volosin.

"But of course." Volosin produced one, and I set to work patching my mate up as best I could with the limited supplies.

Ben made a strangled noise when I applied traction to put the compound fracture into a semblance of where it belonged. Wolf healing meant I had to do that sooner rather than later, or it would heal all wrong.

"Rum," Ben said between clenched teeth. "Now."

"It was well done, *vilkas*," Volosin said, handing him a tall glass filled with Bacardi 151 over ice. "At first I thought you had made a great error, but I did not entirely realize your skill at hand-to-hand combat. Your reputation notwithstanding."

"Most people don't, until they're in the middle of it," Ben said. "Still. Ow. That was my first serious fight with another wolf since the first guy."

"Would you like medical attention?" Volosin asked. "The veterinarian at my pit bull rescue could see to it, and ask no awkward questions."

Ben eyed the broken arm sourly. "Probably a good idea. I wouldn't like it to heal crooked." He drained the glass and held it out for another rum, then a third, and a fourth—and finally relaxed. "Hoo, that's better." His grin was weary and sardonic. "They look at me and see 'small, unassuming baby seal,' not 'former Army Ranger with a chip on his shoulder.' Gave Brimhall a nasty shock."

"He deserved it," I said. "All those things he said. I'm glad you broke his nose."

"Crushed his heel and busted his arm pretty good too. That'll take a while to heal even for a werewolf." Ben lifted an eyebrow at Volosin. "So. Looks like you can kick Larsen off your set with no repercussions. You got someone lined up to take his place?"

"I have someone in mind, yes, if she would like the part." Volosin eyed me. "She, too, did well on this job and should be rewarded."

I froze. "Me?"

"You. You were convincing in your subterfuge, and I have no doubt you can hold your own for action sequences. The part was written for a man, but—" He waved his hand. "That is of no importance."

"You won't rewrite it so I'm the damn love interest? I hate that."

He looked puzzled. "Oh, but I thought—"

"No."

Both he and Ben stared at me.

"No," I repeated. "I won't do it. Explain to me why in every damn action movie, if there's a woman at all, she doesn't get to just kick ass and take names, but there's gotta be a romance in there. It's dumb, it's out of place, and there's no reason for it except a lack of creativity on the part of the writers. If you have something where I don't gotta kiss someone just because the audience expects it, give me a call. Otherwise, no."

"You are an unusual woman, Janni Lockwood," Volosin said, rubbing his chin. He nodded decisively. "Done, then. I will make what small revisions it will need right away. And you will not have to play a romantic part."

I blinked a little, and stuttered. "Well. I guess I'll say a tentative yes to that?"

"Good." He smiled and clapped his hands, once. "I also have another script in development. Again, written for a male lead. But I think we can tailor it for you instead. A heist movie. No love interest, just good friends. What do you say?"

Warily, I said, "Friends. No benefits?"

"No benefits. We start filming in six months, after we finish the current one. Tell me yes."

"I. Well. I'd . . . have to see the scripts first, of course." Ben had a slow grin going, and I took his hand. "But. Pending that. Thank you?"

"Excellent! I will email you the scripts tomorrow, but keep in mind that they will change a little—not much!—from their present form." He smiled and shook my hand, then Ben's. "It was a pleasure doing business with you both."

"Thank you, Mr. Volosin." I was breathless. "Thanks so much."

"I envy you your wife, Mr. Lockwood," Volosin said. "She is a remarkable lady."

Ben wrapped an arm around my waist, just a tiny bit possessive. I liked it. "Just goes to show that the women run our lives, man." He buried his nose in my hair and inhaled. "I wouldn't have it any other way."

ABOUT THE AUTHOR

JULIE FROST writes every shade of speculative fiction and lives in Utah with her family—six guinea pigs, three humans, a tripod calico cat, and a kitten who thinks she's a warrior princess—and a collection of anteaters and Oaxacan carvings, some of which intersect. In her (ha!) spare time, she enjoys birdwatching and wildlife photography.

Her short fiction has appeared in *Writers of the Future Vol. 32*, *The District of Wonders*, *Cosmos*, *Unlikely Story*, *Plasma Frequency*, *Stupefying Stories*, and many other venues. Her first novel, *Pack Dynamics*, was released in 2015 by WordFire Press. "Bad Actors" takes place in the universe of that novel, not long after the events therein.

She whines about writing, a lot at http://agilebrit.livejournal.com/. You can connect with her on Twitter @JulieCFrost, or on Facebook at julie.frost.7967. She also has an Amazon page as Julie Frost.

ABOUT THE STORY

"Bad Actors" was difficult for me to write. This story is set in the universe of my novel *Pack Dynamics*, and I'd often thought I needed to write a story from Janni's point of view, focusing on her hopes and dreams and what she wants, along with how she deals with her husband's Bundle o' Issues. However, anyone who knows me also knows that (for whatever reason) I have a hard time writing female POV stories. I can write Ben in my sleep. Janni, not so much.

It was written as part of a short-story NaNoWriMo push where I challenged myself to write several short stories totaling fifty thousand words in a month. In January, not November, because November is a non-starter for a project of that magnitude, at least for me. I sat down and outlined it, as one does, and then when it was its turn I scribbled the thing. It actually came together pretty well, in my opinion . . .

And then came the edits for the anthology you're holding in your hand.

Our Dr. Bob is a taskmaster, yo. He gave me a lot of editorial comments, some of which I followed and some of which I didn't. Part of the issue was that I had just put the finishing touches on Book Two of *Pack Dynamics*, and I hadn't decided where this story fell in the canon. If it came after, they'd know what a bad alpha looks like--and think and react accordingly. If it came before, well, they're new at this whole "supernatural clientele" thing.

I decided that it comes between the first and second books, and so Ben and Janni, being newly minted werewolves, make some mistakes and have some misunderstandings about the new world they've been thrust into. So they're learning, along with the reader. I hope that you, dear reader, will enjoy the ride.

What is beauty? Where does it lie?
In the eye, in the heart, in the soul?
Is it the potential within us that others desire for themselves?
Or is it accepting one is worthy of love?

....

IN THE HEART OF
THE FLESH

SCOTT R. PARKIN

Beauty isn't skin deep. It's not in the skin at all, but in the cells of the
skin and the bones and the organs. Not on the surface but in the heart
of the flesh, in a gene pattern that was a mistake of nature until Everett's
Virus reversed the error and made me beautiful.

Beauty is in the fertility granted by an XXY chromosome—a
broken X that made me something a little more than a man but a little less
than a woman. Beauty is in the fact that I'm one of only two thousand fertile
women on the planet.

It's just short of six o'clock—time to start working the crowd.
Amber is up on stage one. She's petite like a china doll, with small, firm
breasts that complement her tiny figure. She uses the poles on the corners
of the stage, gripping them with her arms or legs and spinning around first
one, then the other. She shaves and her bare pubis shows only occasionally
as she moves. The men lean forward, but they see little. I wish I had her skill.

Most tables are already filled and all the couches are. The crowd
mostly ignores Amber. They're waiting for me.

I hurry along the back wall, toward the mirrored stage door. I always do a stage dance before I mingle so I can gauge the crowd. It's a different game each night. I usually start with a man; the right one will not only buy a drink and a lap dance, but a bed dance as well. The best ones come with friends. They like the attention and pay well to keep it coming.

Sometimes I pick a woman. She'll scrutinize my body, as if fertility is visible to the naked eye, that by looking at my flesh she can see what's been taken from her. She can almost make me feel sorry for her.

Almost.

The crowd murmurs as I walk past. I won't look at faces until I'm on stage. I keep my eyes up. They're not interested in *me* and they can't have me; they want Jasmine.

The walls are punctuated by picture frames enclosing mirrored glass decorated with silhouettes of men and women coupling. I smile at the glass and wink; Andrew, the club manager, is behind the glass. I blow kisses at each window. We have enough security behind that wall to stop a riot.

I slip into the green room and shrug out of my long jacket. I dress quickly—a white bikini and a sequined wrap. Sometimes I can convince myself that I'm attractive if not beautiful, but tonight all I see is straight hips, flat chest, heavy dark hair on my arms and legs and belly. I used to shave, tried to look as appealing as I could—at least to myself. But not anymore.

They come to see my flesh because it's rare, not pleasing.

Amber's music ends and I hear a smattering of applause. Amber skips down the steps from the stage as the door whispers shut. There's frustration in her green eyes. "Your turn," she says.

"It'll warm up," I say.

Her eyes flash, then she nods and pretends to be comforted. "Yeah, I think it will. Knock 'em out."

I should hate Amber for her beauty, but she's the only dancer who treats me like a person. She must've been kind even before Everett's. I wish I'd known her then.

My song starts and Jeremy announces me. "Club XTreme is pleased to present Jasmine!" I hear an audible murmur and chairs scuffing the carpet. Amber sighs but doesn't look up. I'm angry for her, and that gives me the energy I need to put myself on display. Again.

I've picked a slow song with a strong bass push, and I let the music pull me out into the middle of the stage. I turn a slow circle, my arms lifted and spread as though worshiping a god of fertility. I look at the men at the table nearest the stage; they lean forward, lips parted in anticipation. A woman leans back in her chair and pretends nonchalance, but I see tension in the lines of her shoulders as the men around her gawk. She's pretty, with a trim figure and long brown hair. Finally she turns to stare at me and I see her confusion.

I reach back and flick the catch on my top with one hand, shake the straps off my shoulders while holding the thin cloth to my chest with the other hand, then I let it flutter to the ground. I run my hands over my neck and chest, then caress my slight breasts and fondle my tiny nipples. Warm air from overhead vents heats the stage, but every time the front door opens a cool breeze with the scent of diesel exhaust and the must of this morning's rain penetrates the warmth and I shiver as my skin pimples. It's not unpleasant.

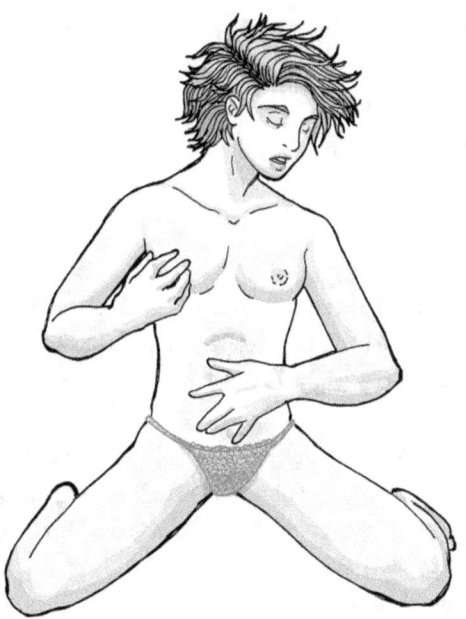

I turn again, then squat down with my knees wide apart and rub my hands along the insides of my thighs. I hook my thumbs in the waist of my panties and stand up, pulling the elastic away from my hips, pulling down enough to stretch the cloth but not enough to reveal myself.

The men stare at my hips, waiting—they're interested only in that part of me. The women look at my chest or into my eyes, but their gazes are as cold as the men's are hot.

I move to the back of the stage, toward the door. As I take the faceted knob in my right hand I pull my panties down to reveal the curve of my ass but no more as I step through and pull it closed behind me.

I hear muffled groans as the music ends. But they will stay until they see what they came to see. Even then they will be disappointed—to the naked eye my body is just like their wives' and girlfriends' and mistresses' bodies. Just flesh.

I dress quickly and peek at the crowd through a crack in the door. I know most of them here tonight—good customers, but the same old fare.

I'm ready to step out when I see someone different. He sits in the couch just outside the door and I see him reflected in the mirrors on the opposite wall. He is tall, with dark brown hair, round glasses, and a bushy van dyke beard. His eyes look up at the dancer's face, not down at her crotch. He watches but he is not entranced.

He's my target for tonight.

YOU LEARN YOU'RE different the day you turn six. You're taking a bubble bath and Mommy comes in. You fling soapy foam, and she laughs. The bubbles float in little globs, like islands on a shallow sea. Mommy kneels by the tub and rinses your hair.

You stand and Mommy wraps you in a big soft towel. You dry yourself and give the towel back to Mommy, who hangs it on the bar on the back of the door. When she turns around, her smile fades and her eyes frown.

"Are you okay, baby?" Mommy asks.

You laugh and shake your head so water flips off your hair. "No, Mommy," you say, "I'm all wet!"

Mommy grabs your arm and pulls you up on the cold toilet seat. She looks at your private parts, touches you.

"Does that hurt?" Mommy asks.

You squirm. "No," you say in a small voice.

Mommy pokes you and asks questions, then sends you to your room to get dressed. You're afraid now. Partly because Mommy touched your private places even though she's said you should never let anyone touch you there. Mostly, you're afraid because Mommy's afraid.

That afternoon you see a doctor who touches you more, but not gently like Mommy did. He pulls and spreads you, makes you lie down with your legs apart and puts things in you, cold metal that hurts. Mommy and Daddy stay away, do nothing to stop it. You refuse to cry even though you really want to.

Over the coming days Mommy and Daddy say little to you or to each other. Finally, Mommy comes to talk to you in your room.

"Reenie, honey, you need to go to the hospital again."

You try to be brave, but your lip quivers and tears slip from your eyes. "No. Please," you whisper.

Mommy hugs you close. "I'm sorry, Reenie-baby, but you have to. You have a problem with your . . . with your privates and the doctor is going to fix it."

You begin to cry. "Is it going to hurt, like last time?"

"No, honey. The doctor will stick you with a needle, then you'll fall asleep. When you wake up everything will be okay."

You frown. "I don't want a shot—they hurt."

Mommy touches your face. "I'm sorry. But it has to happen. It has to."

You understand the look in Mommy's eyes; it will do no good to argue. "Okay," you whisper.

"We'll leave first thing in the morning. I love you, honey." She hurries out of the room.

That night you try to figure out what's wrong. Everyone asked if it hurt, but it never did. If you squeeze some places it gives you a dull ache in your stomach, but that's normal—it's always been that way, though that part used to be inside and only started poking out a couple of weeks ago.

You go to the hospital. They have you breathe from a mask with tubes and hoses like scuba divers wear, then ask you to count backward from a hundred. You tell them it's hard to count forward to a hundred, how are you gonna do it backward? You hear laughing as if from a long way away, and then there's darkness.

When you wake up your privates hurt and when you reach down you find that you're covered in bandages and a little tube runs from under them into a bag. The nurse tells you it's okay to pee whenever you need, that the tube will carry it to the bag and everything will be okay. The nurse is right; it goes through the tube into the bag without any effort on your part.

They take the bandages off two days later and say you now have to go to the bathroom like normal, then you go home. Mommy and Daddy smile and tell you everything is okay now.

That night you touch yourself where it hurts most and find that parts of you are gone, the parts Mommy was worried about, the parts the doctor tugged on and squeezed the most.

You wait weeks, then months and don't say anything. But the parts never grow back, and Mommy and Daddy seem to think that's okay. But you know better. They've removed part of you, made you less than you were before.

They said it was going to be okay, but it's not; you can't imagine it ever will be again.

"BLACK LEATHER COAT on couch one bought you a drink." Andrew points at the man I've already chosen. I'm never wrong.

I cross the room and smile as heads turn. I can feel their attention like a breeze on my back, but no one will touch. A guy tried to take me once a couple months ago, grabbed me on my way out to the car after work. The club muscle beat him until I thought he was dead; there was more blood on the pavement than I thought possible from only one man.

There have been others—taggers, stage door Johnnies, ordinary men willing to die for a chance to have a viable child—but I have protection and never see them. I've seen scuffles in corners of the club; I ignore them and don't think about it.

I walk up to the couch. The man in the leather coat is watching the next dancer—a Polynesian girl who calls herself Lotus. She is thick and soft, with big, big breasts that seem like they should pull her over forward. I wait until the dance ends and the man looks up at me.

"My name is Jasmine," I say and reach down to the small round cocktail table in front of the couch. A fresh glass of soda water with a twist of lime sits next to a Diet Coke; I take the soda water. "Thanks. I get really thirsty when I dance." I point at the couch. "May I sit?"

The man moves over a little. "Sure," he says.

I sit down and cross my legs, then snuggle in close to him and put my hand on his chest. His breath smells like mint and Diet Coke. He sits straight up and down, stiff; but he looks me in the face and smiles. He says, "Hi."

"What's your name?" I ask.

"Philip Astin," he says and offers a hand.

I smile and shake his hand. "Is this your first time in a dance club?" I ask.

"Is it that obvious?" I nod and he laughs. "I've always wondered what went on inside these places."

"What you see is what you get. Pretty straight-forward," I say. "So what brought you here to Club XTreme?"

"I saw it on my way to the hotel," he says. I wait for him to mention the name of the hotel and his room number. He shrugs. "That's it," he says. "I was just curious.

I smile but he's beginning to make me nervous. "Do you know who I am?" I ask.

"The waiter said your name is Jasmine."

I nod and wait for a reaction, but there is none. Nothing. My stage name is well known since the plague, and my occupation is even better known.

No one comes here because they're curious about clubs in general. He's playing a game. I want to know what kind.

"So why did you buy me a drink?"

He shrugs. "I got the impression that's what you're supposed to do. The waiter said you pay to dance and make your money back on tips and drinks." He smiles. "I just wanted to do my part."

It irritates me that I can't find his angle. I grind my teeth and gasp as my sore tooth sends a jolt through my jaw.

"Are you okay?"

"Just a bad tooth," I say.

"If you just take an aspirin, it might feel a little better. It works surprisingly well."

I stand up. I don't know why I should care whether this man wants me or not, but it's suddenly very important that he react, that he look at my ugly body with the same lust as the others.

"Part of the drink is a lap dance," I say. "Do you know what that is?" He shakes his head. "You sit there and I dance for you. Put your hands flat on the cushions while I dance. Keep your mouth closed until I finish. Otherwise, just watch and enjoy."

A new song has started. Usually I wait until a song is half-way through before I do a lap dance, but I don't care this time. He will react correctly if it takes two songs.

I step between his knees and touch his hair, his face, his chest, letting my hand drop down and away, brushing his thigh.

I sit on one of his legs and put my arms around his neck, push my chest in his face and slowly stand up. His beard is soft and tickles a little as it moves down my chest, catches in my top, then brushes my ribs, my belly. It feels sensuous, tingly. It makes me angry.

I stand up on the couch and straddle him, push my pubis in his face, just for a moment, then I pull back. There are things he can't do during a lap dance; there are also things I can't do. I look down; nothing.

I slide off to one side and put one leg behind his neck, the other across his lap. I arch my hips up and pump them up and down while I let the leg in his lap move up toward his waist. I look at him and his eyes are locked on my face. Finally, his eyes flick down to my crotch then back up to my face. I touch him with my leg and there is a swelling. But his eyes are still soft—it's just a natural reaction, a physical betrayal.

The song ends and he smiles. "That was quite an experience," he says. "Thank you."

I should say something, but I'm confused. "I have to get ready," I say and turn away.

I hurry to the back of the room, to the office door between two mirrors, and slam the door shut behind me. "Watch the guy on couch one. There's something wrong with him."

Andrew nods toward the glass next to the door. "I watched the whole time and he never did anything."

"That's the point! It's not natural." Tears form in my eyes and I wipe them away. I am not a weepy child; I'm a professional. "Just watch him."

Andrew nods and I turn to leave. As the door closes behind me, I hear him mutter, "It's not that unusual, Irene."

MOM DOESN'T TALK about it again until you're eleven. You bring home a note about the special girls-only science class tomorrow. You go into the science lab and there's paper across the window on the door, and the blinds are pulled. The teacher shows a film about the changes the girls will soon experience.

Mom reads the note and sits for a long moment before she looks up. "You don't have to go to this if you don't want to."

"Why not? It's for all the girls."

Mom sighs. "We've never talked much about it, Reenie, but you aren't exactly like the other girls. There's a good chance you will never have the same . . . changes as the others." She looks down at her hands then back up. "You've always been different from the other girls, you know that."

You bite your lip, but you can't stop the words from spilling out. "Maybe because I'm not a girl at all? Maybe because I'm really a boy and you goofed up when I was six and picked the wrong way?"

Mom stands up. "You will not speak that way to me, Irene Olkewicz!" She blinks a few times, then the anger drops from her face. "You're a girl, Reenie—don't ever doubt that. Your body made a mistake and grew some things that don't belong to girls. But you *are* a girl; you have all of what makes a girl."

"Then why don't you want me to go tomorrow?" you ask.

Mom hugs you. "I never said you shouldn't go, I just said you don't have to if you don't want." She holds your shoulders. "You're a girl, but it's possible that it might take longer for you to change from a girl to a woman—or it might not happen at all. It's our fault—mine and your father's—not yours. We're sorry."

"I'm going," you say and walk out.

You know more than your parents imagine. You found the medical reports in the crawl space, in an old trunk with a broken lock. You took notes of things to look up at the library, things like XXY and intersex and Mediero's Syndrome. You learned that you were really a boy even though you had a full XX chromosome set; the presence of the Y made you a boy no matter how many Xs you had. Intersex meant you were once both a boy and a girl. Mediero's Syndrome is a special case of something called Klinefelter's Syndrome that happens when you're both XXY and intersex and your body splits the difference and gives you all the parts of both boys and girls.

The report said you had a full set of female organs and that the best choice was raise you as a girl. Perhaps your parents weren't wrong after all.

Still, you can't help but wonder.

You end up going to the special class and learning all the things you already taught yourself from books. You smile when they talk about pubic hair—you started getting that months ago; maybe it will all work out right after all.

Time passes and nothing happens. By twelve, most of the other girls are changing shape. Their hips are widening and many have developed breasts. You're still as straight and shapeless as the boys.

By fourteen *all* the other girls have begun to develop. In gym class some use their period as an excuse to not take showers. You pretend. By fifteen all of the girls have their period and all have at least swellings of breasts. You look the same as you did when you were eleven, except that your pubic hair has developed into a wide, black patch and you have grown heavy, dark hair on your arms and legs and upper lip. By sixteen the other girls notice your mannish figure and abundance of hair. But they especially notice your utter lack of breasts and call you names like "flat face" and "the cliff"—names that mean nothing to the boys, but that mark you as a target to the girls.

You lose your virginity at sixteen. You're damaged and decide to take advantage of it. There are always boys who don't care who they bang, and you gain a reputation as an easy lay. And then only as a thing, an object. Even the popular guys practice with you, though none ever look at you except under the sheets.

By the time you turn seventeen, you understand that your only value is in giving sex and the fact that you'll never get pregnant. But you can do the rest of it, and if that's all there is, then that's what you'll take.

Through it all, your parents are silent. Your father acts like you aren't even there, and your mom treats you like a guest or a stranger. After a while, you decide they're right. You have to rely on yourself.

No one else cares.

FOR MY NEXT dance I cut straight to the chase. In ten seconds I strip off my panties and bra and stand with arms and legs out, listening to the hoots of men throughout the club. Philip is looking up at me.

I face him and rub my hands over my body, down my torso and up the insides of my thighs. I sit down and point my feet at him, then spread my legs wide and run my hands up my thighs again, stopping just short of touching myself. I roll over on hands and knees and point my ass at him. Through it all he looks in my eyes or doesn't look at all beyond curious glances.

A man on the other side of the house shouts and tosses a folded bill up on the stage. It's a twenty. I turn to that end of the stage and do the same moves that I did for Philip. The men hoot and yell and fling more money up on the stage. But I keep my eyes on Philip, looking for any sign that he is interested in my sex, in my fertility—any sign that he's like these others.

The dance ends and I exit the stage. I walk past couch one without looking down, then head out into the house and work the crowd. I give a half-dozen bed dances at a hundred dollars—I am fully nude as I writhe on the bed while the patron sits on chair six feet away. I give a half-dozen lap dances and a dozen table dances at fifty per. The men's eyes are always glazed by thoughts they think secret—fantasies of productive sex that will reassure them of their manhood.

There's nothing I can say or do for them, so I dance.

Near ten o'clock Amber takes me aside. "Are you going to talk to him?" she asks.

"Who?" I ask without looking at her.

She says nothing and I finally glance up; she smiles. "He might be real."

"No," I shake my head.

"It is possible," she whispers, then Amber hugs me and whisks away, past couch one. She hesitates just a moment, then moves off into the darkness and is lost in a haze of cigarette smoke.

She's right. I have to face this man. He's made this a bad night. Though I've made as much money as ever, tonight it's unsatisfying. I want to know why.

I sit down next to him and reach for my drink. It's watery and warm, the fizz long since lost in melted ice. I say, "Hi," and take a long drink.

"Hi," he says. "How's your tooth?"

I blink. "What?"

"You said your tooth was sore. Did you try the aspirin?"

I nod. "Yeah. It worked. It feels fine."

We sit in silence for a moment, and I'm not uncomfortable for the lack of words. I don't need to entertain this one—I didn't know how.

After a few quiet seconds he says, "Why do you dance? You don't need to. You could pick your situation; every wealthy family in the world would pay to make you happy."

So he does know who I am. Bastard.

"If I take money it's wrong."

He raises an eyebrow. "And working here isn't?"

"They can't touch me. I control the situation."

"Don't you feel some kind of responsibility?" he says.

I laugh and make a picture frame with my hands. "Irene Olkewicz's Womb: National Historic Site." I drop my hands. "The Fed tried, then backed off when I agreed to give them my eggs every 26 days. The Fed sells them to privileged families, then sells them the hormones that'll let their broken bodies carry to term. Sometimes." I look down and sigh. "Now the Fed just reminds me of my 'duty to humanity' to procreate and replenish the supply of future American mothers." I nod toward a big man seated near the front door. "And I let them post their guards to make sure I don't get hurt."

"I'm surprised they even let you do it."

I raise an eyebrow. "This is America. They can't stop me."

"That won't work for long."

I stare. He actually cares.

"I'll deal with it. That's what I do."

He touches my hand and says, "I'm sorry."

He reaches into the inside pocket of his coat and I notice his wedding ring; usually the married men take their rings off before they come into the club.

He pulls out a wallet and opens it. "A family is a wonderful thing—the best thing in the world. I have a little girl. Her name is Kimberly."

She's a beautiful child, with a big smile and rosy cheeks. Her hair is dark, almost black, and she looks five years old.

I say, "She was caught in the plague." It's not a question.

He sighs. "She was two. All I can hope is that science comes up with some answers."

We talk—about families and the plague and what might happen in the next few years. We talk about its effect on normal women, at their utter inability to produce viable eggs or carry to term; about the cruelty of a weak virus that did its work, then died out. Andrew signals. It's time for my last dance of the night. I stand up.

I look at the framed glass over the couch. The silhouette is a man and a woman holding hands and walking together, the only picture in the club that isn't about sex. I glance down at Philip and it occurs to me that it does have to do with sex, but with an important difference. It's the difference between fucking and making love. I smile at Philip.

"I'll be back in a minute," I say and move to the stage.

The men at table one look back at him, hard jealousy on their faces. I smile. For once they have good cause.

YOU'RE TWENTY-TWO WHEN the plague hits. It's a viral mutation of Anthrax that attacks only female pigs and humans; they call it Everett's Virus after the man who isolated it.

In only three months the damage is done.

You wake up at two a.m. four months after the outbreak with cramps that make you double over and push on your hips as hard you can. The pain passes and you sit, crying quietly. You feel wetness between your legs and find that it's blood.

You go to the emergency room. You know about the plague, know that there's nothing it can do to damage your non-existent fertility. You wait hours to be seen—women line the halls seeking reassurance that they have somehow escaped the plague's effects. One by one they leave with ashen faces.

When you make it into the examining room, the doctor looks up with a haggard face, her own loss etched into her features. "I can't tell you what you want to hear," she says.

You shake your head. "That's not why I'm here. There are cramps and blood. It hurts."

The doctor examines you, then stands up. "I'll be back in a minute," she says and hurries out of the room. In a moment she's back with two other doctors, followed by a half-dozen lab techs carting equipment. They poke, prod, draw blood, analyze, and discuss.

Finally she takes you aside. "I've looked at your history; have you been sterile all your life?" You nod and the doctor half-laughs, then turns serious.

"Not anymore. The pain and blood are all part of a normal, healthy period."

You hear a buzzing in the hallway and see one of the technicians—a man—talking to a small knot of people and waving his hand toward your examining room. Then he looks up and for a moment it's as though he were gazing at a precious toy, a wanted thing. You're not a person or even a patient. Just meat.

They make appointments for you to come back so they can study you, find out why you are now fertile when everyone else is not. It's more than you can think about at the moment. As you walk down the hallway, though, you begin to understand. Women on both sides of the hall stare at you, dark anger in their eyes. They look at your flat chest, your gangly limbs. They shake their heads, and a few whisper as you go by. "Freak."

You drive home. Nothing has changed, it never will. Before, you were an outcast for your sterility; now, for your fertility. You will never be one of these people, never belong among them. You feel your heart go cold and know it will never thaw.

I DANCE, BUT the edge is gone. The crowd still screams and flings money at the stage, but now I feel wrong. The air is rank with the smell of sweaty bodies, with the musk of lust. I keep covered for as long as I can. When I do strip I turn my back and show them only a little, and then for only an instant.

The song ends and I rush off stage, change out of my costume and hurry out. He's not there. I go to the door and look for an occupied car, for someone pulling onto the street. Nothing.

I turn to go inside and Andrew stands there. "Looking for the black leather coat on couch one?" he asks.

I nod. "His name is Philip." Andrew offers his arm.

We go to his office. I stand quietly for a moment, then say, "I would have done anything for him."

Andrew sighs. "That's why he left, I think."

My body shakes as I think about what might have been. For a moment I see it dispassionately as though it were someone else's life. Then it hits me.

Philip cared about Irene Olkewicz, not Jasmine.

It *was* possible.

The ache in my stomach grows. Has legitimate anger blinded me to something better? God knows nearly twenty years of hurt have led to nothing worth knowing. Is there really another choice?

For the first time I can remember I'm not angry at the world in general, but at those who have actually hurt me. I see that most haven't. I try to decide what that means.

Andrew doesn't say anything. I'm glad.

He's right, of course. If Philip had stayed it would have led to something more. Eventually I would have wondered if the whole thing had been a scam, a skillful manipulation. I suspect I'll never see him again.

Suddenly I want to talk to Amber. I frown. No, her name is Mary Harvey; I want to talk to Mary. I want to talk to a person, not a role or a name or a façade. I need to find out if there really is a difference.

She's in the dressing room, changed and ready to go. She studies my face. "Irene?" She sets down her bag, steps across the room and takes my hand. "Are you okay?"

I nod, start to speak, cough, and try again. "I think . . . I mean . . ." I take a deep breath. "I don't know."

Mary reaches out, pulls me close. "It's okay, Irene."

I didn't understand how hard I had worked to keep myself safe until Mary Harvey hugged me and the tears finally came. Tears for all the things that had been lost through the years, for the pain and the anger and the sorrow. Tears for Mary Harvey and the mindless virus that had robbed her of so much. She deserved none of it.

And tears for myself, because I didn't deserve it either. None of us did; not even those who were privileged before.

The world suffered enough from the aftermath of a horrible disease. It did no good to be part of either the suffering or the disease.

I had a choice.

There's a knock at the house door and I hear Andrew's voice. "Are you okay? Do I need to come in?"

Mary steps back. "You want to talk some more?"

I nod and she picks up her bag and fishes her car keys out of a side pocket. "Whenever you're ready," she says and steps out the back.

I open the door for Andrew. He's alone, and I can see honest concern on his face.

"I'll see you tomorrow night," I say before he can speak. "I'm good."

I push through the back door and into the cool, clear night. It must have rained during the show. Everything glistens and the air smells clean. Mary pulls up in her silver coupe and pushes open the passenger door. I hesitate only for an instant, then step in.

"You want to stop somewhere, or is canned soup at home okay?" Mary asks.

I realize I have no idea where she lives or if she has a family. I've worked so hard to keep a safe, polite distance that I never bothered to learn even the simplest facts about her life outside Club Xtreme. Or Andrew's. I pretended it was professionalism, but it was really simple cowardice.

Even then, they were both there when I needed them.

They *are* my friends; it's time I get to know them. And, perhaps, learn how to *be* a friend, as well.

"Soup sounds good," I say.

ABOUT THE AUTHOR

SCOTT R. PARKIN is an author, publisher, and critic as well as co-host of the *Stories for Nerds* podcast. Scott has sold more than forty short stories to a wide variety of venues in science fiction, fantasy, literary-academic, romance, slice of life, and other genres. Recent sales include both *1st and Starlight* and *2nd and Starlight*, *A Kiss Is Still a Kiss*, *Digital Fantasy Fiction*, and the *Fiction River* anthology series. He's won prizes in a variety of contests and has also appeared in *Marion Zimmer Bradley's Fantasy Magazine* and *Galaxy*. He also records audio books when he has the chance.

Scott remains the most nearly successful, almost prize-winning, author in *Writers of the Future* contest history. Over a period of nearly twenty-five years, he earned more than a dozen honorable mentions, nine Semi-finalists, and a record-breaking five Finalists in the contest before finally being selected as a contest winner in *Writers of the Future Vol. 31* with his experimental short "Purposes Made for Alien Minds." You can find a selection of his stories on Amazon.com under the name Scott R. Parkin. He is also on Facebook as Scott Parkin.

ABOUT THE STORY

"In the Heart of the Flesh" arose out of a combination of a business trip, interest in the impact of biology on perception, and a thought exercise on the nature of beauty. It is the second of my five Finalists in the *Writers of the Future* contest, and represents the turning point where I began to understand the short story form and started to consistently write publishable fiction.

I've always been fascinated by the ways that physical form and individual biochemistry can impact both self-perception and how others treat us. I'm also fascinated by the arbitrary ways that time, place, and culture play into coloring our perceptions of social value.

For example, for much of human history feminine beauty has been defined in terms of youth, evidence of sexual readiness, and signs of wealth. Pre-Renaissance European art tended to portray feminine beauty as generally short, pale-white, and pudgy, whereas modern concepts focus on taller, thinner, more tanned, and athletic women. In both cases, the basis of beauty seems to center on visible evidence of a social concept of wealth:

idle time and the pursuits available to those who are not required to work for their sustenance.

That idea led me to consider my own appreciation of precious metals and gemstones. I vastly prefer rich blue stones to diamonds, and silver or platinum to gold. So what made one gem more inherently valuable than another? The short answer is scarcity. Gold is far rarer than silver, and sapphires far more common than diamonds. Likewise, wealthy idleness was (until that last century) uncommon; and thus we've tended to focus our concepts of beauty on that which is most rare.

I've noodled on these thoughts for years, but didn't generate a story idea until I visited the Microsoft campus a couple of decades back to attend a development conference (I'm a computer technologist by trade). On my way back to the hotel one evening, I noticed a strip club with a neon "XXXtreme" sign on the roof. Many disparate ideas that I had considered over the years snapped into place; and the narrative simply appeared to me as a completed piece in that single, startling instant.

What conditions might cause someone who had always been perceived as ugly to suddenly be seen as beautiful? What impact would that sudden desirability have on her own psyche after a lifetime of being told she was beneath notice? How might that social whiplash further injure her, and what might her responses be?

This is one of the few stories I've written that sprung fully-formed into my mind. I normally take a far more workmanlike and pragmatic approach where I develop the plot and themes as I go and play the question-game to generate the details. This tale also led to the most frustratingly positive rejection I've ever received when the editor said she loved it and wanted to buy it—but she had just bought another story that was too similar. If only I had submitted two weeks earlier . . .

Which underscores one of the most important things for aspiring authors to keep in mind: often we're writing at a professional level for quite a while before we catch the right editor on the right day, and finally get that break. A year after receiving this rejection I gave up in despair and stopped writing. When I came back a dozen years later, it took me only two years to win a prize in the *Writers of the Future* contest and to sell eight of my next ten stories to national and international publishers.

You can't win if you're not in the game.

I hope you enjoyed reading "In the Heart of the Flesh" as much as I enjoyed writing it.

From creation to the world's end, the story of a warrior and a blade,
and the strength of love.
A tale of Jewish mysticism.

....

SHATTERED VESSELS

KARY ENGLISH AND
ROBERT B. FINEGOLD, M.D.

I

If I live to tell this tale to my children, I will say it was the dagger that both saved and took my life, but I want you to know here and now that this is a lie.

Kindness saved me.

II

IN A LONG-AGO time, in the city of Nineveh on the banks of the river Tigris, my name was Aššur. True, I held other names during the six-and-twenty centuries that followed. Some I took for myself, and others I was given—Luminous, Light-bringer, Loukas—and one whispered by a dread voice only I could hear: *Shevirah*, the breaker of vessels.

This name I rejected in the end, closed my ears to it when it hissed like the scratching of talons inside my skull. *Shevirah* also means "fragile," but I only thought of this much later.

In the days of Nineveh, I had been a warrior, the greatest of my generation, then greatest of my age. Armies gathered to me. Kings trembled at the thunder of my chariots and feared the hiss of my arrows through their skies. I swept walled cities and whole realms into my cestus-wrapped hands. My sword and lance dripped wine-dark with the blood of their soldiers and sons.

I brought order to a barbarous age of the world, and my empire became legend. Strength gathered to me, and in time, I knew I was *Gevurah*, the vessel of strength, of action, of strict justice.

But my mortal form aged. With age came weakness, and with weakness, temptation. My strength was tested time and time again by protests, skirmishes, and finally, by rebellion.

Nineveh fell.

Amid the spires of smoke and scalding flame, amid the fading screams of the victors and the vanquished, I lay where my men and I had been cut down. I sought to stanch the flow of blood, but my wound was deep, and I fell back, my face turned to the sky. A starless black night crouched over me, and around me shadows gathered.

A sibilant voice issued forth from the shadows, soft and dry like the susurrus of the desert. At first I thought it was the wind, but its sighs formed words inside my head, offering me life and strength eternal in return for a task—one for which I was uniquely proficient.

And it offered me a blade.

III

IN THE BEGINNING, ten vessels, called sephirot, *were formed to guide Creation, and to bridge the mortal and the Divine. But where there was to be Form, the Unformed, called Tohu or Chaos, was also brought into being.*

When Divine Light filled the vessels to enact Creation, the vessels shattered. Their broken shards plummeted to Earth, each shard carrying a spark of Divine Light, and there, in the depths of Creation, the sparks were buried.

Yet the shards did not perish, for their purpose was to unite Creation. In time, the shards of Wisdom gathered in the wise, the shards of Kindness in the kind, and so on, until each of the vessels was reformed.

Against this, the Tohu raged.

Every time the shards assembled in a human host, the Unformed sent me to shatter the vessel again.

And again.

And again, through all the lands and all the ages of the world.

IV

THE DAGGER ITSELF was a thing of ethereal beauty, a delicate blade of Damascene steel, its surface smooth but with a mottled pattern like flowing water. Its handle of spiraled horn had been polished until it glowed like sunlight through amber. It was the finest artistry of humankind joined to the ineffable beauty of nature.

But this was merely a seeming.

Was it magical? Of course it was. Just as a man's soul lies encased within his flesh, so too the Tohu blade held the essence of the Unformed, of Chaos.

Ah, the blade. If only it could sever memory as cleanly as it shattered the sephirot and severed the souls that fostered them.

V

TEN ARE THE vessels, the sacred sephirot, which briefly held the Divine Light. Their names are *Chochmah, Binah, Daat, Chesed, Gevurah, Tiphereth, Netzach, Hod, Yesod,* and *Malkuth.* And their essences are Wisdom, Understanding, Knowledge, Kindness, Strength, Beauty, Endurance, Splendor, Generation, and Manifestation.

When the shards of these vessels gathered in human hosts, the sparks joined as a single flame, reaching to bridge the chasm between Creation and the Divine. It was then that I'd slay them, destroying the bridge and shattering each vessel anew.

And down through the centuries, I had found them all.

All save one.

VI

THE TOHU BLADE led me to a stone cottage on the south side of the Pyrenees some 500 years after the Cathar crusade. I had crossed the peaks in autumn, a foolhardy venture, but I was enamored by their stark beauty and confident in my strength. My pride and my geas bound me.

Standing atop a cliff, I inhaled the mountain air. It crackled down my throat, as cold as the evening star sputtering alight in the east. In the heavens, an eagle gyred, mirrored below in a tarn whose still water reflected the roseate glow of the sky. A thatch-roofed cottage huddled at the edge of a broad meadow near the tarn's banks, and a pen of gathered stones held a snowdrift of sheep nestled flank to flank.

Whether it was the fading light, my own lack of caution, or the tranquility of the scene so disparate with my nature, I do not know. But when the eagle, lord of its dominion, shrieked its victory over the fading sun, I stumbled and fell off the cliff.

The wind was a raging river against my face. It streamed through my hair and set my great cloak flapping as loud as a murder of ravens. I had but a moment to register surprise and, oddly, humor.

I felt nothing when I struck.

A SOFT WET cloth laved my cheeks and brow. I shivered. Opening my eyes proved futile. They were as heavy as armor and resisted my efforts, permitting but a glimpse of pale light in which nothing was distinguishable.

More of my senses returned. Warmth and the crackle of a fire. The smell of spiced broth. But they were driven from my consciousness by a leaden pressure that expanded through my flesh until I feared I would explode.

Pain!

Just when I feared it would tear me apart, the pain retreated. By some means it was contained, held apart from me.

A woman's voice spoke. "Easy, *Aita*. Lie quiet. All is well." It was a breathy voice, soft, reassuring. "Drink."

Drink? I was swaddled like an infant in bandages and blankets. They had been wrapped about me so I would not move and re-injure myself. Nor could I lift my head. How then could I drink?

Soft lips touched mine, barely a feather's caress, and then a rich broth dribbled into my mouth. It was like tasting sunshine. Its warmth spread through me, seeming to knit bones and soothe flesh.

I didn't know whether she was a maid or a crone, nor did I care. When she drew away, all warmth fled with her like a cloud passing before the sun. I felt a yearning, a nostalgic hollowing within my breast. I *knew* her, and recalled the pain of our parting in the heavens long ago.

She pressed a creased leaf, sharp-edged but pliant, against my lips. Bittersweet oil seeped onto my tongue and soon my senses retreated. My thoughts slowed even as I recalled her name.

Chesed.

I**N THE DAYS** that followed, I discovered that Chesed, in her current form, was neither young nor old. No grey streaked her hair, which was the malt gold-brown of autumn fields, but small lines creased the corners of her eyes when the hearth fire cast shadows within them. She lived alone with her small herd upon her cultivated mountain pasture. This had made her lean, but not gaunt. Her face was a bit long, and her nose thin but prominent. Among the elite of the courts and palaces, few would notice her.

She was beautiful.

It took me weeks to heal, and even then I fell back into fever from time to time. Chesed cared for me without complaint, only once asking, *"Zein da zure izena? Non biza zara?"* What is your name? Where do you live?

But I could not speak. This frightened me greatly. I clawed at my throat until she clasped my hands and forced me to look into her eyes. They were as blue and placid as the mountain tarn outside her door.

"You have no injury to your throat," she said, "but the fall has knocked the voice from your head. Your voice is resting, healing." She passed her fingers through my hair. Her touch was light upon my temple, but it set my heart pounding. "You've a hard head. Strong," she added, a smile teasing her lips, "like an aurochs."

Soon, I could hobble about on a crutch, and I followed Chesed like one of her sheep. I helped her harvest the last of the autumn squash, and pulled the last turnips. Winter cabbages grew in ordered rows reminiscent of the *Etz Chaim*, the Tree of Life on which the Divine vessels had once been arrayed.

Chesed, however, did not know the truth of her own essence. Kindness was present in her every word and act, but she called herself only Nahia, ignorant of her true nature and import.

The blade knew, however.

I had not touched it since my fall. Wrapped tight in oilskin at the bottom of my pack and hidden under my cot bed, it had lain quiescent. But as I grew stronger, the whispers of the Tohu blade returned.

When the first frost limned the stalks of the field and cast arabesques on the window glass, the blade's voice became incessant and demanding. Although I had lost my own voice, its fierce utterances were ever-present. In the gloaming of early evening and in the chill dark before dawn, its sibilant hiss drowned out my thoughts. I'd sit hunched over my chair or upon my straw cot, clutching my head.

Chesed would brew feverfew tea and hold me until these fits passed and the blade's mad voice faded. My mind became a battleground between myself and the Tohu blade; but battlefields were my mother's milk and I was Strength incarnate. Still, if not for Nahia, for Chesed, I would have succumbed.

After the winter solstice, when the days lengthened even as the cold deepened, the blade's voice stilled. I actually laughed, foolishly laughed, recalling the ecstasy I'd known an age before of a warrior's triumph over an adversary.

On yet another night, as spring drew near, I recalled another type of ecstasy, one that is shared.

An unexpected arctic blast sent temperatures plummeting across the mountain pasture. Newly formed shoots snapped and the tarn crackled as it refroze. We hustled the sheep inside the cottage, secured the door and stoked the fire.

Cold pressed in upon us. Rime formed on the interior walls of the cottage. We drew our blankets nearer the hearth, surrounded by the tumult and pervasive smell of wet sheep.

Stillness settled on the world both inside and out, a peaceful silence undisturbed save for the crackling of the fire and the soft bleats of the animals in their sleep.

Huddled together, the herb-scented plumes of our breath mingling, Chesed and I made love.

MY DREAMS WERE of the blade, and the startled, wide-eyed faces of those I'd killed. Netzach had been a taciturn scholar in Rhodes, then a whore in Lyons. Hod, a purveyor of perfumes in Marrakesh and a soldier in Samarkand. Tiphereth, a blind poet in Delphi, an artist's child in Amsterdam, and . . . *so many others.*

The blade sang as it slid into them, a soft discordant jangling of untuned strings. Looking into my victims' eyes, I watched their souls shatter. The shards of their vessels dispersed back into Creation, their sparks flaring up and fading into the night. Their blood, warm and silky, spiraled down the horn handle of the blade and coated my hand as red as my cestus of old.

Blood spiraled down the horn handle of the blade.

Chesed's body sprawled across the stones fronting the hearth. Her left arm lay outstretched, unmoving, her fingers blackening in the embers of the fire. Her eyes stared at me, through me, and up through the thatched roof of the cottage now weighted with snow.

The Tohu blade pierced her chest.

I stood, stepped back, and slipped in the intestines of a ram. The slaughtered carcasses of Nahia's herd covered the cottage floor. Blood and entrails were everywhere—the floor, the walls, the windows. *The stench of it . . .*

I stumbled out the door and vomited into the snow. The bitter cold slapped my face and naked breast.

I tilted my head to the sky and screamed.

The eagle shrieked in chorus, and our cries echoed, mockingly, in the valley.

VII

I buried Nahia in her garden. Nahia. Not Chesed. Chesed was scattered again, and Nahia was dead with no hope of return.

The ground was frozen and the burial took time. When I had finished, my bones ached and I, the essence of Strength, was weakened by the effort and by my loss.

Her animals I burned in a pyre. At first I'd thought to burn them and the cottage together, but it did not feel right. Instead, I scrubbed the blood and filth from the floor and hearthstones, and left the cottage tidy and welcoming, as Nahia would have liked it.

The blade was silent while I did this. Not a single whisper disturbed me.

My dreams that evening, horrible as they were, were wholly my own. But when I took the dagger out onto the frozen tarn and began cutting through the ice, it woke and fought me. Images of the glories I'd achieved and those that still awaited me were followed by visions of horrible doom if I did not submit and honor our pact.

There is one thing about the terrible experiences we suffer in life. If we survive them, they make us stronger, more resilient.

I broke through the ice to water that held the memory of its glacial forebear, and then I dropped the stone-weighted dagger into its depths. I thought I heard it laugh as it sank. Later, I discovered why.

I could not leave the valley.

About three miles from the cottage, I felt unnaturally winded. By five I couldn't breathe. I could draw breath, but I got no vitality from it. My mouth opened and closed like a bass in a fisherman's creel, and I was just as caught. I returned to the cottage and salvaged what I could from the pyre.

It was a long winter.

When spring finally prevailed, I dove into the tarn and, after many attempts, recovered the blade.

But the war between us had begun.

I would kill no more.

VIII

The dawn of the current age found me in San Francisco. In the three interminable centuries since I'd slain Nahia, I'd resisted the blade. The steel still keened for blood, but the hilt no longer warmed to my touch for my bloodlust had died with Nahia. Unquenched, the dagger's song was often angry like the buzzing of wasps, or mournful as the night wind—which is why I hesitated when Shlomo Spielman, the vessel of Yesod, asked me to meet him at the library in Little Russia.

The library gave off a disreputable air. An empty lot filled with jimson weed, needles, and empty vodka bottles lounged against its eastern flank. Old scaffolding caged the exterior with white-painted poles worn to a dingy gray and sagging boards spaced too far apart to give shelter from the frequent rain. Above the scaffolding, the library's façade glowed in the fading daylight, recalling its once gilded splendor.

Shlomo was a squat man, with cheeks round as a gnome's, and thick round spectacles that magnified his eyes, giving him an owl-like appearance. A *kippah* of brocaded blue topped his head, encircled by the final remnants of his once-black hair. His thin lips creased into a tentative smile.

Shlomo should have been dead by my hand long ago. The blade had drawn me to him in Brooklyn when he was a scrawny but brilliant Yeshiva student with an unorthodox eye for one of the Rebbe's daughters. But like the master who led his proverbial horse, the Chaos blade could not make me drink. Instead of killing Shlomo, I'd enlisted him.

We met again when I first arrived in San Francisco two years earlier. Shlomo still affected some outward show of his Judaism, such as the *kippah*, but he was no longer *frum*. His headband and beads and leather vest were more Haight-Ashbury than Hasidic. By then, he not only knew that he was Yesod, but also which vessel I was and the nature of the dagger I carried.

Today, he leaned against the back wall of the library, beside a set of cracked concrete steps. These led up to a heavily varnished oak door over which a caged lantern hung like a vulture, bare-bulbed, with one glass pane broken. The small side street was empty and bleached of color save for an amber beam of the day's last light slanting across the wall. A bottle clattered in a nearby alley, followed by the yowl of a cat. Then there was only silence.

"*Gamal?*" Shlomo asked, holding out an open pack of Camels. A square of white paper had been slipped beneath the cellophane, printed with a promise of death followed by a numerical offer of assistance. The letters were Cyrillic. Ukrainian, perhaps, or Kyrgyz. They could have been Aramaic, Persian, Phoenician, Punjabi, or Sanskrit—the difference mattered little, for my nature rendered all words intelligible to me. As it did for Shlomo.

"*Todah,*" I answered. "Thanks."

Our fingers touched briefly. There was a soft snap, like a spark of static electricity. He quickly withdrew his hand, leaving the stem of one cigarette caught between my finger and thumb like a tiny magic wand. He laughed nervously.

Beneath my coat, the dagger twisted in its sheath and whispered for Shlomo's blood. My fingers twitched. I stilled them.

I raised the cigarette to my lips, and Shlomo lit it. "These things will kill us," he said.

I chuckled. It helped. But being so close to him again, I felt the blade's hunger, its rage, its unrelenting desire to shatter him.

Shlomo spoke quickly. "I found her."

The blade's voice stopped, crushed beneath my will.

The sound of distant traffic rose and fell, sirocco-like. I sniffed and smelled the acrid scent of stale urine, old paint, and rotting wood. A dry breeze carried the last of the day's warmth across my forehead and set dust motes swirling like stars.

Shlomo looked at my face. He nodded at my control, and his own face let go of its tension. "She's inside," he said.

I brushed past him and pulled open the door. Looking back, I asked, "Does she know who she is?"

He nodded again.

"Does she . . ." I paused. "What does she remember?"

His face saddened. "Everything."

The hallway was unlit. I passed a few varnished wooden doors with brass name plaques dulled by time before I entered the library proper. Archways opened into high-ceilinged rooms with dark glass chandeliers and cloth-draped tables, reading chairs, and bookshelves. Everywhere was the sarcophagus smell of old papyrus and dust and memory. Abruptly the passage ended.

I stood in a great hall like a hollowed out ziggurat. Its walls rose up past three tiers of mezzanines to a painted dome ceiling where a great round window glistened with sunlight like the eye of God. The spectacle was vertiginous. For a moment, I thought I might fall upward into it.

A soft voice said, "*Aita?*"

Chesed straightened from where she leaned at the librarians' desk at the center of the room. She was a dark-skinned young woman, neither thin nor overly heavy. She was buxom but demure in a loose-fitting chartreuse blouse and denim jeans. Her left arm was bent across her chest. It looked small and withered, its hand dangling limply, but she affected no self-consciousness.

I grasped her hand gently and fell to my knees before her.

"Forgive me," I said. Unbidden, tears wet my cheeks.

A touch like angora lifted my chin and our eyes met. Hers were auburn and flecked with gold. They lifted slightly as she smiled. "There is nothing to forgive," she said, raising me to my feet.

A man's voice, deep and resonant said, "All happens for a purpose."

I whirled, the dagger springing to my hand. It whispered fiercely. A dissonant chord like the clang of warped cymbals echoed in the great hall.

The man who spoke regarded the Chaos blade, and his lips flattened more with curiosity than with fear. He raised his eyes to mine. They were blue and piercing. He wore a white shirt, open at the neck, with its sleeves rolled up to his elbows. His arms and chest were hairy, and he'd a thick unruly mane and prominent brow ridges.

"I am Chochmah," he said, but that which dwelt inside me already knew his name: *Wisdom*, the first sephira.

He'd caught me by surprise, and the Tohu blade nearly tugged me to him. It took much of my strength to draw it back. Its song like a war-cry rent through centuries of memory, recalling the sack of Alexandria and later, Constantinople. How swiftly the dagger had come to my hand then, how deftly it had dipped and drunk in a dance of blood and death. I had given in to it eagerly then . . . but I would not do so now.

With effort, I sheathed the blade. It twisted in my fingers and nearly cut me, but I expected this and escaped hurt. Having denied the blade for so long, the blood it now sought was often my own.

Chochmah nodded in silent approval, and then repeated, "All that happens happens for a purpose."

Sweat beaded and cooled upon my brow. "What are you talking about?"

He placed his hands in his pockets and smiled. "We are the stuff of Creation, *not* of the Infinite. Do you understand?" He said this as if it were enough.

I shook my head.

"How do you contain the Infinite within the Finite?" he asked.

I felt suddenly weak and began to tremble.

Chesed's right hand slid around me and gently clasped my chest. She leaned against me. Her warm breath laved the nape of my neck.

Chochmah pointed to the blade softly moaning in its sheath. "The Tohu blade is Damascus steel is it not?" His eyes seemed luminous, and the deepening blue of the sky through the domed glass ceiling reflected in his own. "We were too fragile to hold the Divine Light. We needed to become both flexible and hard, forgiving and resilient. How is this achieved?" He leaned forward, not waiting for me to answer, which was as well, for I was unable to speak.

"Steel must be tempered," he whispered, "hardened by passage through fire. You, aided by this blade, were *our* furnace."

From the shadows between the library stacks, the others came. Men. Women. And one child. Six in all. There was nothing distinctive about them. They could have been any group of people passing in the street, awaiting a train, or shopping at the mall.

But what burned inside them was brilliant.

Like to like, I could see the multitudes of their sparks swirling and intertwining in a great dance, flowing like a river, strong yet yielding.

I cried out and would have fallen had not Chesed and Yesod supported me.

Then I did fall. My knee struck the tiled floor with a loud crack. Pain shot up my leg, and I heard Chesed cry out. The warmth of her body against my back was gone.

A devil's symphony of squealing bagpipes, blatting horns, and discordant strings filled the pyramid of the great hall.

Yesod stood in front of me. His eyes were wild, his lips curled back in a rictal grin, his right arm was thrust up toward the distant eye of the skylight.

And in his hand he held the Tohu blade.

YESOD STARED AT the dagger, enraptured. When he lowered his head to look at me, his eyes were dark pits. No colored iris or rim of white, they held only an ebony blackness.

Chesed gasped, and Yesod's eyes darted to her.

With a cry of rage and triumph, he thrust the Chaos blade toward her chest. The blade sang, its song like the clamor of my chariots of old, drowning out the others' shouts and cries of warning—and then it stilled. All sound stilled.

I felt . . . *odd*. Looking down, I found I was standing between Yesod and Chesed, the dagger buried hilt-deep in my breast.

I grasped the horn handle and tugged it free. It felt like pulling a gob of phlegm from my throat. Then it was out, and a sense of pervasive peace filled me.

The very last thing I saw was the Tohu blade shattering into a thousand shards.

IX

IT TOOK THEM thirty-six years to find me, and by then I was remembering who I was. Chesed had not aged. She had decided to wait for me. The others were more or less the same. Yesod cried, and hugged me fiercely every time we met, but I told him it was fine. I felt stronger than ever.

I did. We all did.

Chochmah led us. We did good works that inspired others, a cascade that after millennia of finite ethical steps seemed, at last, poised to bring a new age of Man, one joining the Divine to Creation.

X

THE OLD COTTAGE in the high meadows of the southern Pyrenees was still there. Chesed and I returned to it for a time. We spent our days in the fields and garden, and occasionally swam in the cold tarn. At night, we'd huddle and make love before the fire.

On an evening when the moon was a Cheshire crescent, a nightingale trilled and whistled to it from the thatched roof of the hut. It was a new roof, with rafters of new timber and freshly plastered walls. Across the room, a refrigerator hummed. I turned toward the snapping fire and placed my palm on the warm stones fronting the hearth.

"You are very quiet, my love," Chesed said. She carried a wicker basket under her right arm, her hair bound in a red kerchief. She studied me, but kindly. She knew my thoughts, or at least some of them.

She set the basket down and folded her skirt beneath her to sit beside me, placing her good hand atop mine—atop the place where I had slain her.

"Let the memory rest," she said. "We're together now, forever. It's done."

Our eyes met. "Is it?"

Her eyebrows twitched. "How is it not? Creation and the Divine are linked again."

"Yes," I said. "And yet . . . Creation was drawn out of Chaos, and Form from the Unformed. Creation cannot exist without Chaos." I paused, took in a breath and slowly released it. "If the vessels of Creation can shatter and reform, *why not the blade?*"

She pursed her lips, and then laughed. It was a song more beautiful than the nightingale's. She rapped my skull with her knuckles. "You think

too much," she said. "There are *better* memories we can relive beside this hearth, *Aita*."

She leaned forward and kissed me.

And it was Heaven.

ABOUT THE AUTHORS

KARY ENGLISH grew up in the snowy Midwest where she avoided siblings and frostbite by reading book after book in a warm corner behind a recliner chair. She blames her only high school detention on Douglas Adams, whose *The Hitchhiker's Guide to the Galaxy* made her laugh out loud while reading it behind the covers of her geometry textbook.

Today, Kary still spends most of her time with her head in the clouds and her nose in a book. To the great relief of her parents, she seems to be making a living at it. Her greatest ambition is to make her own work detention-worthy.

A Hugo and Campbell award Finalist, Kary is a *Writers of the Future* contest Winner whose work has appeared in *Daily Science Fiction, Grantville Gazette's Universe Annex, Writers of the Future Vol. 31*, and *Galaxy's Edge*.

You can find Kary on Facebook or at www.KaryEnglish.com.

ROBERT B. FINEGOLD, MD is a retired radiologist from Maine and a multiple *Writers of the Future* contest Finalist whose stories of science fiction, fantasy, and Yiddishkeit have appeared in markets such as *Galaxy's Edge* magazine, *Giganotosaurus*, and *CRES*, as well as in the *Starlight, Mysterion, Robotica*, and Neil Clarke's *More Human Than Human* anthologies. He is the assistant editor of the *Myths, Legends, and Fairy Tales* section of *Cosmic Roots and Eldritch Shores*. Find his musings at robertbfinegold.com, on Twitter at @DocHistory, and on Facebook at Robert B Finegold's Kvells and Kvetchings.

ABOUT THE STORY

KARY ENGLISH: So, there I was, sitting at a blue-draped table at the *Writers of the Future* workshop while Tim Powers handed me a pack of Camels. This, he told me, was to be the inspiration for my 24-hour story. I've never smoked, and if I did, I was pretty sure my cig of choice would be something other than Camels.

Undaunted, I examined the package further. It was empty save for a few, brown tobacco shavings that were too old to have any smell. A small rectangle of paper with writing on it had been slipped under the cellophane on the back of the package. The language was Norwegian, which I know enough of to understand that the message was a warning about the dangers of smoking, complete with a phone number if the smoker wanted help.

So not just Camels, *Norwegian* Camels.

Fortunately for me, my brain is a squirrel cage of free associations. Camels. Alice the Camel. Camels and needles. The camel's nose is in the tent. Tents? Bedouins and camels. Hebrew tribes in the desert. Hebrew? *Now we're getting somewhere.*

Ages ago as a cheeky undergrad, I'd taken a graduate-level seminar in Hebrew mysticism. We read the Zohar, tales of merkabah mysticism, and Gershom Scholem's writings on Lurianic Kabbalah. I tugged at a thread and found a memory: Hebrew for camel is *gamal*. My squirrels, however, had shoved the camels aside in favor of a Lurianic romp through the Tree of Life.

At this point, my *Writers of the Future* cohort set off on a field trip to a library in Little Armenia. On the way, we passed a vacant lot full of weeds and empty liquor bottles, and a walkway covered with dilapidated scaffolding. The library books were mostly in Russian, and the dour-faced librarian wore a *kippah* embroidered in delft blue. Though I couldn't read the books, a cover illustration of a dagger with a spiral hilt caught my eye.

At this point, I had all the elements of my story. Ten chapters, I thought, one for each sephira on the Tree of Life. I sped through the first five chapters only to hit a wall in chapter six. Though I'd gone on to doctoral studies in comparative religion, I didn't know enough Kabbalah to finish the story. I had an ending in mind, but I wasn't sure it fit the tradition, and if it didn't, I ran the risk of being ridiculous, offensive, or both. What I needed was a co-author, preferably an excellent writer who was steeped in Jewish tradition.

Lucky for me I'd been beta reading for fellow contest aspirant Bob Finegold. Not only did he possess the knowledge I lacked, but his work is both lyrical and hauntingly beautiful. With nary a thought for the mixing of metaphors, I decided to use my "Phone a Friend" lifeline and fired off an email to Bob.

DR. BOB: *"Hmm, would you like to co-write a story?"*

This was the subject title of the email I received from 2015 Hugo award and Campbell "best new writer" award nominee, and 1st place *Writers of the Future* contest Winner, Kary English; and I received this email *while* she was attending the WOTF Winners workshop and Gala.

Heart racing, my response was, *"Hell, yeah!"*

But before I wrote her back, I thought I should read the body of her email. True, it would not matter to me if she wished to write about the migratory patterns of vertiginous Martian penguins or the Calvinist philosophical musings of a paramecium in a drying puddle . . . to co-write a story with the talented author of "Totaled" and "Poseidon's Eyes"?

Again, "Hell, yeah!" But first . . . Kary wrote:

> I'm concerned that the very act of trying to make something akin to a fairy tale retelling out of Lurianic Kabballah might be offensive from beginning to end, and if that's the case, I don't want a single living soul to see this.

> Not to imply that you're dead, of course. ;) But with you, I trust you enough to tell me that if something like this just isn't done, in which case I will apologize abjectly. But if you think it's OK, here's the idea . . .

> I'm writing from the point of view of Severity, who murdered Kindness, and in so doing received the first spark of regret that allowed him to grow, heal, and see the error of his ways. Simple, right? Well, not so much.

> The story is flash length, with 10 chapters, one for each sephira. I have not tried to make each chapter reflect the theme of each sephira. That feels a bit beyond me at present. I'm stuck at about chapter six, and it's because I don't know the source material well enough. Perhaps you do? See, I could have Severity end his own life in penance for what he's done; but if I do, he's shattered another vessel and that's bad. And, not knowing what to do with Severity, I can't write the end.

> So, would you like to help? Would you like to sign on as co-author?

Intrigued, I finally did manage a more sedate reply:

> Fairy tales derived from Kabbalah? That's *my* shtick, as you know. ;) I don't think I've offended anyone—yet.
>
> My *two shekels* for writing from such source material are: (1) be honest and accurate when you draw upon your sources; and (2) don't preach. Use the material as a frame, a loom, to weave universal themes of love and loss, justice, and the internal war that rages within each of us between our *yetzer hara* (our evil inclination) and our *yetzer tov* (our inclination for good).
>
> I like your use of the *Etz Chaim* ("Tree of Life," the ten *sephirot*) as the frame on which to craft your story, although how you will have "10 chapters" in a flash fiction length I can't envision. I am sure you will surprise and delight me. *Gevurah* (Severity) lies half-way down the Kabbalistic Tree, halfway between G-d, Blessed be He, and Man/Creation. Gevurah represents Strength and Judgment and Awe of G-d and is balanced by *Chesed* (Kindness), much as there is no Justice without Mercy. If Severity has murdered/killed Kindness, he is off-balance—as is the connection between G-d and Man. Like the conflict between Isaac and Esau, and Joseph and his brothers, there will be no resolution (or redemption) until this balance is restored.
>
> But, perhaps, I digress. I don't know how much help I will be for you. My stories grow "vaster than empires and more slow." Quick turnaround is not my forte. I, of course, am very willing (and humbled that you'd consider me) to read what you've written and offer you my thoughts in hope of igniting and elevating *your* "spark." :)

And so our collaboration began. With my own Yiddisher inspiration set aflame like a *ner tamid,* I read her flash outline and notes and sent her a 4700 word 1st draft in, miraculously for me, a mere 48 hours. I.e. Before she could change her mind. Just sayin'. When opportunity knocks with fresh challah and wine, don't wait.

"Shattered Vessels" appeared in *Galaxy's Edge* magazine #19, March-April 2016.

Postscript: I'm pleased to share our little tale earned a "good stuff" nod from Gardner Dozois in his "Summation: 2016" review in The Year's Best Science Fiction: 34th Annual Collection [St. Martin's Press, 2017].

ACKNOWLEDGEMENT

The authors wish to extend their appreciation to:

DAVID FARLAND
JONI LABAQUI
and
L. RON HUBBARD'S WRITERS OF THE FUTURE CONTEST

http://www.writersofthefuture.com/

for encouraging new authors toward excellence,
and fostering the friendships that result among its participants,
inclusive of the authors whose works compose this book

THE STARLIGHT ANTHOLOGIES

1ST AND STARLIGHT

Edited by Sky Mckinnon

From contemporary to high fantasy, from hard science fiction to the wildly experimental.

14 stories that explore the breadth of possibilities within speculative fiction.

Available as EBook and Print Editions from fine retailers

future finalists
publishing

www.futurefinalists.com/anthologies

THE STARLIGHT ANTHOLOGIES

2ND AND STARLIGHT

Edited by Dustin Adams

Be transported! To a future where androids fight our wars, to deep space to solve a murder, to magical lands where fiancés are transformed into... cows.

11 stories to astonish, delight, and touch your heart on the corner of *2nd and Starlight.*

Available as **EBook and** Print Editions

future finalists
publishing

www.futurefinalists.com/anthologies

THE STARLIGHT ANTHOLOGIES

3RD AND STARLIGHT

Edited by Robert B. Finegold

Also available as an **EBook** and as an Audiobook
narrated by Scott R. Parkin

"This street is unlike any other."
14 tales of wonder and heart by new voices
in science fiction and fantasy.

future finalists
publishing

www.futurefinalists.com/anthologies